The Great Lake Terror

*To a wonderful woman "Ms. Lilly"
From the Auther
"Tony Faceson"
2009.*

The Great Lake Terror

Tony Faceson

Copyright © 2009 by Tony Faceson.

ISBN: Hardcover   978-1-4415-8105-1
          Softcover   978-1-4415-8104-4

All rights reserved. No part of this book may be reproduced or transmitted in any form or by any means, electronic or mechanical, including photocopying, recording, or by any information storage and retrieval system, without permission in writing from the copyright owner.

This is a work of fiction. Names, characters, places and incidents either are the product of the author's imagination or are used fictitiously, and any resemblance to any actual persons, living or dead, events, or locales is entirely coincidental.

This book was printed in the United States of America.

To order additional copies of this book, contact:
Xlibris Corporation
1-888-795-4274
www.Xlibris.com
Orders@Xlibris.com

SYNOPSIS

ONCE UPON A time, in a small secluded town called Saginaw, Michigan, five teenagers had played the wrong dangerous game that lifted a soul from a dark secret. In the process the town was developing strange, mysterious, paranormal murders that humanity could never dream of, which spun out of control. The vileness of Mary Swartz lost soul atrociously inherit the Saginaw Wood's Ghost Trail, and every oak leaf that came with it by this being the second time this town had been traumatized, from the twelve counts of murders that were committed by a very disturbed man named Norman Gandy. So whoever encounters with Mary Swartz plans of vengeance or deadly massacre terror curse.

MUST SURELY DIE . . . . . . !

This is where the figment of the imagination fall's victim to the unknown and unexplained, some games just aren't meant to EVER BE PLAYED.

Tony Faceson

Discovery Date: 6/25/74   MOTION PICTURE/FICTION NOVEL.

PROLOGUE

TABITHA BAILEY AND Maria Gates are best of friends attending summer school together. Tabitha is nine years old and Maria is nine and a half years old, and while everyone who attended summer school was outside having recreation jump roping, playing kick ball, hop scotch, swinging on swings, and running around screaming enjoying themselves. Maria and Tabitha were alone playing on the Merry-Go-Round taking turns spinning each other. Once Tabitha gave Maria another hard push, she turned around to glance up at one of the top windows of the school being very convinced she felt something gazing out the window at her When Tabitha paced off toward the school building, Maria quickly shouted out. "Tabitha, where are you going?" Tabitha immediately stopped in her tracks to yell back "I'm going inside to go use the restroom, I'll be back." "You better come straight back, so you won't get into any trouble." "I will, just don't let the teachers know where I went." Tabitha pointed out. Then she took back off running toward the building. When Tabitha entered the school building, she immediately turned around with adrenaline pumping in her veins, until she realized it was only the closing door slamming behind her. Tabitha slowly turned back around with a sigh while throwing her right palm up to her chest, when she saw something quickly pace across the top main floor landing and whatever it was she couldn't quite make out, being that it paced across so quickly and swiftly. Tabitha slowly eased her way up the steps, while suddenly realizing how the school felt so empty and vacant. She was use to seeing a hallway full of teachers, parents and school kids walking by in honorable straight lines up and down the hallways, but summer school was nothing like regular school, she thought while stopping on the last step before the top landing. Tabitha slowly pocked her head around the left corner of the stair casing wall with her left hand pressed against it to make sure no one was waiting for her arrival. Once she surveyed half the hallway being closed off by a metal closed locked fence she started looking to the right of her only to observe the vision she once saw when she first entered inside the school building vanishing off into the girls restroom area. "What was that?" She exclaimed, while growing even more anxious to find out what it could be. Once Tabitha gut checked her, for a test of courage, she slowly tiptoed onward toward the girl's restroom with urgency in her step. The minute she made it to the entrance of the restroom, she immediately glanced back over her left shoulder with her right shoulder leaned against the wall before taking a speculated glance inside the restroom walk way making sure no one was standing at the far end of the long spacious hallway seeing what she was doing. Once Tabitha saw the coast was clear. She slowly tucked her hair behind her right ear lobe to peek inside the restroom entrance doorway, and then proceeded along into the short walkway before entering inside the stall area. Tabitha stopped in her tracks when she observed a few oak leaves scattered amongst the floor, while saying curiously enough. "Oak leaves . . . , what are these doing in the building?" Then she stared ahead before entering the stall area. Once Tabitha made it fully inside, she immediately yelled out. "Is anyone in here!" moments later she surveyed the scene. Tabitha also felt it was sort of strange and unusual for the restroom light to be completely out, although there was sunlight shinning from the small square windows which gave her enough light to see with. Tabitha swiftly turned around toward the left far corner, once she heard some fluttering sounds on the other side of the corner wall. Tabitha was momentarily rooted to her spot listening to the sound getting louder she then broke her train of thought as she slowly stepped toward the corner. Once she made it to the corner, she suddenly felt like she couldn't move another inch from being afraid of what she may encounter, but then she also thought it was either now or never to see what it may could be that has grabbed her attention all the way from the playground to the restroom. Tabitha counted up to three inside her mind, before finally edging her head around the corner. Tabitha instantly felt her heart skip a beat when her eye's grew bulging wide with fright, once she finally witnessed up close with her very own eye's, oak leaves swirling in a gruesomely, forming at least six feet tall. Tabitha was so shocked with disbelief. She didn't know if she should take off running or scream out for someone's help, but instead she spooked out and started walking backwards from the gruesome leaves, as they were gradually maneuvering toward her. "What are you . . . !" She babbled out walking backwards. Tabitha screamed from the top of her lungs when the leaves dove at her. The leaves was slicing her entire body and clothing, as they continued swarming completely around her body, till suddenly she was elevated high in the air and powerfully flung into the concrete wall. Blood splattered everywhere from the impact of her bloody raw exposed flesh. The Macabre leaves vanished presumably out the girl's restroom, down the long hallway, and out the window. Once Maria realized her friend Tabitha hadn't returned like she promised, she decided to go after her when she heard the teacher's warning that they only had less than fifteen minutes left of recess. The moment Maria came through the school building door she quickly strode up to the main floor landing. When she made it to the top floor she immediately glanced both ways down the hallway and shouted "Tabitha! Where are you?!" Then she headed off toward the girls restroom when she didn't get any reply, remembering Tabitha telling her she was going to go use the student restroom. Maria was a mighty brave little girl, and it also wasn't too many things that could scare her, plus she always wanted to dress up in the scariest costumes. Making it to the girl's restroom entrance she didn't hesitate not one minute in noticing the scattered oak leaves amongst the walkway. Maria once again shouted out when she looked forward into the restroom area. "Tabitha, are you in there? We need to get back out to the playground, before we get ourselves into a lot of trouble!" Maria slowly started walking into the stall area with an abstruse expression on her face when she didn't get any response back from Tabitha, once she was inside she immediately noticed shreds of clothing scattered all about on the floor which made her feel breathlessly oppressive knowing one hundred percent those was the clothes of Tabitha's. Maria's nerves stood out in coruscating agony, once she realized it was blood puddles also amongst the scattered clothing, when she stepped up closer focusing her eyes she glanced up sniffing from her nostril with her attention focused toward the right hand side corner wall, then she suddenly started smelling a strong blood stench in the air coming from the opposite corner. Maria slowly crept over to the corner with the right palm over her nose and mouth area, but when she slowly eased her head around the wall she stepped out into the open with her eyes glued to Tabitha's body. Then suddenly she yelled furiously with a high lament scram. Maria couldn't believe she was seeing the skinned corpse of her best friend's body lying on the floor in the puddle of her own blood, with her two arms broken underneath her. All the teachers had focused their attention to the school building, once they all heard a high lament scream, as they witnessed raven birds flying away from the top of the school building from Maria's voice echoing out.

CHAPTER ONE

MARIA GREW UP to be a very beautiful Hispanic and Italian woman with a very beautiful skin tone complexion, of butterscotch with long soft silky brown hair that perfectly matched the color of her eyes, plus she graduated college and earned a degree in paranormal activities, which also earned her a job at the Los Angeles Paranormal Secret Society O.F.P.A. Office. Maria became a paranormal activity advocate to find who or what may had been the cause of her best friend's death, but on this very day she was working late in the office preparing to give the Bailey Family a home visit, back in her hometown of Michigan. Maria's boss Mr. Kirk W. Wallace came walking out of his office calling it a night from a long day of work, and as he approached her he said "Maria. I guess I'm a call it a night and hopefully your transfer goes through while you're out of state for a few days to the Baileys residence. So have fun, oh yeah, just to remind you, I'm going to be in 29 Palms, California in a day or so, on the case of that missing kid, Bryan Smith. I promised an old friend of mine by the name of Captain Aversa at the Morongo Basin District." "Oh yea. I remember you saying that in yesterday's meeting, you have a fun trip also sir." Maria said politely with a friendly smile. "Thank you, and I sure will Mrs. Gates, don't you work late." Mr. Wallace stated advancing away and out the front door. Maria spun back around toward the computer to type up the American Airline website to purchase a flight ticket off her credit card to Michigan, in the process the buildings security guard Mr. Murphy came walking inside the office form his cigarette break outside to inform her that he was also about to punch out on the clock. "Excuse me Mrs. Gates. I was stopping by to make your aware that my shift is about to be over, so would you be okay alone?" Maria swiveled her chair around and said with assurance "Sure, Mr. Murphy. I was just making some final adjustments on my airline ticket. You go right ahead, I'll lock up behind me" "I sure appreciate it Mrs. Gates, well have a delightful trip and I'll see you when you make it back to us." Mr. Murphy said gently "And have a safe trip home to sir." "I sure will, goodnight." He countered back putting his security jacket on then proceeded out the door. After time went by Maria calmly leaned back in her computer chair after closing the windows on her computer and once her and Bobby wedding photo popped up on the screen saver, she rubbed her temples with both hands soothing her thoughts. To avoid the over lapping images of her best friend Tabitha's murder. "Oh Maria, get a hold of yourself." She said with a low tone followed by a visual sigh. When Maria got up after preparing herself to go home and pack a few things to take with her on her airplane flight. She took a quick glance back at her computer screen saver that gleamed in the darkness of the office. She turned the lights out then closed and locked the main door behind her.

CHAPTER TWO

WHEN MARIA MADE it off the American Airline in her home town of Michigan, she was approached by a short slender built middle age man in his early fifties, with a brown goatee mustache. "Hello Mrs. Gates. I'm the Bailey's family chauffeur, my name is Mr. John Adams. May I assist you with your belongings?" Mr. Adams greeted himself very politely. "Sure, why not." She replied with a friendly smile. Maria thought to herself when they made it to the Bailey's limo. Mr. Adams looks a little younger than what Tabitha's mom assured her to look for. The second Mr. Adams nicely placed her luggage inside the limo trunk he quickly approached the passenger back door with a slight bow while angling his hand toward the inside of the limo with generosity. "Thank you." She acknowledged pleasantly while climbing inside. While the evening sun was approaching its peak of setting, Maria leaned up out of her dream panting strongly, from dreaming that something or someone was tagging along the outside of the limo staring through the tinted window watching her sleep. She quickly got relieved when she saw Mr. Adams looking at her through the rearview mirror. "Is everything alright, Mrs. Gates?" He curiously asked after seeing her alarming actions. "Sure, everything's okay, it was just a little dream that's all." Maria assured him. "Well we have five minutes, or so to the Bailey's residence, we'll be pulling up shortly now."

When Mr. Adams finally turned on the Bailey's family mansion estate they purchased from some of the money they won from the Michigan town school district law suit. He suddenly came to a complete stop in front of their mansion. Maria quickly slid her hair behind both her earlobes, as Mr. Adams was opening the passenger back door saying. "Welcome to the Bailey's mansion." Followed by a short bow. While Maria was getting out the limo a golden retriever came storming out the two big fine wooden doors, as a young lady in her early thirties came walking outside, down the steps wiping her hands off on her pink and yellow flower apron to greet Maria. "Hello, Mrs." Maria immediately said with a friendly leer standing outside the limo. "Hello, Madam. I'm Mrs. Cindy Adams the Bailey's family maid." Mrs. Adams greeted her while extending her hand out to give her soft pleasant handshake. "It's nice to meet you, and I'm Mrs. Gates." "Oh, I know who you are I'm fond of you. You're the lady who captured that crazy murderous guy Norman Gandy years ago. The man that killed and raped those twelve innocent little kids and tortured them in the deepest of the Ghost Trail Woods." Mrs. Adams said with strong enthusiasm. Maria forced a smile on her face then said with a little humor in her voice. "Yup. That's me." "Shall I take you in the Bailey's residence, so you can meet up with Mrs. Bailey, Madam?" "Sure, that'll be perfect." Maria divulged agreeably then she glanced at her luggage. "Don't worry about your luggage Madam. I'll handle it for you." Mr. Adams assured Maria when she glanced over at her belongings. Once Maria and Mrs. Adams entered inside the Bailey's home, Maria couldn't help but to keep looking around, noticing how beautiful and high vaulted their ceilings are, as they both continued up the big spacious hallway that leads to the family room where Mrs. Bailey was waiting for her arrival. "Excuse me Madam, your guest Mrs. Gates has arrived." Mrs. Adams said taking a short bow at Mrs. Bailey and Maria then she walked off. Mrs. Bailey got bright eyed when she saw how beautiful Maria grew up to be sense the last time she seen her nineteen years ago, before Maria moved to California after her daughter Tabitha's funeral. Maria and Mrs. Bailey immediately hugged each other, as if they both had been waiting for the same exact moment to come. "Oh my God! You grew up to be a beautiful young lady Maria." Mrs. Bailey said, when she leaned back away from Maria with both hands planted on both her shoulders then she embraced Maria with another tight hug. Tears began to roll down from Mrs. Bailey eye's while they both continued to hug. "Don't cry Mrs. Bailey. You're going to make me cry." Maria consoled her when she heard her sobbing. "But why my Tabby had to die?" Mrs. Bailey blurted out in tears. "I don't know Mrs. Bailey, but I do know one thing. I'll make sure one way or another, whatever had did this to Tabitha would be tracked down dead or alive." Maria said with sincerity. While Mr. Adams was outside gathering up Maria's belongings, he decided to snoop into her things, once he realized one of her zippers on her luggage was unzipped wide open that contained her occupation profile, and business cards. Mr. Adams quickly reached inside the open zipper part of the luggage bag to pull out her folder. Once he opened it. He reached into one of the pockets to grab a business card that read. "Maria Gates O.F.P.A Investigator Unit." Then he immediately placed the card back inside the folder pocket and quickly slid the folder back into the suitcase using strength behind the zipper to close it, he saw Jason come storming out the front door shouting out Buddy's name. After Maria and Mrs. Bailey had their quick conversation, Mrs. Bailey decided to call out Mrs. Adams name to have her escort Maria to her temporary living quarters. "Mrs. Adams!" Mrs. Bailey called out. "Yes, Mrs. Bailey." Mrs. Adams replied coming through the family room door. "Yes could you please escort Maria to her living quarters? This my daughter Tabitha's best friend and she's like a daughter to me, so I want her to be treated as if she's my very own." "Sure Mrs. Bailey, no problem at all." Mrs. Adams agreed ebulliently. When Maria and Mrs. Adams made it to Maria's living quarters. Mrs. Adams explained where everything was. "Okay, here we go. Here's your wardrobe closet to place your things inside, over here is your private bathroom, and if you need anymore sheets, towels or blankets. Please feel free to let me know, also dinner is expected to be served at 9:30 sharp. Is there anything else I can do for you Mrs. Gates?" "Oh no, you did fine. I think I can handle everything else from here." Maria countered back quickly. "Great. Have a good evening Madam." Mrs. Adams said then walked away. The moment Mrs. Adams walked out the room, Maria went up to the guest room window that looks out to a beautiful lake in the back of their mansion, that also had a Black and Grey two tone cigar motor speed boat tied alongside of the dock. "Excuse me Madam. Sorry to bother you; here's your things." Mr. Adams said very genially when he stepped inside Maria's room delivering her luggage. "Oh thank you Mr. Adams. You been very kind." She noted. Right before leaving out the room Mr. Adams stopped at the door to say. "Excuse me Madam once again. If you don't mind me asking, are you a detective of some sort?" "Yes, but why would you ask me that?" Mr. Adams immediately felt it may have been the wrong thing to ask, for digging into her personal life. "No reason, Mrs. Gates, good evening." He said then took off. Maria said to herself "Young looking for his age, but strange."

Then she immediately realized when she stepped over to her luggage that her pouch was zipped closed, which she thought was strange knowing she usually kept it zipped open, being it was a such an old luggage bag that has been through the ringer and back, and it has always gotten stuck till she came up with the conclusion to keep it open for quick access. "Hum. That's weird." She said thoughtfully to herself.

CHAPTER THREE

THIRTY MINUTES BEFORE dinner time came around, Maria decided to freshen up a little after she took a long hot relaxing bath, from the long airplane flight she took, but while standing in the mirror putting on her eyeliner, she quickly flinched out of reflex when the light bulb began to flicker on and off, before cutting off completely. "Wait, what's going on?" She said thickly, while quickly jetting off to the Baileys dining room, to explain the light bulb incident. Maria strode up the hallway then suddenly glanced back from feeling she was being watched by whatever she didn't quite understand. She made it into the dining room area where Mrs. Bailey and Mrs. Adams was having a discussion, she came into their eye view and openly came out and said "Excuse me for any interruptions Mrs. Bailey and Mrs. Adams, but my living quarter seems to have a power shortage in the bathroom." "Oh dear, well when the men come in I will have one of them to find the problem." Mrs. Bailey answered with a sincere but concerned smile. With that said Maria returned to her living quarters.

Ten minutes later, Mr. Adams arrived with Mr. Bailey from picking him up from the town Tavern after he had a few drinks, but this time more than usual with the celebration of the Labor Day Holidays. The moment Mr. Bailey came staggering through the main front door with a bag and a sip or two left of Don Perion inside his glass. He stood in the doorway after closing the door with the heel part of his right foot then he shouted out. "Jason!" "Yes, Dad?" Jason answered immediately then him and his dog Buddy came striding down the steps. The second Jason got to the bottom landing Mr. Bailey said. "Here, son, I got a present for you and Buddy, it's a season bone and a couple of X-box games, now don't be up playing that damn game all night. You know how much your mom hates that." Mr. Bailey reached inside the bag and pulled out Buddy's seasoned bone and placing it into his mouth. Then handed Jason the bag with the games inside. Seconds later Jason and Buddy strode off back up stairs. As Jason shouted out with excitement "Yeah, my Dad's the greatest!" Mr. Bailey nodded his head with a smile then gulped the rest of the Dom Pérignon down his throat before staggering off to their family room. Mrs. Bailey stopped Mr. Adams when he came walking through the dining room area to grab him something refreshing to drink. "Excuse me, John." "Yes, Madam?" "Mrs. Gates living quarters bathroom light shorted out on her. Is it anyway you could take a quick look down in the cellar to find out if a fuse blew or what the problem may be?" she asked frankly enough. "I sure can Madam. I'll get right on it immediately." He agreed then took off toward the basement door. When Mr. Adams opened the cellar door he reached from the flashlight that was hanging on a plastic hook on the door. He proceeded to slowly walk down the steps with the flashlight glaring in front of him, remembering it's been a long time sense he has been down in this part of the house. His mind flashed back to the last time he entered the cellar and that day somehow the door of the cellar slammed shut and caused him to be trapped. Till this day its still unfathomable to him on what could have caused that to happen. Once he made it to the bottom landing of the cellar, he quickly turned around rooted indecisively to his spot with the flashlight glared to the far back wall. He immediately had a creeping suspicion he wasn't alone in the cellar, and even though he felt that way he wanted to hurry and check the fuses. Mr. Adams turned back around and commenced along toward the fuse box, the closer he got a vial smell began to fill his nostrils it was a strong fetor smell which soiled the air, he waved the flashlight from one section to another of the cellar searching from where the smell could be coming from. It finally came upon a dead decomposed rat on a mouse trap below the fuse box. "Yeah, you wasn't so lucky this time, we finally caught you." Mr. Adams pointed out in a whisper, placing his left palm over his mouth and nose with the flashlight raised in between his right arm pit shinning directly at the fuse box. When he opened the box to examine the fuses, his hair started standing up on the back of his neck from the feeling of fright of being down in the cellar by himself. The minute he pointed the flashlight toward the fuses scanning down the line, he panicked, turned around, eyes bulging wide, glaring the light on all three walls thinking he heard something, but once he realized nothing was in plain view, he focused his attention back to the fuse box raising a skeptical eyebrow and a frown saying thoughtfully. "Hum, there's not one fuse blown that I can see." Hurriedly closing the box and striding back up the stairs. Out of the cellar Mr. Adams instantly felt relieved to be back in the part of the house that felt like civilization to him. Mr. Adams approached Mr. and Mrs. Bailey with a smile, while they all were having their dinner. Mr. Adams started to explain the situation. "Excuse me Sir and Madam, but I did a scan over all the fuses and I didn't discover not one fuse blown." "Well that's strange. That never happened to our power lines before. Thank you, John. I'll see about calling the power company tomorrow." Mrs. Bailey said with disbelief. "Yes Madam. Is there anything else I need to do?" Mr. Bailey glanced over to John saying. "No John. That'll be all, matter fact you can rest for the rest of the evening if you like." Mr. Adams bowed a short bow then walked off to the kitchen taking Mr. Bailey on his offer. While everyone continued enjoying their seasoned steaks and salad, Mrs. Adams prepared for them. Mrs. Bailey kept noticing her husband head nodding, until she finally spoke out. "Tim, Honey, I think you should call it a night, we don't want you to land your head in your plate." Mr. Bailey slowly raised his head while opening his eye's wide open recoiling his vision. He was so intoxicated from all the drinks he had drunk. He didn't hesitate not one minute in sliding his chair back away from the table, realizing it was a good idea. "Well Maria. You sure grew up to be a beautiful productive young lady, and I can guarantee you'll always have a place in our hearts, as if you're our very own daughter." Mr. Bailey said conversationally when he stood up on his two feet. Maria couldn't stop blushing from Mr. Bailey's comment then she said as he stepped around the table to Jason. "Thank you Mr. Bailey. It's good to know, I'll always would be in you guys hearts." Mr. Bailey managed a smile on his face before focusing his attention down to Jason. "And Jason, don't you be up late playing your new x-box games." Jason immediately cut his dad off by saying. "Oh no, cause I know how much mom hates that." Jason caused his mother to toss up a quick smile at his acknowledgment. Mr. Bailey went over to kiss his lovely wife forehead. He staggered back catching himself then he tossed up a solute remembering when he was in the marines, after that he faced bowed staggering off. After dinner was over, Jason and Buddy ditched off to his room to play his new bike game before his bedtime. Maria and Mrs. Bailey on the other hand went inside the family room with their grape Welch wine. They were drinking out of fancy champagne glasses, and time went by while they both were having a girly conversation with each other. Maria started to notice a sympathetic look on Mrs. Bailey's face, as if she was keeping a secret from a best friend for years, but when a tear came rolling down Mrs. Bailey's cheek unexpectedly, she glanced up at Maria to say. "I have something to show and tell you Maria, could you please excuse me for a minute?" Maria gave her a nod of approval. Mrs. Bailey opened the antique wall cabinet and pulled out a stack of old newspapers. Maria immediately placed her half empty cup of wine on the coffee table, when Mrs. Bailey returned sitting next to her. Maria reached out to grab the newspaper article Mrs. Bailey was handing her, and once she received the newspaper in hand. She read inside her mind the name of "Amy Bailey". Maria tossed up a confused look and she continued to read along. The news paper article read out. In the deepest of the Michigan woods, three male teenagers came up missing, one female teenager by the name of Amy Bailey was murdered from her throat being slashed as her body was gruesomely skinned, the other female by the name of Darla Phelps survived with major cuts and bruises, who ended up getting checked into the California Patton State Hospital. No motives on who was responsible for these teenager's disappearance and death. Maria closed the news paper article looking teary eyed, but after she regained her composer she said throatily. "Did your other kids ever get the chance to meet their older sister, Mrs. Bailey?" Mrs. Bailey face expression still didn't hold not a shred of humor, until she spoke out and said. "I never could build myself up to tell Tabby and Jason. I didn't won't them to be scared for the rest of their lives like I am, and when my Tabitha had gotten brutally murdered, it made me feel as if it was a curse of some sort." Maria eyes lifted with apprehension before saying. "Oh, I see. Mrs. Bailey, do you have a pen and a scratch piece of paper I could use to right some info down?" "Sure." Mrs. Bailey countered quickly getting up. A few seconds later she returned with a note pad and pen. When Mrs. Bailey reclaimed her seat, she guzzled her glass of wine down, while Maria jotted down Darla's name and location back at Patton State Hospital. A few minutes later Maria called it a night and went off to her living quarters. The moment she stepped through the door she noticed her bathroom light on. "Wait a minute, that light went out on me earlier, but now its back on? Maybe Mr. Adams came and double checked it for me." She said real low to herself, shoving the thought out of her mind so she could prepare for a goodnight sleep. Sense the couple of glasses of grape wine seemed to relax her while taking her flower top off. Standing there naked she felt the feeling of being watched again through the window. Once Maria changed and had gotten into bed, she decided it was a good idea to leave the bathroom light on while she slept.

CHAPTER FOUR

ONCE THE VERY next day arrived, Maria decided to give her boss Lieutenant Mr. Kirk W. Wallace a phone call on her new findings. She got from Mrs. Bailey last night about her daughter Amy Bailey's murder. She scrolled down the stored phone number list, pushing the green send button. After a few rings, Mr. Wallace picked up and said in a very professional tone. "Hello, this is the O.F.P.A. unit, Lt. Wallace speaking, how can I help you?" "Hello, Sir." "Oh, hello Maria." He said recognizing her voice. "Sorry to bother you sir, but I was calling to let you know about some valuable news I discovered last night." "What's that Maria?" Maria conversationally continued. "I just found out that Mrs. Bailey had an older daughter by the name of Amy Bailey that was brutally murdered. Plus there's a friend of hers by the name of Darla Phelps whom is a survivor victim, and currently is being housed and evaluated at the California Patton State Hospital as we speak." "You know what, Maria. I think it'll be a great thing to go have an interview with that young lady, see if she could give up a story on what happened. I also got an old colleague by the name of Mr. Richard Owens, who was on that case nearly a decade ago. Matter of fact, he retired before the case was ever solved, so I'll give you his address and number for future reference that way you could call him when ever you get a chance." "So you always knew that the Bailey's had an older daughter?"

Maria curiously asked. "Yeah, pretty much." He replied shortly. "Alright, what's Mr. Owens number and address?" "His address is 9107 State Road, and his house number is 555-1805, got that?" "Got it, Sir." She said sharply, closing up her folder of notes. "Oh, before I forget, which I meant to tell you when I first realized it was you, that your transfer to Michigan went through, so sometime this evening I'll fax all the information to the office there to have you all set to go, and I'm here to tell you it'll be great to work from the privacy of your own home. So congratulations Maria. Also don't forget I'm not going to be here when you return in the next day or so, 'cause I'm taking off to 29 Palms for that missing kid case, so your weekly and bonus check summed into one will be inside your desk. It will be there when you get here, Alright?" "Alright Sir." She agreed with a smile before disconnecting the line. Maria closed and clamped her cell phone and replaced it back to the clip on her waistline. Walking up the hallway that leads to the main staircase one of the guestroom doors slightly closed on its own, being engrossed in her thoughts it went unnoticed by her. Mr. and Mrs. Bailey were down stairs inside the family room discussing how long Buddy was barking endlessly at the most highest agitated voice. "Hello Mrs. Bailey. Hello Mr. Bailey." She greeted when she came walking into the family room to join them. "Oh hello, Maria, would you like a nice cup of hot raspberry tea?" Mrs. Bailey asked with a friendly leer. "Sure, that'll be just what I need." "So did you get a good night sleep, over all the loud unnecessary barking Buddy was doing? I can assure you he never acted in such a manner as he did. And I do apologize for any inconvenience to your relaxation as well." Mrs. Bailey conversationally apologized. "Oh, no problem. I actually slept like a baby." Maria over exaggerated, holding back her real thought. "Well it's nice to hear that." Mrs. Bailey added. Maria grabbed the hot cup of tea Mrs. Bailey handed her to and took a small sip, then added three sugar cubes to the flavor. "You don't mind if I take this to go to the room, do you? I was needing to go over a few notes, if you don't mind." "Sure. Why certainly Maria, be our guest." Mr. Bailey said when he lifted the Sunday newspaper down. As time went by, Maria was up stairs in her living quarters going over her notes, and making more notes on what questions to ask Darla Phelps. When she realized it was dark outside, she knew she had lost herself in time, she decided to go to bed especially before Buddy started up again.

Jason was still up late playing his new "Excite Bike" game he got. The television slowly started developing static, until a vision of a girl with a rope tied around her neck flickered on his television screen, interrupting his game. "Whoa! What was that?" he muttered then he got sidetracked when his game flicked back on still in motion, forgetting what had just happened. The game was over and Jason restarted it, a strange scrapping sound came from the closed guest room across the hallway. Since Jason was a brave little boy for his age, and he never got scared when he looked at scary movies, being his dad always let it be known that the scary parts was all fixed and made up. But for the third repeatedly scrapping sound Jason witnessed hearing made him put his game on pause thinking it may be Buddy trapped in the room, without knowing that Mr. Adams was instructed to lock Buddy in the garage. Jason slowly eased his head out looking both ways before stepping out into the hallway, making sure it was all clear, walked over to the closed guestroom while his hand reaches out to the door knob to open the door, he says in a low tone "Buddy, come here boy." Hand on the door knob and turning it to open he gives three short whistles, as the door opens he anticipates Buddy's furry self to be there. He had a confused expression when Buddy didn't come trampling from the room. Jason slowly stood up on his tiptoe's to flick the light switch on feeling convinced that the strange scrapping sounds came from this guest room with out a doubt. When he realized that the light switch didn't have any power surging through it, he squinted into the room lowering his arm down from the light switch and cautiously steps over to the guest room bed. "Buddy, come here boy." He called out kneeling down along the bed to take a quick glance underneath it, remembering Buddy loves resting underneath all the beds in the mansion. While Jason was on both knee's peeking underneath the bed, the window was slowly rising on its own. As the air breezed through the thin see through curtains, Jason sat upright stifling a gasp, in hearing the guestroom door slam, his attention focused on the slam of the door in pure darkness, oak leaves came bristly through the window. A shadow appeared extending in height, hopping up on two feet he shouted out for his dad while running full speed to the private bathroom. Once inside he was too late in closing the door behind him, the macabre oak leaves entered after him, slamming the bathroom door and attacked Jason. The vileness spirit of Mary Swartz within the Macabre oak leaves went to torturing Jason to death. With each leave slicing into Jason's body and then coming back for seconds got deeper and deeper, cutting Jason's body into pieces. Jason busts his head on the soap ledge on the wall as he falls backwards into the tub. Minutes later he was dead, the door opened on its own allowing Mary's s spirit of leaves to escape out the guestroom window, disappearing into the darkness.

When morning time arrived, Mrs. Bailey was sitting at the dining room table sipping on a hot cup of coffee, as is her normal morning ritual, reading a Forbes magazine. Mr. Adams let Buddy out of the garage for the early part of the day. Buddy came excitedly galloping in full speed through the open kitchen door and through the dining room, heading toward the staircase. "Slow down old dog." Mrs. Bailey yelled, when Buddy came storming pass her. The second Buddy made it to the top landing where Jason's bedroom's located, he galloped to the guest room closed door squealing and sniffing, until he began to bark in a high pitched troublesome bark, repeatedly. He sensed something was wrong, behind the closed door. Mrs. Bailey quickly lowered her hot cup of coffee from her lips saying low to herself. "Let me get up and go wake Jason up for school, before Buddy does." Placing her cup of coffee and the Forbes magazine down on the table, she took off to the staircase. When making it to the top landing she noticed Buddy sniffing beneath the bottom seal on the guest room door. Easing her head into Jason's room with a confused expression growing on her face as she took in the scene of his room, not only was he not sound asleep in his bed but it was still neatly made up, and his video game on pause. "Hum. Where's Jason?" Coming out of Jason's room she stepped over to the guestroom where Buddy is still sniffing and impatiently scratching on the door. "What's gotten into you, boy?" Mrs. Bailey asked meekly enough while turning the doorknob. Door opened Buddy went storming inside and straight to the bathroom's ajar door barking endlessly. Mrs. Bailey's walked over to the private bathroom, a frown forming on her face from the nasty smell, which reminded her of death, filled the air as she got closer. She reached her hand out slowly pushing the door open in order to turn on the light switch, when the light clicked on a piercing scream bubbled from Mrs. Bailey's stomach to her throat and out her mouth as her heart broke into a million tiny pieces. He dear son, her baby, her third born child's body sliced into pieces as he laid in a puddle of blood inside the tub with one leg dangling over the rim of the tub. Maria's head snapped up right out of her sleep all attention focused on the entrance door. Quickly got dressed and rushed downstairs.

Nearly an hour later after the Michigan town Coroner pulled off with Jason's body, the Saginaw Michigan police officer's a Mr. Corporal Mitchell and his lady partner was wrapping up their last report from Maria. "I promise Officers, I didn't hear a thing in the middle of the night. I must had fallen asleep at least about nine p.m. or so giving myself a head start on some rest." She explained truthfully with no exaggeration in her voice. "Thank you for your time and cooperation Mrs. Gates. Here's a business card to contact us if you wish too." Corporal Mitchell said, handing her a business card, then shouted out with authority in his voice. "Come on guys lets wrap things up!"

CHAPTER FIVE

THE VERY NEXT evening when Maria made it on her scheduled airplane flight, she got a disturbing phone call from the Bailey's family maid. "Hello Investigator Mrs., Gates speaking, how can I help you?" "Mrs. Gates, this is Mrs. Adams. I called to terribly say less than an hour ago I found Mrs. Bailey hung in the cellar from the steal water pipes with one of their brand new dock ropes." "Oh my God. This can't be!" Maria cried out in disbelief. "But I was just calling to inform you, gotta go!" Mrs. Adams said in a hurry and nervously. "Wait! Wait!" Maria blurted out before Mrs. Adams disconnected the line. Maria wiped the tears from her eyes while trying to control her mood then thought to herself. The Bailey family had gone through a lot and from all the pressure built up from their three kids being murdered caused Mrs. Bailey to take her own life or did the killer strike again? She thought insanely to herself sitting in the far seat to the window feeling the plane taking off. Maria figured she needed not to think harshly and relax her thoughts before she caused her own self to go crazy. As time elapsed by and the airplane was still flying in motion through the cloud of darkness. Maria leaned comfortably back in her sleep having rapid eye movement trying to awake when she began to hear tapping and scrapping sounds outside the window behind the shade blind. Suddenly she popped her eyes wide open panting with sweat beads on her forehead once she heard a solid thud sound tap against the thick window. Maria got her panting under control while she cautiously eased her hand up to the blind and began to lift it up. She flinched back with fear and a sigh loud enough to wake the elderly lady that was sitting in the row right beside her with a tight grip on her purse. When she discovered the same vision she once saw in the back window of the Bailey family limo. "Excuse me, ma'am. I just had a bad dream, sorry to wake you." Maria apologized. "It's quite alright darling. I get a little queasy sometimes when I fly myself." Maria forced a smile on her face, then snuggled herself back into her pillow sighing before drifting back off to sleep. Once daylight arrived, the airline made a perfect landing at LAX Airport. As fast as she could Maria exited the plane feeling happy they all made it to their destination safely and all in one piece. When she made it to the vehicle storage ticket employee, she reached in her purse to give him her vehicle storage ticket for her SUV she stored there before taking off to the Bailey family mansion. "I'll be right back in a jiffy ma'am." The storage ticket man assured her. Less than five minutes later, she saw her SUV pulling through the fence stopping right beside her. "Here you go ma'am, your all ready to go." The ticket man said politely climbing out the driver seat. "Thank you." She countered back climbing inside then sped off the LAX Airport grounds. An hour later Maria exited the Waterman exit in San Bernardino less than two miles away from Patton State Hospital off Baseline Avenue. When she arrived on the parking lot and parked she killed the engine and observed an African American middle aged man walking toward her vehicle in his hospital white coat. "Excuse me sir. Do you have time for me to ask you a question?" Maria shouted out to get his attention. She got out the vehicle with keys and a note pad in hand to meet him at the back of her truck where he stopped in his tracks. "Good morning. How can I help you?" He greeted her with a warm smile and a firm handshake. "Thank you. I was needing to have an interview with a young lady by the name of Darla Renee Phelps, and I also wanted to know if you all still had this such person housed here at this facility." "Oh do we? I could never forget she's here, matter of fact she's the looniest patient we had housed here sense that one kid Jamie Stuart who killed his mother, father, plus two little brothers back in 1986. But this Darla Phelps character just takes the cake and smears it all over the wall." "Well that describes she's still here." "Oh yeah!" he added. "Thank you sir, and may I ask what's your name?" "Sure. It's Mr. Abraham, oh by the way if you do go in there to interview her, please stop at the information desk cause trust me they don't like unexpected visitors here. And last but not least, try not to get her all wound up, we had a pretty calm day with her so far. She's usually kicking and pounding on the door. Talking about some girl trying to take her body and soul. Nighttime is when all the fun around here begins. Have fun!" He said tucking his hands in his pockets walking off. When Maria finally made it inside the building a secretary behind the information desk greeted her with a smile. "Hello Mrs. Welcome to California Patton State Hospital, how can I assist you?" Maria approached the Information desk and said "Hello my name is Mrs. Gates, I'm an investigator from the O.F.P.A. Office and I was needing to have an interview with one of your patients by the name of Darla Renee Phelps, if I could." "Sure, can I please check your I.D.?" Once Maria handed over her investigator I.D. to the secretary, she thought to herself, this was the very first time she ever stepped a foot inside a crazy hospital, well there's a first for everything. When the secretary handed back her I.D. she began tapping on the computer keys to pop up Darla's name and room number, then said while pulling out a visitor pass from the counter drawer. "Ok, here she go, she's in room #213B, right down this hallway fourth door on your left. Is there anything else I can assist you with Mrs. Gates?" the secretary asked professionally. "No thank you. This shall be it." Maria replied calmly. "Great. I'll send an assistant right behind you to let you in the room. Thank you for visiting Patton State Hospital." The second Maria made it through the corridor she couldn't believe what she was seeing when observing the hallway full of patients, walking around freely it was if the hallway was full of zombies. Maria nervously jerked out of reflex when a young lady patient named Kimberly came up behind her and tapped her on the shoulder saying when Maria glanced back. "Are you my mother?" then Kimberly moved along in front of her. "No, now if you'll excuse me!" Maria somewhat demanded gruffly. By the time she made it to Darla's door #213B, an elderly lady came walking through the corridor with a ring full of master skeleton keys that opens the room doors from the inside and out. "Hello ma'am. I'm Ms. Maple, what room would you like me to assist you with?" "It'll be this one right here #213B, Darla Phelps if I'm not mistaking. Thank you." Maria said managing a weak smile moving to the side, so Ms. Maple could open the door. When Ms. Maple opened the door, Maria frowned deeply as if the room had been sealed closed like a can once the door was open and the strong urine stench smell blew toward her nostrils like a fan when she went stepping inside. "Everything else is up to you, ma'am. Just scream if you need any more assistance." Ms. Maple said with a taste of enthusiasm, then closed and locked Maria inside the room with Darla. Maria noticed Darla crouched down in the far left corner of the room, with her arms tightly braced around both legs touching each other, while she rocked back and forth with a blank stare at the floor softly humming. Maria also didn't hesitate in noticing redness developing in her eyes through her spread long bangs partially hanging over her facial area. "Hello Darla. My name is Mrs. Gates I'm an investigator from the O.F.P.A. Office, and I'm not here to harm you. All I want to do is get a report from you." Maria glanced over to the right of her and spotted a wooden chair that all the counselor's use when they come to talk to their patients. "May I?" she said placing the chair in the middle of the floor facing Darla taking a seat. Darla didn't grunt a reply she just kept on humming and rocking without saying a word. Maria trailed her eyes right below Darla where she was in a crouch position. When noticed a goldish color puddle beneath her. "Darla, did you urinate on yourself?" Maria asked curiously enough focusing back to her eyes what little she could see through Darla bangs then continued. "Don't be afraid, Darla, and the quicker I ask you these questions, the quicker I'll be on my way." Maria then opened her folder of notes and clicked her pen. "Darla, do you remember a young lady by the name of Amy Bailey?" Darla stop rocking in mind motion slowly raising her head up to Maria gaze, when she heard Maria mention her friend Amy Bailey's name. "She use to be a friend of yours, do you remember?" Maria coached her. "That's my friend Amy standing right beside you." Darla said dryly pointing then eased her arm down. Maria glanced on both sides her saying with strange intensity. "Darla that's nonsense, don't believe that. There's no one else in this room besides you and I." Although Maria could admit goose bumps nearly covered her entire body, and even down to warm place of her pleasant nest, but then again she was also happy to hear Darla raspy voice for the very first time. Maria quickly flipped to a clear page on her note pad when she heard Darla starting up a conversation on her own. "I told Amy we needed to leave because it was getting dark, but Chris wanted us to keep following him to Mike and Carlos and his seating area in the woods to play a game. Once we all made it to where we was going, Carlos came running up behind us saying he was having a funny feeling about something. As he further on explained to us. He stayed back a little ways skipping round rocks across the shallow lake, when a funny vibe filled his senses, though he couldn't distinguish what he was feeling. Chris ends up telling him he was lying and trying to chicken out, but as we all agreed to sit down Indian style in a circle. Chris explained to us if we say the words 'Mary wake up' once a piece, she'll appear within seconds." Darla stopped her conversation for a second to sigh and started back up rocking. "I tried to whisper to Amy lets go, and we needed to make it home, but she just ignored me and that's when Chris yelled out 'Mary wake up' for the first time, Carlos said it the second time and Mikey for the third, on my turn I told them I wasn't in any mood to play this game. I didn't want everyone to call me chicken when we made it to school the next day and I wanted my boyfriend Chris to think I was brave so I ended up saying 'Mary wake up' for the fourth time. I glanced over to Chris and watched him nod his head as a sign of bravery on what I did. Amy saw that the guys respected me for being brave so she blurted out those same words for the fifth time. I'm not gonna lie, at first nothing happened until we realized the wind started blowing. The guys freaked out and started running when they seen leaves trailing each other and molding into body form. At that point Amy and myself took off running in a whole different direction than them. I couldn't believe they ran off and left us like that. Amy and I ran a few yards away, I glanced back and saw Amy being snatched completely in the air about fifteen feet high, and slammed into a tree by the oak leaves. I guess that's when I ended up tripping over a brick twisting my ankle as my head came crashing down on the ground. I must of gotten knocked out unconscious cause that's really all I know or at least remember." Darla added looking unsure. "So what you're telling me, is, you all played a dangerous game that lifted a curse?" Maria calmly asked. Darla just shrugged her shoulders as if she wasn't sure then her eyes suddenly got bulging wide sliding herself deeply in the corner staring blankly in the air with total fright in her eyes, while breaking out in a loud scream of words. "No, Please don't kill me, please don't kill me!" At the moment Maria saw her screaming and kicking at the air, hallucinating something was approaching her, she dropped her folder of notes and rushed over to Darla to comfort her. Seconds later Maria heard the door unlock and open. Mr. Abraham and Ms. Maple came rushing inside from the noise Darla was making. Ms. Maple paced over to Darla and gave her a shot in her arm to calm her actions. "That's it Mrs. Gates, your visit is now terminated at this moment!" Mr. Abraham snorted then continued. "I sat there and told you not to get her all wound up, sorry but you'll have to vacate the premises." Maria stood upright from picking up her folder and pen open mouth then said moodily enough. "I beg your pardon!" Raising her right palm stopping her conversation deciding it would be a great idea to leave, so she could change her clothes and take a hot shower before she got to the office. Being her entire left knee slid into Darla's urine puddle she made beneath her. Maria was sitting inside her SUV with the engine on looking over her notes saying beneath her breath "Chris made them play a Mary game, could this be the girl I keep visioning inside my nightmares?" Maria closed her folder, put the gear into reverse upon noticing Mr. Abraham standing at the main entrance door, holding it open with his foot and arms crossed making sure she pulled off the lot. Pulling into the AMPM to get gas, she decided to make an out of state phone call to Mr. Richard Owens. After three continuous rings she heard a deep voice say "Hello, Mr. Owens speaking, how can I help you?" "Hello, Mr. Owens, my name is Mrs. Gates and I'm an employee from the O.F.P.A. Office. I was told by my boss Mr. Kirk W. Wallace that it'll be okay to give you a ring." "Oh yeah. I was just informed by Mr. Wallace yesterday evening that you'll be giving me a call." Maria screwed the gas cap on, and got into the drivers seat. "So how can I help you, Mrs. Gates?" he said helpfully "You can call me Maria if you like." "Well sense you made that clear you can call me Richard from now on." "Well actually I was wanting to know are you familiar with a young lady by the name of Amy Bailey?" Maria asked firmly while pulling away from the pump terminal when a vehicle honked its horn for her spot. "Oh yeah, oh yeah. I'm well over familiar with the Baileys case." Richard assured her. "Great because I'm now assigned to these cases that the O.F.P.A. Office decided to reopen from all the strange paranormal activities, that's been reappearing in the past month or so." "I see Maria, so basically your needing my help in this matter?" He asked thoughtfully. "I'm afraid to bother you with it sir, but that's correct." "Well Maria, I have sort of given up but I can't never let the O.F.P.A. Office down, so I'll be delighted to join forces with you and like they always said two heads are better than one, living heads that is." Richard said laughing at his own joke. "Oh you will." Maria said surprised. "I sure will Mrs. Gates, but only under one condition. You be the boss and lead the way." He added forgetting "I mean Maria." She smiled then said. "No problem sir. Thank you Richard, well I'm going to stop by the office after I clean up a little and pack a few things to move back to Michigan. Is there anyway I could meet up with you once I settled in?" "Sure, that'll be great. See you then Maria and have a safe trip." "I sure will, Richard, bye." Maria accelerated on the gas closing her cell phone. A few hours later after she went home to clean up, she made it to the O.F.P.A. Office, cleared her desk getting her check and then making her way to Twenty-nine Palms on the missing kid case. Maria was caught off guard by all her colleagues as Ms. Carolyn and the rest of her co-workers came walking up with a candle lit cake saying all at the same time. "We're going to miss you Mrs. Gates!" Maria's palms came up to her face and mouth area and wailed lowering her hands down. "You guys shouldn't have." Mr. Murphy came walking up with a Polaroid photo of all the co-workers and himself. "Here you go Mrs. Gates. This is something to remind us by." Maria stood up to grab the photo and gave him a friendly embrace in appreciation.

CHAPTER SIX

IT WAS TWO weeks later after Maria, Bobby and their six year old daughter Antonia was all settled in their new home in Michigan. Maria thought it would be a good idea to give Richard a call to finally meet up with him sense Antonia was off to her new school, and Bobby was at his new law firm office. She dialed Richard's number which he snatched up the phone on the first ring. "Hello, Mr. Owens speaking." "Hello Richard, this is Maria." "Oh hello Maria. How things going?" "Great. I was just calling you to let you know I'll be over shortly. If it was still okay with you." Maria said "Sure, sure. This would be a perfect time. I guess I'll be expecting you." "Thanks Richard, see you in a half an hour." Disconnecting the line, she then called Bobby at his office to inform him to pick Antonia up from school on his way home. Maria pulled up slowly into Richard's driveway, causing all four of his Rottweiler dogs to barking at her presence. Cutting off the SUV and approaching the door, Richard opened it right as she was about to knock. "Other than hearing your dogs bark how did you know I was about to knock on the door?" She asked curiously, thinking to herself that Richard reminds her of the actor Bruce Willis who played in the Die Hard movie. Richard didn't say a word, he just angled his left hand toward his three television monitors neatly settled on a table next to his computer desk. "Oh I see." She said stepping inside. Richard grabbed her coat and hung it on the coat stand, then offered. "May I get you a cold drink Maria or perhaps some coffee?" "No thank you. You have a nice home Richard. You live here alone?" Maria commented easily. "Yes. It's just me and my four dogs." "How long you been on those murder cases in the past." She asked standing in the middle of the living room floor. "Well actually it seemed forever, matter of fact, I haven't yet solved any. Let me show you an example." He angled his hand to escort her over to his blue room where he keeps all the victims photos. When Richard opened the Blue room door, Maria couldn't believe what she was seeing. It was nearly a hundred photos of missing victims posted all around the rooms walls, and quite a few animals. "All these photos you see Maria, are unsolved cases that's dying for closure wanting to be solved and as for me not understood." "You got to be kidding me." She said blankly and sharply. "No. I wish I was. Even some of the victim's pets got worse treatment than their owners." Richard explained stiffly angling his hand back to the living room.

Keith Duncan was a Caucasian kid who lived at home with his mother and father, plus his little sister, named Mandy. Keith is fourteen years old and his little sister is eight years old. Keith someday wanted to be a Horror actor, and all his practicing had been implemented on towards scaring his mom and his little sister. When Keith and his dad came pulling up in their driveway from the town grocery store where they went to get some Idaho potatoes, car shine for the mini van and a scary monster mask, he purchased with his own allowance money. Keith came through the front door and went storming up the stairs to his room to avoid his little sister Mandy from seeing what he had in his hand. She was sitting Indian style in the middle of the living room floor looking at Dora the Explorer DVD. Mrs. Duncan was sitting at the small round table by the laundry room basement door looking at a Martha Stuart cookbook, waiting for the laundry to dry. Mr. Duncan went back outside after bringing in the groceries to wash his fourth pride and joy and put tire shine on his wheels that he bought when they went to visit his mother-n-law in Indianapolis, Indiana. Keith was up stairs in his room preparing to do one of his practical scares of the day on his sister, who was still giggling happily in the living room looking at TV. Out of nowhere a sound of metal hitting the floor in his closet caught Keith's attention as he was about place the monster mask over his head. "What was that?" He said after flinching at the noise from the closet. He slowly tiptoed his way over to the closet door with the mask raised up to his forehead and making it to the door calmly reached out to grab the knob.

Maria and Richard was sitting at his dinner table going over the story she had gotten from Darla, but right when she was about to go to the findings, Richard stopped her and said "let me get us something cold to drink before we get into the good part." "Sure, that'll be fine." She ended up agreeing. Noticing that Richard would look much younger if he'd only cut his uneven beard. For a Caucasian man in his early fifties he still had a very strong frame about himself. "Here you go. These Coca Colas nearly was frozen." "These are perfect, shall proceed on?" Maria asked while he reclaimed his seat at the table. "Sure. Give it your best shot." "Well Richard, Darla explained to me she told Amy Bailey they needed to leave cause it was getting dark, but Chris wanted them to keep following him to Mikey, Carlos and his sitting area to play out a game. She said once they all made it to where they were traveling to, Carlos came running up behind them saying he was having a funny feeling about something, as he further on explained to them it was when he stayed back a little ways skipping rocks across the shallow lake. He had got a funny vibe, but couldn't understand what it was. Darla said Chris told him he was lying, and was just trying to chicken out, but as they all agreed to sit down in Indian style in a circle. Chris explained to them if they all said "Mary wake up" once apiece, she'll appear in seconds. Darla said she tried whispering to Amy once again they needed to make it back home. But Amy just ignored her and that's when Chris yelled out the words "Mary wake up." followed by Carlos, Mikey, on Darla's turn she told them she wasn't in any mood in playing the game. Then again she didn't want to want everyone to call her chicken at school the next day, and in wanting her boyfriend Chris to think she's brave she said it for the fourth time. She said she glanced over at Chris and he nodded his head up and down at her as a sign of bravery. Darla further on explained Amy saw the guys acknowledged her for being brave so Amy blurted out "Mary wake up" for the fifth time." Maria stopped her conversation to focus her attention over to Richard's living room window, when the sound of the dogs barking at something reached her ears, which sort of reminded her of Buddy from the Bailey's mansion. Richard paced over to his three camera TV's. monitors to see what was causing his watch dogs to act the way they was, he observed his dogs sitting calm like nothing ever happened. He went and took a speculated glance out the front door, then returned back to his seat raising down his skeptical eye brow. "What was that all about?" "I honestly don't know. They usually don't bark out of spite." Richard assured her. "I guess we could get back to the story, before it gets late. Well at first Darla said nothing happened, until they seen the wind blowing then the guys got up and took off running when they saw oak leaves bodily forming. At that point Amy and she took off running from the leaves which caused them to run in a different direction than the guys, and once Amy and she ran a few yards away. She took a glance back and witnessed Amy being snatched completely in the air about fifteen feet high and powerfully slammed into a tree from the leaves. She tripped over a brick twisting her ankle causing her head to crash to the ground and basically that's all she remembered." "You mean to tell me Maria, all this nonsense started over a Mary game?" Richard asked curiously. "Yes sir, a little after I was born." She agreed. "Well, well, well. These kids now days, will get their hand stuck in a coconut shell if they see any candy in it." Maria didn't comment back, she just laughed heartily from what Richard said with a straight face, and she couldn't deny it wasn't true.

After Keith flung the closet door wide open, as if expected to catch something off guard. He found it very abstruse seeing his clothes in motion swinging on hangers then abruptly stopping. "Oh no! My baseball cards are all scattered and out of order." He relented once he saw his baseball cards scattered all over the closet floor. "Besides, how did this metal box fall from the top shelf anyway?" He thought curiously, gathering up all the baseball cards so he can go scare his little sister down stairs in the living room. With the cards all picked up and placed back inside the metal box, putting it on the top shelf and closing the closet door. Keith slowly crept down the steps with his right hand pressed against the wall to lighten his every step, so Mandy couldn't hear him coming down the stairs. Once he made it down to the bottom landing where Mandy was seated in the middle of the floor unaware of his presence, he mounted his back up against the outer side of the living room wall. Mandy leaned halfway around staring affronted at the living room door walkway when she thought she heard something. But after surveying the scene she focused her full attention back to Dora the Explorer on the TV. Keith thought he blew his cover by snatching his mask down over his face to cause the thick rubber to making a snapping sound. When it didn't he started breathing hard beneath the thick rubber feeling like he was becoming as one with the monster mask. Counting up to five in his mind he jumped out into the open of the living room walkway and yelled "Rahh, Rahh, Rahh." Mandy nearly panicked from being caught off guard. Screaming to the top of her lungs, she dashed off for cover behind their big sofa. Keith jumped on the couch steadily growling leaning menacingly over the backside and when he saw her staring up at him with her eyes big and round with fright, he once again yelled out. "Rahh." Causing her to take off running with a much louder scream, thinking her big brother Keith finally turned into a monster. She made it to the kitchen where Mrs. Duncan was still fumbling through Martha Stuart's cookbook she shouted out. "Mom! Keith turned into a monster, and he scaring me!" Mrs. Duncan pulled Mandy to her side when Keith came walking through the kitchen walkway, causing Mrs. Duncan to jump herself then she saw the cruel monster mask over his head. "What in the?" She wondered. "It's only me, mom!" Keith assured her, taking off the mask. "Keith! You go take that mask and put it away, right this minute young man. How dare you scare your sister like that, when all this crazy stuff going around?" She fumed. "Yes ma'am." Keith said dryly heading out the door.

 Maria stood up from the table after telling Richard, she'll meet up with him a little later, 'cause she needed to make it home to cook dinner for her family. "Well, Maria. It was a pleasure meeting you, and once again. I'm more than happy to work with you on this unsolved mystery." Richard stated handing her coat over to her. "Like wise, Richard. Bye." Making it into her SUV Maria honked her horn reversing out the driveway. Darkness was coming about while she was steady traveling up Spawlding Road, until suddenly she caught a blowout on one of her tires. Maria immediately pulled along side the road of cornfield's that spreads out amongst the entire road. "Shit. Just what I need, a blowout in the middle of nowhere! Amongst nothing!" She snapped, hitting the steering wheel. Maria threw the gear into park, and killed the engine before exiting the vehicle, when she saw headlights on another vehicle approaching quickly. Once Maria made it to the yellow middle divider, she lively started waving her arms trying to get the driver attention, but needless to say the driver kept going. "I can't believe him. He just totally ignored me. Like I wasn't even standing here!" She complained going back to her S.U.V. When Maria sat in the driver seat, she thought it would be a good idea to call her husband Bobby at home. After dialing their home extension, she heard Bobby pick up and say. "Hello. This is the Gates residence." "Bobby, Honey. I called to let you know, I just caught a blowout five miles away from where we live. Babe, the bottom line is I'm stuck." She said disparagingly. "I'll be there in a jiffy babe, but first. Look in the back beneath the floor board and strike up a couple of those emergency flair's." He instructed her in the dark." She said then exited the vehicle to do exactly what her husband demanded her to do, once they disconnected the line. Maria struck the first flair then the second, when she heard something in the woods across the street from her, she glanced over and caught in the tree's shaking like the old movie. She saw called the Predator, when that invisible creature was down trotting in the trees jumping amongst them. "What was that?" She muttered placing the flair down on the ground behind the SUV to pace back over the driver seat. Maria powered all the windows up and the doors locked. Then started rocking her right leg while tapping a rhythm on her steering wheel while gradually looking around her saying underneath her breath. "Hurry Bobby, Hurry." As time elapsed by Maria discovered some bright headlights glaring in her rearview mirror, causing her to squint both eyes. The lights gleamed so bright she couldn't see the make of the car nor catch the identity of the driver that exited the vehicle. Maria flinched taking her eyes of the rearview mirror focusing them over to the driver side window letting out a sigh of relief when she saw her husband. Unlocking the doors to step out and give Bobby a firm hug. "Oh Bobby, you had my heart racing." "I got here as quick as I could." He said hugging her back then added. "Babe, go sit in the car with our little princess while your King fixes the flat." Assuring her with a warm smile. In less than five minutes the tire was changed and they was up and gone to the safety zone.

It was the next day when Keith decided to take the short cut home from school, through a sheet of woods. He stopped in his tracks rooted to his spot looking all around him, he heard twigs on the ground breaking and crumbling in a distance, like someone was stepping over them heading toward his direction. The wind slightly started blowing and his senses got feverishly heightened. He saw a pile of oak leaves dancing on the ground trailing toward him. Keith took off running in full speed like he was Carl Lewis, not slowing down one bit, till he made it out of the woods and on the road that leads straight to his house. The second he made it out of the woods and onto the road he took a glance back at the path way making sure nothing wasn't following him. Arching over with both hands posted on his knees trying to get his senses under control and catch his breath. Keith's heart was beating like a racehorse who just won the World Gold Cup at the Kentucky Derby. His breathing under control he paced off along the road. The further he went the closer his house came into view. He noticed his mom and dad wasn't home, plus that pretty much meant his little sister Mandy wasn't home from her after school daycare either. Making it to the front porch, he bent down to grab the key underneath the mat. His mom left it there for him for times when he made it home before them. Wasting no time he opened the door and locking the door behind him once inside. Walking over to their living room window to take a peek out and see if he can see anything. "It didn't look as if anything is wrong." He said closing the curtain taking off to the kitchen to read the chore list on the refrigerator, his mom made out. Keith got half way through the dishes, turned off the faucet with a glimmer of doubt in his eyes, wondering if he heard something in the other part of the house. Slowly creeping his way out of the kitchen and into the area where their stairs are located only stopping when he noticed his signature N.B.A. Pacer Basketball that was signed by Reggie Miller the night he and his dad went to the Indianapolis, Indiana finals game against the Los Angeles Lakers. "Wait a minute. This basketball couldn't of bounced down the steps on its own." He realized staring at the top landing of the staircase and although Keith had a taste for horror. It didn't stop him from feeling vulnerable inside his own home while thinking this was the second time today feeling the way he felt. While his eyes remained glued to the top landing of the staircase, he slowly started up them then stopped in the middle of the fleet of steps when he noticed a slight breeze coming through the staircase. He flinched and blinked his eyes when he heard something fall to the ground in one of the rooms. "Now I heard that!" He thought to himself.

This is what it may feel like playing in a horror film, but only the feeling he was experiencing was all so real he further thought traveling the rest of the way up. Keith made it to the top landing, noticed Benjamin's dog chain hanging from a nail on the wall of the hallway. Benjamin was their German Shepherd dog they ended up giving to his Grandmother as a watch dog around her suburban Indiana. Home she purchased nearly six months ago, although he knew the dog chain couldn't do much he also figured it beats nothing at all. Keith reached up to take the chain off the nail then quickly wrapped it half way around his right hand for a tighter grip. Taking off slowly looking into each one of the doors as he passed moving along to his room, where the breeze was the strongest at. Making it to his room, noticing something wasn't right he saw his big Disneyland picture flat on the ground and his window prompt wide open with a few oak leaves scattered on the floor, and on the window ledge. "Who's here? You need to show yourself now, before I call the police!" he scuffed out loud, slowly walking inside heading up to the window to close it. Keith walked straight up to the window without noticing his closet door being halfway open. Struggling to close the window he suddenly had a strange feeling he wasn't inside the room alone. Goosebumps grew on both sides of his cheeks. "Keith. Now how you going close the window with a chain wrapped around your hand?" he said to himself raising his arms down along his side. The minute he was about to turn around from hearing something from the closet area. He was quickly snatched off his feet, causing his chin to slam right to the floor. "Ah!" Keith shouted with his arms stretched out in front of him with the chain still wrapped around his hand. The Macrebra oak leaves dragged him into the closet and wrapped the chain around his neck hanging him from the steal hanger pool. The chain sliced through his neck tearing his skin. Keith kept choking and sobbing till he went into state of shock with his legs kicking from the strangulation. The more leaves kept whirling around his body, the more blood kept gushing out from each rip on his flesh. Once Keith was dead as the last air ceased out of his lung's the leaves settled then escaped out the open closet and out the window leaving his body nude and deadly exposed with blood dripping from his corpse.

 An hour later when Keith's mom, dad, and sister Mandy made it home, Mrs. Duncan stood at the bottom of the staircase to yell out for him, Mr.

Duncan was laying Mandy on their sofa. "Keith we're home, come and eat your Mc. Donald's!" When she didn't get a response she goes over to the dining room table to sit the bag down. She walked back to the bottom landing of the staircase and yelled out once more "Keith you better not be trying to scare us, young man!" "Jenny, go see what that kid is up to, 'cause I know he made it home. His basketball is sitting right there by the door." Mr. Duncan instructed her, besides he didn't want to go up and down the steps with his artificial leg if he didn't have to. "Alright honey." She agreed, taking off up the steps. Making it to the top landing she shivered at the chilled air that lingered through the hallway from Keith's bedroom window. "Why its so cold up here?" she thought underneath her breath as she moved alone. Mrs. Duncan immediately felt queasy and nervous with horrid suspicion that something was wrong. "Keith!" she shouted out once more as her voice held a conspiratorial note. Slowly turning into his room gazing straight a head over to the wide open window, then screamed with a loud screeching sound once she observed a puddle of blood soaked into his carpet, and Keith hanging from the closet steal pole with the chain wrapped around his neck. "Oh God! Darell come quick!" she screamed out when her heart sank. When Mr. Duncan heard his wife scream echo throughout the house he limply strode up to Keith's bedroom. "What the hell! Who did this to my son?" He yelled with a instinctive grab in his voice. When he came storming through the door and saw his son in the deadly condition he was in.

The very next day as Maria was sitting at home unpacking a few more things, she got a call from the secretary at the Saginaw Michigan O.F.P.A. Office up dating her on the latest news. Maria placed the stack of picture frames back down in the box, upon hearing the phone ringing. "Hello. Investigator Mrs. Gates speaking, how can I help you?" She answered professionally, when she picked up. "Hello Mrs. Gates and Good Afternoon. This is Amanda Mason over at the office, sorry to bother you Mrs. Gates, but I was told to call you to let you know the update on yesterdays evening news, of the latest paranormal murder victim." "Thank you, please continue." "Yesterday evening a little boy named Keith Duncan was found brutally murdered and Corporal Mitchell notified us on the findings when they discovered it wasn't a common murder." "Thank you Ms. Mason, that was highly appreciated, also thank you for your professional studying in this matter." Maria pointed out. "Oh yeah, Mrs. Gates, would you be needing the victims address?" "Sure that'll be great. Let me grab a pen and some scratch paper. Okay what is it?" "Okay its 65722 N. Durgin Road, have a great day Mrs. Gates." "You too, Ms. Mason. Bye." Maria said before disconnecting the line to dial Richard's number. "Hello. Richard Owens speaking." "Hello, Richard." "Oh hello, Maria. I was just thinking about giving you a ring to let you know I got those radio walkie-talkie's I told you about yesterday." "Good, but I also called you to let you know a little boy was found in his house murdered yesterday evening." "Good gracious these murders is popping up outta no where again!" Richard said surprisingly. "Well I'll be over first thing in the morning to sit and talk with you and also to pick up one of the radios." "Sounds like a plan to me Maria." "But Richard this town is sure losing its Michigan vibe, I know that much. Okay I'll see you tomorrow." "Bye" he said shortly before hanging up. Once Maria got off the phone she went to the kitchen to give their cat Jasper some cat food, plus she also couldn't get the thought out of her mind on what happened to Mrs. Bailey and her kids. At the kitchen counter she took a deep breath inward then exhaled from the thought crazily distracting her mind.

At noon the time next day her and Richard was sitting at this dining room table drinking hot coffee going over some supporting documents. Old photo's of victims that were never found. Richard got up from the table to grab the radio walkie-talkie's from his living room coat closet shelf then returned to the table. "Alright, here's yours. We'll just keep them on channel twenty-two, that way if one of us gets out of range, it'll still pick up full frequency." He explained before handing her one. Maria grabbed the radio from his hand then said through the receiver when she turned it on. "Testing, testing 1, 2, 3, Testing." And once she heard her own voice echoing through Richard's receiver, she snatched her cell phone from her clip on her waistline when she felt it vibrate. "Excuse me Richard. Hello, Investigator Mrs. Gates speaking, how can I help you?" "Hello Maria, how's things coming along on you new assignment?" "Oh hello, Mr. Wallace. Actually it feels great to be back in the heart of my old town, what you got cooking?" "Well, I was calling to see if you could put me in your work schedule to I.D. a few bodies to see if they match your case load, cause these are some mysterious murder victims." "Oh, they look that bad?" "Yeah, I'm afraid so." Mr. Wallace admitted. "Alright. How soon you'd like for me to be on the next plane?" "It ain't no rush, hell, they are already dead. How bout three to four days?" "That sounds great, sir." She agreed ebulliently. "Alright, see you then Maria and have a safe trip on your flight." Maria closed her cell phone and said to Richard. "Richard. It maybe a change of plans for a few days." "Why, what's going on?" he asked "That was Mr. Wallace, and he needs me to make a positive I.D. on some murder victims in 29 Palms California, to make sure their not my case load of mysterious murders." "Oh, I see." Richard acknowledged calmly, as he continued "Just make sure you carry your radio out there with you, so we can stay in contact full fledge." "I sure will. Let's go over a few more of these documents and photo's before I take back off." "Oh yeah, where were we?" he said shuffling through the rest of the photos.

Natalie Louis and David Louis is brother and sister. Natalie is eighteen years old and David is twelve years old. Natalie has a bipolar disorder that keeps her high tempered at David from any and everything he did. "I got to get out of this old lady's house, before I end up in someone's prison for killing that boy!" Natalie said out loud to herself while tapping on her computer keys logging onto the chat line to talk to her new friend Darius. David was outside Natalie's bedroom door peeking his head inside her room, crotched down eavesdropping, but he accidentally laughed out loud from her comment. Natalie quickly swiveled around in her computer chair to storm over to the door when she heard him laughing heartedly. "Mom . . . ! You better keep that little boy away from my room, before I accidentally kill him. And I mean it!" David happy expression suddenly turned serious, while hauling ass away, down the steps, and then with force her door slammed closed.

Darla raced out of bed and ran over to her door barefooted, once she heard the corridor opening and closing."

Natalie Louis and David Louis are brother and sister. Natalie is eighteen years old and David is twelve years old. Natalie has a bipolar disorder that keeps her high tempered at David with any and everything he does. "I got to get out of this old lady's house, before I end up in some bodies jail for killing that boy!" Natalie said out loud to herself, tapping on her computer keys going into the chat line to talk to her new friend Darius. David was outside her door peeking his head inside her room, crouched down ease dropping. Accidentally laughing out loud from her comment, Natalie swiveled around in her computer chair, got up and stormed over to the door, "Mom! You better keep this little boy away from my room before I accidentally kill him and I mean it!" David's happy expression turned serious as he stood up on his feet and raced down the stairs when seeing her stomping towards him. Reaching the bottom of the stairs her door slammed jam tight.

Darla raced out of bed and ran over to her door bare footed, once she heard the corridor opening and closing. "Ms. Dorothy. I need to talk to you." Darla yelled out behind the door. Although Ms. Dorothy kept going, she did take Darla yelling into consideration by yelling back. "Wait Darla. I have to start from the far end tonight."

A little while later after Darla paced back and forth inside her room, she quickly ran over to the door when she heard Ms. Dorothy asking another patient one door down from her, was he alright? "Darla what seems to be the problem?" Ms Dorothy asked Darla when she stepped up to Darla's window. "You have to let me out of here, she's trying to take my soul . . . !" Darla explained vigorously. "That's non-sense Darla. There's no one in the room with you, and I'll advise you to calm down on your own, or I'll give you something that'll help you and trust me it wouldn't be a very beautiful sight, nor feeling." Said Ms. Dorothy before walking off to finish up her loggings on the rest of the patience. "What, you can't leave me here . . . !" Darla said franticly then she kicked the door with five continuous kicks with her bare feet. The second Ms Dorothy made it back to the front where the staff and guard room is located. Mr. Dalton stuck his head out the door with a pack of coffee filter's in his hand saying. "What's going on back there?" Ms. Dorothy stopped right before entering the break room that sits straight across the hall from the security room, took a deep breath be for responding. "It's that damn Darla again. She don't appeal to me as the same young lady back in the day when she first arrived her, besides her eyes are starting to develop redness to them like she tried to strangle herself or something." "He suggested. "Sure, why not. Maybe she'll listen to you." Dorothy insisted. Mr. Dalton placed the coffee filter inside the maker, seconds later he took off to Darla's room. Darla kicked the wooden chair over inside her room, then she quickly stepped over to the door to peek out the square window that peer out into the half lit hallway, once she heard the corridor's closing again. Mr. Dalton had his flashlight blared out in front of him as if his soul knew how frighten he was. Once Mr. Dalton made it to Darla's door he glanced directly in her blood spotted eye's saying. "Darla, what's all this commotion and banging on the door about?" Darla eyes grew bright then she yelled out with a serious voice. "I need to be let out of here Mr. Dalton. She said she needs my body to damn the world for what happen to her. She wants to be born again, damn it . . . !" "Now, now, Darla. You know that's not possible. I thought you was already being put up to have a hearing with Mrs. Kathleen Craig in the next day or so." Darla pounded her fist against the door before snapping. "We don't have time for that do you understand? We're all going to die. Mary going to kill me, Mary's going to kill you, Mary's going to kill Ms. Dorothy, Mary's going to kill Mrs. Kathleen, Mary's out to kill all of us . . . !" Darla's eyes got extremely red when she mentioned Mary's name five times without realizing it. "Darla what's wrong with your eyes anyways. Did you try to strangle yourself?" Mr. Dalton asked with concern rippling through his voice. "Go to hell . . . , you sonofabitch!" Darla blurted out deviously frowning, then she spat at the window. Mr. Dalton flinched back out of reflex when he saw her spit coming at him like 3-D landing on the opposite side of the glass. Mr. Dalton's face expression hardened before saying soberly. "Oh yeah . . . , that's really going to help you!" Then he walked off heading back to the guard room to pour a cup of fresh, hot, coffee leaving Darla to deal with her issue's herself.

CHAPTER SEVEN

NATALIE WAS INSIDE her room preparing to take her nightly hot shower, while David was occupied in their living room finishing up his last few math problems for homework and getting ready to watch his weekly television show "The Shield" to see Michael Chiklis who plays Detective Vic Mackey. "David don't you be up late to where you can't wake up on time for school tomorrow, and make sure you turn out all the lights before you got to bed." Mrs. Louis reminded him. "I will, oh Mom!." "Yes, David" "You forgot to sign my paperwork for our fieldtrip to the Ballet show." "I'll sign it early in the morning, so leave it on the dining room table." she said walking off to her room. Natalie stood in her bedroom window with her house coat covering her nakedness waiting for the shower water to get steaming hot and while she surveillance the scene out side her window, she noticed a pile of oak leaves trailing each other underneath the garage corner night light. "It sure looks windy out there." She said thoughtfully, walking up to her bathroom mirror to take down her long blond hair she inherited from her mom. Natalie was very beautiful with pretty straight teeth and water blue eyes that sometimes turned into the shade of bluish green when she get fired up at David. When she saw the steam she hung her house coat on the hook then stepped inside the tub leaving the bathroom door open so the steam could easily escape and wouldn't fog up the mirror. Once David start looking at this T.V. show the Shield. He immediately felt he was being watched through the opening of their living room curtain so he quickly rived the T.V. so he wouldn't miss not one scene of the show and once he stoop up from his dads recliner chair, whom passed away when his vehicle crashed into a phone poll on his way home from their family business. David slowly spread the curtains so he wouldn't cause any attention to himself, but once he didn't see anyone directly staring through the window, he cuffed his hands on the window focusing his attention toward the star casing when he heard a door slamming up stairs, saying to himself. "Do she ever get tired of slamming doors around here?" Then shook his head going back over to the recliner chair to un-tivo his show to pick up where he left off at. Natalie pushed the shower curtain open, when she heard her bathroom door slamming closed for what reason she didn't know. "I'm gonna kill that little kid, I tell you!" She said without humor in her voice turning the cold and hot water off. When Natalie stepped out the tub, she quickly through her house coat over her nakedness, and wrapped a towel around her wet hair. She easily noticed a terrain of air breezing underneath her bathroom door seal, when she was wrapping the towel around her head. "Boy its getting cold in here all of a sudden." She thought dryly. Once Natalie opened the bathroom door, her expression turned grave when she saw her window prompted wide open. "I just know he didn't!" She scoffed, taking off out the room to confront him. David's nerves jerked, when he heard Natalie charging down the steps and not saying a single word, once she came barging into the living room to give him a pretty hard thump on his head. "What the, MOM!" He yelled, standing up with his hand on his head looking at her angrily. "What's all this racket about?" Mrs. Louis said sharply coming out her room and up the hallway, when she heard them in the living room arguing. "Mom! Natalie came down the stairs and hit me for no reason." David once again yelled. "No Mom, this little turd of yours came in my room slammed my bathroom door, and raised my window up while I was in the shower!" Natalie explained then popped David in the head once more. "Little, pervert!" "Ouch!" David shouted. "Natalie stop it, and don't call your brother that!" Mrs. Louis snarled. "But its true!" Natalie added. "Mom, I want my lick back!" David concluded. "That's enough David. Why don't you go an prepare yourself for bed." Mrs. Louis suggested. "That's not fair. I didn't even do anything!" He pondered going off to his room. "And you young lady, need to find other things to accommodate your attitude with him all the time, instead of resorting to putting your hands on him all the time. You're a grown lady now!" "Fine! Jump all down my throat all the time, why don't you!" Natalie said seriously, then went off to her room to finish getting ready for bed. Mrs. Louis stood there watching her walk off and said thoughtfully underneath her breath. "Lord have mercy on me. I don't know what I'm going to do with those two." She visually sighed, then went to cut the living room light out.

* * *

When Morning time arrived at Patton State Hospital, Mrs. Kathleen Craig was going up to patients doors giving them qualifying news. Darla's neighbor across the hall, Kimberly Tuscan, sat upright on her bed when she heard the day time security guard let Mrs. Craig inside her room. "Hello Kimberly. I'm Mrs. Craig the supervisor of Patton State Hospital. Today I'm here to let you know you'll be up for release in two weeks, under these circumstances though." Mrs. Craig took a seat on the wooden chair, and continued. "You're not to sneak employees' master keys from them anymore, being it shows on my report you've had numerous disciplines on that particular matter in the past few years since being a patient here at Patton State." Mrs. Craig stopped her conversation momentarily to quickly proof read over her notes, making sure she wasn't forgetting anymore don'ts. "Well Ms. Tuscan, that seems to be all. Do you fully understand what I've just explained to you?" "Yes ma'am, I'm fully aware. Is it time to eat?" Kimberly asked. "No not quite. They'll be feeding shortly Ms. Tuscan." "Thanks." Kimberly said forcing a smile. Mrs. Craig stepped over to the door and said. "Well Ms. Tuscan be on your best behavior, cause believe me. They'll be watching." The security guard immediately opened the door, when he heard three continuous knocks on the it. The second Kimberly heard the guard locking the door. She reached inside her mattress to grab the master skeleton key she had hide inside her mattress. Darla stepped up to her door, once she heard Kimberly's door close for the second time. Kimberly paced over to the door gazing across the hallway over to Darla, and displayed the key to her. Darla immediately got amped with excitement, once she realized what Kimberly was waving up to the window. "Give it to me!" She yelled out to her, Kimberly quickly raised her index finger up to her lips, and said "Shhhhh. I'll give it to you later."

* * *

David was on the school bus peering out the window looking mind-boggled on what he experienced last night, when he suddenly felt watched through their living room window. He also was mind-boggled about the slamming door, and the window mysteriously being raised that he had gotten blamed for. Goose-bumps appeared on the back of his neck and on both of his arm's from even thinking about last night. When the bus driver yield onto the public school grounds. David quickly communicated his senses. Natalie was still lying in bed staring blankly at her hot pink ceiling going over everything that happen last night. At 2:00 am in the morning she witnessed her lamp fall to the floor from her nightstand, waking her up out of her sleep. She also witnessed her bedroom door mysteriously turning in a 180 degrees before coming in a complete stop. After Natalie scanned through her entire mind on what happen last night in the wee-hours of the night. The sounding bell from their Grandfather clock snapped her out of her thought. "Alright, Alright. I hear you." she said to herself, when she heard her stomach growling like a small tiger cub. Once Natalie slipped her slippers and house coat on, she immediately went walking out the room to eat breakfast her mom placed in the microwave for her before taking off to work. The house was so quiet and settled, she could nearly hear the birds outside singing to each-other on perfect notes, she thought while making her way down the steps heading to the kitchen. When Natalie made it down stairs to the living room, she felt inexpressibly relieved to see their wasn't anything out of place from what happen last night. When Natalie made it to the kitchen. She pushed the timer on the microwave to warm her food, after that she went over to the sink to grab a fork from the dish-rack. While Natalie was rinsing the fork off with hot water, she stared affronted out the kitchen window that faces their wooden garage. The longer she stared.

She thought it was far too restrictive not to notice the two garage doors swinging freely, when normally it stayed closed by 2 by 4, which was now lying flat on the ground. "Hold on . . . , that garage been closed ever since dad died." she thought insanely before walking off to make sure all the doors and windows locked and secured.

* * *

Mr. Kirk Wallace had just pulled up on the side street called Two Mile Road after being called by officer Dixon to come and I.D a disemboweled body, that was found on the top of the mountain called the Chocolate Drop. "What do we have here Deputy?" Mr. Wallace asked sharply, while approaching the covered body lying on the ground. Mr. Dixon closed his memo pad, and placed his pen inside his shirt pocket, then said while bending down to view the body with Mr. Wallace. "Well I can't tell you off hand how long this body been buried on the top of that mountain, but we couldn't afford wrapping things up until you arrived to make some adjustments on our findings. "Oh God. What in the world . . ." Mr. Wallace said feeling unreasonably and uncomfortable when he saw the chopped up body. After viewing the body Mr. Wallace said while grabbing a handkerchief from his back pocket to cover his mouth and nose area. "Well it's quite certain this is a Mexican kid and I'm looking for a white kid, but either way. You guys have a murder crime scene, and a strong investigation to get on." "That's what we do have sir. Thank you for dropping by Mr. Wallace." "No problem Deputy Dixon. It's all my pleasure, It's all my pleasure." Mr. Wallace said softly taking off walking back to his truck and as he was walking. He Was thinking about how the boy's family going to feel about not only their son has been found murdered, but chopped up as well. Another officer stepped up to Officer Dixon saying with a wide a wake tone of voice. "So what he say about the body, was it the kid he was searching for?" Mr. Dixon stared directly at Mr. Wallace, then said without a touch of humor. "He realized this was a Hispanic kid and not a white kid, so apparently it's not him and we're stuck with this stupid ass investigation. Mr. Wallace dialed Maria's number on his cell phone while pulling up on Frosty Freeze parking lot to speak with her before going inside to eat lunch. After several continuous rings Maria finally answered.

"Hello, Mrs. Gates speaking." "Hello Maria. I keep forgetting time is like three hours difference from California to Saginaw, Michigan. I'm sorry did I awake you?" He sincerely apologized. "No sir. I just combing my daughter's hair before she takes off to school. How things going your way?" Maria said with the that's about to turn grave. "As much as I hate to mention this on an empty stomach. No more than ten minutes ago. The 29 Palms California Deputies discovered a chopped up body of a Hispanic kid on the top of a mountain called the chocolate drop." "Oh my . . . , well that surely wasn't good to hear." Maria relented. "Basically that's all I called to bug you with, and also to let you know I'm still expecting you. So I'll see you when you get here." "You sure will. I guess I'll talk to you later." She assured him before disconnecting the line.

* * *

Darla was having a dream that caused her to scream, kick, toss and turn from dreaming Mary Swartz spirit was hovering over her body while she slept, till a in house nurse rushed into the room to stick a syringe inside her arm. "Darla. You need to calm down, there's nothing to be afraid of." Ms. Stuart assured her, ejecting the syringe from her arm. Moments later slobber started dripping from the corner of Darla's mouth as her eyes closed slowly, then suddenly wide when the medicine shot straight to her brain.

* * *

Evening time in Saginaw, Michigan. Natalie was in the kitchen finishing up the quick dinner she prepared for her mother and brother. Once Mrs. Louis came through the front door, she placed her purse and knit bag on their big sofa." Natalie I'm home . . . ! Did David make it home from school yet?" "I'm in the kitchen!" Natalie yelled back. When Mrs. Louis came through the kitchen entrance way, she tossed up a smile when she smelled the seasoned roast beef and onions lingering in the air. "It sure smells good in here." Mrs. Louis commented with the truth. Natalie squirted water from a water bottle on a mustard spot while saying. "What you was saying mom?" "I was asking did David make it home yet, cause I got a phone call from his Principle while I was at the shop, he said David feel asleep in class and woke up screaming. I've never had any teacher's call me about his demeanor before." I think his bus is going to be late again mom." Natalie concluded, turning the gas down on the stove.

Once five minutes passed. Mrs. Louis and Natalie heard David entering the house, heading straight for his bedroom. "There he go right there mom." Natalie said in the sense of getting him in trouble. With a thoughtful expression and conscious eyes. Mrs. Louis said glancing toward the kitchen entrance way. "Yes he's guilty. He have never went up to his room without turning that darn television on." When Mrs. Louis made it to the bottom of the stair casing, she didn't waste anytime in shouting out to him. "David . . . , You come down these steps right this minute young man!" "Ma'am . . ." He answered while walking down the steps. "What's this about you falling asleep in class, then waking up screaming at the top of your lungs?" David stopped on the third step before the landing, where his mother was standing with her right hand relaxed on her waist waiting for an explanation. "I was tired mom, and I ended up dreaming I was left in the entire school by myself, being chased by a girl that had a rope around her neck. It looked as if she was dead." David said with 100% truth rippling through his voice. "Well you need to apologize to your entire classmates for your alarming actions, startling everyone with that out burst scream of yours." Mrs. Louis said. "Yes ma'am." He agreed absently. "Good, and dinner will be served shortly so go and prepare for dinner in a few." She noted.

* * *

When night time arrived. Natalie, David and Mrs. Louis was finishing up the last bites of their meals, talking about the strange issue's that been going on around their home. Natalie added to her conversation. "And mom, that's not the least of it. I Think your son here got something to do with the barn doors being left wide open, for someone to come and steal dad's things we placed inside it." "It is . . . , well why you didn't tell me this earlier?" Mrs. Louis said with unrestrained bitterness. After giving a second thought on what Natalie had just said. She quickly bald up her napkin, placed it on her plate, then hurried off to see if Natalie was telling the truth. When Mrs. Louis made it to the kitchen window she stood their momentarily with her bottom lip dropped to the floor from seeing Natalie wasn't lying, nor exaggerating about the barn doors being wide open to the public. Once Mrs. Louis communicated her senses she went back to the dining room table where Natalie and David was sitting quietly for the very first time without arguing. "Well that's strange. Those doors hadn't been open ever sense we put you guy's dad things in there for safe keeping." "Mom. Personally I think your son is trying to spook us out of here." Natalie snorted. "Natalie don't you start with him already." Mrs. Louis said somewhat thickly. "Yeah blame it all on me like always." David said with ease, then he added. "But mom, last night when I was looking at the television show The Shield. I sort of felt watched through the living room window." After hearing David's story, Natalie quickly raised her head with a burning stare at Mrs. Louis saying. "Mom. Now that could be dad." Natalie exaggerated "That's non-sense. Your Dad is resting in peace." Mrs. Louis corrected them picking up the dirty dishes from the table carrying them off to the sink to wash, and to avoid reminiscing about their Dad.

* * *

Richard swiveled around in his computer chair with his attention glued to the Blueroom door, when he heard sounds of crumbling paper coming from the room. "Now what is God's mother name could that be?" He wondered, then focused his attention over to his three TV. Cameras monitors, before he slowly crept and couldn't believe what he was seeing with his very own eye's. He witnessed each one of the missing and murdered victims pictures falling dominoly off the wall one after the other as he stood there in amazement thinking to himself, "It's been a long time since the first couple of incidents that made him connect not one, not two but three TV. camera monitors up around his house. At first he thought the walls were sweating and the tape couldn't no longer hold, but that wasn't the case. The walls were totally dry he realized.

* * *

Mr. Dalton was letting the last day time nurse out the main entrance door, when he said, "You have a safe trip home, Ms. Bowden." "I sure will, Sir. Have a great night." She countered back. Once Ms. Bowden walked off. Mr. Dalton quickly locked and chained the doors to serge all the power in the hallways to the night lights. When the night lights came on Kimberly quickly put her shoes on, reached into her mattress to grab the skeleton key to give Darla like she promised. She approached the door took a glance out her square window into the hallway looking both ways making sure the coast was clear, before she risked the chance in getting caught in opening the door. Once she unlocked and opened the door she slowly eased her head out just to be safe, remembering Mrs. Craig's final words "They'll be watching." but when she saw the hallway was deserted, she tiptoed over to Darla's door to take a peek inside her window only to see Darla still dozed off from the medication Ms. Stuart had given her. Kimberly glanced back over her right shoulder thinking that she should have closed her door, but then she thought she didn't have time to waste. So she slid the key into the lock and opened Darla's door, then quickly frowned when she got a strong smell of the urine stench in the air inside her room. Once she stepped inside she hurriedly walked over to Darla's bed. "Darla wake up, its Kim, you have to lock me back inside my room before they come and do their midnight log in." She instructed tapping her on the shoulder. Darla slowly opened both eyes and once Kimberly saw she was coming around, she assisted her in raising upright placing Darla's left arm around her shoulder blade for leverage to walk her over to the door. When they made it to the door, Kimberly double check Darla making sure she could stand on her own, before taking a peek out the door to make sure no one was out there. "Come on Darla, the coast is clear." She waved her hand to her before they both paced over to her room to lock her inside. The second Darla locked Kimberly inside her room, she said sluggishly "Thanks Kim, you will always be my best friend." Then sluggishly crept back over to her room locking her own self inside.

* * *

Everyone finally took off to their rooms, preparing for bed, while Mrs. Louis decided to sit in her chair in her bedroom to knit a blanket for her hobby craft business they owned, until suddenly she flinched out of reflex from being caught off guard once a thick branch from the big tree that sits right outside her bedroom window came crashing through from the strong wind outside. "Good gracious! What in the world is going on out there?" She said surprisingly, placing her blanket and crochet on the chair. She stood up to storm out the room. "Natalie and David, you both come here immediately!" she yelled up the stairs from the bottom landing. A few seconds later Natalie and David came striding down the steps with their pajama's and tennis shoes on. "What was that noise, Mom?" Natalie asked when they made it to the bottom landing looking questionly. "The wind caused a tree branch to plow through my window, and I need to go out there to make sure nothing else is damaged." Mrs. Louis announced stiffly. "Mom, we're going out there with you." Natalie assured her soberly. Then David rushed over to the coat closet next to the front door to grab his aluminum bat for protection. Natalie normally would of said something negative about his quick decision but she also figured it was a great idea for what reason she didn't know. Mrs. Louis cautiously opened the front door and immediately saw trash scattered all over their lawn. "Jesus, what a mess." she said thoughtfully, before stepping out the door. Once they all proceeded out the front door. Natalie reached out behind Mrs. Louis to clutch her shirt in a firm grip. David on the other hand stood five feet behind them with his bat elevated in a batters position full alert. Looking all around him as they moved along toward the left side of the house, but right when Natalie and Mrs. Louis turned the corner the trash can fell to the ground catching David's full attention. "Shit! What was that?" He blurted out accidentally turning around with the bat ready to swing and him rooted to his spot, surveying the other end of the house where the trash can was turned over. Once David realized it was only the trash can, he focused his eyes on a trail of oak leaves trailing toward him on the ground then calmly turned back around to catch up with his mom and sister, thinking it wasn't anything unusual. When he was immediately snatched off his feet by the oak leaves as his aluminum bat went air-borne landing a few feet away from him. When David fell to his stomach on the ground, he quickly tried to recover by getting up while frightfully screaming out to his mom, but the leaves snatched him back to the ground and dragged him on his back into the barn. A pitch fork laid on the ground with the iron forks pointing toward the entrance. The oak leaves flew David right into the pitch fork and the second David's shoulders went into the pitch fork, blood gushed out from his mouth, as his body jerked the barn doors slammed closed on its own. "Mom, where's David?" Natalie asked curiously when she heard a loud closing door sound. Once Mrs. Louis realized what Natalie just said, she turned around maneuvering Natalie to the side, and sped off back around to the front of the house. Natalie immediately thought David was trying to scare them, so she just moved along to the back of the house where her mom's room sits, below David's, to see how bad the damage was. Mrs. Louis easily noticed David's bat lying on the ground when she made it to the front of the house, and thought it was very strange to only see his bat and not him. Then she raced through the front door to yell up the stairs "David! Are you up there?" "Mom!" Natalie yelled out from the back of the house. Mrs. Louis stormed back out the front door when she heard Natalie holler. "Natalie! Where are you?" Mrs. Louis yelled out, when she made it back along side of the house where she left off at. "I'm in the back of the house!" Natalie responded. When Mrs. Louis made it to Natalie she glanced to where Natalie was pointing. "Look Mom, he maybe in his room, look at his light." Mrs. Louis' frown deepened when she saw his bedroom light flickering on and off. "Natalie stay put. I'm going to go and see about this." And if David was in fact up in his room flickering his light, he's in big trouble for not answering her when she called out to him in the first place, she thought. Traveling back around the house, Mrs. Louis didn't hesitate traveling straight up the stairs when she made it inside dying to catch him playing with the light. Mrs. Louis slowed down when she made it to the top landing, seeing David's light boldly flickering through the jarred opening of his door. "David!" she called out slowly moving toward his bedroom. "David, you better not be messing around!" She said, slowly easing his door open with her right hand. Once she noticed he wasn't in his room, she immediately gazed at the light switch on his wall only to see the light switch was down on off, as the bedroom light continued boldly flickering. "No way." She said thoughtfully racing over to the window. Natalie turned around looking over her right shoulder when the thought accrued to her in her mind that the barn door wasn't swinging freely any longer. She then focused her attention back up to David's room when she heard her mom struggling to open his window to further assist Natalie on what to do but while she struggled at the window a pile of oak leaves trailed through David's bedroom door entering inside the room with her. "Oh God!" Mrs. Louis screeched, snatching her hands from the window turning around. "What's going on Mom?" When she saw her mom panicky turning around. "What is this?" Mrs. Louis blankly thought in disbelief seeing the oak leaves gradually whirling then they end up diving savagely at her. Mrs. Louis yelled out a high lament scream froze standing by the window as blood splattered across David's window from the attack of the oak leaves in the flickering light. Natalie screamed out. "Mom!" once she witnessed blood splatter across the window. Then the gruesome leaves un-covered Mrs. Louis's raw skinned exposed corpse once they settled to make the escape while Natalie nerves jerked with erratic violence causing her to faint falling to the ground.

* * *

A few hours later while Richard was still up late looking at television the TV. program he was watching was interrupted with a breaking news brief on the Louis Family incident. Richard quickly grabbed his cordless phone from the coffee table to dial Maria's extension, and after four continuous rings. He heard Maria soft sleepy voice say "Hello." "Maria, I'm terribly sorry for waking you out of your sleep, but you gotta turn to channel forty-two." Maria didn't say another word she just leaned upright in her bed with her back rested against the base board, grabbed the remote control off the night stand on her side of the bed, then clicked the wall plasma thirty-six inch TV. on to channel forty-two. Bobby woke up outta his sleep and heard her sigh saying "What's wrong Babe, and who's that calling this time of the night?" He asked re-burying his head back into the pillow falling back to sleep without waiting for her reply but right when she was about to answer she cut her conversation short once she heard him snoring like a new born baby. "Hello Maria, you still there?" "Yes, I'm sorry. I'm still here." She answered. As they both continued to watch the news cast lady do her coverage report. Maria said with a pockmarked face expression. "I know I didn't just hear her say. The young lady's mother and brother mysteriously got murdered, besides their only twenty to thirty minutes away from where I live, Richard." Then she powered her TV. off once a Carls Jr. commercial popped up after the breaking news coverage. "Well Maria, although I'm sorry for waking you out of your beauty sleep, I have one more thing to tell you. Earlier today when I was searching the web, something weird happened in my Blueroom." "It did?" she said concerned enough without malice in her voice. "Yes it did. I witnessed each and every last one of my missing and murdered victims photo's fall from the wall one behind the other." "No way." Maria snorted. "Yes, way." He wailed a reply then continued. "But I'm going to let you go Maria. I know you got a long day ahead of you." "Thanks Richard, for waking me up to catch the news and for being on your tippy toes about everything. Good night." Goodnight, Maria." Once they disconnected the line Maria slumped back down in bed, reached out to cut the lamp off then tossed up a smile of comfort when Bobby placed his arm over her in the darkness.

* * *

Kimberly immediately woke up out of sleep, when she heard a noise coming from Darla's dark room and to her it sounded like someone was lifting the metal bed up and constantly slamming the leg poles to the floor, it also made her rush to the toilet but once Kimberly started urinating she realized the noise stopped, as she sat there staring at the floor contemplating the urine sound releasing inside the toilet. Once she was finished she wiped herself and washed her hands, although she was namby-pamby she still was a clean freak. Darla's eyes popped wide open while laying stretched out on her back as the possession of Mary was surely within her. Kimberly rushed back over to her bed to play it off like she was asleep, when she realized Mr. Dalton was flashing the light in each patients window trying to detect where the loud noise had came from, that had woke him up. Darla quickly closed her eyes when Mary sensed he was about to flash the flashlight inside her pitch dark room, cause the possession of Mary Swartz had now given Darla razor intelligence, mega strength, super-natural calcium in her fingernails that made them strong and razor sharp. Darla was a very petite woman whom normally wasn't strong at all. The average weight she normally could lift was forty-five to fifty pounds, but the possession of Mary within her increased that nearly two hundred and fifty more human weight pounds extra, allowing her to lift up to three hundred pounds with her bare hands with no problem. When Mr. Dalton didn't see anything out of place or unusual inside Darla's room, he did to himself "I must have been dreaming, oh well" then he pushed the thought out of his mind disappearing back through the corridor. Kimberly immediately slid her feet inside her shoes to go to the door, when she heard the corridor door closing to peer over to Darla's room and she couldn't quite distinguish much from Darla's room being pitch dark when looking at her window. She said to herself "I hope Darla's o-okay in there." Then she exhaled going over to her bed to go to sleep. An hour later Mr. Dalton was out cold in a deep sleep again with his portable radio blasting out loud old school oldies on 96.2 fm. Ms. Dorothy was also asleep inside the staff room across the hall from the security office with the laptop computer open with her head rested on her folded arms on the table in front of it. The light in Darla's room clicked on by itself. The second her eyes popped open then she slowly rose up from the waist with the skeleton master key tightly gripped in her hand to let herself out. Darla slowly stepped over to the door bare footed, and without hesitation she stuck the key inside the universal door lock. Once she pushed the door wide open she took off through the corridor heading for the kitchen. The music from Mr. Daltons radio echoed throughout the entire hallway, Darla easily noticed. Finally making it to the kitchen she stuck the key inside the lock, and watched the door pop open pots, pans, big spoons, strainers and meat cleaver knives was hanging from a steal pot holder ring on hooks from the ceilings she noticed making her way over to them. She also wasn't in any mood for cite seeing, nor was she in any mood for playing around, she reached up to grab the wooden handle meat cleaver that wouldn't trace her finger prints. Walking out the kitchen with the key in one hand and the sharp meat cleaver in the other heading for her mission that wasn't impossible. Ms. Dorothy lifted her head still half asleep to wipe the drool from her mouth, and slid the laptop computer a little ways from her positioning her arms and head back on the table. Darla was walking with determined steps toward the office looking deviously through the strands of her bangs hanging over her forehead with not one percentage of regret on what she was about to do. She also was getting more irritated as the radio in Mr. Dalton's office was sounding off the tunes. Mr. Dalton was leaned back on the two hind leg's of his chair with both his feet propped upon the desk with his fingers interlocked on his stomach. Darla slipped her way inside the staff office unheard and un-noticed quietly creeping her way on the backside of Ms. Dorothy with thinly veiled hatred in her eyes and once she made it on the backside of Ms. Dorothy she quickly placed the skeleton key in her mouth holding it in place with her yellowish teeth, then grabbed Ms. Dorothy's hair with her free hand pulling her head back toward her which made Ms. Dorothy's eyes open bulging wide in total fright. "What the . . . !" Ms. Dorothy said appearing honestly startled while Darla ferociously sliced her throat cutting off her words once the meat cleaver slit through her wind pipe like cheese causing blood to squirt all across the laptop screen like a water balloon that just been poked with a needle. Darla immediately released Ms. Dorothy's hair from her tight grasp when she realized she was dead causing Ms. Dorothy's head to crash down freely to the floor head first, and without remorse Darla went walking strongly out the staff office heading over to the security room. Once she made it inside she stood silently next to the desk where Mr. Dalton's legs was stretched out on top scrutinizing his face while he slept, till suddenly she placed the skeleton key in her mouth bracing it back down with her teeth elevating the meat cleaver high in the air with both hands tightly gripped around the wooden handle. Darla displayed her yellow teeth then came down with a powerful chop on his right ankle making him give out a tremendous loud scream that echoed throughout the entire building going into state of shock from the pain of the meat cleaver chopping his foot off from the ankle. Once his chair fell backwards and his body landed on the floor. Darla straddled over him, grabbed his head up by his hair and went hacking away at his neck dislocating it from his shoulders, she released it from her hand dropping the meat cleaver from her tight grasp. The murder weapon laid a few feet away from his body then she slowly took off back up the spacious half lit hallway with the key in her hand. Kimberly slid her shoes on racing over to the door when she heard the corridor slamming closed. Then she saw Darla walking blankly back to her open room with her shirt full of blood. "Darla! Are you alright?" Darla just kept on walking not hearing Kimberly. "Well that was rude, she didn't answer. I knew I shouldn't have given her that master key, oh well. I better get some sleep its going to be morning here soon." Kimberly concluded, when she saw Darla close and locked herself back in her room. Darla immediately took her shirt off and flushed it down the strong titanium toilet, and stood there momentarily with her bra still attached.

* * *

Once morning time arrived Patton State Hospital was flooded with San Bernardino County Sheriffs, and Homicide Detectives running around investigating patients. The outside parking scene with nothing but news van's with stretch satellite polls standing straight up on top of them. Mrs. Kathleen Craig and Homicide Detective Mr. Riley was walking door to door to all the patients rooms, but when they made it to Darla's door. She was standing there with a blank stare out the square window peering and breathing through the strands of her shabby bangs. When Detective Mr. Riley stopped in his tracks in front of her door, he said to Mrs. Craig "Well I know she couldn't of been the one that committed the murders, especially on such a big guy like Mr. Dalton as puny as she looks. Hell it looks like she ain't here now, but then again. You never could be quite sure, cause look how small Bruce Lee was. I guess you see where I'm going with that." "You mean my patient Darla could be a murder suspect? I don't think that's possible. She's actually on my good patient list believe or not, besides the only thing she did to get a write up was urinate all over the hallway floor, and we all here don't count pounding and kicking on the door they all do that, plus as we speak, once things sort of clear up and become business as usual I'll be giving her the qualifying news that we recommended her to be release, shall we proceed?" Mrs. Craig said conversationally. Darla just kept staring straight ahead without blinking, as they both proceeded along. By the time Mrs. Craig and Detective Riley made it to the last room on Darla's row. Deputy Ross came through the corridor saying with relief. "Oh, here you are Detective. I was looking all over the building for you, by the way. We've yet came up with Jack. The only thing we seem to have right now is two victim's brutally murdered and a potential murder weapon that can't even detect fingerprints. I'm also here to tell you who ever committed these murders was a damn good smart killer cause we don't even have foul play of entrance into the building unless it was done from within." "Thank you Deputy, just fax the report to my office." Mr. Riley concluded, while angling his hands toward the grey corridor for him and Mrs. Craig to walk through them first.

* * *

Maria was packing up her few last things preparing to fly into Palm Springs California Airport when Bobby and Antonia came through their bedroom door. "You all set to go, Honey?" "Good thing its the weekend or mommy wouldn't be set to go no where." She said charmingly to them both then she bent down on her knees and brushed her nose back and forth with Antonia's saying. "Give mommy a kiss you going to be on your best behavior for Dad?" Antonia nodded her head yes with a smile. "Alright. Now Mommy ready to go, come on you guys. Out, out, out." Maria suggested sweetly, when she stood up from Antonia straight ahead gaze to her. As time elapse by and they all gotten out of the car at the Saginaw Michigan Airport. Antonia started crying from the top of her lungs when she saw her mother was bout to depart from them. Maria quickly released her roller luggage handle to bend down and give her a tight embracement hug and a mother kiss. "Mommy will be right back honey. I'm just going on a business trip and you'll be fine with dad for a couple of days, if that. Can mommy count on you to be a big girl?" Maria said smiling wiping away her running tears from her soft cheeks. Maria stood up and gave Bobby a passionate kiss once she heard her airline door number sounding off the boarding her flight. "Bye Babe. Trust me, we'll be fine. Oh hold on. don't forget this." Bobby reached through the driver window of their charger to grab her walkie-talkie radio then handed it over to her. "Oh yeah. I can't forget this." She said reaching out for it, followed by giving him a peck on his lips, before taking off through the sliding door's with her luggage.

* * *

It was business all over again at Patton State Hospital while Mrs. Kathleen Craig was finishing up her qualifying news list letting patients know when they was going to be released, and lucky for most of them. The new bill prop 188 passed allowing in house patients to be released without any parents or family supervision under the new law Sacramento California verses Webber. Darla sat upright like an arrow on her bed when Mrs. Craig stepped inside her room. "Hello, Darla." She greeted, hearing the door close and look behind her by the daytime security guard. Darla just sat there without grunting a reply. "Darla remember me, Mrs. Craig, the Patton State Head Supervisor? Well, today I'm here to give you some important good news. We all here at Patton State Hospital decided to release you at Twelve p.m. tomorrow afternoon, due to your good behavior here at Patton. And as I'm here reviewing over your behavior folder, I can't think of anything prejudice to hold you here any longer past your original release date, so I'm wishing you a safe trip back to your hometown Michigan, and good luck with your life decisions. Alright?" Mrs. Craig said pleasantly. Darla still didn't say a word. All she did was nod her head up and down with acknowledgement. "Great, oh yeah. you'll be released with the clothes you'll be dressed in, another pair of changing clothes, a two hundred dollar check and some hygiene. So have fun . . ." Mrs. Craig said then she tapped on the door to be let out so she could escape the strong urine smell, but the moment the door was opened by the security. Darla said with a quiet, soft, raspy, creepy whisper. "Oh I will . . ." Seconds later after the door was locked. Darla closed her eyes and went into a meditation mode. Meanwhile Mrs. Craig stood outside Darla's door saying to Mr. Thompson. "I shall admit Mr. Thompson. Darla do look sort of spooky with her hair covering her face like a wild woman. But it's her prerogative. She can do what she wanna do." She teased, thinking about one of Bobby Brown's new edition debut's on an old album, then tapped him on the shoulder with her folder walking off. Kimberly walked away from the door after ease-dropping on their conversation.

CHAPTER EIGHT

WHEN MARIA GOT off the plane that end up giving them nearly a five hour lay over for repair and service in Las Vegas. She was immediately relieved, when she saw Mr. Wallace standing colleagues of the Los Angeles O.F.P.A. Office. "There you go. We was worried sick about you! Especially from all these terrorist acts on these planes that shocking the nation now a days." Mr. Wallace pointed out, when he saw her walking through the terminal door's. "We sort of had a little delay at Las Vegas Airport, but good thing I made it." She admitted a little breathlessly. "Shall I, Mrs. Gates?" Edwin asked politely, reaching out for her luggage. "Sure, why not?" Maria replied. "Are you getting taller, Edwin, or am I getting shorter?" She added. Every last one of them laughed at her sense of humor. They all continued out the sliding doors to the parking lot where the vehicles was lined up in front of the terminals. "Palm Springs is a beautiful. A little hot though for this time of the year, and believe it or not, this is how it looks and feels." Maria said conversationally, climbing in the passenger seat of Mr. Wallace unit Excursion truck. "Oh, and believe me, its a hell a lot better scenery than where we're going. I can bet you that." Mr. Wallace said sharply closing his driver door. As time went by all three of the Units Excursion trucks convoyed the steep hill through Morongo 62 highway. Their highlight on the ride was Fire trucks and Morongo Basin Ambulances, assisting their emergency help on a turned over auto zone tool truck off the side of the road. Maria leaned up in her seat making sure she got a good glimpse, as they slowly drove passed the accident. "What a beautiful scene already, huh?" Mr. Wallace said with a little humor. "It certainly is." She added her thought with a blemish grin widening on her face. After the truck accelerated up the highway's steep hill, Maria spotted a Circle K Gas Station sign up ahead, and requested to stop there for some Sunflower Seeds and something cold to drink. Once all three vehicles parked side by side in front of the Circle K, Maria immediately made her way inside to the back wall to grab her favorite Coca-Cola drink, then quickly went to the snack rack to grab a bag of seasoned Sunflower Seeds. While Maria waited in line surveillance the store seeing if it was something else she would like to purchase. She spotted the newspaper rack on the outside of the potato chip lane, and couldn't believe what she was reading on the headline which read out in big bold letters. "TWO MURDER'S, ONE WEAPON, NO SUSPECTS." Then she placed the newspaper on the counter, so the cashier lady could scan it. "Isn't that something?" She said to Maria. "It really is, and I can't believe it." Maria responded looking amazed taking another quick scan over the bold letter's. "That'll be, $2.35, ma'am. Out of $5.00, and here's your change $2.65. Have a great day." "You too. Thank you." Maria replied pleasantly. Before walking away. The moment she hopped back in the passenger seat she placed the newspaper on Mr. Wallace's lap. "You won't believe it." She said with a serious leer. "Wait. Wasn't you just there?" He asked, once he read the headline. "Yes. I sure was, but I didn't see anything out of place, except a bunch of patients looking helpless." "Yeah, this world today. Is most definitely coming to an end." Mr. Wallace said, handing her the newspaper back while pulling off the lot. As all three Excursion Unit vehicles convoyed along, people were pointing and waving their hands out their car's remember seeing Mr. Wallace on the news coverage for Bryan Smith, when he first arrived for the mission. "I see your popular." Maria teased. "Yeah, only in a small town though." He admitted smiling while reaching for his CB Radio to let the other crew know they was heading straight to their rooms at Motel 6 and start fresh first thing in the morning, sense they was a little behind from the delay on Maria's airline flight.

* * *

Richard decided to radio Maria for a testing, and also to see if she made it to California safely. "Richard, to Maria, over." Maria grabbed her Walkie-talkie when she heard his deep voice echoing through her receiver. "This Maria, copy." "I didn't want much. I was just giving you a radio testing, and making sure you made it safely, over." "Yes. I most definitely made it with the exception of a delay of five hours in Vegas for repair, over." "Well, that's all I wanted, over." "Oh Richard. I just read inside the newspaper today stating two murders have been committed inside of Patton State Hospital with no suspect's." "Is that so? This world is coming to an end." "That's the exact same thing, Mr. Wallace said, over." "See, there you go. Well, I'll be keeping in touch, have fun, over and out." Richard concluded. "Over and out." She responded easily.

* * *

The next day evening the Patton State Transportation Officer sat and waited inside the airport lobby, watching Darla take off inside her airplane flight and once everybody was strapped down for safety and the airplane was lifting off. Other customers on the airplane started whispering amongst themselves on how spooky Darla was looking with her long bangs hanging down over her forehead. A flight attendant lady approached her asking if she would like any peanuts or anything soft to drink, but Darla didn't comment or say a word, she just quietly gazed at the seat head rest in front of her. "If you don't mind me asking, did someone hurt you ma'am?" The flight attendant curiously asked, when she discovered redness in Darla's eye's through the strands of her scattered bangs, that was looking quite noticeable. But still yet Darla didn't grunt a reply as if the questions weren't being asked. "Oh Well." The flight attendant said moving along to the next customer, realizing Darla wasn't in any mood for conversation. The flight attendant tossed up a welcome smile at the next lady customer behind Darla and greeted her. "Thank you, ma'am, for choosing Michigan Airlines. Would you like to have some peanuts or a refreshing drink?" "Sure. That'll be fine, oh by the way, she's not very talkative is she?" The lady customer pointed out whirling her right index finger up to her temple as a sign for craziness to Darla. Across the way in Darla's row one little girl was standing up in her seat giving her mother a hard time about staying buckled down for take off, until her mother said moodily enough. "Alright, Kelley. I'm going to make you sit over there by that crazy lady if you don't do what I ask you and stay seated." Kelley trailed her eyes over to where her mom was pointing at Darla and said objectively. "I don't wanna sit over there!" "Well I guess you better sit down, young lady." her mom directed her in a demanding tone of voice. As time elapse four hours later. The pilot came over the P.A. System and said. "Hello, everyone. This is your Chief Pilot Mr. Earl Wilson, and we'll be landing here less than five minutes into Saginaw Michigan Airport so please make sure you don't leave any trash on the floor to keep a healthier and much cleaner airline, also make sure no kids is left behind, just kidding. Thank you for choosing Michigan airlines, please fly again." he pronounced firmly with a sense of humor. Everyone vacated the airplane when it came at its terminal. Darla was the very last person to exit the plane leaving her extra clothes, hygiene, and her two hundred dollar gate fee check from Patton State in the bag sitting on the seat next to where she was sitting alone. "Mom, look at that lady's nails and hair!" Johnny said when he saw Darla coming through the sliding doors inside the lobby. "Johnny, those are fake lee press on nails and mind your own business for a change." Wanda said. Darla came through one sliding door, bumped into a man's shoulder boldly out the other. Hey watch it, fucking bitch!" He shouted out moodily to her when she bumped into him heading out the sliding doors.

* * *

"Did you have a good night sleep in your room, Maria?" Lieutenant Wallace asked her smoothly, while she climbed into the passenger seat. "Sure. I slept like a new born baby, after Scartatic's went off the Sci-Fi Channel." "I see I'm not the only one who loves the Sci-Fi Channel." Mr. Wallace said thoughtfully. "No, I guess you're not." She responded with an encouraging smile. "Alright, here they go turning the corner now." Mr. Wallace said powering his driver window down once he saw the other guys pulling up, then he yelled out the window when they pulled right beside him. "It took you guys long enough, what the ladies stayed in too late?" "I sure wished they did Lieutenant." Edwin said playfully, then waved his hand giving Mr. Wallace the signal to pull off first. As they all traveled a little ways up the 62 Highway Maria said blankly staring out the passenger window scoping the scenery. "Well at least 29 Palms is much bigger and more populated than Joshua Tree, California." Then trailed her head back to Kentucky Fried Chicken when they passed it thinking from her stomach. "Yeah, and a hell of a lot bigger if you ask me." Mr. Wallace added, lighting up his Marlboro cigarette, when they all finally made it to Joshua Tree Sheriff's Station, that sits next door to the Highway CHP Station. Mr. Wallace fired up his second cigarette and said. "Well I better run inside and get the Morg key from Captain Aversa. I'll be right out in a flash." Mr. Wallace stopped in his tracks when he came through the Sheriff Station door, saying thoughtfully. "Shit! Where's my manor's?" Then he re-opened the door to flip his cigarette out. "Hello, Mrs. Wade. Is the Captain In?" "He sure is Lieutenant Wallace." She said politely buzzing him in. "Thank you." He said shortly with a friendly leer. "Hello Lieutenant Wallace. I take it your looking for the Captain, well he's right over there." "And I was just about to pass him up. Thank you Mrs. Morales." "No problem, sir. Have a nice day." Mrs. Morales said with a warm smile, and he smiled back stepping over to the Captain. "Hello Captain." "Mr. Baker, I'll have to phone you back in just a bit sir, bye." The Captain said before hanging up the phone. "Hello, Lieutenant Wallace." They both greeted each other with a firm handshake. "I was just stopping by to get the Morg key from you, and you didn't have to discontinue your phone conversations." "All hell, that conversation wasn't nothing. I was dying for a way out anyways. Oh yeah. I'm a little bit of a step ahead of you. I got two uniform Deputies already there waiting on you guys to assist you in." "Well if I would of known that, it sure would of saved some lunch time." Mr. Wallace admitted. "My, my, my, Mr. Aversa confessed. "Well, let me catch up. I don't want those guys to be waiting on me all day." Mr. Wallace gave up a solute, before trailing off, then he tapped on Mrs. Moralas cubicle wall as he strolled pass. "Bye!" She shouted out continuing back talking over the switchboard. Mr. Wallace visually sighed when he climbed inside the driver seat and said. "Well this was a waste of a stop." Then fired up the engine. "Why you say that?" Maria asked. "He already got two uniform Deputies there waiting on us, to assist us inside." "Yeah, it sure was." She said absently before he pulled off.

* * *

Darla nearly got hit by a Mini Van, causing the driver to swerve and shout out the window. "Get the hell out of the street cunt, before you get run over . . . !" Darla didn't pay him any mind. She just kept on walking along the deserted road, until a country elderly man came pulling up alongside her. "Hey young lady, do you need a lift I'm guaranteed I'll be the last vehicle riding down this here road, at least for the next thirty to forty minutes or so?" The old man shouted out the half raised window, then he immediately stopped his station wagon when she stopped in her tracks. Mr. Billy Miles reached over to the passenger door to welcome Darla inside, But once he seen she was taking him up on his offer he quickly pulled his false teeth from his oil-infested flannel work shirt pocket, instantly popping them inside his mouth. Once Darla was inside the passenger seat and he pulled off heading up the road. He started up a conversation. "My name is Billy Miles. What's your name sweetie?" Darla didn't muffle a sound gazing straight ahead. "I know one thing, you sure had a mighty long journey up this here road." He continued with a country accent. "And how far you were going, if you don't mind me asking?"

* * *

Eddie and Samantha was girlfriends and boyfriend, also soon to be married on Christmas Day. The both of them was camping buddies that shared the same passion for the out door wilderness and blending in with mother nature. "Are you going to help me with this tent, or what Sam?" Eddie asked meekly. "Yes as long as you put it up a little closer to the lake, so it could give off a little more breeze this time." Samantha responded somewhat moodily. "Boy aren't we a little edgy today. Is it that time of the month, Sam?" "You know what, you fucking put it up yourself. I'm going to go look for fire sticks." She said with an edgy tone of voice arching her butt in the air, then tapped it with her right palm before stomping off. "Good, this is a man's job anyways. Just make sure you bring back dry ones this time, before we go without fire again!" Eddie yelled out with confidence, than he said beneath his breath thoughtfully. "Now how did I put this up last time?" "Why do guys always have their heads stuck up their ass, and try to make it seem like their balls much bigger than what they are? When half the time there too busy complaining more than women, and they're the most dominate ones. Geez." She complained under her breath, advancing away searching for fire sticks.

* * *

"Do you even gotta place to go?" Billy Miles asked Darla. "Well if not, I got a little place you can shack at for a few days." He added while sizing her up and licking his lips applying moisture to them. "What you like doing on your spare time, if you don't mind me butting in?" He continued reaching his hand over to her leg slowly to rub the upper part of her thigh while at the same time watching the road. Darla slowly turned her head toward him with her bothersome eyes peering through the thick strands of her bangs softly breathing irritably. "You like this don't you, what the cat got your tongue?" He asked with a firm smile, then Darla angrily reached over with a growl, grabbing him by his throat with her right hand. Mr. Miles stomped down on his brakes reaching at her hand with his own, once he felt her nails sinking into his flesh. The Station Wagon jack knifed sliding off the road, as Darla ripped his adams apple out from his throat. The vehicle went slamming into a tree coming to a complete stop. Her hand snatched away from his throat once her head went crashing into the dash board from the powerful impact to the tree. Mr. Billy Miles was dead before the wreckage, his head laid pressed against the horn. Darla slowly recovered with only a knot on her forehead sitting upright while the steam was escaping from the radiator, and the horn blaring endlessly. Once fully recovered from the dizziness, she reached out for the door handle then turned her whole body side ways on the seat and took a powerful kick with both her feet at the half raised window. Glass shattered everywhere then she climbed out the window frame disappearing within the Saginaw Michigan woods.

* * *

Maria suddenly gotten chills looking at the first body the Morongo Basin Police Department found, with the head completely chopped off from its body. "Well Maria, you think you can with stand another peek at our next body?" Mr. Wallace asked her. "Sure, but it sure wouldn't of hurt if we would of eaten breakfast, before we started." She replied wit a little humor. "Alright, here we go." Once Mr. Wallace pulled the rack out from the wall. It was a big sigh in the room when every one saw how small the body bag was then he slowly un-zipped the bag. But the more he un-zipped it, the strong stench smell came lingering through their mask. Maria leaned over the badly decomposed chopped body. Carefully examining its body parts where they been cut and severed precisely then said. "No, this is not one either, Lieutenant." She assured him. "What makes you so sure, Maria?" "Well its plain to see, whoever committed this murder actually took their time slicing away at his body parts cause the bones is to smooth where the parts been severed away." "Oh, I see. Well you sure know your job, Mrs. Gates." Mr. Wallace complimented her. "Do you have anymore bodies for me to examine, Lieutenant?" She asked, and was very relieved when he came up with the conclusion. "Well, I did, but those two bodies was identified as a common murder wit no doubt. Those guys they found in the car up the street from 29 Palms Tires was robbed in Redlands, California, and was driven to 29 Palms to burn them in their vehicle to cover up the murder scene, so yeah, we're pretty much squared away on that case. You guys ready to warp things up?" Everybody heard the door slamming closed from Maria excusing herself to the restroom to vomit. Maria couldn't believe she was throwing up knowing she seen way more disturbing images in her time working for the O.F.P.A. Office, then she also thought. "Its because I probably needed to eat something first." The thought pushed to the back of her mind when one of the Deputies knocked on the restroom door asking if she was alright? "Yes, I'm perfectly fine thanks. I'll be out in a minute!" Maria was pretty happy she always kept a traveling tooth brush and toothpaste inside her purse for times like this. Lieutenant Wallace approached the officer standing outside the restroom door to say "Deputy Snider, stand post to show Mrs. Gates out, we'll be outside having a cigarette break waiting." "You got it, sir." Deputy Snider agreed. Despite all the throwing up Maria had done, she felt inexpressibly relieved when she got through brushing her teeth. Deputy Snider stood up straight away from the wall, once he saw the door opening and the light click off. "Where's everyone else?" She asked soberly. "Their all waiting on us out front. You sure your o-okay, Mrs. Gates?" He asked concerned. "Sure, It was just a little upset stomach, that's all." She assured him, as they both took off walking beside each other heading out the building. "Shall we eat now?" Maria shouted out to everyone managing a smile showing them everything was o-okay. "We sure in the hell can. My treat to Denny's!" Mr. Wallace yelled out.

* * *

Back at Saginaw Michigan on the news many residences didn't get a chance to catch what had just been aired which was Norman Gandy, Alfred Carbajal and Juan Tucker had just escaped the Saginaw Michigan State Prison Officers, while they was being transported to a medical facility earlier, and they could possibly be armed and dangerous.

* * *

Darla was still traveling in the Saginaw woods trailing through the broken twigs and fallen leaves all scattered amongst the ground. The possession of Mary Swartz totally took over her imagination and soul leaving her with no remembrance of the immediate family she had left. The only thing left of Darla was 75% her image and her soul was 100% Mary Swartz with total vengeance on mankind as we know it. For the repayment of her death and soul that never settled from everyone's calling full darkness was no more than forty-five minutes away, and was forthcoming very quickly. "Great, I'm all finished. Now that looks like a sturdy seven foot tall tent. "What you think Sam?" Eddie asked proudly with both hand's placed on his waistline. Samantha stood up from the pile of fire sticks, gazed over at the tent to say with a little humor in her voice. "It looks like the same sturdy seven foot tall tent we been putting up for the last past five years." Then she immediately bent back over facing away from him with her butt sexually arched in the air, gathering all the sticks in a pile. Eddie shook his head smiling staring straight over at her bending over gathering the fire sticks together. He thought to himself, "He was a very lucky man whom was having the opportunity to marry a very beautiful Canadian and Caucasian woman, with a peach olive complexion, nice set of small lips, treacherous hips, brownish hair, and hazel nut color eyes." That loved him no matter how much an asshole she felt he was. "Sam."

He said finally. "Yes, Ed?" She answered pleasantly, standing up right to face him. "Wouldn't it be great if we stayed out camping in the woods all weekend?" "Yes it would, as long as you don't be acting childish, and scare the shit out of me again, to cause me to camp out in the Jeep in front of the camping ground public restroom on the lot." She reminded him about the past. "I was just trying to have a little fun. God always said, stay a kid at heart Babe, and I'm sorry once more since someone seems not to be able to forgive or forget." Eddie apologized. Sam withdrew her attention from his words to say. "Well for future reference. One can only forgive ones stupidity, but one can't forgive his or her action's cause actions speaks louder than words when you scare the shit out of them." Then she quickly bent down, picked up a solid, smooth, round rock immediately tossing it at him with a disgruntled look. "Alright, alright . . . !" He downsized, then pleaded. "Can I please make it up to you babe?" Samantha's veins didn't pulse a beat as her expression soften, before racing into his boney, hairy arm's and ashy elbows. Right when Samantha's lips met his. Eddie's eye's got bulging wide, then both their eye's dimmed closed on a magical cue while they passionately kissed.

*   *   *

While the rest of the crew was enjoying themselves in their rooms at Motel 6. Mr. Wallace was sitting at the wooden round table inside Maria's room having a business discussion with her. Maria was up dating him on all the strange murders that had been popping up crazily all over Saginaw, such as the Bailey's and the Louis family murders. "So at this point Lieutenant. I'm not Quite sure on what's causing all these murders. But This one thing I do know for sure sir. I'm professionally trained to get down to the bottom of things." She rested with a serious expression. "I know you will Maria. Hell, you're the best I got in this darn business and of all the thirty years I been in this Paranormal Investigation Union. I've never thought a beautiful woman would become the top Advocate in the Paranormal Mystery Dept. Mr. Wallace stop a moment to recollect his thoughts, then continued. "And Maria your someone I see that's very prompt in everything you do and take on, besides I knew you wouldn't let me down by not coming out here on this extra assignment which was quick compared to the miles you've traveled and that let's me know I have the best woman on my team." No sooner when Mr. Wallace finished his last words he belched lifting his cup up to his lips. Maria merely grinned before asking curiously enough. "What else is in that cup Mr. Wallace, besides juice?" no-peep-no-sound Mr. Wallace tipped his cup back up to his lips to take another sip instead. "Well Maria. Let me leave you bee, so you can catch that early flight to get back to that beautiful little twin of yours. Cause boy do I have plenty work on my hands around here in Twenty-nine Palms California." "Alright Lieutenant. Goodnight and it was nice chatting with you." Maria said as she watched him staggered out the room, closing the door behind him. Once Mr. Wallace was gone and considerate to be out her hair. Maria secured the door, paced over to the bed, got under the thick cover and cold sheets, reached over to click the lamp off and ended the night by snuggling her head into the feather soft Sleep Hour Pillow.

* * *

Samantha and Eddie were inside the tent making love to each other. Eddie had her laid in a missionary position rubbing his arrow up against her dream catcher, until he finally got sucked inside. Her dream catcher was so warm it nearly warmed his entire naked body within an instant. Samantha bottom lip started shuddering once he lifted his weight to come down on her clitories at an angle with the lower part of his stomach braising up against her mound. He continued thrusting in and out. "Sam, I love you." "Oh Eddie, I love you too keep making love to me. Oohhh . . . , it feel so good while you rock hard inside of me." she admitted giving him an affectionate smile. When Eddie rested his chest upon her exposed perky breast to ease some weight, he felt her nipples sticking up an half inch sinking into his bare, pale chest. Then Samantha directed him to lift up so she could pull her legs up to her head in a double-jointed position to allow him to go deeper inside her wet, warm, pussy just how he liked it, while she continued nibbling down on his earlobe and just as saying how much he enjoyed her he kept on pounding away at what he loves best. Eddie held her leg's with one hand behind her left knee with his right hand behind the other. Darla was still traveling strongly through the Saginaw woods as darkness finally settled in, until suddenly she stopped in her tracks on the other side of the shallow lake, when she observed camp fire burning. The possession of Mary also gave her eye vision capability to see through the pitch darkness of the night like a hungry wolf hunting for his prey. After she stood their gazing across the lake with vengeance in her heart, she immediately went walking the lake, and the further she kept walking through the water. The deeper it had gotten, until finally the gut of it was up to her chin. Darla's five foot seven inch height was to her advantage to with stand the deepness without going under. Eddie slumped himself over on the right side of Samantha taking a deep breath from all the work he just put in trying to rest up for a second round. "So Eddie, you would rather have a girl instead of a boy, if I ever gotten pregnant?" "Yes, I sure would love to have a little girl before a boy, so she could take up all the beautiful features of her mom." He agreed ebulliently. Darla was now less than twenty yards away from the dry shore on the other side, as her shoes continued sinking into the soft mud on the bottom of the lake. Right when Eddie was about to warm Samantha back up by placing his hand on her dream catcher, he suddenly stopped when the swish should of water caught his attention. "Wait a minute Sam. Did you hear that?" He asked while quickly ejecting his right hand off her clean shaved mound. "You talking about that air pressure? That was my vagina stupid." "No! I know what that was, see there it goes again. Tell me you didn't hear it that time?" He said seriously. "See, here we go again. Just like last time when you played that same scary role that ended up making me sleep in the jeep while you slept in this tent by yourself." Samantha reminded him once more. Darla finally made it to dry land, camouflaging herself on the far side of the tent. Eddie started scrambling around trying to locate the flashlight in the clutterness of their cubby little space. "What are you tweaking on?" Samantha asked sharply. "Tweaking? I'm here trying to find the darn flashlight, so I can check things out." He continued heatedly enough. Samantha eased her left hand along side her while lying on her back, and when she grabbed the flashlight, she immediately clicked it on pointing it directly in his eyes laughing. "Give me this! You knew where it was the entire time!" Eddie said with no humor in his voice frowning skeptically at her. "Don't look at me like that. I was just seeing how long you were going to tweak along."

She continued when she saw him sliding on his jeans only. "Aren't you going to put your shirt, socks and underwear on too?" Then she immediately covered her nakedness with the blanket, when he ignored her opening the tent entrance. "Close the tent back. We don't want any night crawlers creeping in, you know." She scoffed. Eddie zipped the tent closed then stood up rooted to his spot scanning the area while hearing crickets all around him. Clicking the flashlight on while walking off cautiously along side their tent to take a speculated glance on the backside, Samantha irritably rolled over on her stomach and covered her entire body and head with the blanket trying to relax, so when Eddie comes back inside they could finish where they left off. The second Eddie made it to the backside, he quickly turned toward the lake with the flashlight blaring on the water, mistaking the noise he heard, without knowing it, it was Darla stepping down on broken twigs on the ground, then he quickly turned back around. When he heard foot steps approach behind him landing the light closely blaring into Darla's partially blood shot eye's. Everything happened quickly. He opened his mouth to shout a warning out to Samantha when Darla grasped his throat cutting off his windpipe and elevating him off his feet. Eddie threw the flashlight at Darla and it struck her on her forehead, her head jerked back just a tiny bit, but it didn't interfere with the plan she has in store for him. When Eddie saw that that didn't do anything to her, fear formed in his eyes and his hands started clawing at her hand and arm that was around his neck, while his feet were kicking beneath him. Darla didn't let up on her grip. Shaking convulsively, eyes rolling into the back of his head, with the coloration of his face turning purple, Darla powerfully punched him in his chest with a closed fist and ripped his heart out in plain view. Samantha's eyes popped right open under the blanket once she heard the bare skin slap sound from Darla punching Eddie's chest. Thick blood gushed out of his mouth and into Darla's face and hair, as he started choking on his own blood. When Darla released him from her tight grasp with his heart hanging out his chest by a few main arteries and veins, Samantha snatched the cover from her head, when she heard something heavy hitting the ground. "Eddie. What's going on out there? I already warned you about what'll happen again if you try to scare me!" Samantha shouted, staring straight at the tent where the flashlight outside on the ground faced. "Eddie I'm so warning you!" Samantha quickly slid her panties and bra on figuring it'll be best to go out there to see what's the hold up and she didn't bother putting on her shirt or her pants. Instead, she grabbed the comforter blanket to cover up. Samantha zipped the tent open and cautiously eased her head out to call for him once more. "Eddie, where are you?" She sat there for a moment with her head sticking out gazing straight ahead studying to see if she could hear him but once she couldn't detect a sound, she stepped out wrapping the blanket around her thinking it would have been wise to put on some shoes. Tossing the thought out her head realizing it wasn't the first time she stepped out the tent bare footed. Darla quietly tucked away on the opposite side of the tent when she heard Samantha thinking out loud to herself as she approached Eddie's body lying on the ground, and the first thought flashed through Samantha's mind was "He's going out his way again to scare the living shit out of her." As she got closer she said "Eddie, that's it. Sense you wanna waste your damn time, lying on the ground instead of lying in the tent going half on a baby, once again I'll sleep in the jeep!" Then racing over to his body saying while tapping her foot up against his leg. "Did you hear what I just said? Idiot!" But when he didn't budge she trailed her eyes to the ground where the flashlight was still glared on a puddle then she raised her eyebrow skeptically bending down to raise his body to the side, then screamed when she saw not only it was a puddle, but a puddle of blood. Darla quietly crept up behind her unnoticed standing there with her right hand elevated in a swinging position. "Oh God! Oh God!" Samantha cried out, trying to calm her nerves from seeing Eddie's heart hanging out from his chest with eyes stiffly locked to the back of his head. She stood there stunned momentarily not really knowing what's going on at the same time trying not to panic, but once Darla shadow moved, it caught her attention then she glanced out the corner of her eye to the ground only to find two shadows. Then she frightfully turned around hoping she was hallucinating, but she let out a scream that echoed through the woods when she saw Darla was about to strike at her. Samantha took off in full speed only leaving Darla to connect with the blanket ran along. She didn't notice she was running in the woods with nothing on, but panties and a bra. She ran at least fifteen to twenty yards away from the camping site, and suddenly stopped to hide behind a oak tree mounting her back up against it trying to slow her strong panting while peeking back around the tree. "Hum, I don't see anyone, why didn't she run after me?" Samantha broke her thought when she heard an owl fly away from the tree. "Oh God, look at my feet. I must be scared. I didn't even notice their bruised. There ain't no way I'll be able to travel any further without shoe's, so I don't have any choice but to make it back to the tent and grab my clothes, shoes and jeep keys to get out of here. Alright Sam, on the count of three, run like hell back to the tent." She whispered glancing down at her feet, then started to count 1, 2, 3, and took off running. The further she ran along, the more her stride was turning into a limp from all the broken twigs and rocks damaging her feet. She slowed down to stop thinking she saw someone ditch off behind a tree in the woods twenty feet away from her while she carefully scoped out the scenery she said thoughtfully. "I can't believe what's going on that person killed Eddie. Is this actually happening? Sam you got to really be a sick bitch back tracking for some clothes." Then she communicated her senses and took off fast walking the rest of the way. When she finally made it up to the tent she said trying to avoid from looking at Eddie's body on the ground. "I'm gonna go crazy in the morning." With all the intensity built up she didn't waste no time reaching half her body inside the tent to grab her, shirt, pants, shoes and the jacket with the Jeep keys inside. "Hurry Sam, hurry up." She mumbled under her breath, once everything was in her arms she needed, she dropped her shoes to the ground to rush fully slide on her pants with her shirt and jacket gripped in hand, then she slid her shoes on the wrong feet. "Come on Sam, get a grip of yourself." She said thoughtfully sliding her feet into the right shoes, and tossed her shirt and jacket on. She took off through the trail that leads to the parking lot. A little ways through the trail she immediately stopped in her tracks hallucinating thinking she heard someone walking stiffly behind her from hearing broken branches snapping on the ground beneath someone's feet other than her own, but once she realized no on wasn't behind her. She proceeded along with a little more urgency in her step. "Shit! What was that?" She said curiously, stopping in her tracks again with a glimmer of fright in her eyes looking all around her. Then she took off, limping, the rest of the way through the trail once she heard the foot steps boldly heading toward her. She realized when the Jeep came in plain view parked in front of the public restroom it wasn't enough time to unlock the door, hop inside, and take off, so she just hurried right passed it rushing inside the restroom area to hide off. She panicked and got confused on which stall she should pick to hide herself off inside, until finally she chose the fifth stall at the end. "Damn it Sam! That was too loud." She said with a whisper once she closed the stall door and climbed up on the toilet rim settling into a crouched position, so the psychopath killer wouldn't see her feet. Her heart started racing from not getting the correct oxygen it was needing, and all at the same time her feet was aching to the core of the bone inside her shoe's. Darla came storming inside the restroom stopping in her tracks at the first stall door, then jabbed it open with her left hand moving along to the next one. Samantha eyes extended bulging wide. When she heard the first stall door get jabbed open, then the next one, then the third one, and once she gazed blankly at the stall door lock bar, she couldn't believe she forgot to lock it. The second she reached out to lock the stall door, she snatched her hand back placing it over her mouth, when she heard the fourth stall door next to her get jabbed open, as she immediately braced herself thinking within seconds the door is going to fly open and she'll face the killer eye to eye to be killed. Samantha stayed crouched down on the toilet taking short breaths looking unsure on why the stall door hadn't come flying open then the thought vanished when she heard a loud shattered glass sound outside the building. "Now what was that?" She said thoughtfully from not knowing it was Darla who busted the Jeep's back window out. Every second felt like an hour, till finally she eased one foot down from the toilet, then the next one then she gut checked herself for a test of courage before she opened the stall door. "Well Sam. Its either you do or you don't, but either way you sure in hell can't use the restroom." She whispered, the door was open she tiptoed slowly pass each stall peering over to them making sure she wasn't walking herself into a trap, and to her it seemed as if all the life entered back into her, regaining her strength. Letting out a deep breath upon not seeing anyone waiting on her in anyone of them. Everything was to quiet she noticed while making her way up to the front entrance doorway, and once she placed her back on the inside wall she coached herself. "Alright Sam, ease your head out and if you don't see her make a run for the Jeep." Samantha exhaled visually then peeked her head out to scan the parking lot. The Jeep was less than fifteen feet away from where she stood contemplating to run out from behind the inside restroom wall. "On the count of three, take off running Sam. 1, 2, 3." She counted and she was off running to the Jeep. She nervously started fumbling with the key ring trying to locate the door key when she made it to the driver door. "Good gracious, here it goes." She said placing the key inside the door lock, seconds later sob's of blood gushed out from her open mouth. Darla had crept up from the far side of the public restroom and plunged the crow bar pointed tip through her lower back. The blow was so powerful, the pointed end came ripping out from her stomach. Darla lifted her body two feet from the ground with her two hands tightly gripped on the back handle and once the last breath emptied out of Samantha's lungs, Darla released her hands from the crow bar, causing the Jeep door mirror to break off once Samantha's head came crashing down on it. Her body's dead weight dropped heavily to the pavement with the bar still pierced through her backside. Darla slowly turned her head side ways, then vanished from the light that illuminated from the corners of the public restroom back off into the Saginaw woods that she now owned.

CHAPTER NINE

THE NEXT DAY when Maria made it home from meeting up with Mr. Wallace in 29 Palms, California. Detective Avery finally decided to phone her and update her on the latest. Maria was seemingly enjoying the moment stretched out on their living room couch, until her cell phone on her waist line started ringing. "Hello. Investigator Gates speaking. How can I help you?" She answered cutting the ring short. "Good evening Mrs. Gates, this is Homicide Detective Avery." "Oh Hello, Mr. Avery." She confirmed with a smile, sitting upright. "I was told to call you, and update you on the few murders that was discovered." "Please continue." "Well yesterday evening before sun down, a young lady by the name of Billy James Miles, dead, crashed into a tree with his Adams apple snatched out of his throat." Maria swallowed as he continued. "Also, a couple of campers found two other campers murdered in the Saginaw woods camping ground, by the name of Eddie Stewart and Samantha Morris." "So you guys came up with the conclusion these wasn't common murders?" She asked soberly. "Well, to tell you the truth Mrs. Gates. There's no significant clues to strike up right now on whose doing the paranormal ones or the common murders at this point." "Well make sure you keep me informed Detective." "Sure thing Mrs. Gates, I'll be staying in contact. Bye." "Bye." She said, then closed and hooked her phone back to the clip reminding herself about what she promised Mrs. Bailey when she was alive, and that was she'll do anything to catch the person or thing whose responsible for the killings. Just like she promised the town, she'll eventually catch the Saginaw killer Norman A. Gandy when she in fact did.

* * *

Darla discovered an old abandoned house dead smack in the middle of the woods surrounded by oak trees with a old busted down water well in front of it. Stepping up to the door, she forcefully pushed it wide open stepping inside and the house was really empty, with a condemned old furniture stench smell in the air. She immediately took a seat on the floor with her back up against the left hand side wall. That supports the door frame staring blankly at the inner part of the house with her legs stretched out in front of her. As time elapsed by while still standing on the floor with the appetite of three hard working hungry men, she slowly turned her head facing the rabbit that came resting inside the open doorway. Keeping herself in the dark shade of the boarded window, she savagely reached out snatching the rabbit up by its neck like a human animal trap. The scared rabbit kept jerking its hind legs trying to break loose from her grasp, until she gruesomely bit a nice size chunk from its neck. You could actually hear the gristle sound while she chewed going in for a second bite. Flinging the remainder of the rabbit in the middle of the floor as she blankly chewed on the raw meat with blood dripping from the corner of her mouth. When done, she vacated the abandoned house traveling through the woods heading for the road. "Yah!!! Mommy's home!" Antonia yelled from the backseat when she saw the living room curtains open, as her and Bobby came pulling up in the driveway. The second Bobby opened their front door she went storming straight to the study room shouting. "Mommy, mommy, you home!" "Mommy sure is, give me a kiss. Where's Daddy?" Maria asked with a smile, and once she saw Bobby coming through the door she said. "Oh, there he is." "Hey honey, how was your trip?" He asked concerned bending toward her to give her a kiss. "It went pretty well. If you're counting no extra cases to my load, and seeing chopped up bodies good." Bobby sat right beside her saying in a whisper, with a skeptical grin. "Honey. Don't say that." Then nodded his head toward Antonia. Maria cuffed her mouth with her right palm saying, after lowering her voice. "Babe. I seriously forgot." Being that they always been careful on their conversations around Antonia, cause she thought her mom was only a Animal Patrol Officer. Everyone focused over to the door once they heard the bell dangling around their cat Jasper's neck, when he came prancing through the study room door to jump on Maria's lap. "I know, Jasper. Mommy forgot to feed you." She said thoughtfully rubbing his fur. "Can I feed him mommy, please?" "You sure can. Come along little girl." Maria answered, standing up letting Jasper leaped out from her hands. Bobby stepped over to the door angling his hand out saying. "After you ladies." Then he made Maria skip up from giving her a tap on her butt. After Maria opened a con of fancy cat food, and placing it in Jasper's bowl. She accompanied Bobby on their living room sofa while Antonia stayed in the kitchen area to watch Jasper eat his food like she normally had. When Maria sat right beside Bobby on the sofa, he nuzzled close to study her beautiful delicate face, making her hazel brown eyes twitch as they're lips met. Slowly closing her eyes once her heart started racing from the passionate kiss they stole from each other.

* * *

Later on that evening while Darla was walking down Clifton road coming from the Saginaw woods, a family in a green Suburban truck sped right passed her. "Honey wait, turn around. I think that was Chris's old girlfriend Darla Phelps." Mrs. Cunningham said surprisingly. "It can't be! That girl is 3,800 miles away from here in a crazy hospital in California." Otis challenged looking unsure in the rearview mirror. "Ok. Maybe she was, but now she's back. Otis honey, just turn around and if it's not her we could always do another u-turn and head home." "All sugar, shit." He hedged, decreasing his speed to yield to the side of the road doing a u-turn. Stephanie their 8 year old daughter was sound asleep in the middle passenger seat buckled down, and their fourteen year old daughter Rachael was sitting right beside her bobbing her head to the music from her head phones, until she saw her dad pulling over doing a u-turn. Mr. Otis floored the gas pedal heading back toward Darla. Mrs. Clair squinted her eyes powering down the passenger window peering over at Darla on the opposite side of the road as they passed her, then Otis pulled over and did another u-turn, and came slowly pulling up beside her. "Darla, it's me. Chris's mom Mrs. Cunningham, you remember me? Your old boyfriend's mom!" Mrs. Clair yelled out the passenger window looking back at managing a smile then she reached back to the back passenger door where Darla was standing on the outside of it looking straight ahead, but when the door opened, Mr. Otis babbled out to his wife, "Honey, what are you doing? We're . . . !" His words cut short when Darla climbed in sitting right beside Stephanie their 8 year old daughter. "Honey, drive off, lets take her to our house, at least to clean her up. She's a mess." "Clair, I don't know about this you're forever picking up something off the side of the road." He said, looking in his door mirror seeing if it's safe to merge back onto the road. "Honey, I know what you're talking about, besides she's not an animal. She's our deceased son Chris's old girlfriend, watch the road!" Clair huffed when he stared blankly at her. "Oh, she smells!" Rachael blurted out, placing the head phones back on her neck and raising her right palm up to her nose and mouth area. "Rachel turned her gaze from her mother to Darla and said with a friendly leer. "Hi. I'm Rachel, and this is my sleeping little sister Stephanie." Darla didn't grunt a reply at all, she just stared forward through her shaggy long dirty bangs. "Mom . . . , you'll just have to excuse me on what I have to say. This woman looks spooky." Rachael added, while tightening herself down inside her seat so she could study Darla and watch every move she made. Mrs. Clair didn't care to contest her daughter opinion cause she sort of thought the same thing, she could admit. The moment Darla closed the door, and Otis yield back onto the road. Rachael was nodding her head while at the same time placing her IPod earphones back on her ears to drain her parents out from their constant argument sense they left the pumpkin patch fieldtrip with Stephanie's school. Once seven minutes exactly went pass and they all came pulling up in their driveway beside their boat called Caesar Wind. Mrs. Clair said to Darla with the calmest leer ever. "Alright Darla. You've always been welcome into our home, but the last time you was here years ago. You stole my white, gold, twenty-five diamond special made necklace I had gotten on my fourth anniversary. But, your still more than welcome to some clean clothes that you can change into, so you can get out of those horrible clothes your wearing that smells like mothballs and stray, wet dogs. "Now you want talk about the poor girl, geez." Mr. Otis concluded, shaking his head climbing out of the truck and once everyone made it through the front door, their cat Angel came prancing up with eagerness brushing her body up against Darla's leg, but out of reflex and off guard. Darla kicked her air-borne into the wall. "What's wrong breathing like that?" Rachael yelled furiously racing to Angel's aid. Mrs. Clair raced over to Angel right behind her. "Darla! what's gotten into you? Clair said then added when Rachael dropped Angel from her arm's running off to her room. "Rachael! Why you drop her like that?" Then her expression hardening seconds later Angel stopped breathing. "Oh my God, Angel's dead." Mrs. Clair said with a disbelieving look. Rachael opened her door when she heard her mom announced Angel was dead. Then shouted with her head sticking out the door. "See she killed Angel, you never listen!" Mrs. Clair's nerves skipped a beat when she heard Rachael's room door slam. "See what did I tell you. First you bring home a stray dog that ripped the bottom of your couch away, now you bring home Darla that killed your daughters thirteenth birthday present." Mr. Otis reminded her with a tease. "Ah Otis put a fucking sock in it!" She exploded then continued. "Besides, she didn't mean it. She did it out of reflex, Angel must of frightened her." "Ah shit! Leave that cat there, I'll get it. Just go on continuing acting naive." He countered while walking pass her to place Stephanie in her bed so she could finish napping. "Fine! Come on Darla, so I can get you cleaned up." Otis marched straight into the kitchen after he laid Stephanie in her bed to grab a plastic trash bag to place Angel inside. Darla was walking slowly behind Mrs. Clair heading to the bedroom, until suddenly she halted in front of Stephanie's bedroom door that once was Chris's bedroom before he came up missing and never was found; and it wasn't the fact Darla remembered, it was the possession of Mary that knew, and controlled her membrane of thoughts. "Come on Darla, and yes that use to be Chris's room." Mrs. Clair reminded her waving her to the room so she could get cleaned up. Darla's nails was starting to gradually grow at a steady pace and at a abnormal length from all the strength and calcium building up in her body. Her nails would soon be at a lengthy one inch and razor sharp. The moment Darla stepped through their bedroom door. Mrs. Clair already had a blouse, black stretch pants, and some leg warmer boots that she never had gotten the chance to wear, laid out on the bed. "Here Darla, I've never been into fashion of course you may remember, but there clean and warm, which pretty which pretty much counts." Then she guided her into their private bathroom so she could get cleaned up, and usually Darla would have been the shy type to not let anyone see her naked, but instead she started ripping her shirt off. "Wait Darla, don't tear your shirt! What all that place do place do to you?" She asked looking questioningly at her then further insisted. "Here, let me help you." Once Darla was naked, Mrs. Clair turned the shower on and stepped out of the bathroom when Darla stepped into the shower.

* * *

Night time arrived, and Darla was sitting on the floor between Mrs. Clair's legs in Indian style getting her hair combed, Mrs. Clair built herself up to ask her a question. "Excuse me Darla, this ain't none of my business, but how did you get the pink eye?" She finally asked, leaning on the right of her waiting on a answer. Darla still continually sat quiet. The possession of Mary within Darla was very smart with intelligence and knew all the right times to strike or to remain calm. Mrs. Clair also wanted to ask her what happened to Chris and the others, beside hearing that phony story shed given the authorities years ago. But she continued to stroking through Darla's hair with the comb with a blank stare, until she heard three continuous knocks on her bedroom door. "Come in!" "Mom, I'm going to sleep early tonight, and tell me she's not sleeping in my room." Rachael said clearly enough. "Darling, she didn't mean to do what she didn't, so get over it." "Get over it! Mom she killed Angel, she was like a family member to us. I guess that's what we get for you not ever taking dad's advice on things, so you're the one who needs to get over it!" Rachael snapped. Mrs. Clair fumed raising a skeptical eyebrow. "I beg your pardon, young lady? Go to your room at once, and I think it would be a good idea to go to bed early!" Rachael suddenly fumed with a silent expression stomping off to her room. "Where you going, Darla?" Mrs. Clair wondered when she saw Darla slowly walking out the room. She whispered softly. "Oh Well, it ain't like she's never been in our home and spent many nights, besides she's probably tired of sitting underneath my nose, knowing we never got along when her and Chris was dating." Then she thought quietly in mind. "Could Darla actually know where Chris's body is?" Mr. Otis was in the living room having a few beers' sitting in his reclining chair looking at the Los Angeles Lakers take on the New York Knicks on their big screen, until he suddenly felt watched. "Darla, what made you want to stand right there at the corner of the hallway and stare?" Then he cracked another beer open. "You can't be creeping up on people, and believe me you done already caused enough damage around here for one day. That's for certain." he added while looking at her standing border line of the living room and hallway. Darla immediately took off out the front door leaving it wide open. "Darla! Sugar come quick, so you won't think I'm the one who ran her off!" He shouted out to his wife from the beginning of the hallway. Mrs. Clair came pacing out their bedroom saying while she approached him. "Where she run off too?" Mr. Otis didn't say a word. He just pointed to the open door, then immediately stepped out the way going back over to his chair once he heard the crowd on television got amped up, from Coby Bryant's slam dunk on Rasheed Wallace. "Darla come back! You can't be out walking around in the middle of the night." Mrs. Clair yelled from the porch sounding concerned. "Aww she'll be back! Where else could she go to make problems this time of night?" Mr. Otis concluded, looking at his wife stepping back inside the house. "Oh, now you want her around!" She pronounced firmly, slamming the front door leaving it unlocked then moodily paced off to Stephanie's room to lay her in Rachael's. "Honey, I'm still considered a pain in the ass remember?" He yelled from his chair. Then laughed heartily when he heard her comment back saying. "We know this already! "Aww hell. I guess I'll leave the front door unlocked and sleep in the living room just in case she do decide to come back in the middle of the night." Otis said to himself cutting the volume up a notch.

* * *

Shelly Ciera and Patrick Hughs was an engaged couple at home celebrating Shelly's birthday with a little dinner and a few drinks amongst themselves. "Thank you Babe for cooking and preparing this lovely dinner for my birthday. I can't imagine anyone of my birthdays being as important as this one." She noted very excitedly. "But its plenty more to come, Babe.

I can guarantee you that, if I have something to do with it." He assured her with a smile. Darla was about twenty minutes into the woods from the Cunningham's residence, when she discovered Shelly and Patrick's house sitting off the lakeside fifty feet away. Darla boldly kicked their gate open entering their backyard in the root of the darkness while Shelly got up from the tale to go make something to drink at their private bar. "Babe! Make two of those while your over there and I'll clear the table off so we can relax in the living room to have a few drinks." Patrick suggested. Shelly dropped three ice cubs a piece in both their glass before pouring Mudslides and Martel over them. "It'll be right over here waiting on you Honey. Just like I will." She pointed out firmly, making her way over to the sofa that's faced away from their dinning room area, and sliding patio door." Give me one more hot second, and I'll be right there to accompany you!" Patrick placed the dirty dishes inside the fresh dish water, then went walking inside the living room. "Now where were we?" He asked concerned, reaching for his drink from her hand taking a seat beside her. "We were talking about how the rest of my birthdays will turn out o be just as good as this one. If you had anything to do wit it." She reminded him. "Oh yeah, your right, and shall we toast to that?" Looking into each others eyes as they clung their glasses together for remembrance. Once they both took a sip from their glasses they placed them on the cup holders on the coffee table. Then Shelly decided to heat things up by lying long ways on the sofa pulling him to her command. Darla slowly crept on to the patio door relaxing her face up against the glass stalking as they fore played. After Patrick planted several kisses on her lips, he stayed down a for long one curiously peeking out the corner of his eyes at their big mirror, that reflects the patio door while Shelly's eyes was closed when Darla observed Patrick looking at her through the mirror she paced along side their house. Patrick blankly raised up from Shelly's lips mistaking her saw someone standing at their patio door. When she felt him release his kiss she immediately opened her eyes pulling her head away from his. "What are you tripping on?" She asked curiously following his gaze coming from the mirror to stare back into his eyes for an explanation. "Nothing Babe. I just thought I saw something that's all." He assured her, going in for another kiss working his way down to her throat while at the same time opening her shirt exposing her cleavage with his hand. Shelly's body started tingling with escalating desire as she sounded off soft moans. Darla eased herself back up to the sliding patio door breathing strongly. Patrick kept kissing away at her breast playing it off looking out the corner of his eyes again trying not to cause any attention to himself, and ended up seeing the exact same looming presence in the outside darkness peering through the patio door. Once Darla realized he was gazing straight at her through the mirror again. She scampered away on the left side of the house in the darkness. "That's it, I am not seeing things!" He said seriously standing up on his feet heading back to the kitchen counter. Shelly sat upright fixing her shirt over her cleavage saying. "What are you talking about?" Patrick snatched the butcher knife from the knife holder and tiptoed his way over to the patio door. "Ah, hah! Just like I figured. I see vapor mist from somebody's breath on the glass!" "What?" Shelly said sounding confused with a disbelieving look. Patrick clicked the patio door unlocked to step out and check things out. "You are serious, aren't you?" she protested, looking over at him from the living room sofa. Patrick still didn't grunt a reply. He just continued out on the patio and stopped in his tracks with his eyes bulging wide with the butcher knife pointed out in front of him. Once he made sure the yard empty. He took off toward their shed to make sure it was still locked. "Hum, well the shed is still locked." He whispered, jerking the padlock then took off toward the left corner of the house. Darla was waiting in the dark like a pride of lions hunting in the middle of the night with her right hand elevated high to cause a deadly low with her razor sharp nails. Patrick stopped three feet away from the corner turning toward the patio door once he heard Shelly say. "It ain't nobody, but the Boogieman! You're just scared to make love to me!" Then she took off toward their bedroom. He wanted to comment back, but he couldn't get the right words out in time so he just went back inside locking the patio door behind him, and placed the butcher knife on the table heading to the room. Shelly took her shirt and skirt off then hopped under the cover sliding her g-string panties and bra off. When Patrick stepped over to their bed still trying to find all the correct words to say. She dropped her panties on the floor starting up a conversation with her bra still in hand. "Patrick, we both agreed tonight we wasn't going to wait all the way to we got married to have sex and your outside in the dark being a ghost buster with a butcher knife." He then caught the bra in his hand, she threw it when it came sliding down from his face, and once he placed her bra on their straw chair. He stripped down to his boxers and socks and climbed in the bed under the covers. It was all the his idea when they first started dating to make a pact with each other to wait and have sex after marriage, being he was the one that is a virgin in their relationship. Shelly straddled her naked body on top of him to crack the shell he was deeply hiding inside with a little more foreplay and although his shaft started rising from the soft skin of her nakedness. It still didn't remove the worried expression from him feeling confident he saw someone's reflection and vapor mist from their breath on the patio door. Darla paced away from the patio door once she realized it was locked, then peered through each one of the windows she approached and once she located their bedroom, she just stood there ease dropping on them. Shelly thought it was very worsening, the way he laid there like he was dead to the world staring at the ceiling coming to the conclusion inside his mind. He still forgot to check along side their house, and until then he could never find his mojo to make love to her. Shelly raised up from kissing his neck when she felt his veins clutching and pumping from deeply thinking. "Oh Patrick, I swear!" she barked shortly un-straddling herself from him. Patrick wanted to shout out to her "no" and to keep doing what she was doing, but then he also thought. "This was his chance to go check on the side of the house and once he got up to put his clothes on she fumed. "Fine! Don't have sex with me then. I'll just go right to sleep, and if I wake up in the middle of the night, I'll just oh never mind!" She cut herself off holding back her real thought that she'll do it herself. She angrily crossed her arms over the pillow resting her head on her arms faced away from him. "Shelly, I'm just going to check out one more place to ease my conscience, and when I return we can make love how you want, when you want, and where you want." He added after putting on his clothes and shoes before walking away. "And I promise you it wouldn't be no more talk when I return." Shelly sighed visually turning her head toward the door, once he went walking out heading to the kitchen table where he placed the knife. "I can't believe, he's actually serious about going back outside to ghost hunt." She snorted staring at the jarred door listening to him slide open the patio door. Darla raced away from their window rooting herself back to her spot inside the dark corner of the house while Patrick slowly stepped back out onto the patio with the butcher knife, heading to where Darla was impatiently waiting to strike. Stopping in his tracks with his attention focused to the back fence of their yard mistaking he heard something. "Aww maybe its nothing." He whispered dryly and proceeded along. The second Darla saw his shadow approaching on the ground she came charging out from the darkness like a human animal in rage with a growl. "Ahhh!" He yelled out from being caught off guard swinging the butcher knife landing it in her right shoulder. Darla came down with her sharp nails at his throat hitting a main artery with a powerful blow that laid him helpless. Blood squirted from his deep open wound as he laid choking to death on his own blood. Darla didn't even notice she was wounded as blood warmly ran down her arm and her finger tips. The blood from her arm was dripping so badly once she entered the house through the open patio door. Blood dripped from her finger nails and onto the dining room carpet as she headed toward their hallway. She slowly crept up the hallway stopping at the first bedroom ajar then boldly jabbed it open as expecting to catch Shelly lying in bed. Shelly popped her eyes wide open still faced toward their half open door and yelled out. "Yeah, yeah. I'm just as pissed as your are!" Mistaking it was Patrick whom punched the door open. Darla stopped rooted to her spot once she heard Shelly's voice echo through their cracked bedroom door, she crept up to their guest restroom that was a few feet away from Shelly's and Patrick's room, and hid herself off inside the pitch darkness of it. Shelly lifted her head from the pillow when she observed Darla's Shadow swiftly scamper away on the hallway wall outside their bedroom door. "Wait a minute. That didn't look like Patrick's shadow!" She concluded easily knowing one hundred percent the shadow she further thought insanely. When Shelly eased out of bed she bent over naked to grab her g-string panties from the floor, and once she grabbed her bra from the chair and swapped it on. She turned half her body toward the door feeling queasy and nervous." What the heck is the doing?" She complained underneath her breath when she heard a scrapping sound that made her teeth grind, till it suddenly stopped. Shelly ran both her index fingers along the sides of the crotch part of her panty line rushed both feet inside her fuzzy shoes then headed out the room. "Patrick!" She called out on the outside of the guest restroom door peering into the darkness looking directly into Darla's eyes without noticing it, then proceeded up to the bedroom door Darla jabbed open. She stuck her head inside the room to take a speculated glance, then slowly crept her way to the dining room area. The minute she turned the corner she noticed their patio door wide open trailing her eyes down to the carpet letting out a slight shiver from the open patio door. "What is that!" She thought out loud frowning when she discovered reddish scattered spots amongst their dining room carpet. Shelly stood upright feeling breathlessly oppressive with her senses feverishly heightened from the long scrapping sound around the corner in their hallway and as the scrapping sound was getting closer, she shouted staring at the corner from the dining room area. "Patrick, you are so dead, you can't imagine how pissed off I am with you!" Then she continued standing there with a confused expression once the noise came to a mute on the other side of the corner but she got even more eager to find out what was causing the scrapping sound. Once she built herself up she tiptoed her way up to the wall stopping right before turning the corner. "1, 2, 3" she counted. Then gave out a high extreme scream, when she saw Darla with her bloody nails elevated with a grizzly hatred expression and murder in her eyes. Shelly took off like speed lightening leaving her shoes in the direction she was facing storming out the patio in full speed behind her so she couldn't escape. Shelly blanked out so bad. She didn't even recognize Patrick's body on the ground on the far right of her, as she fled toward their back gate. Darla was right on her heel when Shelly tripped bare footed in a hole that an animal had started digging at some point trying to dig underneath their gate. When she tried to get up Darla straddled over her back and gave her a deadly blow to the right side of her face. The powerful blow left four big deep lacerations to her jaw bone, as her neck snapped over out of socket. Darla stood upright from her back to reach down and grab her legs with both hands to drag her like a crash test doll to the lake. After dragging her body up to the water, she lifted Shelly's legs by her ankles spun around and flung her petite body into the lake then walked off vanishing into the darkness.

* * *

Mrs. Clair was just now coming from the bathroom from taking a long hot shower after touching Darla's smelly cloths and ended up tossing then in the trash can, noticing that there was dried blood on them. A though raced through her mind. "Darla may after all had something to do with my son's disappearance, cause I'm not sure as hell isn't going to buy it now from seeing blood on her pants. Hum maybe I'll just stay up a little longer in Stephanie's room sense she's asleep in Rachael's cause God knows I can't stand to sleep in the room with Otis tonight after he nearly drank eight beers." she said underneath her breath cutting all the lights off, and headed to Stephanie's room. Darla was heading back toward the Cunningham's residence and doing some tremendous breathing amped up to kill again, as if killing became a natural born hobby. Mrs. Clair couldn't stop entwining her brain thinking about the day when the homicide detectives knocked on her door and told her about the horrible news that changed her life forever, that her son was missing or could possibly be dead somewhere. "Oh Clair, get that thought out your mind." she quietly told herself. As time passed by, Mrs. Clair extended her eyes open wide in the darkness once she heard their front door open but never closing. She stayed lying there in Stephanie's bed gazing straight out to the dark hallway through the open door contemplating if that's what she heard. Darla stood in the door way looking around before she took off toward the bedroom area but once she entered the hallway she stumbled over one of Angels cat squeeze toys making a growl sound underneath her breath. Mrs. Clair's eyes soberly opened wider when she heard the noise from the cat toy. Seeing Darla's shadow creep past Stephanie's doorway, Mrs. Clair quickly tiptoed up to the door and when she clicked the bedroom light on that blared through the hallway she said. "What are you doing, Darla?" Darla stopped facing the door with her hand froze extended out on Rachael's door knob. "What was you about to do, kill my daughter too?" Clair pressed stepping into the hallway. Darla let out a low unexpectant angry sigh turning around taking off fast passing her while swatting Mrs. Clair's hand from her shoulder when she tried stopping her. "Shit!" Mrs. Clair groaned. Feeling the sting and seeing her hand bleeding from Darla's nails leaving a open cut, she quickly closed and dead bolted their front door leaving her back on it thinking with her head tilted up to the ceiling. "What possibly would of happened if she never decided to stay up until she came back? God only you know what's gotten into that girl, only you know." She whispered underneath her breath heading to their bathroom medicine cabinet for a ban aid.

* * *

The very next morning Shelly's sister Lavina Ciera was crazily ringing their phone from out of state to wish her a Happy Birthday and let them know what time her daughter will be expected on the airplane flight. Shelly daughter was seven years old when Shelly first met Patrick at the town fair four years ago. "Now I know, she was expecting me to call this morning!" Lavina hedged tapping her nails on their nightstand humming a tune while listening to the never ending rings from no one answering. "Well that's strange, the answering machine isn't even picking up so she couldn't be on the computer, besides here it is seven o'clock in the morning something got to be wrong, and whatever it is, I'm not waiting around to find out." She pointed out disconnecting the line to dial 911. "Emergency 911, how can I direct your call?" the male switchboard operator said. "Yes, could you quickly direct me to the Saginaw Michigan emergency 911 please?" Lavina replied. "I sure can man. Thank you for using emergency 911, hereby your request." "Saginaw emergency 911, please state your emergency." The lady operator said professionally. "Hello my name is Lavina Ciera and I'm calling from the Show-Me-State Missouri. I'm here reporting an emergency call from my big sister Shelly Ciera's home there in Saginaw Michigan." she excitedly explained. "Slow down ma'am, so what do you think is possibly wrong at this residence?" "My sister had always answered her phone on the second ring, and if she didn't her answering machine would pick up to intercept the call, because she worked from the privacy of her own home for Kays make-up." "Now what are you requesting, ma'am?" "Well with no further delays I'm requesting for you to send some authorities over to her residence immediately to be safe than sorry, because I have her eleven year old daughter whom was expected by her mom to be on the nine o'clock air flight." "Alright, do me a favor, don't put your niece on the flight just yet, wait until we figure out what's going on." The operator insisted helpfully. "Yes ma'am, I won't." Lavina assured her. "Fine, sit tight and we'll send someone out to the residence, but first please state her address." The operator started tapping on the computer keys when Lavina said. "Its, 5552 E. Dearborn Lane." "Alright ma'am, that'll be it. Thank you for calling emergency 911, we'll send someone right now." "Thank you very much, ma'am." Lavina said politely before hanging up.

* * *

Less than twenty minutes later after Lavina's emergency request, Corporal Mitchell and Officer Herd pulled up in Shelly and Patrick's driveway with their emergency code three lights flashing. "I'll go cover the backside, Corporal!" Officer Herd yelled out, racing alongside their house with her nine millimeter extended out in front of her. Corporal Mitchell immediately raced up to their front door, and rang their doorbell three times while grabbing his radio receiver from the strap of his uniform. "Corporal Mitchell, go head." "Corporal. I just observed a body of a male ten feet of the open patio in the back of the house, over." Officer Herd pronounced. "Alright stand by don't approach the house yet. I'm on my way over." He instructed with the sting of authority rippling through his voice. "That's a copy sir, over and out." Officer Herd swallowed dryly standing up against the house with her weapon pointed in the air as Corporal Mitchell came racing up to Patrick's body making a positive I.D. that he was dead, then raced to his partner side to instruct the positions they needed to perform, after he radio in for emergency back up units. "This badge number 1312. I'm requesting emergency back up at 5552 Dearborn Lane, over." "That's affirmative sir. I'm sending back up right now." Corporal Mitchell strapped the receiver back to his strap and said. "Alright, Herd. I'm going in first to see if it's a code thirty, so just stay a little ways behind just in case if it's not clear." he demanded. "That's affirmative, sir." she agreed ebulliently. Then her frown depend when she saw him take off inside through the open patio. "This is the S.M.P.D., is anyone in the house." He yelled out with his voice holding a professional note. Once he was rejected with silence, he slowly proceeded onward with his weapon extended but when he saw spots of dry blood and a pair of pink house shoes a few feet from where he was standing. He once again yelled while slowly entering the hallway.

"I repeat, is anyone in the house?" He turned toward Officer Herd and gave her a silent sign language that he was about to go for the back after pointing down at the blood spots and house shoes. He didn't hesitate at all in noticing the deep four scrap marks stretched all the way down the hallway wall and once he entered the hallway "Good God, what did this?" He whispered thoughtfully moving cautiously along and once he saw the coast was clear in the first bedroom, he slowly crept his way up to the guest restroom. Mr. Mitchell reached his arm inside the restroom to click the light on, then took a second glance at the restroom mirror when he noticed the same deep marks straight across it. He was being very observing by rubbing his left hand fingers along the marks to see how deep they was but once the sirens from the emergency units rang out in the background coming closer, he communicated his senses and continued up to Shelly and Patrick's bedroom. He eased the door open wider with his left foot with his hand gripped tighter around his weapon for foul play, being that was the last available room to search. Right when the door opened wider, all he saw was clothes scattered beside the bed and more shoes as he slowly took in the room. The whole back up unit team rushed to the back of the house when Officer Herd notified them by radio their position. Corporal Mitchell came calmly walking back toward the dining room area with his weapon placed in his holster, confirming the inside of the house is a code thirty clearance. Once the house and the backyard was covered with the back up unit, Officer Drake noticed something a few yards out into the lake floating in the water, and once he was closer he shouted out. "its most definitely a body you guys!" Then in a rush he took off his shoes, socks, and rolled up his pant legs going in the water. "Oh God!" he pondered as he reached for Shelly and saw her pale raw face and deep lacerations. Nearly an hour later when both bodies was taken away to the morgue by the Saginaw County Coroner, and the house had been yellow taped when the forensic unit arrived to do their investigation. Homicide Detective Gary Grant from the forensic office cut out three patches from the carpet to take to the Investigation forensic office for identification testing. "Alright guys, it's a rap. Let's start clearing this place out!" He shouted to everyone.

* * *

Mr. Otis grabbed his wrapped ham and cheese sandwich from their kitchen counter taking back off to work from his lunch break, while his daughters was at school, and his wife was still off to work. "A few more hours than you can come back home and catch the Lakers play at home again, but this time against the Wizards." He reminded himself underneath his breath, tapping in forty four twelve on their Brinks Alarm System to arm all windows and doors to their home the second he climbed in the driver seat of his work meat truck from the slaughter house. He clipped his cell phone on the sun visor, fired the engine up and took off up the road heading back to work. Mr. Otis drove up the road three quarters of a mile from their house, when he had to yield to the side of the road where he observed Darla standing in place staring affronted at the Saginaw woods. He reversed his work truck back to where she was standing, as if she didn't have any acknowledgement of a running over size truck pulling up parking beside her. "Darla what's going on now, and what are you staring at? I know one thing you better hurry up and make a decision about hoping in this truck, cause time is ticking away and I need to get back to the slaughter house in fifteen minutes!" He yelled out the rolled down passenger window. Darla opened her eyes slowly turning around, heading toward the passenger door. Mr. Otis reached out to assist her by opening the door from the inside knowing she wasn't all there anymore, and once she climbed in slamming the door closed. He pulled off saying "Hell, knock the hedges off the son of a bitch, why don't ya! Darla that place at Patton State sure did a number on you, so where were you heading? All I forgot you wasn't or shall I say where you want to be dropped off at? Well here goes this silent game again. Ah shit!" He yelled, when an overgrown buck came from out of no where stopping dead smack in the middle of his lane, and even though he slammed on his brakes. It was to late, the truck plowed right over it sliding to a complete stop at a jack knife angle. Darla's hands were still mounted against the dash board bracing herself from the impact of the Buck being hit. Mr. Otis visually sighed glancing in his wide driver door mirror looking at the Buck jerking his hind legs going into shock with a crushed rib cage. "Are you alright, Darla?" He asked, climbing out without waiting around for any reply to see up close for himself what type of condition the Buck was in. The truck Mr. Otis was driving was big and white and sort of reminded him of a lays potato chip truck. Once he noticed the Buck breathing had stopped, he quickly headed back to the truck to grab his cell phone clipped to his sun visor and when he opened the door to grab his cell phone he didn't even notice Darla exit the vehicle leaving the passenger door wide open. Darla raised the back door latch bar open and once it was open she saw all type of meat hooks and other slaughter materials, raising up on her toes to grab a meat hook from the inside door grapping it in her hand tightly. Mr. Otis finally got reception from his antenna being broke off, then he dialed 911 standing in his driver side door faced away from the Buck behind him. "Emergency 911. How can I assist your emergency?" "Yes, my name is Otis Cunningham. I was traveling up the road on N. Kenly, when a Buck ran out in the middle of the lane, and I hate say it, but that's when I struck him. So . . ." He cut his conversation short when he heard foot steps approaching behind him, but as he slowly turned around he said, "Darla, what are you . . . Ah!" "Sir! What's going o, are you there?" The operator lady pressed, then the phone disconnected. "All emergency units we have a foul play in progress on N. Kenly Road, and I need a patrol response team in route!" The operator voice ranged out through the emergency units receivers. Darla dragged Mr. Otis's body with the large meat hook she plunged completely through his upper back bone, leaving a thick trail of blood from the driver door to the back of the truck. She lifted the upper part of his dead weight body inside the truck first, then flung his bottom half afterwards, them closed both doors when she heard sirens sounding off in the far background. Darla disappeared in the afternoon sun, and into the heart of the Saginaw woods the small town exist inside. She was trailing through the woods like a human lawn mower stepping over fallen twigs, leaves, tree bark and dirt making her escape. Ten minutes later patrol vehicles raced up from both directions on Kenly Road responding to the emergency call. Tires screeched one after another as police vehicles kept arriving at the scene some officers jumped out their vehicles confused on why they didn't see anyone except a dead Buck in the road, and a jack knife meat truck with the passenger and driver doors open. "You guys, come quick! Its a trail of blood right here from the driver door, to the back." Officer Scott said pointing to the back doors of the truck. Officers aimed their weapons out in front of them while he raised the bar swinging the doors open. Then he jumped out of firing reach saying in disbelief. "What in the hell?" Seconds later two plain unmarked cars pulled up yielding off the side of the road then Officer Pax said "Great, just in time. Here comes Detective Avery." "Hello gentlemen, what we have here?" Detective Avery asked with his face expression hardening. Once he saw the town meat man Mr. Otis Cunningham's dead as a door knob. "Oh Lord All Mighty. What is this town up to?" he continued dryly. "Detective Avery, who in the world would want to do a thing, like this?" Officer Pax curiously asked. "Well, when I got radioed by Mrs. Spears at the main switchboard, she informed me she clearly heard Mr. Cunningham holler out the name, Darla." He answered truthfully.

CHAPTER TEN

LATER THAT SAME evening when Mrs. Clair and Stephanie pulled up their driveway wondering why Rachael hadn't come running out the house like she normally had, Mrs. Clair glanced over at the screen door and noticed a white piece of paper stuck in the opening part. "Come on Steph, and grab your back pack." She said exiting the vehicle making her way up to the screen door to read the note that said. "Mom this Rachael, Wendy's mom picked me up to go over their house for a little while, cause its Wendy's sisters birthday. I'll be home at seven o'clock p.m. she said, Love Rachael your Daughter." The second she opened their door, she quickly ran over to their alarm code pad to press forty-four-twelve to disarm the house alarm, and thought it was also odd not seeing Otis home at this time of day looking at his basketball games on TV. "No Stephanie, go place your book bag in your room, what mommy say about dropping it on the floor as soon as you step through the door?" Stephanie sluggishly picked the back pack string up from the floor and dragged it all the way to her room. Mrs. Clair stared at her blankly nodding her head then stepped over to their answering machine. "One message. I wonder who this may had been?" She said curiously enough pushing the playback button on the answering machine. "You have one new message. Beep!" Hello Mrs. Cunningham. This homicide detective Mr. Avery, and I'm sorry you missed my call." Mrs. Clair grew a worried expression on her face as she continued listening. "But this is very urgent that you contact me as soon as possible, its concerning your husband Mr. Otis Cunningham. My number is five-five-five-six-zero-five-zero, I'll be waiting to hear from you. Bye." "You have no more messages." the machine reminded her. "I knew something was wrong. I hope he didn't get hurt on the job, this evening." She mumbled underneath her breath, picking up the phone to dial Detective Avery's number. After three continuous rings she heard him say. "Hello, Detective Avery speaking, how can I help you?" "Hello Detective Avery, this Mrs. Clair Cunningham, I called you as soon as I received your message regarding my husband." She said with concern and sharply "Oh yeah. I really don't know how to put this out to you Mrs. Cunningham, but I hate to say Your husband was murdered earlier this afternoon." "He WHAT! No, this has to be some sort of mistaken identity." She snapped with one single tear rolling unexpectantly from the corner of her right eye. "No ma'am, I wish I was. Your husband works for Jakes Slaughterhouse, correct?" "yes, that's correct." She confirmed shortly. "Yes ma'am, that's him and I'm totally sorry for having to be the one to break this sort of news to you Mrs. Cunningham, but it lead me no choice." He said somewhat pleadingly. "Thank you very much Mr. Avery, every things fine. I just don't know how the girls gonna take the news, that's all." she mentioned while fighting back her crying and sobbing. "I'll keep in contact Mrs. Cunningham and I'm terribly sorry." "That'll be great, bye." She said managing a fake smile hanging up for not being able to hold back the sound that's followed by tears. Just like the quick flash of lightening, then comes the silent and suddenly the sonic crackle boom behind it all. "What's wrong mommy and why you crying like that?" Stephanie asked walking up when she heard and saw her mom break down. Mrs. Clair tears was so detrimental it made Stephanie break out in tears without even knowing what's going on.

* * *

Once nighttime finally arrived, Tracy, Alice, Donna, Tiffany and Katrina was all attending Jessica's pajama party over her house. Every last one of the girls had been screaming and shouting endlessly sense they arrived after school. Jessica's mom thought about taking two three hundred milligram Aspirin's to support the headache she was fast developing reminded herself on how her mom may had felt when she use to have those type of parties herself. "Girls, could you please consider being a little bit quieter?" Mrs. Motley sighed then continued. "At least stop the stumping around!" She walked away to the kitchen rubbing her temples. "You guys, stop running, stop running!" Jessica fervently yelled, at the same time seemingly enjoying the moment herself. All the girls sat and lounged on the floor stilly laughing and giggling taking her into consideration.

* * *

Darla finally stopped to sit down and rest by a wide forty foot tall tree, and it was no doubt she was completely turned into a massacre killer with no point of return, also it had been plenty of years since Mary Swartz waited for her killer day in court so she could rest in peace and find closure, but the wait was no longer needed. She was well walking and alive inside the body of Darla's and decided to hold court in the streets alone on her own by cursing the entire town and damning it to hell. The Saginaw town of Michigan had finally gotten their taste of the spectral legend of the exorcist. The paranormal was becoming normal in their world, but on a much higher rector scale of unpredicted murders with no boundaries or sympathy for no one. This was a different type of exorcist where the figment of the imagination from a derange woman fell victim of Mary's lost soul for vengeance. As her should was called through the ritual for her spirit to wake up and cross over from the unknown.

* * *

"Jessica, you and one of the girls volunteer to come down to the kitchen to get you all some fruit punch, potato chips and cookies before it get late!" Ms. Motley yelled up the stairs once more, then walked back off to the kitchen. "yah . . . !" All the girls shouted. "I'll help you, Jessica." Tiffany insisted "Alright, come on." Jessica agreed skipping out the room while Tiffany followed lead both girls came storming into the kitchen from playing the game. "The last one make it in the kitchen, is a rotten egg." "Whoa, Whoa, Whoa! Girls slow down." Ms. Motley whined. "You're the rotten egg, Jessica!" Tiffany teased. "Mom. Can we have all of these cookies, please?" Jessica pleaded. "Yes, as long as you girls be a little quieter up there." she agreed under a certain condition to reason with the girls." "Ok, we will!" Jessica promised, sealing the deal by carrying the gallon of punch and cups while tiffany carried the potato chips and cookies disappearing back up the stairs to finish enjoying themselves. Ms. Motley's little pug nose female dog named "Mechi" came prancing in the kitchen, when she heard the dog bowl being refilled. Mechi sort of reminded people of the little talking dog in Men in Black with Will Smith. "Lazy old dog. Girl that's all you do is eat, and fart. You don't go outside or nothing." Ms. Motley scoffed, nodding her head. "Guess what. After we eat our snacks, I know a game we can play that's scary." Donna mentioned sounding very convinced. "What type of game, Donna?" Katrina asked. "Yeah, what type of game?" Jessica asked afterwards sounding very interested. "Well I don't exactly know if it works, but my brother was talking to a friend that was spending the night over our house, and I over heard him saying that he know a scary game they could play only if it was five of then, or else it wouldn't work." she explained. "And who was the one coming up with this game?" Jessica wondered. "My brother." Donna answered shortly "Well, it's six of us. Which is well over enough so what do we have to do?" Katrina curiously asked again. Donna visually sighed putting her cup of punch down in front of her, where they all was sitting in a circle. The rest of the girl's attention got focused in when they all saw Donna preparing herself to explain finally. "Alright, like I said at first. I don't know if it works or not, but if five of us go in the closet with the light out to say the name Mary and word wake up once a piece she'll appear." Donna finally explained the game. "You believe that phony stuff, how someone going to appear outta nowhere? Your brother probably said that knowing you was eavesdropping." Alice said meekly enough. Donna for a moment stared in self doubt thinking she could of been right, but she wasn't bound to let Ms. Know it all know that. "Well there's only one way to find out, now isn't there?" Donna said sarcastically with a lopsided grin. "Well I'm not doing it!." Alice noted, looking around the other girls to see if they was going to stand halt with her on not playing the game. "Well." I'm in."

Jessica said. "I'm in, also." Donna agreed. "I'm in." Tiffany followed. "I'm in, of course." Tracey stated. Once it got to Katrina, she silently looked around seeing everyone staring at her and said. "Well I guess I'm in too." "Yes! I mean great." Jessica exclaimed excitedly, then corrected herself calmly looking at everyone. This was Jessica right type of game. She always loved being scared, spooked or frightened, especially to spice things up for her pajama part before bedtime. "You sure you don't wanna join in with us?" Jessica asked Alice with a friendly leer, once everyone headed to the closet. "Nope! I'll be right here eating the rest of my chips, have fun." she objected with a false smile. "Alright." Jessica said then went to join all the rest of the girls in the closet. Donna quietly closed the closet door, but left it barely cracked and said. "Alright, before we cut the light out, let's get order here. Who wants to be first, second, third, fourth and fifth?" "I'll be first." Jessica claimed. "I'll be second." Tracey followed. "I'll be third." Donna countered. "Shhh." Jessica said airily with her right index finger up to he lips, with her left hand relaxed on the light switch. "Alright, Alright." Donna agreed ebulliently to be quieter. "I'll be fourth." Katrina said. "And I'm lucky number five, huh." Tiffany snarled. "Is everybody ready?" Jessica asked preparing to turn the light out. The rest of the girls shook their heads with approval then braced themselves once the darkness surrounded them. "Here goes nothing. Mary wake up!" Jessica didn't waste no time starting things off. "Mary wake up!" Tracy said. "Mary wake up!" Donna said being number three. "Mary wake up!" Katrina followed. Being the fourth person to say it. Once again they all got a little excited from the intensity building up from Tiffany hesitating. "Alright. Mary wake up!" Alice crunched down on a ruffle potato chips instantly when she fearfully flinched from hearing the closet door slamming closed. All the girls gave out a scared cry then Jessica flipped the light switch on in time to see the last big jagged sharp piece of glass fall out her closet door mirror frame shattering into the rest of the broken particles on the floor. Once they all communicated their senses looking at one another. Everybody freaked out in disbelief running out the closet leaving the light on. Darla's eyes popped wide open, when Mary heard the calling of her name, and immediately directed Darla to take off walking to the calling. Once Mary's soul heard the calling of her name, she has the full capacity to guide the body to its rightful destination as if she was traveling in spirit alone without the flesh. "Oh God, did you guys see that?" Jessica said trembling like the rest of the girls was and even Alice sort of had a little tremble within her from hearing the closet door slamming and the loud sound of the mirror shattering right after. "Jessica what was that noise? It sounded like a window had been broken!" Ms. Motley shouted traveling up the stairs. "Sort of, but not really though!" Jessica answered Ms. Motley entered the bedroom and wailed. "What you mean sort of but not really though?" It wasn't my window, it was my closet mirror." She admitted. "Your closet mirror!" she repeated heatedly rushing over to the closet. "That's it girls, everyone off to bed and no getting up unless someone needs water or to use the down stairs restroom. You got some explaining to do in the morning young lady, and make sure this closet stays closed until I clean up this mess in the morning. Do everyone got that?" Ms. Motley said clicking the closet light out closing the door. Jessica said. "Yes, ma'am." While the rest of the girls choirly said at once. "Yes, Ms. Motley!" Ms. Motley produced a smile. "Good!" Then pulled the bedroom door halfway closed when she walked out. "I told you it was something scary." Donna croaked with a confirming smile. "Ooh. I don't never wanna play that game anymore." Jessica said nodding her head with a short blank stare at the closet door.

* * *

Once time elapsed by and all the girls including Ms. Motley had been asleep nearly two hours. Mechi furiously came storming out from the basement door that's located in the kitchen and up to the kitchen back door constantly barking at something she felt threatened by. Ms. Motley was trying her best to wake up, once she heard the barking noise not only rang out in her deep sleep, but from the wear and tear of the two three hundred milligrams pills she took that made her feel drowsy. But she finally broke her sleep when she realized it was Mechi barking with her one of a kind bark, which really became noticeable when normally she didn't bark at all half the time. "What has gotten into that crazy old dog of mine?" She wondered tossing the covers to the side to slid her tiny feet into her house slippers. Mechi pranced over to Ms. Motley when she saw her presence in the darkness walking through the hallway. She raced back over to the kitchen door, but only to sniff at the bottom of the seal this time. "What's going on girl, what's out there?" she asked. Then thought to herself while peeking through the door blinds, "Like you'll be able to tell me." "Well, its sort of hard to tell through this dirty old window, now isn't it Karen?" She whispered to herself unlocking the chain and the knob to take a quick peek out the door, but the second the door was cracked Mechi impatiently squeezed and sprinted out the door in top speed into the darkness. "Mechi!" she yelled shortly. Then continued. "That old dog, go her nerves all twisted tonight, now she decided to go outside in the middle of the night, but I gotta go out and get her before something hungry do." She sighed visually walking over to the kitchen light seitch to put it on while she grabbed the flashlight from her closet. Darla quickly snatched Mechi up from the ground to snap her neck out of socket like a chop stick, and flung her to the side traveling up to the open kitchen door. Once she made it to the door she glanced straight in and paced over to the open basement door barely closing it behind her. Ms. Motley turned around with alertness when she heard the snap sound when Darla closed the basement door. "Let me hurry up and go out there, and find this darn dog so I can get some rest." She said thoughtfully heading out the room with the flashlight.

* * *

Maria was still up late at twelve o'clock in the morning going over a few things that she needed to discuss with Richard tomorrow evening being very exhausted. She leaned back in her chair at the computer desk lifting her reading glasses to rub her eyes from feeling the first sign of tiredness, then snatched them off. Hearing a loud sound of a plate or glass bursting to the floor in the kitchen. "What was that?" She said curiously pushing her roller chair away from the desk to focus in on anymore disturbing sounds. The intruder quiet like a mouse crept up the stairs and into the Antonia's closet where she was restfully sound asleep. The intruder broke into their home through the half open kitchen window while everyone was away on their daily schedule but was immediately forced to hide out in their kitchen food pantry when they were heard in. Maria slowly eased her head out the study room door to glance down the hallway toward the kitchen. Bobby was already up and out of his sleep. Once he heard the exact same noise and when he slipped his shoes on and house coat he instantly went to Antonia's door only to confirm she was still sound asleep With the hallway light half blaring on her face. When he made it to the bottom of the stair casing and saw Maria in the hallway cautiously creeping toward the kitchen, he whispered out to her. "Honey, go grab the nine millimeter from the study desk locked drawer." Once the handgun was in her hand, she made haste back to him where he stood waiting. "Babe, now go upstairs and keep an eye on Antonia, until I clear things down here." He demanded with a whisper. Maria didn't give no sign of rejection, she just took off doing exactly what he insisted her to do. Bobby proceeded toward the kitchen with the nine millimeter pointed out in front to him with his right index finger slightly relaxed on the trigger. He made it to the kitchen, discovered one of their see-through plates on the floor between the prep counter and sink. "Hmm, how this happen?" He wondered, then angled the handgun out in front of him making his way over to their open pantry room, not noticing that it had been open the entire time they have been home. Maria was gently placing Antonia's soft hair behind her left ear and thinking to herself. "She'll do anything in her power to protect her family from any harm, if she lived to tell it." Bobby slowly extended his left arm out to ease the pantry door open a little wider to make sure no one was hiding behind it, and when he saw it was clear, he headed toward the living room only to find the curtains moving. Bobby kept easing his way closer and closer with the gun extended out in front of him. Standing two feet away from away from the curtain's he took a deep breath and snatched the curtain open. "Damn it Jasper, you could of gotten yourself killed!" Jasper glanced into Bobby's eyes purring. "It's clear, Honey!" Bobby shouted. Maria kissed Antonia on her forehead and slid the cover up to her neck. The second she made it down stairs Bobby said. "It was only Jasper, Honey. He must of ran across the sink counter causing the plate to fall then hid behind the curtain." Maria went over to the curtain to pick up Jasper, and said, "You broke mommy's plate, bad boy!" then stroked his fur repeatedly before releasing him from her arms. Bobby sat on the sofa ejecting the bullet from the chamber to slid it back into the magazine slot. "Here Hon. I guess the goes back where it belongs." He stated, handing her the gun with the Barrow facing toward him. Maria stepped on the backside of the sofa where he was sitting leaning toward him to say, "Well I guess I'll go back in the study room and clean things up to prepare for bed." She calmly planted a soft kiss on his jaw, before she walked off. Bobby stared at her curvy hips until she disappeared into the hallway. Then he nodded his head with a smile clicking their sixty-four inch television on, until she was ready to go hit the haystack for the night. Bobby smiled to himself thinking about what he just said in his mind, which was something his old man use to say to substitute the word bed. Then his smile instantly vanished, hearing his daughters soft voice behind him saying. "Daddy, it was a man in my room!" bobby jumped up from the sofa racing around to the backside to grab her in his arms then rushed her to the study room. Maria flinched out of reflex, when seeing Bobby charging through the door with Antonia in his arms. "Babe, take Antonia, she said she saw a man in her room." He breathlessly whispered then rushed over to grab the gun from the drawer and with weapon in hand he cocked the active bullet back into the chamber standing faced away from her and Antonia. Maria couldn't still believe what she just hear him say. "Bobby!" she stopped shortly once she saw him leaving out closing the door behind him with the gun in his hand, and all she wanted to tell him was to be careful and she loved him. Bobby tiptoed his way up the steps to keep from causing attention to himself. At the top landing he didn't waste no time placing his back up against the hallway wall that supports Antonia's room easing his way up to her door entrance. He noticed a strong draft breezing through her doorway and that's what made him tightly grip the rubber handle with both hands building his courage up a little higher to make a move for it. He jumped into the door pointing his weapon in all directions that was possible while observing her window raised wide open like her walk in closet. Bobby checked the closet and under the bed he placed the gun into his front waste line to raise her window down and lock it. He took off directly to their room afterwards making sure the intruder didn't change his hiding position, but only to find the intruder vanished presumably when he confirmed the upstairs was clear.

* * *

A few hours later, when Ms. Motley went back to sleep after she searched all around the house for Mechi and couldn't find her, Darla was still down in the dark basement clicking all the power fuse switches off. Then she stepped over to a homemade table to grab a wooden handle weed sickle from it taking off with it along her side traveling up the steps. Each one of the steps squeaked beneath the pressure of her feet making her way to the top. Darla extended her arm out for the door knob, she twisted the knob and pushed the door open, and on her way to accomplish her mission. As her vision in the dark was extremely vivid like a cat, Darla by passed Ms. Motley's bedroom closed door and crept up the carpet steps. Tiffany kept tossing and turning from the time she had fallen asleep mind boggled about what they all experienced inside Jessica's closet the minute she called out the name. But her eyes finally opened wide penetrating the darkness of the room, when the pressure settled at her bladder indicating she needed to urinate. Three of the girls was on Jessica's bed sleep, while her, Katrina and Donna was laying right beside each other sprawled out on pallets on the floor below the bed. Tiffany stared at the door peering through the crack of it, once she thought she saw something on the outside swiftly pace away from it. "Donna wake up. I think I saw something out there in the hallway." She whispered. Donna raised up in her sleep changing her position in the opposite direction and once Tiffany realized Donna dozed off back to sleep from hearing her snoring. She slowly raised the cover over her head to see if whatever she saw would go away while saying beneath her breath. "I know I'm not dreaming, or am I?" But being over excited was starting to make her feel she needed to use the restroom even more. "Yeah, maybe if I go down stairs to use the restroom, I'll probably be able to get some relax sleep." She eased the cover from her head coming to the conclusion what she once saw may had been a figment of her imagination like her mom use to have her believe. Darla was standing off in the darkness of the hallway waiting in the dark with the wooden handle weed sickle firmly gripped in her hand. Tiffany tossed the cover off her raising up with a visual sigh taking a glance at everyone enjoying their sleep, then she thought for a minute, she should wake someone to see if they would escort her to the down stairs restroom, but then the thought flew out her mind. Knowing that each one of the girls, including herself love to talk about people in school especially when it came down to someone being a chicken. Tiffany finally stood up on her two feet making her way over to the door where the light switch was located. "Hum. That's strange, there's no power in this light switch." She said thoughtfully then figured it wasn't no need to be wasting more time with precaution. "So no exaggerating, get your butt down stairs to use the restroom and don't wake Ms. Motley up." She coached herself, stepping out into the hallway managing a frown on her expression when she smelled something faintly. "What is that horrible smell?" She said in a low voice slowly heading toward the starting point of the stair casing. Darla was gazing straight at her still being un-noticed as Tiffany walked right pass her in the darkness. Making it to the seventh step down she stopped rooted to her spot looking over her shoulder back at the top landing and squinted her eyes seeing someone's presence heading toward her from the top. She panicky raced down the rest of the steps to hide herself off into the living room beside Ms. Mostley's big sofa, thinking to herself on her knees trying to control her breathing. Darla tuned in on the panting Tiffany didn't notice she was giving out, as the serge power of the house filtered every sound. The house was so quiet, you could hear the Grandfather clock second hand ticking away. Darla quietly entered into the living room and the closer she had gotten to Tiffany the clearer her panting had became. Tiffany screamed out to Ms. Motley when Darla snatched her up by her hair while she kicked for dear life with her hands on Darla's arm trying to break loose from her tight grip. Tiffany's mind was thinking that "If they say the name Mary wake up once a piece she'll appear, and she did." and rest of any thoughts were no longer when Darla chopped her neck off with the sickle and all brain function ceased. Darla released Tiffany's hair from her grasp, dropped the weed sickle right beside her body and escaped out the back door into the night. Five minutes later Ms. Motley broke through her sleep again from dreaming her daughter Jessica was hollering out "Get out the way Mom!" as a bus was speeding toward her non-stop, like the movie Speed. Ms. Motley rushed out of the bed when she glanced over at her digital clock on her nightstand, and easily noticed it was completely turned off. "What happened to the power? I know I paid my bills on time." She reminded herself, making her way over to the window to make sure it wasn't another silent storm remembering it once happened before, due to a power line being struck by lightning. "Well, it sure isn't storming. Now where did I put that flashlight? Oh gee'z, I forgot that quick that it wasn't any power." she pondered when she reached for her bedroom light switch and didn't get no power. "Good, here it is. I must had gotten up to fast." She whispered, heading out the room with the flashlight blared out in front of her. Ms. Motley passed the living room entrance upon noticing her kitchen door swinging. "Oh my. Now I know I locked and closed this back door before I went back to bed, or did I?" the she turned with a sigh, she turned around when she heard a squeak sound behind her from the basement door moving when she closed the kitchen door. "Its was only the air pressure." She told herself then headed back through the hallway that leads to the living room and the stair casing. When she made it to the doorway of the living room. She pointed the flashlight toward the stair casing first then immediately blared the light to the dark shadow she saw laying in the middle of the living room floor. "What's that?" She said amazingly enough slowly walking over to what appeared to be a small body the closer she got. "Tiffany?" She said softly with disbelief, then screamed to the top of her lungs as the flashlight dropped to the ground when she threw both palms up to her cheeks from seeing Tiffany's head barely hanging on by a limb. All the girls raised up out of their sleep nearly at the same time once they heard the high lament scream from Ms. Motley echoing through the house.

* * *

The next morning after Bobby took off to work, and dropped Antonia off to school like he normally had, Maria tossed her piece of Apple Butter toast onto her plate racing off to the study room to catch the phone call. "Hello, Paranormal Investigator Mrs. Gates speaking, How can I help you?" she answered professionally "Hello Mrs. Gates, this if Forensic Detective Mr. Gary Grant. I'm terribly sorry for bothering you at this early hour of the day, but we have some extraordinary news we need to release to you. This may change your whole path of investigation on the mysterious murder cases for now on, if I shall add." Maria Blankly plunged down on her computer chair preparing herself for the news, sense Mr. Grant said it that way she thought. Then she asked curiously when she heard him fumbling through some papers on the other end. "And what may that be, sir?" "Ok, here we go, yesterday morning two victims by the name of Ms. Shelly Ciera and Mr. Patrick Hughs was found murdered and in the process of the investigation at the crime scene we confiscated blood samples from the victims carpet and office less than an hour ago." Mr. Grant paused while Maria impatiently said. "I can't even imagine Mr. Grant, but I sure would love to know. "Alright, here it is, the test revealed to us, the D.N.A. blood samples we've confiscated from the victims dining room carpet was or shall I say is one hundred percent the deceased girl Mary Swarts." He said soberly. "Wait, wait, wait. Did you say the blood was from the deceased girl Mary Swartz, by any chance?" She asked with a bit of nausea gripped at her stomach. "Yes, Ma'am, that's correct." He assured her. "Mr. Grant. Is there anyway you could fax me a copy of the D.N.A. testing for the O.F.P.A. Office records?" "Sure, that'll be no problem Mrs. Gates, what's the fax number? And I'll see that it gets to you immediately." Mr. Grant agreed with no problem. "Got it Mrs. Gates. I'll fax a copy immediately, have a blessed day ma'am." He said politely before disconnecting the line. Moments later while Maria was gathering up her notes she had sorted out to discuss with Richard, she heard the fax machine spitting out the test results. "There we go, perfect timing." She said pleasantly, snatching the copies from the printout tray, then headed out the room and off to Richard's house.

* * *

Darla returned back to the house inside the Saginaw woods the town decided to call the Ghost Trial woods from when Norman Gandy kidnapped and murdered all those innocent little kids inside that very same house he use to own. Once she stepped inside she took a glance at the decomposed rabbit she once killed while walking pass it traveling toward the stair casing. The house was so condemned. The nails in the steps had gotten loose from the wood rotting throughout the years. Once she made it to the top landing she immediately went to the bathroom area that sat at the front of the house at the end of the hallway, she kneeled down sitting in the corner behind the door with her back up against the wall with her legs stretched out in front of her. She just sat there staring with a blank stare at the bathroom window and the cracked spots that was exposing the inside of the wall while flies started grouping around her head from the dry blood of victims she murdered. One fly just sat there on her nose un-threatened as if she didn't feel it, nor noticed it while closing her eyes allowing the group of flies to continue to hover around her head.

* * *

"That's exactly what we need to do Maria." Richard said, when she told him the plan she came up with. "Now Richard, as anxious as I was to tell you this, I saved the best for last." She said with a confirming smile reaching inside her folder pocket to pull out the faxed information she just received. Richard picked up the remote control from the table to mute the volume on the television while she calmly slid the results over to him from the other end of the table, so he could figure it out himself as she sat there wearing a smile with her arms folded in front of her. Richard scanned over the fax documents saying half aware. "Well I see its a D.N.A. testing that had been done, but who's? Oh, wait a minute." He said as he re-read the paperwork to make sure he was reading it correctly. Maria smile got even stronger seeing his eye twitching from acknowledgement. "So the D.N.A. results is the deceased girl, Mary Swarts?" He asked looking amazed. "Yes, sir. This is really outta hands now, Richard." She assured him. "How could this be. when this girl been dead a long time?" He further asked in disbelief. "Well, that's why there's such a thing called Paranormal murders, paranormal people, paranormal mysteries and last but not least paranormal rituals, cause anything possible in this world or put it like this, they discovered outside the orbit one hundred thousand planets and only ten thousand of them have life. That's why I say anything's possible." She logically explained, then danced her eyes where his was planted at the muted television screen. Richard pointed the remote to un-mute the screen to hear what they was rallying about in front of the police station. "My daughter had just been murdered last night over a friend's house attending a pajama party, and the dame police authorities isn't doing a damn thing about it. If any one has nay leads to her killer, please contact me at five-five-five-seven-seven-zero-five." Tiffany's mom angrily presented on live news in front of the S.M.P.D. Station. "Richard, do you think we could make it in time to catch that little girls mom to assure her there is someone doing something about it, and also cares?" "Well its like fifteen to twenty minutes away and I'm sure we could if we leave right now." He concluded. "Well, we're off." she added standing up gathering everything together.

* * *

Maria and Richard was driving through town and as they was passing the Saginaw Police Station, they saw crowds of people who was involved with the rally getting inside their vehicles taking off. Maria pulled along the passenger side of a news center unit van, where a camera man and a lady reporter was packing their things to leave. "Excuse me!" Maria shouted when she came into a complete stop beside the lady reporter. "Oh hello, I'm Linda McCallister. How can I help you?" "Hi, nice to meet you Ms. McCallister. My name is Mrs. Gates, and I'm a Investigator for the O.F.P.A. Office. I was wanting to know if you knew where we could find that little girls mom who was murdered?" Ms. McCallister sat her bag on the front passenger seat, and immediately turned around raising her right hand above her eyes like a sun visor. Then said pointing when she located Tiffany's mom. "There she goes right there in that yellow and white stripe dress, standing on the driver's side of that Lincoln town car talking to that gentleman." "Oh, thank you very much." Maria said with a friendly leer, before her and Richard pulled off to where Tiffany's mom was standing. Maria pulled in a slot directly across from where she was standing talking to a under cover homicide Detective. The second Richard and her came walking up she pulled out her identification saying. "Excuse me for this interruption, but my name is Mrs. Gates. I'm an investigator from the O.F.P.A. Office, and you don't mind if I ask a few questions do you?" "Nice to see you, Mrs. Gates." "Oh, Hello Mr. Avery." "Oh yeah, Ms. Jenkins. This the investigator you really want." Maria tossed up a quick smile from his comment while reaching out to shake Ms. Jenkins hand. "Sure. I got time to answer a few questions, why not." Ms. Jenkins agreed. "Thank you, that sure will be appreciated. Shall we step over here to the trunk of my vehicle?" "Sure, that's fine." The second they all stepped over to Maria's vehicle Mr. Avery grabbed his brief case out front his trunk, then walked off to the main entrance of the police station. "Ok. Here we go, and for the record, this is my partner Mr. Owens." Maria said when she made it back to the back side of her trunk from grabbing her small Sony Digital recorder. "You don't mind if I tape this conversation, do you? Maria asked. "No, be my guess." Maria pushed the record button and said. "Can you please state your full and correct name?" "Now?" Ms. Jenkins asked. "Please." Maria answered her. "Alright, my name is Lorraine Jenkins, and I am the mother of Tiffany Jenkins." "That was perfect, Ms. Jenkins, can you tell us where and how your daughter got murdered?" Ms. Jenkins took a deep breath then exhaled before she started her story. "Well, it was a day or so ago, when my daughter Tiffany and about four other girls was having a pajama party over their friends Jessica's house and all the girls explained to me that they was all up meeting around at night playing some Mary game inside the closet. Jessica told me Tiffany was the fifth person to say Mary wake up." Maria's eyes dilated when she heard the name Mary. "So is that when she was murdered?" Maria asked simply. "They all explained to me nothing happened at that moment but the closet door slamming and the closet mirror shattering." "So did anyone of the kids say they saw her appear?" Maria asked collectively. "As far as what was told to me, no one saw anything, and at point neither of the girls was hurt period. Jessica assured me that every last one of them was inside the room, when they all fell asleep, but you know what, Donna told me Tiffany woke her up out of her sleep in the middle of the night saying she thought she saw someone in the hallway outside Jessica's bedroom door, but Donna didn't pay her any mind." "Oh I see, and that's when she may had gotten up wondering off in the middle of the night." Maria concluded. "You know what, I believe so, cause my daughter's body was found down stairs in the middle of the living room floor." Ms. Jenkins assured them. Maria immediately pushed the stop button and said. "Thank you Ms. Jenkins for sharing this incredible story of your daughter with us, and may God be with her as she rest in peace." Richard wrote his number down on a yellow memo pad, and said when he handed it to her. "Thank you Ms. Jenkins also, here is my number if you find anything else you'll like to discuss with us, don't hesitate not one minute." "Oh, that's my ride right there. Thank you guys for being very sincere in my daughters favor."

"No, Ms. Jenkins. Thank you for your time and strength, it was all our pleasure." Maria assured her. Once Ms. Jenkins pulled off with her ride, and Maria and Richard got in her vehicle she said thoughtfully. "Maybe I should phone Mr. Wallace to see what kind of progress he made so far." Then she whipped out her cell phone and speed dialed his extension as they was pulling off the Michigan Police Department lot. "Hello, you've reached Lt. Wallace, sorry I couldn't catch your call, so if you could please leave your name, time and date you called and I'll be gladly to return your call at my earliest convenience." Maria closed her cell phone without leaving a detailed message, then accelerated on the gas heading back to Richard's house.

CHAPTER ELEVEN

KENT, RICKY, LISA and April was attending the speed boat race later that evening and Kent was worried about the little time he had left with his grandfather's Yukon Denali S.U.V. "Are you guys ready to go? It's getting pretty damn boring here, besides every ones all packing and leaving but us." He let it be known. "Yeah. You right, also its gonna be getting dark soon." Lisa added. Kent and Lisa use to be grade school boyfriend and girlfriend, until she dumped him for kissing one of her friends on the back of the bus, and Ricky and April was always hitting on each other, plus they cared about each other more than anything. It's just no one popped the question yet and the only thing they ever did was hold hands and kiss. Once everyone made it inside the SUV Kent said while turning on the ignition to fire the engine. "Well, I do have a couple of hours with the truck left before its expected back so we'll just cruise a little bit." "That's fine." April agreed, as they was pulling-off the convention grounds heading up Dayton Road. Kent took one hand off the steering wheel to grab the half ounce of Marijuana from his hoody pouch. "Where you get all that Paraphernalia from?" Ricky asked, then shook his head from the passenger seat as both the girls whisper to each other about the guys behind their backs. "I know you haven't been riding around with that stuff, all day!" Lisa snapped, when she realized what Kent was sniffing every time he raised the sack up to his nostrils and being she was the most squared up one inside the truck, that was the main reason why Kent liked her so much to see if he could be the one to break her in. "No, crazy. I just coped it from pot head Jesse for sixty bucks. Ricky, reach in the middle console and see if those three strawberry swishers still in the box." Kent said, then tossed the sandwich bag of bud's on Ricky's lap so he could roll one up. "Yeah, there still here, and whaddaya want me to do with this?" Ricky asked, holding the bag up. "Don't try to act like that sense the girls is here. Mr. I'm the best blunt quickest roller in Saginaw." Kent pronounced sarcastically. Ricky managed a smirk on his face, then peeked out the corner of his eye to the girls in the backseat. Kent grabbed out the insurance paperwork from the middle console, so Ricky could have something to roll the Marijuana cigar on. "Here you go, use this."

* * *

When Maria and Richard made it back from meeting up with Tiffany's mom. Ms. Jenkins, and from riding around, she sparked up another conversation saying. "Richard. I really hope Ms. Jenkins be o-k. I can't believe she told us that little girl Dona came up wit the exact same game. Darla Phelps told me they played a game which was called the Mary game, then the closet door slammed and the mirror shattered." She said conversationally, as they both sat in the SUV in Richard's driveway. "Yeah, Maria. The only thing I can honestly say is we need to get down to business like in a hurry." Richard asked on a rippling sigh. "I guess, I'll call I'm gonna call it an evening. It was nice meeting up with you Maria, and you have a safe trip home with all this madness dominoly going around this town." Maria managed a smile, saying. "Tell me about it. O.K., I'll see you later and keep you updated, and I think its gonna be soon Richard." "That'll be great." Richard exit the SUV then tapped the hood waving his hand bye.

* * *

Once Ricky was through rolling the Marijuana cigar, he passed it over to Kent so he could place the remainder of the Marijuana back in the sandwich bag. Kent quickly placed it behind his right ear saying. "A you guy's I know a place where we can get out, and smoke this at." "Whaddaya mean, we?" Lisa spitted. "I mean, the rest of us that's seventeen years old." Kent joked. "Yeah, right. Just because you guys are three months older than I am doesn't necessary give you the right to down my age because I'm not a pot head." Lisa snorted, then smacked him in the back of his head. "Ouch!" Kent shouted. Right when the sign came up in plain view up the road ahead, Kent smiled happily saying. "Oh yeah, here we go coming up." Then he yield the SUV on the dirt road. "Hold up, Kent. That sign said welcome to the ghost trial road." April said sharply. "All it's not like that, besides never judge a book by its cover." Kent wailed, looking through the rearview mirror at her. "If that's the case, I'm not judging the book bit its cover, I'm just telling you what the cover said." April shot back sounding like a smart alec. "Trust me. It's perfectly safe, besides we're just going to walk the trail until we're finished with the blunt. Quit freaking out." He said calmly, yielding to the side of the road, where he saw previous car tracks in the dirt and the opening trail way that they could enter the woods. After Kent killed the engine, and they all exit the SUV he went around the entire truck to check the doors making sure all the locks worked on the first push of the button. Ricky stopped at the beginning of the Ghost Trail pathway, reached inside his pocket to pull out a wad of toilet tissue to blow his nose, then placed the rest of it back inside his pocket. "Yuck! That sounds gross." Lisa protested, frowning her nose up. "Here, you wanna use it?" He said playfully bringing the hazardous tissue from his nostrils trying to hand it to her. "Stop it!" She fumed flinching away from his reach. Once they all took off walking up the pathway to where they could no longer see Kent's Grandfather's truck. Kent stopped in his tracks saying. "Hold up you guys, let me light this!" Upon lighting the blunt he took a hard pull, then another and held the smoke trapped in his lungs passing it off to Ricky. "I don't mind if I do." Ricky said calmly, grabbing the blunt from Kent's finger tips placing it up to his lips. "This taste pretty damn good. There's no doubt pot head Jesse does have the bomb green." He added, dancing his eyes over to Lisa with the blunt extended out o her. "No! I don't smoke that stuff." She objected. "You have before!" Kent interrupted. "Yeah two years ago, when I was fourteen going on fifteen, besides even then I pulled but didn't inhale."

She replied from Kent's comment. "Now you sounding like that guy, Mr. Bill Clinton. I pulled, but didn't inhale." Kent pronounced firmly. Lisa quickly reached out to punch him in the stomach for the smart comment he made. "Ouch! I hope you don't think you hit soft!" He immediately said with a instinctive grab in his voice. "No! And it gets harder if you don't knock it off!" She assured him, then scoffed. "April, you better not hit that!" "Why not? Its only Marijuana, besides what's the big deal about it? It gotta be good for something. Its legal in my Aunt Emma City San Fransico, matter of fact. She has a medical marijuana card." April explained conversationally. "Kool!" Kent out burst amazingly, with his eyes barely open from the first couple of pulls settling in as he stood there and watched her blow the ashes then hit the blunt. "I can't believe you hit the blunt hard like that!" Lisa exclaimed "No Baby sitting the blunt. Its puff, puff, pass only April." Kent said impatiently. Once Kent received the marijuana blunt back and hit it a couple more times. He slowly eased his head over to where Ricky was blankly staring then tiptoed over to a large oak tree to suffocate the fire on the blunt, when he also observed the two full grown bucks throughout the scattered trees and woods twenty yard away. Kent took a quick glance at the remaining half of the blunt making sure it was completely out, before he slid it into his hoody pouch pocket. Then elevated his right index finger up to his lips to silence everyone, although Lisa wanted to tell him they don't have time to be clowning around she just kept quiet and threw up the expression on her delicate face to April and Ricky. Ricky shrugged his shoulders and nodded his head to her while Kent slowly tiptoed over to a nice size round rock and when he picked it up, he tossed it in the air and caught it to get a good feel of the weight. Everybody stepped off the trail, when they saw him waving them to his side. "Shhh! I'm going to try and hit em, don't say a word." He whispered advancing away from them and a little closer to the bucks where they was going their natural thing. Once he crept his way fifteen feet away from everyone, he cocked his hand back then hummed the rock with all his might at the two Bucks Kent would of struck the smaller one if it didn't duck out of reflex jack knifing his hind legs taking off behind the other one but once he saw the two Bucks scampering away only to stop in plain view ahead. He empty handedly went running after them like he was Tarzan of the Jungle, but instead, he was the high kid in the woods. "Kent! Great you guys." Lisa hollered out cutting herself short. The more the Bucks ran the more Kent ran behind the, until he suddenly stopped realizing he ran to far away from the others where they was no longer in sight. "Come on you two. We need to find him before it get dark. I swear, its something about that guy. That Marijuana must be destroying the rest of his brain cells he got left." Ricky and April laughed heartedly, from the comment she made about him taking off behind her. As they traveled off to the direction Kent ran off too. Everything was starting to look identical the way all the trees were planted along the way, Lisa thought then yelled out in her tracks. "Kent! Where are you?" When Kent heard her choice echo out to him, he echoed back. "I'm over, here!" "Where?" Ricky shouted through his hands to distance his call. "Over here! I'm going to stay right here, so keep shouting out to me and follow my voice!" He suggested. Everyone started turning around in different directions trying to locate where his voice was traveling from. But needless to say they couldn't distinguish much the way his voice continued to echo all around them. "We don't have no choice but to keep heading this way, although that's the direction he ran off too." Lisa suggested, leading them back off on their hunt for high boy then she smiled at the thought. Once a few minutes went by Lisa stopped in her tracks once more to yell out. "Kent, can you hear me!" "Yes, you guys sounding closer!" He responded clearly. "I can hear him real clear from over that direction." Ricky pointed out sounding convinced, leading them off to the direction he pointed to. Less than ten yards more he said to the others. "See just like I knew it, there he goes right there." He said as they stood there for a moment looking at the back side of him. "Kent you are so dead I tell ya!" Lisa yelled while deviously frowning. Kent quickly turned around relieved skipping his way over to them. "Man, I thought I lost you guys." Lisa reached down to pick up a rock that was small enough to cause damaged, and said when she threw it at him. "You did loose us, stupid!" "Alright!" He admitted dodging the flying rock she threw. "Now, would be a great time to leave, don't ya think?" Lisa asked soberly. "Good thought, but which way?" Ricky asked, managing a smirk on his face. "Kent you know your way out of here, don't you?" April asked meekly. Kent glanced over at Lisa and saw the, you better know look, then nodded his head no and braced himself. "You, what!" Everyone exploded at once. Lisa threw her hands on her waist line waiting for an good explanation from him. "Alright. I never been inside the woods all I ever did was park along the road where I just parked and stepped out to chief." He explained himself sounding sincere. "Well somebody better think of something and I mean quick. Kent, I don't know about you sometimes." Lisa huffed. "I think we should head toward this direction." April suggested at they all follow her lead without question. Kent's Grandfather Mr. Stewart and his lovely wife for thirty years Margaret Stewart was waiting outside on their cover porch having a conversation waiting on Kent's return. "Margaret, that boy of Iren's should have been back from that speed boat race along time ago." Iren was one of the very first victims that got murdered a few years ago, whom also was Kent's mom. Mr. and Mrs. Stewart had adopted Kent soon after their daughter was mysteriously murdered. "Charles, he still has thirty more minutes, just be patient." She said with saccharine sweetness. "I'll be patient, alright." He replied, with saccharine bitterness, getting up from his lounge chair to go in the house and look for the number to the emergency vehicle theft office. Just in case Kent decided to joyride a little longer like he done in the past. When he stole their Expedition SUV and drove it to New Jersey with a couple of friends, but for some reason they could never turn him down on this vehicle sense they had it, being they hardly went anywhere except to the town market. Mr. Stewart also figured if they let him use it, he wouldn't have no desire to want to steal it. Mr. Stewart smacks his lips opening the desk where they kept their important papers, and phone books to have the nine-one-one vehicle theft number out and ready.

*   *   *

They all stopped when April said "Oops! I think we're lost, you guys, my bad." She observed a house fifteen to twenty yards ahead of them. "Wait, I never noticed that house being there." Lisa somewhat relented, when she spotted the house herself. "And not only that I have the urge to wanna go potty bad." April said thickly. "Go right ahead. The trees is all yours." Ricky jokingly suggested. "Yeah right, your perverted butt would love that wouldn't you?" She confirmed. "Well, put it like this, April needs to use the restroom, we need to find our way out of here and I need to light the rest of this blunt cause these matches aren't staying light with the wind blowing like this, and maybe we could ask whoever lives there how the hell we get out of here?" Kent said conversationally making a little bit of sense. "what are we still standing here for?" Ricky inquired, walking off toward the house. "I swear. You guys need to stay off that pot, you too April!" Lisa complained, as they took off behind Ricky. April marked Lisa silently by making faces and chattering her fingers together repeatedly against one another as the sign to Kent saying she was a motor mouth. Kent just busted out laughing thinking to himself, April called it on the one. As the house was coming into plain view, Ricky was seeing clearly the house was one hundred percent condemned, and wasn't no way suitable for anyone to be living in. "I hate to say it, but no once could be possible living inside." Ricky said thoughtfully. "You ain't never lied." Lisa agreed ebulliently. "Alright. that only leaves us two alternatives now, that's to light my blunt and for April to use the potty." Kent concluded, while April thought deeply on which could be worst, taking the chance on using the bathroom outside behind a tree like a female pup or to use the bathroom inside the condemned house like a bum? But either way, I'm not sitting my behind down nor waiting any longer she thought. Darla eyes extended wide open when she heard the distant figs crunching and breaking beneath their feet outside the house or her domain shall she call it. "Geez, this house is so old and run down, I can actually smell the rotten wood from it." Lisa pondered. "Even the paint gone from many nights and many storms it with stood." Ricky added, stopping at the beginning of the steps to the porch. Darla quickly stood up on her feet to pace over to the window that looks out to the front of the house, and only saw Kent out a little ways trying to light his marijuana cigar, as the other three was out of eye view below the porch roof. Kent skipped up to everyone and said. "Come on you guys, let's go inside so April can test the waters, I mean use the potty." Then laughed. "Very funny, Dork Almighty!" She shot back managing a smile on her face. "Alright, I'll go in first, so everyone just stand behind a little bit." Ricky volunteered going up the steps. "Shit!" "Be careful Ricky! Did you hurt yourself?" Lisa shouted concerned when she saw his lower leg fall completely through the soft porch wood. "Yeah, a little bit. It'll be ok though, just watch your step." He assured them proceeding along. Lisa turned glancing over her shoulder to confirm how dark it was becoming and came to the conclusion in her mind, that they had probably thirty minutes left till sundown. Then slowly went up the steps behind April. Ricky eased the front door open a little wider to get all the light he could. To glare inside which it didn't quite help any, he thought. Everybody stopped up on the porch, when seeing Ricky's index finger indicating for them to stop as he enters first. The second Lisa glanced down to the porch trying to avoid stepping into the same hole Ricky just made. Ricky rushed back out the door blurting out. "what was that?" Then mysteriously glanced at his right shoe. "What's in there Ricky?" April asked curiously, when she observed him rushing back to the porch. "I don't know. I think I stepped on a dead animal." He answered with a frown, angling himself back toward the door trying it once more. Ricky crept straight over to what he stepped on. "Yep! Just like I figured. Its a dead rabbit." Once everybody finally made it inside, Kent didn't waste no time striking a match to light the end of the half of blunt, then bent down with the light match blaring it on the decomposed rabbit. "Ooh. It stink. Something must gotten a hold to it, maybe a big bad wolf. Naw, I'm just joking, but it do have a nice size hole in its neck." He exaggerated, shaking out the match to take a pull on the blunt. "Here Rick, hold the blunt for me, while I take care of something real quick." He echoed handing over the blunt and making his way over to the far corner. "No way! I know he didn't whip out his Vienna Sausage, and started peeing?" Lisa said turning around laughing to Ricky and April with her hand cuffed over her mouth area. "To bad April can't do this!" He yelled out still faced away using it, and hearing the sound of Kent releasing really made April wanted to do the same. "Where's the restroom at, anyways?" She asked impatiently enough. "Well the way this house is designed, I would think up stairs." Ricky answered helpfully. "Oh great!" She exclaimed with an echo. "Do you need any help?" Ricky asked raising his eyebrows up and down from making a funny jester. "No! Besides I need some tissue and don't even have any." "Oh yes you do." He said pulling out the rest he had left in his pocket. "You are good for something, aren't you?" She said with a little sarcasm in her voice, snatching the tissue paper from his hand before walking off. Darla quietly stepped inside the old dirty tub that had a filthy non-see through green curtain around it, when she heard April mention coming up stairs to use the restroom. "Oh yeah, here Kent you gotta relight this thing it went out." "Yeah. I forgot all about it, give me that. You just let it burn." Kent demanded while feeling good and buzzed. "You forgot, because of those brain cells you smoked up." Lisa and Ricky burst out laughing. April stood there for a moment glancing at the top landing of the stair casing communicating her senses, then when she felt the pressure in her uterus indicating she was running out of time, like the darkness forthcoming quickly outside. She snatched her hand from the stair casing wall that was slowly decaying as age emerged with the house, when pieces of dry wall crumbled beneath her palm that she used to brace herself against the wall for leverage to go up the squeaky steps. She suddenly stopped in the middle of stairs lightly leaning herself to the left to steal a quick peek, before she traveled the rest of the way up. Darla was still rooted to her spot behind the tub curtain waiting for her presence or anyone for that matter and as April proceeded up the steps she realized it wasn't too much sunlight left from the sun going down minute by minute, plus she also thought she needed to hurry up before they never find their way out the woods and be forced to camp out inside the house in the dark. Chills ran down her spine from even thinking about it. "Ooh, it smells up here, ten times worse than down stairs does, or maybe its because down stairs door was wide open to air it out a little, but up here it smells deadly." she whispered to herself, slowly walking along the top landing hallway site seeing. Stopping right outside the door of the first room where four mattresses was turned over with dark spots that appeared to be blood to her. April flinched at the same time throwing her right palm up to her breast with all her attention focused at the beginning of the stairs when she heard Ricky's high pitch voice echo through them saying. "How's everything coming out up there, do you need any help?" "No! I don't any help, besides I can only handle one asshole at a time.!" She assured him, proceeding along. "Ooh, I guess she told you!" Lisa yelled agitatedly then laughed. "Well excuse me, for being a hemorrhoid!" He shot back advancing away from the stairs and back into what use to be the living room part of the house. The second April finally made it to the bathroom doorway she took a deep breath then exhaled thinking she finally made it and she needed to handle her business quick fast and in a hurry, cause night time finally settled with exception of a little more light left she further thought rushing over to the toilet bowl. Once April raised the lid open she didn't see a lick of water in the toilet. The only thing was in it was rust and a dark ring from when there once was water before it evaporated, but she didn't mind it anymore cause she was about to add her own water. April quickly loosened her low rider Apple Bottom Jeans working them down to her knee caps, then decided to stand over the toilet to avoid sitting on to multi-millions of germs releasing all the pressure feeling relieved. Darla was getting very impatient as she stood a few feet away in striking distance, and right when she was about to strike, April cleaned herself with a tissue, and hurriedly pulled her pants up snapping them closed. "Let me see if I can see in this darkness on how to get back to the trail, by looking out the window from up here. Cool, I can see where the woods separates from the dirt road we parked on. Boy, we was way off the direction and . . ." April cut her whisper short, when she saw someone standing right behind her with long hair over her face in the reflection of the window, and the moment she was about to turn around to scream out to someone, Darla came down with a powerful blow with the hand she had highly elevated hitting a main artery in April's neck. April gave out a faint cry when her head hit the edge of the sink knocking one of the polls loose, that supports it to stand leveled. "What was that?" Lisa curiously asked, with a blank expression. "I know!" Ricky exclaimed. "She probably fell through the toilet." Kent joked with an irritating laugh. Ricky sort of managed a smile until he realized that wasn't the case and the sound didn't sound right. "Ricky, go up there and see what's going on, and when you two make it back we'll just have to travel out of here in the darkness." Lisa insisted. "I'll be right back." He said shortly, taking off immediately to the stair casing. Ricky slowly climbed the steps trying not to fall through them, like he did outside on the front porch. Though when he made it in the middle of the stairs he stopped when he heard the sound of something being snatched or broke off. "April! Are you alright?" He yelled, while cautiously making his way up the rest of the steps. "Oh God! What is that smell?" He pondered as he expression deepened once he made it to the top landing. "April, quit joking around and what was that loud thud sound? Watering the toilet pipes is over with!" He shouted out playfully to her once again trying to avoid from walking up on her and catching her sitting on the germ infectious toilet. Ricky squinted his eyes approaching the bathroom door and said with a concerned tone of voice. "April!" then he rushed over to her side where she was stretched out on the floor with her arms crossed extended outward, and when he rolled her over to see what condition she was in, he turned around forgetting that quick of the blood that's beneath her when he heard the squeaking sound of the bathroom door closing and hollered out. "Get out of here you guys!" before Darla plunged one of the sink pipes completely through his neck causing his body to fall helplessly over April's body. "Stop singing that stupid song you just made up. I couldn't hear a single word Ricky just said. What you say Ricky?" Lisa said moodily enough to get Kent to stop it completely, and stomping off from his noise he was making. Kent kept striking up matches every now and then for light, until he realized he needed the few he had left just in case they had to camp out in the woods to light a blunt or two. When Lisa made it to the stairs, she eased her head around the wall upon hearing foot steps slowly coming down the steps. Squinting her eyes into the darkness and making it out that it was someone else other than Ricky and April with long hair. She yelled out in fright taking off running. "Kent run!" Kent was so caught off guard, he deliberately dropped his blunt cigar from his hand hauling ass out the door, down the side porch and disappearing into the woods without taking a second glance back or knowing what he was running for, nor that he was leaving Lisa behind. Lisa hurriedly got up from her left leg falling into the same exact hole Ricky's leg fell through as she heard the hard crumbling steps heading toward her within the house. Once up she dashed off the porch running in full speed as if her leg wasn't at all hurt. It was the urgency of wanting to get away from whoever, or whatever that made her feel instantly numb at the moment. She also didn't get a chance to see which way Kent went, being he had jumped off the side of the porch in a entire different direction than she. Kent was running through the dark woods as the stems that was sticking up from the ground began to cut away at his hands, the more he plowed through them. "Thank God. I got a hoody sweater on." He whispered to himself, coming to a stop to catch his breath behind a nice wide tree he has chosen. Darla has the capability to sense out the direction of her prey, and the only advantage the prey had was the choice to hide and not be seen unless Mary's soul was called upon, as this being the case. "You can hide, but you sure can't run." Lisa got a horrid suspicion on whoever she saw, had murdered Ricky and April up stairs, and it probably was the person who killed that rabbit. She thought insanely while her jogging transformed into a limp from her leg being injured.

* * *

"That's it Margaret. I've given that kid nearly over an hour. I'm calling the cops, and report my damn truck stolen." Mr. Stewart said moodily enough, dialing Emergency nine-one-one. "Hello, Emergency nine-one-one, please state your emergency." The female operator said professionally. "Hello ma'am, my name is Mr. Charles Stewart, and I'm here calling to report my truck has been stolen by my grandson." "Charles! Don't say he stole your truck just tell the lady your grandson and friends was expected back a while ago and you think something maybe wrong cause its totally out of character." "Ma'am, I disregard what I said about my vehicle being stolen. What it is, is my Grandson and a few friends borrowed my black Yukon to attend the yearly speed boat race down at the lake, and they hadn't shown up yet, so I'm just a little skeptical from all this craziness that's been going on around town lately." "I totally agree sir, so you basically want me to put out a APB on your vehicle and a missing person report. Is that what you're asking me Mr. Stewart?" The operator asked, with sympathy strong in her voice. "Yes ma'am. That's exactly what I'm asking for you to do, and it'll be very highly appreciated." He said winning her over. "Alright, sir. I'll pronounce that over the switchboard immediately, but its one more thing before I do." "And what's that ma'am?" "Could you please tell me the main road they may have taken from the convention?" "Let's see, if I'm not mistaken its Dayton Road. That's the road that leads right into and from the Convention they all attended this afternoon." He explained thoughtfully hoping that's the road they chosen. "Thank you, sir. For reporting your emergency nine-one-one and have a great night." She conveyed easily before disconnecting the line. "This is the main Emergency dispatch to badge number thirteen-twelve, come in, sir." "Badge thirteen-twelve, copy." Corporal Mitchell copied immediately. "Hello, sir. I have an emergency APB out on a black Yukon SUV and a missing person report on four teenagers who were last seen at a speed boat convention race. The possible road they may have traveled on would be Dalton Road, over." "That's a copy, ma'am. I'm out in route right now." He assured her busting a u-turn. "Badge thirteen-twelve to sixteen-fifty, over." Corporal Mitchell dispatched through his radio for another unit to join him in route. "sixteen-fifty to thirteen-twelve, copy." Officer Payton countered back promptly. "Yes we have a APB out on a black Yukon SUV and four teenagers possible missing so I'll be needing back up on Dalton Road, over." "That's affirmative sir, over and out." Officer Payton acknowledged clicking on his emergency code three light, and doing just that.

* * *

Darla strode right pass Kent without him being noticed standing behind the tree. "Wait a minute, what a lady doing walking inside the woods this time of night? I think that's a lady, and should I call out to her? She may know the way out of here. I better do something before she disappears." He whispered beneath his breath. "Excuse me ma'am, over here." He yelled out without having the slightest clue if Darla was the killer or not. Facing the other way Darla stopped in her tracks and slowly turned around upon hearing him call out to her. Kent glanced over his shoulder before he stepped off making sure no else was around reaching while inside the hoodie pouch to grab a book of matches. The second he stepped up to her, he struck a match up to her face and said "Excuse me ma'am. All Shit!" He yelled frightened and taking off a neck breaking speed, and Darla took off right after him. Kent ended up jumping late over a log that was stretched fifteen feet along the ground letting out an expectant sigh when he went face first to the dirt then Darla leaped completely over it landing straddled over his back. He tried to get up and recover but it was to late. She grabbed his head back toward her stomach by his hair and sliced his throat with her razor sharp nails before he gave out a loud scream. Lisa stopped in her spot panting strongly, when she heard a male loud lament scream echoing throughout the woods. "Oh God. Who was that!" She said looking all around her and seeing nothing. But endless trees scattered all around her under the cozy moonlight. She was beginning to feel like she was in a documentary, that she once saw called the Blare Witch Project, but only this was real and happening to her. Corporal Mitchell and Officer Payton parked side by side facing in opposite directions on Dayton road going over their plan of operation on making sure no vehicles been banned or ran off the road for any apparent reason. Dayton Road was known for those types of foul play accidents and had became a very remote area ever sense Norman Gandy had walked those parts of the woods years ago. "Alright, Officer Payton, you go ahead and patrol north bound of Dayton Road, and I'll head southward bound." "Got it, sir." He agreed with no problem powering his window up taking off then Corporal Mitchell sped off southward bound as they planned. Lisa got tired of walking so she decided to sit along side a tree with her arms locked around her knees pushing them up against her chest trying to keep warm. Kent was dead on the ground where he had fallen with one leg still propped up on the stretched out tree. He tripped over a blood was pouring constantly from his open wound, his face losing coloration. "Him, let me check down this road perimeter." Corporal Mitchell said softly to himself flipping his cigarette out the window then he yield off Dayton Road once he saw the familiar sign that read "Exit right to the Ghost Trail Road." He decreased his speed down to twenty mile per hour on the dirt road to avoid spitting rocks up beneath his patrol vehicle, saying softly "Bin-go, what do we have here?" then he cut on his bright spot light pulling over five feet behind the black Yukon and placing the light directly on the license plate. "Thirteen-twelve, to Emergency Head Quarter switchboard." He said through his patrol car c-b radio. "Emergency switchboard, go ahead thirteen-twelve." "Yes I wanna run a make on this plate number 3WL1127, and it's a Saginaw Michigan plate on a Yukon black SUV, over." The switchboard officer quickly started tapping on her computer keys to pull up the information then came back over the radio saying. "Hello sir." "Yes, go ahead." "That particular vehicle belongs to a Mr. Charles Stewart sir, over." "Thank you ma'am. That's affirmative, over and out." Corporal Mitchell stepped out his vehicle to make sure the inside of the SUV was a code thirty clearance. Glaring his flashlight through the dark tinted side window. "Thirteen-twelve to sixteen-fifty, over." Speaking through his uniform radio receiver. "Sixteen-fifty to thirteen-twelve, copy." "Yes, I just located the SUV off Dayton and the Ghost Trail Road, as we speak. It's a code thirty clearance on the inside of the vehicle." "I'm on my way sir, over and out." Officer Payton assured him making a u-turn with his code three light on. Then Corporal Mitchell went back to his patrol car to glare his spot light on the passenger side of his vehicle at the entrance of the trail way, so his partner could confirm which way he traveled off too when he arrived. Lisa stood up on her feet looking around contemplating on which way to keep traveling, plus making sure she didn't end up back at the house. The way everything was looking in the dark under the moonlight was making it seem like she was traveling in circles the entire time. "Alright, Lisa. I think you should travel this direction, no wait. I just came from that direction." She whispered confused underneath her breath and heading in the opposite direction she was about to choose. The tree twigs crumbling underneath her every step. Corporal Mitchell turned his flashlight on with his nine millimeter in hand and extended in front of him as he trailed up he visual pathway. Darla was walking through the dark woods with her ears tuned in for any sound of an animal and her human prey that was being hunted by her whom is Lisa. "Please, let me make it out of here alive." Lisa muttered, then thought to herself, she didn't know what was worse being murdered or dying from thirst and starvation, then she laughed heartedly to herself for thinking about it either way with her eyes bulging wide. Lisa was transcending into the first stage of hallucination, thinking she was seeing someone's presence looming in the darkness behind trees ducking off, and freaked out, saying out loud. "What do you want from me?" But once her voice echoed throughout the woods in all directions. Darla and Corporal Mitchell stopped at their spots at the same time re-angling themselves to the direction her voice rang out from. They both wasn't aware it became a race between them both in finding her. Corporal Mitchell finally decided to cut his flashlight off so it wouldn't cause any more attention to him and started using the movement in the darkness tactic he had learned in the Vietnam war, when they dropped the two big farts on Hiroshima in 1945. So he placed his flashlight back through the flashlight ring on his uniform belt and quickly turned his radio volume down once he heard Officer Payton say through the receiver. "Corporal, I'm a few minutes away, over." "That's a copy, over and out." He responded stepping off the trail to blend in with the woods and trees to become one with the darkness. Lisa picked up her pace limping and panting all at the same time, and happy that no one hadn't jumped out from behind one of the tree's around her. Corporal Mitchell quickly placed his back up against the tree he was close too, so he could listen and see if someone was wandering about. Lisa started stumping through the woods a little faster, when she heard someone else's foot steps stepping over broken branches in a distance behind her. Turning around and facing forward in shock. "Oh God!" she cried behind a terrifying sigh, when she discovered someone stepping right in front of her out o nowhere it seemed. "Shhh! I'm an Officer, be very quiet. I got to get you back to my patrol care and out of these woods, follow me." Lisa quickly nodded her head with approval feeling very happy God heard her prayer, and sent a guardian angel to rescue her. She thought amazingly. Officer Payton was traveling up the Ghost Trail Road, parked behind Corporal Mitchell's vehicle with his code three lights flashing, got out his vehicle handgun in hand and extended, and radio in the other hand while moving up the pathway. "Corporal, where's you location, sir, over?" corporal Mitchell grabbed his receiver responding. "I'm southeast about fifty yards off the Ghost Trail, over." "That's a copy sir, over and out." Offer Payton confirmed traveling southeast off the trail with his flashlight glaring. Darla had lost the race by seconds in reaching Lisa before Corporal Mitchell did, as she stood ten yards away in the darkness watching them rush along. She turned her head right and stormed off vanishing presumably in the mist of the Ghost Trail woods like she was a ghost herself. When she say the distant light flashing from officer Payton heading in her direction. "Is that you Officer Payton? And if so, flash your light on and off three times." Corporal Mitchell demanded through his radio receiver. "That's a ten-four little buddy. We're less than thirty feet away from you to the right." He assured Officer Payton, once he saw his flashlight code out his demand. The second Officer Payton met up with him and Lisa he placed his hand gun inside his holster and immediately placed his arms around her shoulders with his coat helping to escort her out the woods. When they all made it to the Trail. Lisa immediately noticed she was heading the right direction the entire time, she thought silently to herself. But when she saw Kent's Grandfathers SUV still parked where they left it, she went into a small shock breaking away from officer Payton arms running out the pathway and up to the truck saying. "No you guys! Kent is still back there lost, we can't just leave him. We have to rescue him!" "Just calm down, young lady. We need to get a quick report from you and looking for anyone in the pure darkness of these woods is totally impossible. We'll have to set up a search team bright early in the morning, but right now we need to get a report from you and some medical attention. Officer Payton, can you call in for an emergency medical unit?" "You got it, sir." "Come on young lady. It's a hell a lot warmer in my patrol car." Corporal Mitchell said reaching out to her. Lisa immediately came to his side to be guided to the patrol car and once she was in the passenger side backseat, he flopped down in the driver seat clicking the dome light on to reach inside his briefcase for his report pamphlet to get Lisa's report on what's going on. "Alright, young lady. If you will, please tell me exactly what's going on from top to bottom." At first Lisa sat there with a blank stare communicating her senses and trying to calm down all the anxiety that was built up in her from getting rescued and not murdered. It was a feeling no one ever could imagine, unless they traveled in the same shoes she just traveled in and survived. Lisa took a deep breath inward then exhaled before she started up her story. "Alright, me, Kent, Ricky and April were attending the speed boat race down at the Dayton Dock, and after the Convention was over, we all agreed to leave instead of sticking around for driver signatures. We were on our way to return Mr. Stewart's truck but Kent decided sense he saved a couple of hours from not staying for signatures, it would be a good idea to smoke a little or to chief he calls it, and just for the record, I don't smoke at all, sir." She corrected then started her story back up where she left off at. "But as calm as it seemed we parked right here to walk the trail for some fresh air, and so they could do their deed. Well, Kent ended up seeing two large size Bucks and decided to throw a rock at them to see if he could hit them, but failed the mission. Then when he saw the same Bucks didn't run off too far and still was in plain view, his high must have kicked in, 'cause he took off after then in full speed, and that's when things got heated. Me, April and Ricky went looking for him when he was no longer in plain view, and after we searched for him a little while and finally found him, we all realized we was far off the trail and at that point lost. April ends up choosing the direction we should take and we ended up being really lost. We came across a house less than fifty yards ahead of us, we thought someone was living there occupying it, until we got close enough to see it was totally condemned and abandoned. April needed to use the restroom and Kent wanted to re-light his marijuana cigar, oh God. I so sound like a snitch right now!" "No young lady. You sound like you're doing the right thing, so please continue. You said April wanted to use the restroom and Kent wanted to relight his marijuana cigar." He reminded her. "Oh yeah. As we all approached the house, Ricky decided to go inside first, but once he stepped on the porch, his leg fell completely through it and when he saw it was only a few scratches on his lower part of his leg, he continued up to the front door entering inside. Then he immediately came storming back out when he stepped on something in the middle of the living room floor. Then he realized it was only a rabbit badly decomposed. Once we all were inside and other than Kent doing something foul like always, April decided to go up stairs to use the restroom while the rest of us waited for her return, but moments later we all heard a loud thud sound that came from up stairs where April went off too use the restroom, and at that point I insisted for Ricky to go see if she was alright, so once they returned we all would take off to find our way back to the truck. Well, when Ricky went up there he ends up shouting out something, I quite couldn't make out from the irritating singing Kent was doing, so I decided to go up there and see what was the hold up myself, but the moment I made it to the stairs, I eased my head around the corner and I saw someone I didn't recognized with long hair over the facial area stiffly heading toward me. I couldn't quite tell if it was a male or female, but I'm for damn certain it wasn't neither one of them and that's when me and Kent ran for our lives." "So where's Kent?" Corporal Mitchell asked concerned. "I don't know, he disappeared. I guess we ended up running separate ways." She answered, looking unsure starting up her conversation again. "Oh Yeah! After a while as I was in the woods hiding, I heard a devastating loud scream echoing through the woods. The type of scream, when you know you're not supposed to be in a certain type of predicament, then I got saved by you and that's pretty much all of what happened, Officer." She said truthfully. "Hold on for one second, Lisa." Corporal Mitchell said powering down his window. "Yes sir, Officer Payton." "I was just letting you know that an ambulance will be here shortly, they made a wrong turn. I guess they got a rookie driver tonight." Corporal Mitchell said with a little humor, then said to Lisa through the rearview mirror. "You're a brave young lady, Lisa. I got your full report down and the ambulance will be arriving soon, so its ok to relax if you like." Lisa nodded yes, then turned her head to the right of her glancing at the dark woods and once Corporal Mitchell stepped out the vehicle to have a conversation with Officer Payton. She calmly eased her head back on the cushion of the backseat to close her eyes feeling relaxed and dehydrated all at the same time. "Well, she didn't necessarily tell me if the others are harmed or not, which that means we'll have to set up a special search team bright and early in the morning, and its only one person I can think of that'll be great to lead the special search team directly to the house with no extra delays." "And who would that be, Corporal?" "The one and only Paranormal Investigator, Mrs. Gates." He answered determined. "Oh yeah!" Less than ten minutes later while they was still talking Darla eased all the way up to the passenger's side of Corporal Mitchell Patrol vehicle unnoticed where Lisa was resting, then she punched her fist completely through the window grabbing Lisa by the throat. Lisa woke up panicky screaming out in fright grabbing at her throat with both hands. "What's going on?" Officer Payton shouted in disbelief taking off behind his partner. Corporal Mitchell immediately snatched the passenger door open and frowning thinking that she was having a nightmare that quick. "What's the matter Lisa?" Corporal Mitchell asked her placing his left hand upon her shoulder to console her that she was perfectly safe. Lisa took a deep breath to catch up with her breathing and said after she deeply exhaled. "I don't know. I guess my muscles got totally relaxed and I drifted off to sleep." "Great, there goes the rookie driver in the ambulance now." Officer Payton teased, flashing his flashlight toward the ambulance driver as if he couldn't see their emergency code three lights flashing. "Good, gracious, he's going to blind someone with that flashlight, enough already." The rookie ambulance driver said to paramedic Ms. Connie. "Come on Ms. Lisa, we gonna get you to a hospital to get you some medical attention." Corporal Mitchell said easing her out the backseat to escort her to the back of the ambulance. And once she was inside she laid back on the gurney so Ms. Connie could strap her down for safety. "Alrighty. Your safe and buckled young lady." Connie assured Lisa and once she was back in the passenger seat she buckled down herself, the rookie driver made a u-turn purposely throwing up soft dirt getting Lisa off to the hospital. "Jackass! Now why would he want to kick up all that dust, knowing we was still standing here?"

Officer Payton complained heatedly. "I don't know, maybe he was getting you back from trying to blind him with that bright flashlight of yours." Corporal Mitchell inquired quickly, then laughed heartedly. When the ambulance yield on Dayton Road from the Ghost Trial Road, and drove a little ways up, the driver pressed down on the horn for three seconds, once Darla appeared in the head lamps of the ambulance barely missing her traveling to the other side by a second. "What the hell! Did you see her?" He whined. "How could I not? When she crossed directly one second in front of us." Ms. Connie said without exaggerated in her voice. "That's the person I saw, right there!" Lisa cried out pointing when she raised up from the gurney seeing Darla out the ambulance back door window just staring looking at the ambulance more along. But Lisa's voice was drained out by the radio, when Ms. Connie raised the volume nodding her head in disbelief as the driver accelerated on the gas.

CHAPTER TWELVE

"WELL I GUESS I'll phone Mrs. Gates on my cell phone to see if she'll be willing to lead the Swat team into the woods first thing in the morning." Officer Mitchell said, reaching for his cell phone from his uniform belt. After he dialed Maria's extension four dissonant rings punctuated her room while she was making her final notes like she normally had. "Hello . . . , Investigator Mrs. Gates speaking. How can I help you?" She professionally answered. "Hello Mrs. Gates This Officer Mitchell. I hope I didn't catch you at a bad time ma'am." "Oh no actually you didn't sir. How can I help you?" "Well, we seem to have a bit of a problem. Do you remember that horrible house deep off in the Saginaw woods along the ghost trail?" Maria smile turned sour not holding a shred of humor while answering. "I sure do. How could I ever forget that devilish house of Norman's, especially after seeing those innocent dead kids tied to those blood stained beds naked." "Yes ma'am that's the house. Well, we have a few teenagers." "Teenagers . . . ?" Maria blurted out cutting his conversation short, then she apologized. "I'm sorry sir for cutting you off, please continue." "No problem Mrs. Gates, but three teenagers earlier this afternoon had gotten lost in the same the woods after attending our yearly speed boat race convention and so far only one of those kids had been found. So I wanted to know would you be delightful to lead our special crew to that house?" "You know what Mr. Mitchell I'll be happy too." She said willingly enough. "Oh you would, thank you so much Mrs. Gates. Oh yeah. My partner officer Payton and a few other officer's are going to be on stand by here while I go to the hospital where the young lady name Lisa is getting Psychiatric treatment. I need to finish my report on this matter so I can have the first and last names of the other missing kids." "That sounds like a plan to me sir. I'll see you and the guys first thing in the morning and I honestly appreciate the breaking news Mr. Mitchell and enjoy the rest of your evening sir, bye." Maria said genuinely before hanging up. Once the phone call was ended Mr. Mitchell closed his phone walking over to officer Payton's vehicle where Mr. Payton was tapping on his patrol car computer keyboard sending the report over to the swat team department. "Yeah it's most definitely a go head. Mrs. Gates more than agreed to lead the swat team to the house first thing in the morning and I need to call for a couple more back up vehicles to come and stand post with you while I go pay our victim Lisa a short visit at the hospital. After that I'll be back to join you guys before my shift is over with, but first. I need to contact Saginaw U.S.A Tow Truck Company to get them out here to tow Mr. Stewart's vehicle to his residence and let him know the findings so far." Mr. Mitchell said conversationally with authority rippling through his voice. Moments later Mr. Mitchell headed off to challenge his mission. Officer Payton on the other hand powered the other three windows down before striking his last match to his cigarette watching Officer Mitchell's break lights glare up in his dark eye pupils.

* * *

Forty five minutes later exactly, Corporal Mitchell arrived at the Stewart's residence with their S.U.V tied down on a flat bed tow truck. Mr. Stewart muted the news channel as soon as Stan the weatherman was about to pronounce it would be thunder showers coming early as tomorrow. "What activities do we have going on out here in the front of the house?" He said opening the door that lead out to the porch. "Hello Mr. Stewart. I'm Corporal Mitchell from the S.P.D. I have some good and bad news to spill on you if you don't mind me saying. "Well hell let me have it." Mr. Stewart said impatiently enough. "Great. Well as you can see the good news is, we returning your vehicle. The bad news is, we found a young lady by the name of Lisa lost in the woods tonight over an hour ago and we haven't confirmed the others whereabouts at this point and time. We believe they could still be lost in the woods trying to find their way out, but this is one thing I can assure you. Bright and early in the morning we're sending in a special response search team. Oh yeah, would you allow me log in your number inside my cell phone so when we do find them I'll be able notify you a.s.a.p.?" Corporal Mitchell asked politely. "Sure why not. It's 555-7001." Mr. Stewart answered quickly. When Mr. Mitchell logged in the last number he said. "Got it and there's your vehicle Mr. Stewart and you have a great night hopefully everything will turn up as good results." "Yeah I really hope you all find them at least my boy." Mr. Stewart said somewhat selfishly. "Oh we will." Mr. Mitchell said, but as he walked off to his patrol vehicle he whispered underneath his onion breath. "What a selfish bastard."

* * *

Bright and early the next morning while all the swat team vehicles were lined up one after each other along side the ghost trail woods, where Kent Grandfather truck was once parked. Maria pulled up and parked her vehicle on the opposite side of the street. Detective Palmer from the M.P.D (Missing person department.) met her in the middle of the dirt road with his index finger pointed down to his clip board. "Good morning Gates. I believe we haven't met before, but I'm Detective Palmer from the missing person department. Here's the other three missing kids names I was instructed by Corporal Mitchell to give you once you arrived. We have two gentlemen by the name of Kent and Ricky and we have a young lady by the name of April Tilly. "Wait you say April Tilly?" She said surprisingly. "Yes I believe that's correct." He confirmed. "That's Father Tilly's daughter if I'm not mistaking and I hope I am." Maria said with a blank stare, then she walked off to forewarn the swat team they were about to get things rocking. "Alright everyone . . . , in about five minutes the search begins." Once her authority of sound was recognized, all the swat men started quickly gearing up while guzzling down their dark coffees that were strong enough to keep a bear up all year round.

When everyone heard Officer Huntz open the back door to one of the artillery swat trunk they all yield into a single file line behind each other to receive their vest and helmets. "O-k guys were pretty much down to our final minutes and once we reach where the trail split up I'll need five guys to search along the opposite direction of it to kill some time, so is everyone ready and prepared?" She said to the huddle of swat men with one hand relaxed on her waistline, while the other hand was relaxed on the handle part of her 9 mm that was snug tightly in her holster. "And we're off!" She instructed them on when she saw everyone nodding their heads with approval. No longer after they made their way to the spilt off the trail where Lisa, Ricky, Kent and April never made it too help them out the woods. Maria silently signaled the first five swat men to move along the opposite direction as planned, while the other five were directed to head off in the same direction she remembered Norman's house would be sitting amongst nothing but oak trees.

* * *

Once Maria and the swat team traveled ten minutes into the woods Norman's rotten old house popped up in plain view like a Friday the 13th Movie, if you know what I mean. Maria immediately got everyone to camouflage themselves amongst a large tree less than 20" feet away. "Here we go guys. I need one guy to work his way to the backside of the house and work his way in, next I'll need two guys to work their way up to the porch to stand post on both sides of the door and last but not least, I'm going to follow you two inside. O-k here we go." Maria said pointing at Officer Harris and his partner. After everyone mission was directed to them, Maria pulled out her 9 mm from her holster trailing right behind the last two swat men as planned. "This is the search swat team, is anyone in this house . . . !" Officer Harris voice echoed through the house vibrating the morally rotten walls, but when he didn't get an immediate response he lead everyone inside. The second the search team made their way to the bottom landing of the stairs Ricky and April once went up but never came down, another Officer voice came blaring through Office Nixon's radio. "Officer Nixon, come in sir." "This is Officer Nixon, Go ahead." "Sir we found a body of a teenage boy. I believe it's one of the missing kids we're searching for. Also we discovered a large sandwich bag of funny grass inside his sweater pocket, over." "Alright, wrap things up from there and make a note of what you guys found, over and out. Did you hear that Mrs. Gates?" "Yes I heard it loud and clear. Well there's no stopping us now let's move along on the count of three. 1-2-3." Maria counted, then they all trailed off behind each other hauling beef rump up the stairs with their weapons extended out in front of them. "Is anyone in the house this is the swat team . . . !" Officer Harris again yelled, before they thoroughly searched the two rooms making their way to the bathroom where Ricky and April bodies would soon be found. When Officer Cannon opened the bathroom door he shouted out. "We got two bodies in the bathroom Mrs. Gates . . . !" Maria communicated her senses standing in the same exact room she once seen little kids tied up naked to beds, but only after tossing the bad image out of her mind she answered back while storming out the room. "I'm on my way . . . !" Maria couldn't believe what she was seeing with her very own eyes when she entered the bathroom area. "Oh, my, God, this is the preacher's daughter April Tilly." She assured them all placing her weapon back into her holster. The Forensic Unit arrived immediately after Ricky and April bodies were found to do their photo shots of the bodies and soon as they were finish Detective Davis kneeled down to try the poll that was sticking out from Ricky's neck. "This is going to be a task pulling this poll out from this kid's neck Mrs. Gates." Mr. Davis said when he felt the poll barely budged from giving it a fare tug. "Why is it so hard to pull the poll out from his neck Detective?" Maria asked curiously enough. Mr. Davis glanced at Maria with a thoughtful expression before saying. "I guess it's from his body being here throughout the entire night, which caused the wound to swell around the poll." He explained truthfully. Maria grabbed a hazard bag from the open box and while holding the bag wide open for Mr. Davis to place the murder weapon inside she said as a joke. "Would it be much to put a little more back arm in to it?" Mr. Davis grunted "Ahhrrr . . ." While pulling at the poll that's stuck inside Ricky's neck until finally he said. "You know what putting a little more back arm in to it did work. Here we go." He pronounced cautiously when he saw the poll was giving way and once it was out he immediately placed it into the hazard bag Maria had extended open. The second Mr. Davis released the poll from his long finger tips. Maria quickly air tight closed the bag before yelling out to everyone who accompany her inside the house. "Everyone one did a perfect job today and as of right now, I'll be heading off to the Forensic Department to get a positive I.D on our murder weapon so we'll know who exactly and what exactly committed these horrible murders, bye . . . !" When Maria made it back to her vehicle and sat down in the driver seat she reached over to the passenger seat to grab her radio. "Maria to Richard over." She said when she pressed the button. Richard quickly pulled the hot coffee from his lips to rush over to his radio when he heard Maria's voice sound off through the receiver part of it. "Richard to Maria copy." his voice echoed back. "Good morning Richard. I was just giving you heads up on me being late for our meeting. I need to confirm something at the Forensic Department over." "That's a copy, over and out." He agreed easily. Moments later Maria did a U-turn taking off to the (F.D) Forensic Department. Once time flew by while Maria was still traveling up the road. She took a speculated glance out the windshield and noticed dark clouds forthcoming quickly right before her bright, brown eyes that just wasn't bright enough to make the clouds go away. "Oh great, it's about to rain on our heads. Lordy, Lordy, Lordy." She muttered turning the volume up on her c-d dash player letting the greatest hits of Michael Jackson sound through out the Bose surround system speakers that came with the car, then she drift out loud with a rest in peace memory of Michael Joseph Jackson. "Mike the world is surely going to miss you. I honestly think you was murdered heart attack my ass." She further mumbled with a sincere thought.

* * *

Swat Team Officer Cannon came walking up to Officer Mitchell patrol car when he seen him pulling up to start a double shift. "Hey stranger we have some good news and of course some bad news, like you've always said." Cannon said with a smile as Mr. Mitchell was exiting his vehicle. "Well don't hold back no more." Mitchell said while he braced his belt upon his waist. Officer Cannon lift his bullet proof vest above his head before explaining. "Alright the good news is we found the other three kids here, dead, smack in the deepest of these woods. "That's great!" Mr. Mitchell blurted out with a smile. "Well don't get to excited." Cannon assured him. "Why not?" said Officer Mitchell asked with a thoughtful expression. "Cause they weren't found alive." Officer Cannon said meekly enough bursting Mr. Mitchell's happy bubble. "What . . . !" Mitchell snapped. Officer Cannon studied Mitchell's uncharacteristic expression continuing. "We've found them, but they all were dead." "This town is coming to a story with no happy endings, gee. Well I guess I'll go take back off before lunch break comes and break the news to the Stewart's like I promised, matter of fact. I'll give Mr. Stewart a call now. Excuse me Officer Cannon and thank you for the results from this here investigation." "You got it sir. I'll meet up with you back at the station." Officer Cannon said with a far well wave when he seen Mr. Mitchell raising his cell phone to his ear.

* * *

Mr. Stewart quickly snatched and closed his reading glasses the second he heard the phone ringing. "Hello." He answered with somewhat a whisper. Mr. Mitchell instantly felt he couldn't bring the strength to himself to tell Mr. Stewart the life changing bad news once he heard the soft sound of hope with' in Mr. Stewart's voice. "Hello. Mr. Stewart this is Officer Mitchell from the S. M. P. D. I don't know how to bring my courage up to pare to tell you this, but they found the other three kids dead." Mr. Stewart released the cordless phone from his sweaty palms causing the battery to slide across the ground once the battery cover popped off from the impact to the floor. "Excuse me Mr. Stewart are you there, excuse me sir are you alright?" Officer Mitchell said after hearing the crashing sound of the broken phone, seconds later he heard a loud cry from Mr. Stewart in the background, then the phone disconnected.

* * *

Maria was happy she made it on time to the Saginaw Forensic Department once she witnessed raindrops splashing against the windshield by the size of the raindrops that falls within the atmosphere of the planet called Titan and believe me those raindrops is three times the size bigger than earths raindrops. "Now why didn't I bring my umbrella out with me this morning knowing the late night news told me it would do so." Maria whispered to herself pacing quickly up to the main entrance and into the building. The moment she entered inside she immediately noticed the information area had a strong, clean, hospital smell to it while being greeted by an African American woman from the information center. "Hello Miss. My name is Mrs. Robinson how can I assist you today?" "Nice to meet you my name is Mrs. Gates and I'm here to speak with Mr. Grant, if he's available that is." "Sure, one moment please. Mr. Grant you have a visitor up front, Mr. Grant you have a visitor up front." Mrs. Robinson announced through the P.A system intercom, before assuring Maria he would be right with her shortly then she directed Maria with an offer to some of their coffee and cherry Danish rolls. Taking Mrs. Robinson up on her offer Maria calmly advanced away over to the refreshment area where everything was set up clean and nicely like a five star hotel. Maria helped herself to a Danish roll, coffee, and a magazine before guiding herself over to the seating area where moments later Mr. Grant came walking through the corridors with his white employee coat on, forensic goggles and gloves. Maria immediately closed the magazine standing up on her two feet when he had approached her. "Hello Mrs. Gates I wasn't expecting it to be you." Mr. Grant said half surprised at the same time politely while taking off his gloves to shake her hand. "I know and it's nice to see you my old good friend, but unfortunately I'm here to see if you could do a fingerprint check while I wait for the results." "And what would that be Mrs. Gates?" "It would be this poll right here that was used in the same exact house I had you to brain storm through all that contaminated evidence on the Norman Gandy vs. Michigan case." "You don't say . . ." Mr. Grant said airily when Maria lifted the clear evidence bag right in front of his face. "Oh gosh what a cruel thing, what a cruel thing I most certainly could Mrs. Gates but it'll probably take every bit of thirty minutes with this new gadget we got donated to us a little after that case was solved, now that I come to think about it." "Oh wow that is a whole lot quicker, I'll wait." "Great, I'll be right back with you shortly." He said taking back off through the corridors. Maria tossed up a friendly smile at Mrs. Robinson claiming her seat, then she restarted the page inside the Entertainment Magazine on the scene of the movie Syriana where George Clooney character gets tortured by terrorist when they yanked out his fingernails with a pair of pliers, also threaten to hack off his head with a handsaw as they ruptured his Dura Mater (The membrane protecting his spinal cord) giving him splitting migraines for a month, which sent him to the hospital for major surgery. Then the article told Maria, that last bit wasn't in the script of things and it was an accident on the set instead. "Oohh . . ." She sighed at the thought of pain and suffering, while softly flipping through the rest of the pages while she continued to waiting patiently for the return of Mr. Grant and his quick findings. Maria could actually hear the rain pouring down hard outside from the lobby area where she was sitting then she thought she'll help herself with a nice hot cup of coffee and sugar, and strawberry cocktail Danish that was individually wrapped in plastic beside their little microwave. After eating a quarter of her Danish roll and all her coffee, but a sip, Mr. Grant came through the corridors raising his latex mouth mask to his forehead, saying while approaching her with the printout in his hand. "Alright, Mrs. Gates. I got finished a little quicker than I though and it was a good thing you did decide to stick around this pleasant place." "so what did you come up with?" She asked somewhat impatiently giving up an encouraging smile. "I don't have the damndest clue who this young lady is but here's your results. I'll let you figure it out." He said firmly looking a little confused. Maria off the top had a feeling once he said young lady it was Mary Swartz, but when she traced her eyes down to the fluorescent yellow marking she couldn't believe what her eyes was showing her. Darla Phelps's name was highlighted with a ninety-nine point nine percent rate. "Thank you very much, Mr. Grant. You can't imagine what great help this is. You don't mind if I keep this do you?" "Like I once said Mrs. Gates we keep everything in the computer file once it prints something out. You're very free to have that copy." He agreed calmly. "Thank you once again sir have a great evening." Mr. Grant slightly bowed then disappeared through the corridors. Maria stopped at the door to disarm her door locks and alarm before running out into the rain. "Ooh they never lied, when they said, when it rain it pours in Saginaw." She declared truthfully once she made it inside her driver seat firing up the engine. While she was driving up the road she couldn't believe how hard it was raining cause once her windshield wipers wiped the running water it immediately recovered the entire window. 'Let me phone Richard to aware him the delay is no longer about our meeting." She said underneath her breath while dialing his number. "Hello this is

Richard Owens speaking." "Hi Richard. I was calling to let you know I was on my way." "Oh that's great because I got an old friend here with me who wanted in on the meeting that's phenomenal in tracking actually he was the very first Indian tracker onthe O.F.P.A. force before he retired." "Sense you've mention Indian don't tell me its Mr. Ethan D. Wichita Mr. Wallace use to brag about?" She said genuinely with a smile. "You nailed it well hurry. We'll be here waiting so we can get this meeting on the roll cause you wouldn't believe how hard it was getting this guy out of a six year retirement." He inquired smiling. "I'm almost close and I got great news to add to our meeting as well. Bye." Maria closed her phone accelerating on the gas.

* * *

Darla was walking along side the road in the pouring down rain when a car yield next to her slowing down in the same pace she was walking to offer her a lift. "Excuse me, do you need a ride somewhere?" Amber said then added. "Its raining too hard for you to be walking you know." Reaching to her right along the seat to open the passenger back door. Amber's boyfriend Johnny pulled a few feet ahead of her coming into a coming into a complete stop so she could get in and Darla didn't hesitate at all hopping into the backseat. Johnny glanced in the rearview mirror and thought she looked strange with her wet hair dangling along her facial area while managing a frown on his expression as Amber started introducing herself to Darla halfway cocked around in the passenger front seat as Johnny slowly yielded back onto the road. "My name is Amber and this is my unpredictable boyfriend Johnny, so where were you heading?" Darla didn't grunt a reply she just stared at Amber through her thick wet bangs. "I see she's not a talkative person." Johnny quoted, glancing his eyes back and forth to the road and mirror keeping an eye on her. "John, maybe she's shy." Amber said changing her focus from him to Darla. "Well do you even got a place to go?" Darla shook her head no. "At least we know she's not death." He said with a little sarcasm. "What's your name, if you don't mind me asking?" Amber asked with a friendly leer. "Mary." Darla finally replied glumly and a little raspy. "Babe, she said her name is Mary." Amber scoffed surprisingly. "Yeah, she smells Mary bad too." He teased pushing the power window buttons cracking the two front windows to release the aroma that smelled faintly. "I'm getting kind of light headed, Amber." "I need you to keep looking at the road too, Johnny." She snorted. "Maybe I need to eat something oh yeah. I think I'll have a slice of Cherry Cheese cake, yeah that's what I'll have." He said thoughtfully with his mouth watering making a left on Sage Road that leads them right to their house and the rain was starting to come down a little harder by the time they end up pulling inside their driveway. "Oh no! I forgot to close the living room window." Amber whined with a skeptical frown and crossing her arms like a big kid who wanted to get on the Superman ride at Six Flags, but couldn't. "That's no big deal Amber." Johnny somewhat consoled her, when he killed the engine. Amber exited the vehicle rushing up to the house to close the living room window, so her sofa her grandmother recently bought her wouldn't get all soaked. Johnny rushed out the vehicle too and not only to avoid from getting soaked but to escape the foul odor Darla was perspiring. "Johnny, you left her in the car." "No, you left her in the car, ah what the hell." He corrected sharply taking off back to the car to show Darla some courtesy by opening her door, then took off running back inside to eat some cheesecake. Amber took another peek from their living room window realizing Darla didn't come running in behind him. "Where's the umbrella Babe?" "I think it's lying on the floor right behind the sofa, at least that's the last place I saw it." He answered then sliced a perfect piece of cheesecake. Amber grabbed the umbrella she opened it with her right foot propping the screen door then went jogging over to the open car doo. "Come on Mary. I need to get you out of this rain before you catch a cold or me one." She suggested extending her arm out to Darla's hand. "Ooh! When was the last time you cut your nails?" Amber said feeling unreasonably uncomfortable when she snatched her hand away from Darla's and decided to place her hand calmly on her right shoulder to ease her out the backseat. Darla finally budged stepping her right foot slowly out the car, then the next one. Amber stepped back a little giving her enough room to help herself out and placed the large umbrella over both their heads escorting her inside the house. "Don't touch that slice of Cheesecake in there sitting on the kitchen counter. I decided to take a quick hot shower to get out these damp clothes, and that way my cheesecake can unthaw." Johnny said advancing away when they came stepping through the door. "Don't nobody want your cheesecake, Johnny." Amber countered with a straight face.

* * *

Maria, Richard and Ethan was sitting around Richard's dining room table discussing past experiences with the O.F.P.A. Office of strange encounters and what the world has to offer, especially with the things some people could see with the naked eye, or something you can't see but are still there and something's one is only gifted enough to encounter with good or bad. "But it's definitely a pleasure to have you back on the team Mr. Wichita." Maria said pleasantly. "No, it's all my pleasure, Maria." He corrected with a friendly smile. Maria smiled back scanning over the contents of the out come from the finger print results then said. "So you guys ready to hear the fantastic news I accomplished this morning?" "Are we ready? We're damn anxiously ready Maria." Richard said with a little humor, while Ethan took a short sip of his ice cold Cranberry juice. "Alright, here it is. The test I had gotten ran today from a sink poll support came back ninety-nine point nine percent that of Darla Renee Phelps." She explained extending her arm out to Richard, so he could see with his very own eyes and pass it to Ethan. "What! You got to be kidding me that young lady is in California Patton State Hospital." Richard relented. "Well at least that's what we thought." Maria concluded. "Well Darn. Don't eat it up, let me see." Ethan demanded with strong enthusiasm. After reading over everything he slid the results over to him. "So that means, Darla is Mary and Mary is Darla, whatever sense that makes." Richard quoted. "Tell me about it." Ethan demurred. "That means the blood that was left behind at Shelly and Patrick's residence is the blood that leaked out from Darla's Body which also means Mary Swartz planted her lost soul seed into Darla and picking her specifically because she was one of the kids who called upon her through the dark secret ritual and Mary plans was to come back for vengeance on her death plus a hell of a lot more. So we have to find Mary Swartz killer before she does to have closure for her. That way her soul could finally rest in peace, but if not and she do retaliate and find her killer herself, we'll have a much greater problem on our hands and that would be Darla and Mary's soul to be lost together forever. Right along with plenty more victims in the process. It would be a little not to drive down to the news center and broadcast Darla's identity now that we honestly know what we're up against." Maria explained. "Yeah. Your most definitely right and that would help a lot." Richard agreed. "Well what'll we waitin on? We can take my vehicle." Ethan concluded standing up tucking his shirt into his pants then grabbed his forty-five automatic from his holster making sure his clip was fully loaded.

CHAPTER THIRTEEN

DARLA WAS SITTING on Amber and Johnny's sofa contemplating how she was going to plan out her attack, while Amber sat beside her scrutinizing her nails. "Johnny, come and look at her nails." She yelled to the kitchen where Johnny finally gotten the chance to enjoy his cheesecake once he was fresh and clean, but he immediately picked the saucer up from the kitchen counter gradually feeding his mouth while entering the living room. Amber went over to grab his hand saying while pulling him over to Darla. "Look Babe. My nails could never look like this, no matter how much milk I drink." "Oh God, you're sick Amber! If you want your nails to be a inch long plus gritty looking." He said thickly with a straight face, then stormed back off to the kitchen shouting. "You need to help her out and cut 'em. Do something for once that's not so gross!" "Yeah, yeah, yeah. Hold on Mary. It would be nice to at least trim them down a little." She suggested, getting up from the sofa to get the nail clippers from the bathroom medicine cabinet. Darla got up from the sofa and deviously crept her way over to the kitchen baseboard where the refrigerator located to the immediate right of the walkway, then Amber came walking back into the living room with a puzzled look, wonder on her face to where Darla went, and then she spotted her standing beside the refrigerator eavesdropping on Johnny while his back was turned looking at his curves magazine and finishing his second piece of cheesecake, unaware Darla was watching him and sizing him up. "Mary what's wrong?" amber asked finally. "Don't tell me she's was just standing there looking at me." Johnny whined "She's a bigger freak than I thought Amber. You and your taste of choice in friends, I tell you." "Come on Mary so we can trim your nails down a little, then we can play a game if you like." Once her and Darla reseated themselves on the sofa, and Amber prepared herself to cut Darla's nails to a much suitable length. The rage was slowly building up in Darla as Mary tried keeping her demeanor calm as possible. Amber placed Darla's hand on her lap and didn't waste no time placing the thumb nail between the nail clipper clamp and snipped it which made Darla quickly snatch her entire hand off Amber's leg while giving out an un-expectant soft growl. "Mary its ok, I'm not going to hurt you." She assured her, while reaching out to lay her hair behind her ear. "Good gracious, what happened to your eyes. Johnny come quick!" Amber yelled with a smile thinking Darla's eyes sort of looked far out and way to cool, being if it wasn't raining cats and dogs outside. She would have been looking strange also with black eyeliner around her eyes, representing black magic. Johnny came walking in the living room to see what his factious girlfriend had wanted, then said sarcastically enough. "Oh, for heavens sake, now you trying to upset my stomach after I've eaten." "No, they look pretty cool like that." Amber huffed. "It looks like she got a bad case of red eye infection.' He said sounding particularly edgy.

* * *

Maria didn't hesitate in noticing the news center building had been added on to become a nice size building sense she been away living in California. "Well, lets go inside and do what we came here for you guys." She said calmly before opening the passenger side door of Ethan Truck, and noticed that the rain had started to slack up as she rushed inside the sliding doors of the news building. It was super busy in the news building with everyone prancing around with stacks of papers in their hands, they all realizing making their way up to the information counter. "Hi. Welcome to Saginaw Michigan News Center. How can I assist you, help or information, ma'am?" Mrs. Piller said gently. "Hello, I'm Paranormal Investigator Gates.

I'm here with a couple of colleagues bring you all here at S.M.N.C. some very valuable information for public safety concerns." "and what would that be, Mrs. Gates?" "That would be on the behalf of these results I have here that the murders that were pronounced earlier this morning about those three kids being found murdered deep in the Ghost Trail Saginaw woods was one hundred percent Darla Renee Phelps who was responsible for the innocent kids murders and may be responsible for many others. Here's the facts." Maria explained convincingly, then slid the results over the counter. "Hum. You don't mind if I Xerox a copy of this, do you Mrs. Gates?" "No, be my guest." Maria agreed ebulliently looking over her shoulder with a smile when she felt Richard pat her right shoulder for the expression of great job. The news assistant Mrs. Pillar came back to the counter sliding Maria the main copy back with a smile while saying. "Mrs. Gates, Thank you for that very important information. I'll see that it'll make it over live air within a hour for breaking news." "Thank you Mrs. Pillar for your generosity in this matter. Have a goodnight." Mrs. Pillar tossed up an even stronger smile at Richard, when he silently raised his hand up to her saying goodbye as thy all walked off toward the sliding doors to exit the building and head back to his house to finish their meeting.

* * *

After all Darla's nails were trimmed down at a normal length still was sharp enough to be used as weapons. Amber talked her into sitting on the floor to play a game with the Ouija Board. "No why you want to play that stupid game again?" Johnny complained easily. "Because this stupid game, is better played on a gloomy day like this, come on Mary lets start before we get entirely interrupted again by Johnny Quest over there. Alright. This how you play. We both place our hands on the play check softly with our fingertips and as the words begin to spell out, normally someone would have to immediately write letters out, but I can remember them so I'll write them out at the end. You ready to begin? Alright lets begin. Ouija Board is there something you need to tell us on a day like this?" She asked then her and Darla's hands started moving from the play check landing onto the letters and Amber repeats them out loud. "B-O-T-H-O-F-Y-O-U-A-R-E-G-O-I-N-G-2-D-I-E-A-J!" Amber quickly took her hands off the play check saying. "Now let me hurry up and write those letters and that number down, before I forget. After writing them she says "Let me see. Both of you are going to die A-J." She said wearing a confused expression then yelled out to Johnny where he was minding his own business playing his Play Station three. Johnny exhaled putting his video game on pause to see what she had wanted and although he never liked to play the board game with her, he never hesitated on racing over to see what the stupid game had to say. "What craziness it had to say this time?" He grunted a reply bending down on his knees in front of them then added. "Amber, before I read off what you wrote down, I want to get this off my conscience." "Excuse us for a second Mary." Amber said to Darla before advancing away over to where he was waiting. "Alright, what is it?" Amber asked Johnny, whispering with his back turned away from Darla who was standing in front of Amber. "Alright Amber. I been trying to ignore the fact that her shirt is all ripped on her upper left shoulder." "You know what, I was noticing that myself." "No, hear me out Amber. Those spots going down the arm of her shirt, isn't just mud spots. I think its dry . . ." Amber cut his sentence short with her index finger up to her lips whispering. "Shhhhh! She just turned and stared at us." Then she yelled out to her when Darla stood up heading toward the closed screen door. "Wait Darla! Where you going?" "That's why I didn't want to say nothing from starts so you wouldn't think I was trying to run another one of your friends away, Babe." He said sounding very sincere. Amber gave him a lopsided grin, before pacing over to the screen door to see where Darla vanished off too inside the sprinkling rain. "There's one thing for certain. We're surrounded by woods and cornfields, so there isn't to many places she could go, not far that is." He pointed out, while Amber continued looking out the screen door. Johnny went over to where Amber laid the piece of paper down of what the Ouija Board spelled out, then his eyes sprawled up in confusion as he began to repeat what he just read. "Both of you are going to die, A-J?" He whispered to himself then turned to Amber saying. "See Babe. This game is reading out some very confusing shit again." Amber closed and locked the big door to join him so they could finish discussing what the devilish Ouija Board spelled out.

* * *

Once night time arrived in Saginaw Michigan, the news center finally decided to broadcast the breaking news report that Maria requested. Mr. Timothy Bailey was standing next to his new personal bar he purchased for his family room but he immediately placed his bottle of Bacardi he was pouring over a glass of ice on the bar. When his football game got interrupted by the report then he quickly placed his glass down rushing over to the big screen plasma TV on the wall, to catch exactly what the news anchor lady was about to announce. "Sorry I interrupted your program we have a very important breaking news brief to bring to the public. A few hours ago, we've just been notified by Paranormal Investigator Mrs. Gates. The three murdered victims that were found earlier this morning was committed by Darla Renee Phelps, and we've yet not received a photo of this suspect. If you have information that could lead us to her arrest please contact the number on the screen." Mr. Adams came knocking on the family room jarred door to notify Mr. Bailey about what he just saw on the kitchen TV. "Come in!" Mr. Bailey yelled. "Oh, excuse me sire, I was just about to aware you on what was being aired, but I see you saw it for yourself. Good day, sir." Mr. Adams said gently proceeding back to what he was doing. Mr. Bailey couldn't believe what he just heard standing there stunned with his hands on his waistline. "I can't believe this. Darla Phelps was my older daughter Amy's best friend, and Mrs. Gates was my younger daughter Tabby's best friend. Does Darla have anything to do with my Amy's murder?" He exhaled visually then continued whispering underneath his breath. "Good, I wish my wife was still alive to see this day, and what more could this little town of 400,000 people can stand?" then he nodded his head laughing with malice, going back over to the far corner where the bar was located.

* * *

Maria, Ethan and Richard finally made it back to Richard's house after driving around town a little from seeing if they could locate Darla out in about on a flute. Maria still didn't have any knowledge what so ever, that her second nightmare was free as a jail bird and well in town walking the streets in the mist of things. "Well Maria, the only way I see us getting closer to Darla is if we immediately get on her trail with our good ole friend Ethan right here. When another sightseeing accrues and believe me, with the way this town gossips, it won't be long for us to get our big break tonight. Moreover, the patterns of murders that been popping up gradually has to better pattern, cause every serial killer has a unique patter. We shall never forget." Richard explained conversationally and sharply. "So basically, we should note the murders that pops up back to back will be Darla's or shall I say Mary's pattern expressing her feelings?" Maria pressed. "Exactly." He replied straight and un-cut.

* * *

"I'm glad it finally stopped raining. Where you think she could of went, Johnny?" Amber asked concerned enough. "I don't know, and if it was left up to me to say anything about her running off. I'll say she could be more than happy to stay where she's at." He replied with an instinctive grab in his voice. "I hope she'll be alright wherever she vanished off too, especially from all these sick people and situations going on around here." "You're always feeling sorry for someone Amber. You just met that lady outside in the rain, over a cold bowl of soup, beside when you were clipping away on her nails it looked as if she wanted to kill you." He said managing a smile upon his face. "I would of said something negative just now Johnny off that comment, but she did give me a look like something else was staring out her pupils with the way they got big and dilated." She admitted kneeling down to the floor to place the Ouija Board back in the box to store it back into their bedroom closet.

* * *

Lieutenant Mr. Wallace pulled inside some complexes called Twenty-nine Palms Apartments coming into a complete stop, once he observed two teenagers walking by the laundry mat. "Excuse me young fella's. My name is Kirk W. Wallace, and I was wanting to know if anyone of you guys saw a young gentleman by the name of Bryan Smith by any chance?" "No sir, we sure haven't." Torey said quickly. Jay-Jay just silently nodded his head no. "Thank you guys. Have a good night." Mr. Wallace accelerated on the gas a little to cruise through the apartments, seeing if he could locate anyone else that possible may have seen him.

* * *

"I just thought about it, Johnny. You could be a real asinine person when you want to be." Amber blurted out coming back into the living room. "Now I got to be stupid. Where did that come from?" He said with shock. "That came from your comment you made a moment ago when you said, I'm always feeling sorry for someone. I guess that explains me meeting you over a piece of Now Later candy you offered me over Tom's house." "I did meet you by offering you a piece of candy at his party, didn't I?" He said amazingly. "Duh . . . !" She replied. "Well I see you loved that flavor." He said with a little sarcasm. "As a matter of fact, I didn't. Your shirt is what brought you to my house." She shot back sarcastically enough. "But either or, Amber. We can't forget, I been on the run from my probation officer for a year now. Which equals warrant, and I shouldn't be running around with some freakazoid with eyes suffused with blood spots. Hell, they'll probably think I put hands and feet on her." He babbled. "No they won't and they already know Johnny Downey isn't going to hurt a fly." Amber teased him basing her conversation on when he didn't fight back at Billiards pool hall with a midget. Johnny couldn't stand a chance to comment back knowing where she was going with the conversation, and all he did was brush his right hand along his goatee beard a few strokes. Then took his Play Station Three off pause with no further comments. Amber lounged back on the sofa with her arms and legs crossed, smiling to herself that she won the argument once again.

* * *

Alfred Carbajal and Juan Tucker was still unlawfully free running astray through Saginaw, a town they know nothing about. "I need to get the hell out of this town homes. And try making it to Houston where my Jina lives." Alfred said as they both was secretly tucked off inside an abandoned house garage. Alfred is a Hispanic guy in his early twenties, height five-eleven, weighting two hundred and fifteen pounds and Juan

Tucker is an African American in his early twenties, standing five-six weighing one hundred and sixty pounds with a dram to be a rapper someday. Until he was sentenced for murdering his younger sister Dina's boyfriend, who got drunk one night and assaulted her because it wasn't anymore ice cubs in their ice trays on that humid summer night. "I feel you man. I need to get down to Atlanta myself to see my fam, so how you think you gonna manage to get all the way down to Texas without being caught?" Juan asked, while taking off his shirt to shake it off from all the dirt clung to it which came from lying on the filthy concrete ground. "Well I sort of have a way." Alfred concluded combing through his hair with his palm brush he stole from the grocery store. Alfred was a low key clumsy type person, whom never mapped out anything he every done. He just did it. "And what way is that? Shit, I wanna know." "Even though I got buzzard luck, I was thinking about catching the Greyhound out of here. I still have a hundred and twenty-five dollars from that lick we did the other day, besides like they always said, if you do things right under peoples nose, they'd never expect a thing or see it coming." Alfred explained. "Man that ain't gonna work, matter of fact, I'm a bust a rhyme for you. Three convicts escaped from the penitentiary It wasn't attend to be until Norman slipped the keys and let us free but me and Carbajal fled staying low key so we won't get apprehended by the police but if you slip, Gee you back in the slam, Gee where you use to be in the man facility." Juan wrapped it up expressionally. "That's right, that's right, I give it to you its tight. Look here, I got a reincarnation Tupac Shukur on the run with me." Alfred said reaching in his pocket to pull out his money so he could count it, while thinking about what Juan just got through rapping about and contemplating if he should take the Greyhound route to Texas.

* * *

As time crept by Johnny and Amber decided to relax in their bedroom to watch a DVD they had rented from Blockbuster Video earlier. Johnny reaches over to the lamp stand to grab the piece of paper Amber wrote on earlier of what the Ouija Board spelled out. "Both of you are going 2 die, A-J. Wait a minute, Amber." Amber sat upright placing her back against the baseboard of the bed saying. "Yeah, what's going on?" "This note isn't reading out, Both of you are going to die, A-J. Its saying both of you are going to die, Amber and Johnny!" "What? Let me take a look at that." The second she received the note in her hands, they both got aghast when they heard a loud thud knock on the screen door. "Who in the hell could that be?" Johnny said brusquely slipping on his tennis shoes just in case it was his probation officer, and if he had to make a run for it. Amber quickly followed right behind him when she tossed the note on the night stand. He couldn't quite distinguish much looking out the peep hole into the outside darkness, so he calmly reached his left hand over to the light switch with his eyes still peering out the peep hole. "What the!" he maundered turning around to Amber open mouthed. "Well, who is it?" she asked curiously enough.

* * *

Richard and Ethan was conversationally talking to one another covering a lot of ground on the precautions they need to be taking while Maria was thinking to herself, she was very proud to have two hard working advocates that was more willing to wanna annihilate Mary Swartz's devilish ways just as well as she did. "I'm ninety percent sure. I'll be able to track her down as soon as the time prevails that is." Ethan assured them both. "I just can't believe, after all these years. It was Mary Swartz's soul creating these mysterious problems the entire time." Richard asserted disbelievingly. "Well its not hard to believe, cause if you look at the world big picture style. We have shadow people, extraterrestrial little people, ghosts, big foots, witch craft, Angelic Angels, the immortal beings attendant upon God, earth shifters." "Alright Maria, I get your point." Richard said with a friendly smile.

* * *

"Johnny, why are you just staring out the peep hole? I asked moments ago who is it?" "Its your disturbed friend again, Mary." He finally answered her dryly stepping away from the closed door so she could take a quick peep herself. Darla was standing stiffly faced away from the door looking out toward the road as Amber impatiently unlocked the door knob once she confirmed it was the truth, and when the door was open she realized the clemency of the weather outside was mild and humid after the rain.

"Mary come in. Where did you run off too?" She asked concerned, opening the screen door, allowing Darla to come inside to get out the dampness. Darla slowly turned around looking creepier than ever with her hair having a insidious look to it, and this time it was a little more tangled than it looked earlier when it was raining. As the door remained open once she stepped in. Johnny once again pulled Amber to the side when a plan popped into his mind on what they should do. "Look Amber, I know you wanna be friends with her, but you'll just have to pass this one opportunity up. She's not looking legit not one bit. And I'm sure you could see that and understand what I'm trying to express to you." He wailed. "I agree Johnny. So what we need to do?" Amber asked with a peep low voice staring directly at his challenging gaze. "What we need to do is call the cops and being I'm wanted for probation violation, I'm gonna have to take a little drive over to Tom's house to give you enough time to get the authorities here to see what they can do about this freak." "Johnny, you starting to really scare me now." She muttered with a touch of hauteur. "Now don't start freaking out. The quicker you get on the horn to call the cops when I leave, the quicker things would be resolved, alright Bunny?" Amber nodded her head with approval, just knowing Johnny wasn't playing around when she heard the word Bunny. "And I promise you I'll drive back in thirty minutes, but you gotta promise me you'll get someone here immediately." He required reaching for her hands placing a peck on her nose. "I promise." "Great." He countered letting her hands reach in his pocket, only to miscalculate his keys was in their bedroom inside his jacket, and once he got them, he was out the door. Amber friendly with a valiant attempt at a smile told Darla she could have a seat, and she'll be with her in a moment. "Feel free to sit where ever you like Mary." She didn't waste another second on doing what she promised Johnny she'd do, making her way over to the phone on the left wall entering into the kitchen, she dialed nine-one-one, heard the phone pick up on the other end on the first ring. "Hello. Emergency nine-one-one, how can I assist your emergency?" The lady operator said professionally. Amber turned faced away from Darla muffling her conversation from her saying to the operator. "Hi, my name is Amber Lynch. I'm calling to make a complaint about a strange, woman sitting in my home by the name Mary. Uhhh!" Amber explained giving out a dreadful sigh of agony after Darla crept behind her with a closed umbrella gripped in her hand and immersing the three inch metal tip through her lower backside. The point end came impinging straight through her spinal cord and into the abdomen part of her body. The operator yelled out sympathetically. "What's going on ma'am, are you there?" But didn't her Amber grunt a reply, all she heard was a horrible brawl sound of choking. Amber's nervous system made her hand clinch tightly onto the phone receiver while her eyes extended widely from the shock she was going through, as she coughed up sobs of blood from her open mouth then the operator heard her body being dropped to the floor clearly when Darla released her grip from the umbrella handle. "Hello ma'am, what's that noise!" The operator assertion was cut short when the line disconnected, and that's when she yelled through the main switch board receiver intercom. "To all emergency units we have a disturbing emergency call with possible foul play involved, and our suspect is a possible woman by the name of Mary. The residence belongs to Amber Lynch on 13013 Sage Road!"

* * *

Bobby suddenly stopped in his tracks heading out their study room door, upon hearing the operator from nine-one-one over the police scanner yelling. "They have a disturbing emergency call with a possible foul play involved, and their suspect is possible a woman by the name of Mary." Quickly walking over to the desk to jot down the information name and address to the residence and picking up the phone to call Maria cell." This is Investigator Mrs. Gates, how can I help you?" "Hello Honey." "Oh, hi Babe. I just opened the phone without looking at the number, oh yeah I just had you in mind also." "Thank you Babe, but listen, I just heard over the police scanner, that an emergency fold play at 13013 Sage Road was in progress, the residence belongs to a Amber Lynch and the possible suspect is a lady by the name of Mary." "Wait Bobby, did you say Mary?" She asked surprisingly. "Yes, I sure did. Honey be careful, will you?" "Babe, I will. I gotta go, love you!" "Love you too!" He replied back, but not in time before she closed her phone hopping on the trail while it was hot. "We got our big break! I knew it was quiet long enough that girl just can't wait." "That was a lead on Darla?" Richard asked standing up on his two feet. "Yes, sir.

The Mary side of her as well, at 13013 Sage Road. I think that's twenty minutes or less from here, but we have to go before our trail gets colder." "Hell, like I always say, what we waiting on?" Ethan said anxiously.

The carteblanche coming from Mary's soul was making Darla powerful and powerful, the more the massacre killing kept going without her being apprehended. As she impetuously moved along through the cornfields making her escape. Ethan screeched both his back tires taking off from Richard's house with adrenaline pumping in his veins to catch Darla hot trail, and put his experience and eyewitness back to work.

* * *

In the meantime, police squad cars came pulling up from all directions with the emergency ambulance unit. Officer Windslow immediately approached the open door and yelled out. "This the S.M.P.D.! Is anyone in the house?" He didn't waste no more time going in once he didn't get any response, with three officers trailing in right behind him with their weapons extended. "I see a corpse right here in the kitchen!" Officer Fox yelled with heartfelt anxiety. "Good gracious! This young lady been murdered, brutally." Officer Viet's scoffed when she saw the umbrella plunged in Amber's back as she laid prone in her blood. Johnny was finally close to their house after finding out Tom wasn't home. He also couldn't think straight knowing he left Amber home alone with a complete stranger, and it was something strange about Mary's appearance. The way her long shaggy hair was always hanging over her facial area like the girl in the movie Grudge and The Ring, but only she had sharp nails and a pair of eyes devilishly suffused with blood spots. He insanely thought to himself with a shiver. Once he saw numerous flashing lights up ahead when he turned on Sage heading toward their house. He said. "Good. I hope they got her, but wait, what the ambulance doing there?" He yielded slowly passing the house when he saw a paramedic and an Officer willing the gurney bed out the house with a sheet completely over the body. Johnny was stunned for a minute, then he hit the steering wheel in disbelief saying. "No, no, no! This can't be happening, she murdered Amber. How could I be so damn naïve to leave her there by herself! How, how, How?" He whined as reality was settling in on him traveling up the road.

CHAPTER FOURTEEN

"QUICK, TURN RIGHT here on Sage, Ethan. I see lights flashing far over there." Maria insisted. "Yeap, that's our spot, Ethan." Richard vouched from the back seat when Ethan made the turn. "We made it here in good timing, nice going, Ethan." She said pleasantly enough. Ethan mustered up a smile, tossing his cigar out the window decreasing his speed while pulling over in front of Amber's house. Maria was very excited but couldn't believe Darla was behind the previous madness that been going on, especially as fragile and very high strung she was. "I'll go around the house to see if I can fell any connection, while you guys see what's going on." Ethan suggested, when they all exited the vehicle crossing the road. The second Ethan made it on the side of the garage facing westward. He closed both eyes with his index finger on his temples to hum his ritual. "Hmm . . . , Iyika Estuma. Hmm . . . Iyika Estuma." He repeated over and over, then opened his eyes once he didn't get any positive mental power reactions, then took off toward the back of the house facing southward into the cornfields repeating the same ritual. Ethan tracked his mind for the energy and once it was right, he squeezed and opened his eyes, feeling all the sense of direction on what path Darla had took making his way over to the edge of the cornfield. "Quick. Let me borrow your flashlight Officer." He yelled, when he saw Maria and Officer Fox approaching the backside. Officer Fox raced to his side handing him his flashlight and once Ethan grabbed the flashlight, glared the light on the moist ground and observed footprints going into the cornfields. "Ah, Ha!" "we have what we need Ethan?" Maria asked sharply. "We sure do, she took off through these cornfields heading southward bound. We can take off heading west to cover the perimeter, head south, then eastward to see if we can locate her." He explained standing upright to hand Officer Fox his flashlight back. "Well, we outta here." Maria said convincingly. Darla was walking on the middle yellow divider off Spawlding road heading westbound along the cornfields, when a man driving a Nissan minivan nearly hit her, while she was making her way back to the side of the road. "Hello, Emergency nine-one-one, how can I assist your emergency?" "Hello, sir, I'm reporting a crazy lady who almost got hit by me just a moment ago from walking in the middle of the road like Froger. I'll advise you to get someone out here quick before she gets herself killed." "What road is this, sir?" "I'm right here traveling eastward on Spawlding Road, but she's heading westward bound on Spawlding." "Than you, sir, for your emergency complaint. We'll send someone out immediately." Once the line was disconnected the operator dispatched an Officer to go out and confirm things. They all nearly slammed their doors at once, then Ethan punched off heading westward bound. Every citizen that drove pass Darla kept taking second glances back knowing it was truly out of place seeing a woman walking by herself down a dark woody area, especially on a road that seems like it'll never end. "I guess I'll turn right here, and start heading southbound." Ethan whispered clicking his blinker on preparing to make a left turn at the stop sign. "Why that young man was just sitting off to the side of the road like that?" Maria asked questioningly noticing Johnny sitting at the corner of the side of the road on his block feeling guilty and while he continued waiting for the emergency unit to clear out from their house he whispered insanely. "It could have been Mary they were rolling out on the gurney. Maybe she freaked out when the authorities arrived, and they shot and killed her. Anybody, but my Amber." He further thought tearing up. "That should be Spawlding Road where those yellow lights flashing up ahead. How could I ever forget that road, from the night my SUV caught a blowout." Maria said thoughtfully. "Once we get up there, I'll bust a left turn heading eastward and we may just get lucky and run right into her." Ethan concluded feeling very convinced and the closer he reached Spawlding road he decreased his speed to make a left turn. Maria reached to unlatch her seat belt preparing to jump out if they did see her. When Richard heard her seat belt unlatch, he grabbed his handgun from his holster with his hands firmly gripped around the rubber handle pointing the nose toward the floor taking it off safely. Ethan glanced into the rearview mirror when hearing the click sound of Richards safety being released then he prepared with alertness himself. "Well. Her we go." Ethan said clicking his left side blinker on making the turn. Maria started anxiously looking on both sided of the road making sure every step of the way was carefully being surveyed. "Slow down just a little Ethan. We don't want to pass her up by any chance." She suggested when Ethan drove a quarter of a block down. Maria squinted her eyes looking ahead of them saying calmly. "I think I see someone, Ethan." Then she braced her hand against the dashboard as he decreased his speed to thirty miles per hour. "You guys, I'm one hundred percent sure that's Darla. Ethan just drive pass her and yield to my side of the road so we won't cause any attention that'll run her off." "So that's how Darla looks?" Richard said blandly staring amazingly. "Well not actually the way her hair is scattered along her facial area, but I'll never forget her figure. Pull over right here Ethan with you hazard light on." She directed and when he did she climbed out the passenger seat. Ethan and Richard didn't hesitate exiting the truck as well. Maria extended her left arm to the side of her flagging them to lay off a little as both their weapons was pointed for a direct target at Darla. Maria also decided to keep her weapon in her holster so Darla wouldn't feel the immediate threat while she approached walking at least fifteen feet behind her with Ethan and Richard steady walking counter clockwise in the middle of the street keeping Maria out of firing range. "Darla! This is Maria Gates, remember me? I'm not her to harm you, but I need you to stop so no one would get hurt!" Darla quickly stopped in her tracks standing faced away and Maria decided to stop in her tracks as well to keep safe distance to not scare her off. "Darla you have to trust me, we're not here to harm you, but you have to come to reality and know Mary isn't who you are! She's just a figment of your imagination, and I understand she's being very influential to exert the vigorous actions within your mind, but . . ." Maria stopped talking when seeing Darla take off in full speed to the right of them into the open cornfield, when hearing the sirens sounding off in the distant background. "Shit!" Maria cursed, snatching her nine millimeter from her holster taking off in full speed behind her. Ethan and Richard took off in separate pathways into the cornfield to cover their search for her. After Darla took off she disappeared instantly. Maria stopped inside the cornfield rooted to her spot looking all around her to see which path she could have taken, saying to herself. "Damn it, Maria! This isn't going to be ease." Then she slowly moved along with her weapon extended. Ethan was so amped up with excitement from anxiously wanting to kill. He couldn't stand a chance to close his eyes and hum his ritual to track her down. Richard on the other hand panicky, turned around pointing his weapon in all directions when he thought he heard the bristle sound from the corn stalks brushing up against each other, but he couldn't make out the direction as his nerves began to jerk with erratic violence with the more he moved along further and being fully aware. He also decided to turn his walkie-talkie volume down; just to be safe instead of sorry if Maria's voice came blaring through the receiver. Officer Nixon turned off his siren as he yielded to the opposite side of the road facing westbound, directly across from Ethan's truck. Ethan yelled to Maria and Richard. "I think she fled this way, I saw someone dash off!" Officer Nixon heard Ethan and exited his patrol car wit his weapon out heading into the cornfield. Darla was close to Officer Nixon, kneeled down a little over to the right of him where he entered quietly waiting, not drawing attention to herself, to creep out of the cornfield to flee across the road to the other side where the woods and trees are. Officer Nixon didn't bother to turn his radio down; instead he pulled his flashlight out holding it in one hand while his weapon was in the other and slowly walked alone. The closer he was getting to Darla without knowing it the more she crouched down lower, but once a limb from the corn stalk snagged on the backside of her shirt he became more conspicuous when the sound echoed closely to him causing him to turn around feeling breathlessly oppressive like he was being preyed upon. He was so frantic; he didn't recognize the light partially glared directly on her face. Panicking he flashed the light all around him making sure no one was creeping up behind him, nor on the side of him. When Darla saw him slowly proceed a few more feet forward. Actively she popped up charging him from the behind catching him off guard, and once he turned around out of reflex to defend himself, she instantly grabbed him by his neck in a sleeper and snapped it with no remorse or regret. He gave out a high lament audible respiration sound that made Richard reach for his radio. "Richard to Maria, over." Maria stopped in her tracks when her nerves jerked from hearing his raspy voice echoing through her radio receiver. "This Maria, go head Richard." She answered while still being on guard to her surroundings. "Did you hear that?" "I heard something but I couldn't make it out." She replied and feeling ambiguously uncertain. "Well, I'm gonna move toward that direction whence it came from, over and out." "Be careful Richard. She's very boisterous bale person at this moment." Whit the Officer dead Darla quickly fled out of the cornfield and into the large body of woods on the other side of the road, vanishing without being seen or noticed. Maria felt it was preposterous to be looking for Darla amongst thousands of cornstalks everywhere. The noise Ethan heard from the Officer made him redirect his path toward the same direction Richard was heading. After covering thirty feet of ground from he was last standing, he whispered out to Ethan, who was a little ways up to the left of him. "Ethan, over here!" Waving his hands to get his attention. Ethan turned with a crouch racing to his side. "You see what I see?" Richard whispered. "You dame right I do. I wonder what's causing the light." "I don't know, but we sure in hell need to find out." Richard countered seriously reaching for his radio. "Richard, to Maria." "This Maria, go ahead." "Meet us east about twenty-five yards away from the road, and we'll keep our eyes open for you. Copy?" "That's a loud and clear, copy." She agreed amiably taking off toward his direction. "You ready, Ethan?" "Ready when you are, Rich." Ethan replied with confidence as they both moved along slowly with their weapons drawn out in front of them and made it to the body Ethan pronounced firmly. "That is a body, matter of fact, its an Officer's body." "Oh God! Darla got a hold of him. That's what we were hearing. It was Darla attacking him!" Richard wailed looking all around them. "It look like his neck has been broken." Ethan said reaching for the officer's radio. "This is Ethan D. Wichita, I'm a Investigator from the O.F.P.A. Office. I'm reporting an Officer down and the location is west Spawlding Road inside the cornfield. I repeat, we have an Officer down on west Spawlding Road inside the cornfield!" Then Richard picked up Officer Nixon's flashlight reaching for his radio to notify Maria. "Maria come in." "Copy, go head." "Can you see the flashlight? I'm all never mind." He said cutting his conversation short when he saw her approaching threw the cornstalks. "What's going on here?" She asked skeptically, when she saw Officer Nixon's body sprawled out on the ground with his neck twisted out of place. "Darla got a hold of him, and the noise we heard was the Officer hollering out in agony." Richard explained dryly.

* * *

It was a week later when Lisa was staring blankly out her up stairs bedroom window mourning and grieving over April, Kent and Ricky. Standing there calmly rubbing her amulet charm she chosen to keep on her neck for remembrance of them all, while thinking it'll be a cold day in heel before she ever stepped another foot on the Ghost Trail, or in the Saginaw woods period. Lisa got herself together, wiping the tear drops from her rosy cheeks, when she heard the three continuous knocks on her door. "It's unlocked!" She yelled soberly facing the door then her eyes got bright seeing Father Tilly at the door, standing right beside him, her mom. She also realized Father Tilly was quite a tall man, especially compared to her mom that was five foot in height. "Honey, I decided to call Father Tilly to come over and speak with you." "Hello Father." Lisa greeted with a friendly smile. "Hello Lisa. It's a God blessing to see you in such good health." He countered back with a warm soothing smile. "I guess I'll leave you two to talk." Lisa's mom said closing the door. Lisa sat on the head of her bed saying. "Have a seat Father." "May I?" H said politely while spinning his black dobster brim hat in his hands claiming a seat. "I'm terribly sorry for what happened to your daughter Father." She said, while wiping the running tears from her cheeks. Father Tilly didn't say a word at the moment. He just reached out to embrace her to his side with his chin softly rested on top of her head, and rubbing her back assuringly saying. "I am too, but she's now in a much better place. Lisa. Then he slowly pulled away so he can scrutinize her face for a moment, thinking he was with the one who was last to see his daughter's beautiful face. "I also came over to give you this locket of my daughter's. It's the picture I took of her at her sixth grade graduation, and she always told me you was her best friend in the whole wide world and someday you two would become school teachers, but its obviously her side that dream vanished with out a trace, so I figured you should have this Lisa." He said with sugar cane sweetness, extending his arms out to place the ten karat locket around her neck. "There. That looks great on you." He said throatily managing a smile on his face to stop himself from tearing up. His eyes trailed down to steal one last look of the locked to see his daughter's million dollar smile, the one he seen through the camera lens when he took the picture. "Father, I'm sorry but I can't except this, cause this is something you should keep forever." She objected pleadingly. "No Lisa. She's your Angel now, please in Gods name." He said pleasantly embracing her with one last hug, before walking off leaving out her room. Lisa laid on her stomach burying her head into the pillows and crying her heart out for the loss of her friends.

* * *

Norman Gandy quickly closed the top lapel part of his coat to his chin disguising himself going into the phone booth like he once did when he called four-one-one to get Maria's new address, though this time he wanted her telephone number. Reaching in his left pocket to pull out a hand full of change and even Canadian tokens he took from an unlocked vehicle floor cup holder tray. Sorting out forty cents, he dropped the rest back into his front pocket, inserted a quarter, dine and nickel into the change slot and pushed four-one-one. After a few beeps he heard a male operator come on the line which caused him to smile to turn hard by wanting it to be another female operator again like the first time, when he talked dirty and nasty to the one who had given him assistance with Maria's address. "Hello information, four-one-one. How can I assist you with information, and what city and state please?" "It would be a number in Saginaw Michigan, I would love to be assisted with." Norman replied with a disguised tone of voice. "Alright. Please state your request sir." "Ok, can I please have the number to Maria Gates? Her address is 15715 Luke Worm Dr." He said getting out his chewed up pencil and his bus schedule to write on. "Thank you. Here's the request and have a nice day sir." A second later an automatic voice operator said. "The number you requested is 555-1001, for an additional charge to." Norman slammed the phone on the hook cutting the voice machine message short still feeling moody about getting a male operator instead of a female one. While neatly folding the bus schedule he stepped out the phone booth. The town of Saginaw really was beginning to be very vindictive from all the crimes and murders that were ninety percent based on vengeance and to the local residence the crimes seem to be ubiquitous as murders popped up back to back like they were existing everywhere all at the same time and although most of the town citizens wanted to move away from all the madness they also wanted to keep the town strength. The way they did when Norman Gandy was the cause of all the torment himself from murdering all those innocents.

* * *

In Twenty-nine Palms California is where Mr. Wallace was still doing his investigation looking for the missing kid Bryan Smith. He threw his Excursion truck in reverse to the street Cienega Dr. where he observed quite a few patrol vehicles and ambulance's and once he pulled up he peered straight at the yellow tape yielding along side a San Bernardino Sheriff car facing in the opposite direction. Deputy Lucas glanced up when he realized he was being flagged by Mr. Wallace to power his window down. "Hey, good morning Lt. Wallace." He said with a grin widening on his face. "Is it really. So what do we have here?" Deputy Lucas marked and closed his incident report book to grunt a reply. "We just found a young man in his early twenty's shot dead in this home. We don't have any suspects at this moment, I hate to say." "Poor little fella." Mr. Wallace grunted, while looking at his gas gauge once it beeped alerting him he was getting low on fuel. "Oh yeah. We was called here to this residence at ten eighteen am from neighbors claiming they heard gun shots at one am this morning. "Well, I'm getting low, you don't mind if I go ahead, and jump back on my tail?" "no, not at all." Deputy Lucas murmured huskily. "Good luck, on the case Deputy." Mr. Wallace said soberly, then pulled off reaching for his pack of Marlboro's snugged by his sun visor. "I know, I know." He said blandly when he heard the low fuel bell sounding off once more.

* * *

A few days later while Bobby was at his Attorney Law Firm walking into his lobby to get a soda out his beverage machine, where clients was patiently waiting glued to the T.V. Bobby even became glued himself when he saw the live news coverage being aired, and as everyone continued watching. They all heard the news anchor lady saying. "It's been three weeks sense Norman Gandy, Juan Tucker and Alfred Carbajal had been free and on the run from escaping the Michigan State Penitentiary Correctional officers, while they were being medially transported to the city hospital. If anyone has any leads to these escaped convicts. Please contact this number on the screen, also we have a strange derange lady by the name of Darla Renee Phelps who is wanted for numerous murders. So please, remember if anyone has any leads to the arrest of these people feel free to contact this toll free number below." Bobby nodded his head going over to the beverage machine saying thoughtfully. "Hum. Norman Gandy escaped and I didn't know he had a pretty ice size birthmark beneath his eye, of God, Maria." He said with an icy tone, snatching his soda from the receiving slot then raced back to his office to phone her. At the office he sat at his desk to dial their home extension. "Here princess, feed Jasper the rest of his cat treats while mommy answers the phone." Maria demanded softly before rushing over to the living room phone. "The Gates residence, Maria speaking." She answered. "I also called to ask Antonia a question, well actually one." He said sounding actually confused. "Hold on honey, she's right here. Let me put the cordless on the unit and press the loud speaker. Put the cat treats down for a second, Princess. Daddy wants to talk to you on the phone." "Hum, mommy?" Antonia said softly racing over to Maria command. "Come around on the side of the sofa so Daddy can talk to you on the loud speaker, honey?" Once again Antonia did exactly what she was told answering. "Hello?" "Hello Princess. Daddy was just wanting to ask you a question, then you can go back to doing what you was doing." Bobby stopped his conversation then threw up his index finger stopping his clerk at the door indicating he'll be with her in a minute. "Honey, you still there?" "Yes, sir." "Do you remember when you saw that man in your room?" Maria scrutinized her expression when Antonia glanced up at her. "Yeah, I was scared Daddy." "It's ok honey. Now could you tell me if he had anything on his face?" Maria's expression turned puzzled while saying. "Go head honey, tell Daddy what you told me the next morning."

Antonia stepped a little closer to the receiver saying. "Daddy. He had dirt under his eyes." "Ah, ok. Thank you Honey, you did great and in another hour Daddy will be off work so I can take you and mommy out to eat. Alright, you can go finish what you was doing. Love you!" "Love you too." She countered back, skipping away to finish feeding Jasper his cat treats. Maria picked the cordless phone back up, causing the loud speaker to automatically shut off. "Hello." "Honey. I'm sure your sitting there thinking what was the questioning all about?" "Well, yes. So what was it about?" She asked incredulously. "Now don't let what I'm about to tell you ruin your evening. About twenty minutes or so ago, the news aired some notifying news to the public. they said three prisoners escaped two Michigan prison guards on a medical trans, and Norman Gandy was among them three." "Wait, wait. You got to be kidding me! So your telling me Norman Gandy the same enormity creep I put away behind bars for life, is now free on the loose, Bobby?" She asked throatily when hearing Norman's name. "That's exactly what I'm telling you Babe, and there's no doubt it was him inside Antonia's room that night." He assured her sincerely. "I was just about to ask you that." She returned calmly. "So Babe. Make sure all the windows are locked inside the house and once my time runs out, here. I'll be there to pick my two young ladies up and take you both to dinner, sounds like a plan?" "Sounds like a plan to me babe, but one more thing." "What's that honey?" He asked concern enough. "Why the news waited this long to air this?" "To be honest with you they may already have. Its just we was to busy to ever catch it on the news." "Yeah, your right. Alright honey, we'll be ready when you pull up. Love you, bye." she said passionately enough disconnecting the line. "Come on, Daddy's little girl. We have to close and lock all the windows like Daddy asked us to do." "Mommy, I wanna feed Jasper." She objected. "No, you can't feed him the entire box at once honey, so come along." Maria commanded gruffly. Antonia glanced back at Jasper seeing if he saw, or realized the extra cat treat she purposely dropped on the floor for him, then faced forward when she saw him biting into it. "You're not sneaky young lady. I saw that extra cat treat you purposely tossed on the floor for him." Antonia gave her mom a sharp scrutinizing look as the nerves in her eye lids jerked from the icy tone in Maria voice. As time elapsed by Maria stood in her bedroom window looking out into the drizzle rain. She was still feeling mind boggled about her nightmare had finally come true about Norman Gandy running loose free, she also started thinking about when Antonia first brought it to her attention. That the strange man she seen creeping out her closet had dirt beneath one of his eyes. Antonia noticed when the hallway light glared onto his face while she played sleep and Maria knew right then the description sounded all too familiar, but she didn't want to further convince herself, she thought dryly.

CHAPTER FIFTHTEEN

B OBBY WAS WRAPPING up his conversation with the last client saying while closing the confidential file. "Okay, Mrs. Hamilton. I'm guaranteed I could get this third D.W.I. reduced down a little further, but you cannot afford to miss another court date. The judge was up my ass with a flashlight about you not showing up for the preliminary hearing, but other than that, everything will be looking good alright?" "Alright, I sure appreciate all the correct counseling you've been giving me Mr. Gates. Thanks a heap, good day." She said with a Benign tone of voice, before excusing herself out his office. Bobby stood on his two feet managing a smile thinking it feels good putting confidence and a smile on his clients faces, then he took a peculated glance at his Rolex watch saying. "Business hours is now over with, and family time has just begun." Clicking his computer off, locking the file cabinet took care of the last of the day duties and out the door he went. To buy some time for his family night out with his two lovely ladies, he opted to take a short cut home. Pulling into the driveway he honked his horn. "Come on, Antonia Daddy's outside waiting on us, an grabbed another one of your dolls." Maria instructed her. Antonia calmly placed her sleeping doll Tinker Bell on the sofa, then raced over to their floor model T.V. to snatch up her cookie monster talking doll that was leaned up against it, and when they both got in the car, Maria gave Bobby a passionate kiss after she glanced in the backseat making sure Antonia had buckled herself down for safety. "Honey you should of saw how quick Princess hopped in the backseat trying to prevent from getting all wet from the rain. It was so cute." "That's mommy Princess." Maria said genially while he was reversing out into the street taking off from the house. Maria faced forward in her seat thinking Antonia couldn't have another sympathetic father on the world other than Bobby, then she snuggled herself deeper into the seat feeling relaxed.

* * *

Alicia Wagner and Michael Stearns was a couple who both agreed to pull off to the side of a dark deserted road that sits within the Saginaw woods. So they could make love inside the car being spontaneous with their love making like they normally had. Sneaking around with one another always had been their cup of tea ever since they were younger, besides that's how Alicia earned his heart from her best friend that everyone hated with a passion in grade school. "You think this is a perfect spot to park Alicia?" He asked meekly. Alicia didn't grunt a reply instead she glanced around, even though she couldn't quite distinguish much through the pitch darkness of the woods that was sprouted out amongst both sided of them. "Yes, I suppose so, as long as there isn't anyone around." She said finally. Alicia is a brunet with an olive skin complexion, dark brown eyes with long brown hair and freckles on her nose and cheek area. Her hair was twirled into a wrap style underneath Michael's hat she wore so it wouldn't get wet. Michael slid the gear into park, killed the engine, and placed his hand softly on her neck covering her lips with his own. Alicia slowly pulled away from his embracement to toss the hat in the backseat, then scrutinized his expression raising her shirt over her head taking it off. The second Michael saw she didn't have a bra on like she normally had to his surprise. He leaned toward her bare naked breast, and circled her light brown nipple with his tongue being a tad bit wet. Then Alicia pulled him on top of her laying back gently on the passenger seat long ways in a missionary position with one leg propped on the dashboard with the other stretched out along the seat. Landing himself between her spreaded legs and steadily kissing away at her breast and stomach, listening to her soft harmony moans. "You making me horny Michael, please me." She said softly with lust building in her eyes gradually. Not saying a word he just chose to talk to her with actions kissing down her stomach where her hair line beneath her bellybutton direct to the wilderness. Calmly lifting up so he could un-button her pants to get a better feel of things, and to also make the mood more tense. The moment her pants and boy cut panties was off and in backseat. His sharp eyes start surveying the scenery of her luscious curves, thighs, breast and her twelve inch waistline that supported her thirty-six inch butt. "Now that you got my clothes off, what are you going do to me?" She asked impatiently. "I'm going to give you what we came here for and all what you deserve, Baby." He responded smoothly, landing a kiss on her naked shaved mound sliding his right index finger inside the warmth of her body and started spelling A-P-H-R-O-D-I-S-I-A-C on her intense clitoris, but once he saw her vagina squirting out cum like a low pressure water fountain while she softly moaned uncontrollable, he raised up saying with a little cum drying on his lips. "Are you ready for me to enter, Baby?" "Yes Babe, yes!" She suggested sweetly. Michael raised upright with his knee on the seat detecting her slight shiver, while he continued struggling at his belt buckle to take his pants off. Alicia was staring into his eyes licking her lips applying moisture to them with both hands massaging both breast, showing him she was good, hot and ready for him to enter inside her rain forest which was also good and wet. Then she widened her legs a little further once she saw him bare naked leaning slowly toward her to join the excitement and right when she felt the tip of his hard shaft, she clinched her vagina muscle from all the intensity that was built up. His muscle man slid in nice and smooth. "Yes, Michael." She whispered in his right ear lobe out of welcome lust. Michael started breathing strongly while landing small passionate kisses on her lips as he continued thrusting his shaft in and out like he was doing it with a grudge until Alicia couldn't keep her legs propped wide open any longer, so she locked both legs around his waistline with her toes spread from the intense sensation. After a while Michael's body started shivering from trying to hold back from climaxing, but it wasn't any stopping it. He quickly withdrew his shaft from her secret garden, and extracted all over her lower stomach. Then he tapped his shaft repeatedly against the mound of her lady lump releasing the reset of his reproductive fluids, while she still was in the missionary position releasing fluids herself. Alicia extended her arms out to pull him toward her, and after he followed her command they both started tongue kissing each other passionately. Michael lifted his body weight off of her bare naked breast holding himself up by the strength of his arms, when he noticed how foggy the car windows got. "You see how steamy our love is together? We fogged up the windows." He whispered to her fervently studying the sexy expression on her face, and the sweat beads on her forehead. Alicia silently turned her head right to glance at the windshield, then nodded her head at his gaze in acknowledgement to his question. "Well, Baby, I think we need to be getting back to the house. Its pitch dark right now." He suggested. "Maybe we should Babe." She agreed with a friendly leer, sitting upright reaching in the backseat for her clothes. Once Michael latched his belt buckle closed, he turned the ignition, firing up the engine, and did a u-turn to head back toward the way they came. Alicia could of sworn she saw someone standing off to the side of the road through her door mirror, and when the brake lights popped up adding light to the darkness, she actually did see someone standing there watching them pull off. "Michael. I could have sworn I saw someone standing behind the car while you were backing up and turning around." "You saw what?" He barked, easing his foot off the gas. "No, NO, don't stop. I was just saying I thought I saw someone that's all, maybe I was mistaken." She replied simply holding back her real thought, she actually did see someone. Michael clicked the dome light off tossing the thought right out of his mind and accelerating on the gas.

* * *

Someone was creeping their way out of Richard's blue room, while he was tapping away at his computer which sat faced the opposite way. He was trying to pop up coast-to-coast radio to listen to George or Art over the Manila Philippines area. He only had one light on which was from the computer screen that lit his face and showing his deep thoughtful expression. He was so drawn into the open line caller on the computer coast-to-coast radio he didn't hear the release latch sound from the blue room door opening, instead he reached out to grab his melting ice water sitting next to the computer. The intruder was slowly creeping up behind Richard like a tiger in the Jungle preying on him, as if he was the first meal of the month. Then a glimmer of comprehension lit Richard's eyes when he saw something, or someone moving behind him in the reflection of the computer screen causing goose bumps to race across his entire neck from seeing the reflection of the shadow elevating the hatchet in the air as he was unable to move then the hatchet came down with a force at his neck. Richard quickly raised up out of his sleep soaked in sweat feeling breathlessly oppressive with his eyes penetrating the darkness, while at the same time realizing it was only a nightmare he was having. But still yet he quickly tossed the cover to the side rushing his feet into his soft cotton interior slippers to check things out in the living room to be safe instead of sorry at all means necessary. Once he opened his bedroom door he noticed a dim glare of light on the end of the hallway that leads into his living room, and for a minute the thought ran across his mind to turn back and grab his forty-five automatic until he convinced himself the strange feeling he had was only from the nightmare he experienced moments ago. Once he made it at the end of the hallway entering inside his living room his face expression tensed. "I left my computer on? I never leave my computer on." He grumbled thoughtfully walking over to the computer desk, not wasting a moment in noticing the glass of water beside the computer just the way he left it, but only it wasn't sitting on a napkin as he vividly remembered. Then he glanced at the digital clock on the bottom of his computer screen saver seeing it was barely going on eleven p.m. "Hum, I must have been tired from cleaning up all that dog poop." He thought dryly taking back off to his room while knowing he wouldn't be able to get no sleep.

* * *

Maria was making her way back down stairs from tucking Antonia into bed, after she tired herself out by chasing Jasper all around the house when they made it back from dinner. Bobby was sitting on the living room sofa looking at the eleven-thirty news finishing off his chicken fingers he brought home from AppleBee's. "Honey. While you're in the kitchen, can you snatch a few of them napkins for me?" He asked her pleasantly.

"I sure can, Mr." Maria responded then came walking around the sofa handing him the napkins he requested. "Thank you, Babe." Maria forced a smile sitting right beside him focusing in on the news. "I wonder what tomorrow's gonna bring?" She said softly with a solemnly gaze at the big screen. Bobby stopped the piece of chicken right before his lips slightly turning his head left of him to study her face expression. "You're not worried about Norman Gandy are you, Honey?" He asked gently. "Of course, I'm worried about him. It'll be wrong saying I wasn't. When in all reality, I am." She replied un-tranquilly. Bobby decided not to take another bit of his left over meal, and just focused in on Maria from seeing her eyes brimming with distress. "Babe. Everything's gonna be completely fine, besides I'm sure the town authorities are doing everything in their power to capture him, I mean them of course." He inquired sympathetically. "Well, until then Bobby. I'm not gonna let down my guard's and keep him in mind." She said with her expression amazingly bland looking directly in his eyes. "I understand Honey. I just don't want this to stress you out, that's all." He assured her with his true thought, then picked a piece of chicken up and finishing his meal.

* * *

The very next morning, Maria drove off to Richard's house after he called her letting it be known he really needed to speak with her face to face as they went over things pertained to this case as well as Maria had a personal topic to discuss herself. Roxy was up on her hind legs with her two front paws propped up on the five foot fence barking from the top of her lungs amping the rest of the dogs up right along with her. Richard rushed out the kitchen and over to the camera monitors as if he wasn't expecting anyone. "Oh Roxy, its only Mary." He said making his way over to the front door. Maria was tossing the dogs cold chicken nuggets Antonia left in the car last night and as they all was growling at each other over the nuggets Richard said. "I wouldn't do that if I was you. They'll be expecting that every time you pull up you know." "Which one is Roxy?" "The only one that doesn't have anything hanging, I shall admit she's the only female amongst them all." He vividly enough indicated stepping outside the door walking up to the fence. Maria laughed delightedly saying. "Stupid ole me, huh?" "Its all gone Roxy, no more!" He yelled frankly, when he observed Roxy cut off tail wagging back and forth then they both headed in the house. Once they was inside Richard grabbed her think jacket and hung it on his coat rack. "Well to start things off last night I had the most weirdest nightmare I've ever had in my entire life. I dreamt I got murdered while sitting at y computer listening to coast-to-coast radio, and to my knowledge, the intruder crept out of my blue room from behind me. Maria, I've been up all morning wrecking my mind, well actually, since last night, wrecking the little raisin in my cranium trying to figure out the identity of the intruder's face. Or it would of been the killers face if it wasn't actually a nightmare. Maria and this is one time I actually can say, Thank God for nightmares, being that it was better to bet that then reality." He conversationally explained when he sat at the table where they normally held their meetings. "So you telling me, you been up all night trying to figure out who it may had been?" "Yes, to be honest, all I can do is be mighty happy it was only but a nightmare. I can't stop saying that." He declared truthfully. "Boy Richard, event though I'm a strong woman in mind and spirit, I think I'll crap in my night gown if I was about to be murdered and noticed it at the last minute." "Yeah, well enough of this murderous talk its time to get down to some capture figurations." "Yeah, you right." Maria agreed easily.

* * *

Juan and Alfred was coming up with the conclusion they both needed to split up and travel in their own separate ways from here on out, instead of traveling together stupidly like the television series Prison Break. "So, where you're going to travel too?" Alfred asked, while bending down tying up his soft sole boots. "To Atlanta City, to my moms. She's the only one I can trust." Juan answered simply. "To your moms. That's the first place they'll check, or will check eventually." "But have you ever thought about that they may think I'm not stupid enough to go there, and may never check?" "No . . . !" Alfred echoed absently. "You didn't have too, I'm going anyways." Juan countered quickly pulling the beak of his ball cap down over his head with both hands. "I'm not even gonna ask you, how you gonna get there." "Please don't, cause that'll be giving up to much information." "Whatever Amigo." "Can a brother get a hug?" Juan said very humanly. Alfred moved forward and embraced him with a bald up fist on his back saying. "I'm gonna miss you dog. Be careful." "Like wise, Homie." Juan countered back as they both un-braced each other and for a minute Juan could of thought he saw a sparkle of a tear drop in Alfred's eyes, but he was out the old abandoned house garage and gone. Alfred ran up to the garage's small window to see if he could see Juan to catch him cause he left a few sheets of paper of some of his rhymes on them, but he was gone with the wind. Then he opened the folded papers and read on the top page corner. "If you picked these papers up to read what I'm saying, then you already know these rhymes is yours. Get rich or die trying like Fifty Cent said, stay safe Alfred and stay away from the Greyhound Bus Line." Alfred glanced up at the window with a smile, then said with alacrity. "Your one good dude, Juan. Be safe Bro."

* * *

"Oh Yeah. I'm going to give the Saginaw School District Supervisor Mr. A. Zimmerman a call requesting an old school list of students that attended school with Mary Swartz back then, at least that'll buy us a little more lead way." Richard inquired. "That would be a good thing to do Richard." Maria advised lightly, placing her pen on the pamphlet showing him she was very interested in his conclusion. "Also, that'll at least let us know who her main targets are." He added. The thing that's mind killing me is, its other innocent victims paying for the past also." "Maria declared truthfully. "Exactly. Its no longer only vengeance, its becoming personally." Richard concluded. "Oh yeah. How could I ever forget this conversation, Richard." She said in a rough gravely tone. "What could that be Maria?" "Bobby told me the news pronounced Norman Gandy and a couple more prisoners escaped the Michigan State Prison Transportation Officers a few weeks ago." "Wait. How I miss that news coverage?" He asked absently. "That's exactly what I thought Richard when my husband brought it to my attention, then we realized, we have been so busy we actually hadn't been paying any attention to the news, well the television period for that matter." "Yeah. That's sounds exactly like what it was, so let me catch up. Now we have a possess woman on a mission for Mary Swartz lost soul, and a disturbed sick bastard that escaped to his damn freedom, and only the devil knows what the hell for." Richard fumed, with a serious expression. Maria gave him a lopsided grin raising a skeptical eyebrow, assuring him he hit it on the nail. "You don't think he's after you for putting him where he belongs?" He asked curiously. "Belong was a big word for six words Richard. But to answer your question truthfully, I think so. And I could never forget those harsh words he was yelling to me in the backseat of the patrol car. And that was I'm going to make you pay for what you done, and heaven isn't going to be able to save you." Maria said wearing a look of frustration after she answered his question, then changed her entire face expression when Richard added as an after thought. "Not if we get him first you're not going to pay." "Well there goes another big word for only two letters this time, and that's "if"." "Maria. I know you're not putting your guards down." "No, I'm most definitely not, I'm just not to fond of a cat and mouse game that's all, besides its bad enough this town of four hundred thousand people and decreasing being haunted by Mary and to top it off their first worst nightmare is on the prowl and uncounted for once again." Maria leaned back in her chair letting out an expelled sigh that breezed through her bangs, then she quickly added, "I'm just afraid for the towns future." "Plus your safety?" Richard countered shortly. Maria's expression was back grave when she glanced up from the table to gaze at his shaky hands. Richard couldn't refuse to acknowledge her frustrated look saying "We'll handle these situations trust me." Then he reached out to grab his cup from the table to guzzle his cup of apple juice down non-stop, preventing Maria from seeing the dry swallow from his Adams apple, and his worried expression from the relapse to memory of his nightmare last night. Once he sat the empty glass back on the table, Maria couldn't help but notice his eye twitching that always put the mood back in its perspective moment, cause she learned that was from him having flashbacks on whatever the cause may be and normally flashbacks means stress, she though with a smile.

* * *

As time went on darkness descended. Juan was steady traveling up a long road trying to hitch a ride, but people paid him no mind as they drove pass him, until a two thousand and five Monte Carlo yielded off to the side of the road, traveling in the same direction he was headed. Juan ran back to pick up his hat which flew off his head, and continued on the car. When he opened the passenger door he couldn't believe how beautiful and petite the driver was with full size lips, nice legs, Carmel complexion, beautiful feet with a Colgate commercial smile. "You need a ride somewhere?" "Oh hi, sure." Juan answered finally while bringing his mind back to reality slumping down in the passenger seat placing his back pack on the floor between his legs. "So what's your name? If you don't mind me asking." Juan appeared honestly startled by her question. She didn't catch by paying more attention to the yielding back onto the road. After staring from her blind side thoughtfully he said. "It's Thomas." "It's nice to meet you Thomas, my name is Carmen." "It's nice to meet you Carmen, and its very nice of you for giving me a lift. You pick up strangers all the time?" "Actually this is my very first time." She answered truthfully. Juan experience a sharp stab of guilt when he thought about what he was going to do in order to take her vehicle so he could have a for sure ride to Atlanta City. "So where you need a lift too?" "How far, you willing to go?" He countered quickly. Carmen's expression turned tense from him answering her question with a question. "That's not the question I asked you." She replied simply. Juan was beginning to wear a look of frustration, while he built his self up for the okie-doke.

CHAPTER SIXTEEN

MARIA JUST MADE it home from sitting with Richard all day talking over notes and issues. The second she stepped through the door she locked it behind her. Glancing over to the far living room wall, she noticed it was three minutes to nine p.m. and realized that was the longest she ever lounged over his house. "Bobby!" She yelled out softly kicking off her shoes. "I'm in the study room, Babe!" Maria placed her folder and purse on the sofa before heading to where he was.

* * *

"You're traveling South!" Carmen exclaimed while looking unconvinced. "Yes, and I'm needing your help." He pointed out quietly hoping she'll do all the right things in cooperating to keep from harming her. "Whadya need me to do?" She asked quite nervously, and while the street lights shown through the windshield onto to her smooth tan legs. Juan tawny eye's kept dancing over her breast cleavage, then he said. "Alright, what I need you to do is drive me to Atlanta City." "You got to be kidding me. There's no way I could drive twelve hours to Atlanta from here and jeopardize my job by not showing up in the morning. Besides I'm refusing!" She charged heatedly. "Now we can do this the easy way or the hard way lady, the decision is yours." Juan said after reaching inside his backpack. Pulled out his dagger knife he found inside the abandoned garage. Carmen swallowed dryly when she saw the weapon firmly gripped in his grasp, then protested softly. "Its not that easy is what I'm saying." "Why not?" He challenged thoughtfully. "Wait a minute. Don't tell me your one of those prisoners their looking form, are you?" Her mouth tightened almost imperceptibly once she noticed he still had his brown prison boots on with a green Khaki suite he stole from Wal-Mart. "That's besides the point right now." He answered bluntly. Carmen immediately glanced into her rearview mirror noticing a car slowing down behind her preparing to stop at the light and once she came into a complete halt at the red light. She threw the gear into park, snatched the driver door open and jumped out. "Lady, come here! Shit!" Juan yelled angrily, when she jumped out then he panicked climbing over in the drivers seat and once he snatched the gear down to drive, the driver door slammed shut and the tires screeched as he took off through the red light. Carmen ran up to the car that was parked behind her screaming out in fright. "That's one of the escaped prisoners their looking for!" She cried out panting strongly.

* * *

Maria stretched herself out along the leather sofa in their study room to relax, while Bobby finished up his business notes for one of his special clients first day of trail the next day. Bobby is one of the best lawyers Saginaw Michigan has. Everyone called him the White Johnny Cochran, being that most of his cases never got a chance to make it to trial. This one is the first one in a long time. His client by the name of Tony Morris did a hit and run after striking an elderly pedestrian man named Gregory Mays. Mr. Mays was lifted fifteen feet in the air and was instantly killed, when he suffered a broken neck and a punctured lung. "Honey. I'm going to check out the eleven thirty nightly news again to see what the weather is gonna be like tomorrow." Maria said moving toward his lips. "Alright Honey, I'll join you in a minute." He said softly as he stole a peek at her sexy walk while she was heading out the door. Upon wrapping up his work he went to accompany her on the living room sofa. Maria patted her right hand on the sofa next to her directing him to snuggle down, then they both tuned their undivided attention to the top story that was being aired. "Hi. I'm Joe Maxey live at the S.M.N.C. Broadcasting today's top story. Less than two hours ago a young lady by the name of Carmen Snider, car was jacked by one of the escaped America's most wanted prisoners, and she bravely jumped out her vehicle at a traffic light. If you have any where abouts where this convict could be located, please contact this toll free number on bottom of the screen." Then Juan's photo popped up on the right hand corner of the television screen. "It's a mad, mad world after all." Maria said with a very affable voice. "Yeah Babe, you most definitely got that right." Bobby agreed laconically.

* * *

The very next day, Juan was less than four hours away traveling from Chattanooga Tennessee to reach Atlanta City. He pressed on the brakes when he came to the steep hill that leads into firecracker city remembering when he was young. Him an a few other friends traveled up to lookout mountain to throw rocks off it at the town that sits right beneath it, then the thought swiftly erased from his mind when he leaned up to sit straight. Once he observed a highway trooper off side the road with his speed detector monitoring the speed of travelers. "Sit up straight Juan, and whatever you do don't panic." He nervously coached himself with a whisper and a few moments after Juan passed the Officers aim. The highway trooper sped out from the soft soil with his emergency code three lights flashing coming from behind in full speed. "Shit! I knew it." He barked frantically, while looking in the rear view mirror pulling over acting civilized and his heart didn't waste anytime sinking to his feet when he saw the highway trooper jet pass pulling over a eighteen wheeler from J.B. Trucking Co. in front of him. Juan sighed when he yielded to a complete stop with heartfelt anxiety. "Damn. That nearly made me shit on myself." He said with relief cautiously proceeding back on the road with his driver side blinker flashing. He was stiff as a board driving pass the patrolman, that was about to give the driver a sobriety test. "Good luck, Mr. Drunk ass!" Juan teased with a smile advancing away.

* * *

The soft kick ball bounced onto the sidewalk from the park playground area, as eight year old Cindi went storming off after it before it bounced in the street. "Thank you, Mr." She said with a benign tone of voice, extending her hands out grabbing the ball from Norman grasp. "Cindi you get back over here, right this moment young lady!" Cindi's mom yelled from the sitting bench. Cindi immediately skipped over to her mom. Norman flipped his collar of his jacket up to his cheeks disguising himself, then scampered away up the side walk vanishing. Mr. Wallace was coming out of Stater Brothers grocery store in Twenty-nine Palms heading back to his Excursion unit truck, when Derrick Akins and his older sister Confy came pulling along side him. "Excuse me, sir." Derrick yelled, from the passenger seat grabbing Mr. Wallace's attention. "Hey, how you guys doing?" Mr. Wallace answered with candor. "Pretty good, sir. My sister and I recognized you from being on the news looking for that missing kid, Bryan Smith, so we waited until you came back out the store." "Hey, pull over for a second along that Excursion truck right there so we can talk." Confy pulled her vehicle into the empty slot on the drivers side of his truck where he stood. Mr. Wallace reminded himself to open his driver side door to his three piece Chester fried chicken on his seat to ask Derrick a few questions on what he's possibly knew about Bryan's where abouts. "So do you know anything his where abouts?" Mr. Wallace asked concern. "Well, something like that." Derrick answered bleakly. "Hell. Don't hold back no longer, let me have it." "To be straight forward with you sir. I just heard through the Twenty-nine Palms gossip, where he possibly could be located." He inquired truthfully, then added. "Matter of fact, follow us, and I'll point out the location. If you don't mind." "If I don't mind? Lead the way." Mr. Wallace concluded, hopping in his truck, firing up the engine and once Confy spotted him waving his arm out the window, she threw her floor shift gear into drive taking off. "I hope this kid knows what he's talking about." Mr. Wallace whispered sharply, accelerating off the Stater Brothers plaza lot behind Confy heading eastbound to the 62 Highway. Confy yield into the middle turning lane preparing her turn on to Larrea Avenue, and when the left turn was made she guided him to the side of the road along the out skirt of some trailer homes. "There aren't any houses right here." Mr. Wallace said skeptically, when he pulled on Confy's side of her vehicle. "Of course not, my brother just said keep heading straight up this road, and right before the street Sunny Slope that's where the rumor stops." Explained, easing her car back into drive with her foot pressed on the brake. Mr. Wallace leaned over deeper into his passenger seat with the window down repeating everything she told him. "Kids, you did a great job. Thank you very much for this vital information." Then he sped off up the curvy street of Larrea Avenue while Confy and Derrick did a u-turn heading back toward the 62 Highway to pick her daughter up from Oasis Elementary School on the Elpeso Drive.

* * *

Maria opened their drawer where she normally kept her nine millimeter hand gun inside the study room, and slid the chrome twenty-one shot magazine into the bottom of the handle. She was preparing to get inside her S.U.V. to ride around to see if she could spot Darla or Norman for that matter, and apprehend them before they decided to take another innocent soul. Once she slid the active bullet into the chamber, she slid the hand gun into her holster and clamped her walkie-talkie to her waistline heading off to her S.U.V. Maria decided it would be a good idea to radio Richard to see if he wanted to join her on her short quest before Antonia made home from school. "Maria to Richard, come in Richard." she obliged when she fired up her S.U.V. reversing out the driveway taking off. Richard rushed out the Blue room to snatch his radio from the battery charger by the computer. Then said "This Richard, go head Maria." "It wasn't nothing to surprising. I was just wondering if you wanted to ride along on my short quest?" "That's affirmative Maria." "That's a copy, over and out."

* * *

After twenty minutes lapsed by, and Richard was finish posting the victims photos that feel off the wall a few days ago. He went walking to his bedroom where his babygirl was located which was his forty-five automatic, babygirl is what he always likes to call it, now he'll be ready when Maria arrives. As he was entering his bedroom he thought to himself. "Persistent and Determine Maria is to catch Darla whom we now know is responsible for the mysterious murders. If only I would have had her on my team back when it all started, this whole matter probably would have been solved by now or a lot of lives would had been spared." Then he thought over all it wasn't any use to be thinking about how things would have been, cause what's done is done and the bottom line is now that they're on teams its finally time to get down to the thick of things. When Maria pulled up in his driveway five minutes later, the dogs alerted him by barking at her presence. She was waiting in her SUV. "Ah hush that noise Roxy. You barking like somebody trying to kill you." He instructed his female watch dog while heading toward the passenger side of Maria's vehicle. "Good afternoon, Mrs. Maria." He greeted closing the passenger door. "Good afternoon, Mr. Richard." She replied back with a identical friendly leer reversing out the driveway.

* * *

When Juan finally made it to Marrietta Cob County, Georgia, he exited the Plumtree Road. "Damn! Shit looks different from the last time I saw this place." He said thoughtfully traveling to the stop sign on top of the ramp. But when he made the right turn he hurried and swerved along side the road, once he heard a Frito Lay truck horn blowing and nearly coming into a collision with him. "Ooh! That was a close call." He said excitedly yielding back on to the road. Juan immediately tuned the radio down when he suddenly realized he was hearing a cell phone sounding off punctuating the backseat area. "Those rings coming from the inside of this car." He said dryly, reaching his hand to the passenger side back floor to grab Carmen's black leather brief bag, in which he just now noticed, seeing how he never looked in the back seat area. Juan placed the brief bag on the passenger seat immediately scrambling his hand inside for the cell phone, although it stopped ringing. "Ahhhh . . . , here we go." He echoed, when he located the phone pulling off from the third light. He took a glance at it and the screen read "Missed Call." Then he happily realized he didn't only come up with a car but a phone as well. It couldn't get any better other than staying a free bird, he thought with a nod. Once he made a left turn at the light, he remembered belatedly. He forgot the directions to his moms house, so he flipped the cell phone open to dial his moms extension and whispered placing the phone to his ear. The phone rung four times then he heard his mom pick up. "Hello." "Momma, this Juan." "Juan. How you call me straight through?" "Momma look, hear me out. I'm on my way right now and I need your help momma. I promise I'll explain to you once I get there, so what I need first is to get the directions again. Alright. I just made a right turn at the Plum Tree exit, and drove down two lights." "You suppose to had made that left at the first light and the Castle Brook Apartments will be around the bend." She explained simply while still being stunned about hearing that he was on his way home. "How you get free son?" "Momma I just did a u-turn, I'm on my way right now. I promise I'll explain to you when I get there." Juan said disconnecting the line accelerating on the gas.

* * *

Maria and Richard had just arrived to the inner part of their town driving slow making sure they was catching everything. "I guess this part of town is going about their normal lives, I see." Richard pointed out clearly enough. "Or should we just wait until we get a call, instead of looking for the problem?" "Well even though we've only been riding around for thirty minutes. I still would say that's a good option." Richard divulged agreeably. Maria made a right on the main road taking off back to Richards house.

* * *

Mean time Juan was just pulling inside the Castle Brook Apartments following behind a U-Haul moving truck entering through the remote control gate, which he thought was perfect timing and when he located his mom parking lot court, he slowed his speed making sure there wasn't any undercover police waiting for his arrival. Juan continued looking around parking the stolen car right in front of his moms apartment building, and once he killed the engine everything suddenly got quiet and vivid. He quickly shoved the cell phone in his right front pocket, snatched the keys from the ignition, and exited the vehicle. Then swiftly strode up to his moms apartment, stopped at the door, inhaled then exhaled then knocked on the door three times with a closed fist. The second Ms. Tucker heard the first knock on the door. She immediately approached it to peek out the peep hole, and once she actually saw it was her son standing on the other side of the door like her dream come true. She breathlessly snatched the door open without delaying any further. "J.T, I can't believe this!" She condoled reaching out hugging him close in disbelief that she was actually touching the baby boy she birthed as miles became air space and years of him being away became a perfect moment. "I really missed you, Momma." He mumbled out teary eyed making his embracement tighter. "I love you too son, and I sure in the heck missed you too." She countered back with a strong Southern accent, leaning back with her hands on his shoulders to scrutinize his face once more. "Come on boy, you get in this house. Come on now!" She said then ten minutes later after Juan and his mom took their seats on the big suede sofa Mrs. Tucker through her left palm up to her mouth area staring at him blankly from the story he was telling her, then she raised her palm down saying. "Son, I'm extremely happy to see you, but I can't believe you escaped the authorities." "I know momma. I guess I wasn't in my right mind at the moment, but when I saw that crazy guy Norman unlocking my cuffs leg shackles with the key, I just took off running behind him and another guy he un-hooked." He responded smoothly. "Well for some reason they haven't checked here yet for you which is a good thing, so what are your plans now that your wanted son?" She asked while staring affronted for his answer. Juan threw up a blank stare looking away from her gaze, then faced back toward her only to reply simply again. "What I had in mind was to stay here for a second or two at least until I figure out other options." "Son, of course you know I been missing you so, but I think you should turn yourself in at least that'll make things lighter on yourself, J.T." "Momma, its not that easy." He objected sincerely. "Why not son?" "Because its more to this a lot more." Juan stopped his conversation to take a deep breath then continued. "Alright, before I got myself in this mess, a group of guys from a gang called Nazi Lowriders was out to kill me for secretly stabbing and killing one of their members after I was rat packed inside the license plate workshop and the guy I killed friend's knew exactly who did it, but they didn't let the guards know cause they were out to get me themselves, momma." Ms. Tucker raised her palm right back up to her mouth, nodding her head slowly in disbelief looking at her son thoughtfully saying. "J.T. that means, if you do end up getting caught for escaping those horrible thugs gonna be still patiently waiting to take your life." Tears started rolling down her Carmel checks while she extended both arms out to give him another hug like when she first opened the door. "Son I don't know where I went wrong it seemed like when your father passed away. I dropped my guards on you and your sisters, cause if I never did that your sister wouldn't never had to do what you did to her no good boyfriend in the first place." A glimmer of comprehension lit Juan's eyes from thinking that it was in fact the truth, what his mom just explained to him. Ms. Tucker finally embraced him to wipe her tears away with both palms. "Momma don't cry, I'll be alright. Its just I can't go back to that place for nothing in this world, so I have to make the best of this freedom I got."

CHAPTER SEVENTEEN

IT WAS THREE days later, when Maria, Bobby and Antonia went out to have dinner with Mr. and Mrs. Barberi at Sizzlers Steakhouse. Mr. Barberi was one of Bobby's new employees at his attorney law firm, who successfully won twenty-five murder trials with Yagmen and Sons Law Firm.

* * *

In the meantime, Norman was fifteen minutes in walking distance away from the Gates residence, walking around their neighborhood grocery store stealing work gloves, and a pack of variety lunchmeat slices, but when he glanced up at the tinted camera bubbles planted throughout the entire store, he realized he should go tuck the items inside his pants in their public restroom, so no one would observe him stealing, nor recognize his identity. The second he made it inside the men's restroom, he started tucking the items away inside his pants legs that was cuffed into his socks. On the way out the restroom door a man gave him an approving look as if he had saw Norman somewhere before, but he continued on to the restroom stall paying Norman no further attention. Norman escaped un-noticed out the store and disappeared off to his mission. Most people remembered Norman Gandy from his corrosive arrogance and sardonic humor back in the days before he became completely mentally disturbed. He would never be the type of person that could walk the streets legally another day in his life, especially being on John Walsh's Americas Most Wanted, and this little hometown of his is surely in for a big surprise with him walking the streets unsupervised and freely.

* * *

Four o'clock on the nose, the Michigan Town School District Supervisor Mr. Zimmerman phoned Richard from his request a couple days ago. Richard was tapping away on his computer keys ignoring the phone ringing endlessly, until he finally pushed himself away from the computer desk in his roller chair snatching the phone up. "Hello, this better be important!" "Hello. How you doing Mr. Owens? This is Mr. Zimmerman the Supervisor of the Saginaw School District." Richard's demeanor changed within an instant saying. "Oh Hello, Mr. Zimmerman. I apologize for that outburst comment I've just made." "Oh. No problem, but it is sort of in the middle of the day, oh yeah. I'm contacting you to let you know the materials you and Mrs. Gates requested is right here in my hands. I have the list of all Mary Swartz classmates and most of them is still living here in town, may I remind you as pioneers. I guess it is kind-a hard moving from a town where most of your family grew up throughout generations." "Yes, that's true. Is there anyway you could fax that list to me as soon as possible? It'll be greatly appreciated, and also thank you for your quick response and professional studying in this matter as well, sir." Richard said politely. "All you don't have to call me sir. I work for a living for Gods sake, but I can fax this material right now if you like." "Sure, that'll be great. My fax number is one-eight-eight-eight-five-five-five-zero-zero-zero-one." "Got it Mr. Owens. Give it about two to three minutes and it'll come up available for you. I hope this will be helpful for you and that lovely lady Mrs. Gates, talk to you later." Right when the phone line was disconnected, Richard got up from his computer chair taking off to his blue room where his fax machine was located and no later after he placed a half a pack of blank paper inside the paper slot. The faxed materials Mr. Zimmerman promised him came printing out the front receiving tray. "Oh yeah, this is big. Maybe we can solve or predict our little problem around here." He said beneath his breath walking out the blue room with the faxed material at his fingertips.

* * *

Darla was in the town cemetery sitting on the ground with her back leaned up against Mary Swartz tombstone resting up, and recouping for her next mission of vengeance on the town while singing and humming real low. "Mary, Mary, here to stay alive, Mary, Mary, soul will never die. Mary, Mary, back for revenge. Mary, Mary, gonna kill all her friends." Darla continued humming the note staring blankly at adult Raven birds a little ways in front of her. The cemetery was one of the most quiet and deserted placed in the town of Saginaw, due to everyone didn't visit on normal occasions thinking it was haunted, cursed and secluded. Since Mary Swartz body was buried there years ago.

* * *

After time flew pass Norman made it to the gates residence standing in the backyard behind their big shade tree that sits exactly in the middle of the yard. He just momentarily stood there camouflaged beside it with one shoulder leaned against it, chewing on his last slice of lunchmeat he stole staring at their patio door.

* * *

Richard decided to dial Maria's extension to let her know about the documents he received from Mr. Zimmerman, but instead her answering machine picked up on the third ring saying. "Hi. This is the Gates residence. Sorry we missed your call, but your call is very important to us. It'll be highly appreciated if you would leave your name, number and the time you called. We promise We promise to return your call at our most earliest convenience." Once he heard the beep, he said. "Sorry, you missed my call Maria. This is Richard calling at four-twenty-five, and I was just calling to inform you that Mr. Zimmerman, the Saginaw School District Supervisor, faxed me those materials we requested, so if you could please give me a call as soon as you receive this message. Bye." Then he pushed the off button to his cordless phone, and immediately placed it on the battery charger. Once he heard the low battery beeping sound indicating low cell.

* * *

Norman quickly dropped the empty lunch meat package on the ground beside the tree, when hearing their phone stop ringing. He rush fully slid his dirty hands inside his gloves, and took off up to their patio door. The house was pretty much dark as the sun was setting by the moment. The kitchen light partially illuminated the living room, Norman could tell while he approached gazing straight ahead through the open blind of the patio and right when he was about to step on the concrete porch, his right foot went sinking in to mud from their water creating puddles on the ground. "Shit! Great, its just my luck." He cursed raising his foot that was covered with mud, then he leaped on the porch avoiding his left foot from sinking as well. He could tell by far they wasn't home and reached out to grab the patio door handle with his gloves on seeing if it was un-locked or not to ease his tuition. "Ok, the patio door is locked. Now that means I have to bust that window out over there." He whispered to himself glancing at the study room window. When he made it over to the window, he tried glancing through the cracked curtain even though he couldn't quite distinguish much from the light turned out inside, and with no further delays. He reached back with his hand balled into a fist, and gave the window a good solid punch. When the window shattered it made a real loud sound that made him be that much quicker in scrapping the glass particles off the window ledge to climb inside. Norman carefully reached his arm inside the hole preventing himself from getting cut up from the inside handle. Then hopped up on the window ledge causing a metal and glass picture frame with Bobby and Maria over their picture table that sits right beneath the window ledge. "Damn it! What the hell wrong with me?" He grumbled, face and quickly tossed it back on the table. He started feeling his way around the room with his eyes wide like a half dollar coins, sense the sun was no longer giving light. "Ahh . . . , here we go." He said with calm felicity, once he felt the study room door knob leads him to the rest of the house. The moment Norman opened the door. He cautiously peeked his head out slowly making sure he wasn't being set up as if someone had been watching him the entire time, and once he saw the coast was clear peering down the darkness of the hallway that was barely being illuminated by the kitchen light. He took off walking up the hallway remembering where the stairs was located from the last time, he broke into their home through their jarred kitchen window., while everyone was away and he was forced to hide himself off inside their food pantry, when he heard them coming through the front door. That's the day he'll never forget when he came creeping out the pantry room, and Jasper caused the plate to shatter onto the floor room being caught off guard. Norman communicated his senses at the bottom landing of the stair casing saying. "Where's that damn cat at? Here kitty, kitty, kitty. "Followed by some ticking sounds that normally catches cats attention. Jasper quickly came prancing down the steps out of no where to his successful cat call. The second Jasper made it to the bottom landing by Normans feet in striking distance, he quickly snatched up into his arms tightly then Norman took off to the kitchen area to grab a butcher knife from the dish rack. Jasper started purring then sensed the sign of danger, once Norman placed the butcher knife in his hand. "It's gonna be alright, kitty. Real soon now." He said then went walking up the stairs with Jasper still tightly in his arms while his hand was firmly gripped on the butcher knife handle with his gloves on. When he reached the top landing, still being cautious. He started opening each door he approached thinking insanely with a whisper. "Hum, you're not in there. Let's see, hell you're not in their either." He continued mumbling to himself as if expecting to find Maria asleep in one of the bedrooms, then he quickly coped and attitude with Jasper, when the thought of him blowing his first chance to destroy the Gates family ran across his mind. "Well, little kitty, you're really about to get it now." He said angrily while his voice held a conspiratorial note, heading back to where the stair casing is located. He made a sudden stop in the hallway before going down facing himself toward the wall with Jasper elevated with his left hand staring momentarily into his big green eyes saying. "Its just gonna hurt for a second." Jasper out of fright struck Normans face with his sharp displayed claws drawing fresh blood from Normans right cheek. "Ah, shit! You damn cat! Yeah, that's gonna let you live!" He whined in pain. Norman grew even more frantic, mad with rage wedging Jasper against the wall, then without any remorse. He immersed the butcher knife completely through his midsection. Jasper gave out a high lament meow agony sound before he died hanging stuck helplessly with a butcher knife plunged through him and into the wall. Once Norman saw blood running from the backside of Jasper down the wall, He smudged two fingers with his gloves on into Jaspers blood and wrote above his head onto the wall. "This should have been you, Bitch!" Then he strode down the steps and out to the front door leaving Jasper dead nailed to the wall with his tongue hanging visual from his mouth.

* * *

Britney Levels and Tara Peers are next door neighbors, were old school best friends with Mary Swartz coming up in grade school years ago. Britney is a very good looking Caucasian woman with straight silky black shoulder length hair, with bluish eyes, five-eight in height, a hundred and thirty pounds with pretty white teeth she always gotten compliments for. She was raised by foster parents. When she was fourteen years old because her natural parents were killed on a airplane flight that was over taken by a Terrorist group and crashed. The house Britney inherited from her foster parents after they passed away was being cursed for participating in their old friend Mary Swartz hanging inside the school girls restroom. Britney was sitting in her living room with her twelve year old daughter, Dorothy and her nine year old daughter Anna. While combing Anna's hair she said. "Dorothy, go close and lock the back yard garage door. It's getting dark." "Do I have to go out there alone, mom?" "Yes, because I don't want your sister catching a cold again with her hair being damp, besides if you would of locked it after you was playing, you wouldn't have to be doing it now. "Yes, ma'am!" Dorothy agreed blandly taking off to do what she was asked.

* * *

Darla broke into the storm basement that's located in the backside of the Sunnyside Mortuary, due to it had gotten a little colder and she had o other place to go. It was totally dark inside the basement once she closed the doors heading down the steps, and when she made it to the bottom landing. She bumped into a stack of guest chairs and with a low growl, she immediately flung the chair out of her path then laid down on the cozy concrete floor on her side with her hands between her legs to keep warm.

* * *

Tara was knocking on Britney's door to come and sit with her cause she got bored sitting in the house by her self with nothing to do. Her husband Nelson took their son and daughter to their grandparents in Cleveland, Ohio, for the weekend to celebrate their Grandmothers birthday. While Britney was in the kitchen putting away the left over food in the refrigerator after she was through doing Anna's hair, Dorothy yelled out. "I'll get it." Jumping off the sofa and racing over to the door. "Hello, Mrs. Peers. Where's Justin and Rhonda?" "Oh, their gone to their grandparents house for the weekend. Is your mom woke?" Tara asked managing a smile. "Dorothy. Who's at the door?" Britney yelled from the kitchen sink. "It's Mrs. Peers, mom!" "Have her to come in Dorothy!" "You can come in and have a seat in the living room, she'll be right with you." "Thank you." She said stepping inside. Tara is a Caucasian and Irish woman, five-nine, one hundred and thirty-five pounds, long dark brown hair, greenish eyes with a dimple chin and low self-esteem that was very attractive. The second Britney came entering inside the living room where she was sitting on the sofa waiting. Britney told Dorothy and Anna to go up to their rooms until her company leave. "What. You mean to tell me your hubby allowed you to come over, and sit with me for a little bit?" "Actually, no. He went to take the kids over to my mother-n-laws house in Ohio. So what you was doing, girl?" What was I doing before I started putting the food away? Oh yeah I just got through combing Anna's tangled hair." Britney answered thoughtfully. "Oh, did you see the news yesterday evening, Girl?" Tara asked excitedly enough. "No, not at all. I be so busy around here, I barely get a chance to catch upon my soap opera "Passion's" why what went on?" Tara scooted back on the sofa with her legs crossed saying. "Its this deranged girl by the name of Darla Phelps, that calls herself Mary." "Hold on. Did you say Mary?" Britney interrupted with a slight discourse expression. "Yeah. That's exactly who I said, but you know that remind me of?" "Who?" "Our old best friend who was hung years ago, Mary Swartz." Britney wanted to say no Tara it was your best friend, but instead she said. "You know what. I was afraid you was going that, isn't that a little bit creepy?" "Yeah. It sure is, but wait, that sounds like the same strange girl or woman years ago on the news, who told the homicide detectives her friends came up missing from playing some Mary game, and that was around the same time all those mysterious murders and disappearances reoccurred." Tara explained clearly. "You exactly right, so this Darla Phelps person is five years younger than we are." "Lets see, we're thirty-eight years old. Yeap, I believe so." Tara agreed.

* * *

It was ten-thirty in the morning, when Bobby, Maria and Antonia made it back home from having their quality time dinner with the Barberis. Once Maria pulled in their driveway killing the engine. Bobby easily noticed light glaring through their jarred front door. "Babe, did you close and lock the front door, before we took off to the Barberis?" Maria sharply glanced over to the front door following his gaze saying. "Of course I did. I know that for a fact." Then she glanced back at him to studying his face expression while reaching through the middle of the front seats to un-strap Antonia. "No, Babe. Hold on for a minute. Wait here with Antonia, while I check things out first." Maria pulled her arm back to her side slumping back into her position following his order. Bobby stepped outside the charger taking off slowly up to the front door, and once he eased the door open with his left palm he didn't hesitate not one minute in noticing muddy footprints on their living room tan carpet, and that's when he knew something was terribly wrong. It was his basic instinct to race off to grab their nine millimeter handgun from the study room for safety. When Bobby made it in the hallway where the stairs begin, he squinted his eyes to the top landing and saw Jasper had been abolished. After seeing that he went into a hostile state of mind storming off to the study room. Bobby clicked the light on then noticed their window had been completely busted out by seeing the curtains breezing freely from the air outside. Then he rushed over to the desk drawer, snatched it open and gripped the gun in his hand. Maria was getting very impatient sitting in the quiet car from not seeing him coming back out to explain to her nothing was wrong, so she stepped out the car locked and armed the vehicle with the alarm remote while Antonia momentarily slept on the backseat. Bobby was on his way up the stairs after noticing more muddy footprints below their picture table where their window was shattered and continued up the steps with the gun drawn out in front of him. Maria came walking through the front door and also realized an intruder had been in their home again from the mud prints on their carpet. "Babe, where are you?" Her voice echoed. Bobby didn't grunt a reply, he just moved along slowly to the top landing and he couldn't help but to stop and read what was written above Jasper's head in blood. "This should have been you, Bitch!" He whispered thoughtfully. When Maria turned toward the top landing of the stair casing where Bobby was standing at the top, she couldn't believe what she was seeing with her very own eyes. "Babe, is that Jasper?" She asked with hype concern, slowly walking up the flight of steps with her eyes glued to the sight of him. Bobby placed the gun in his pants below his stomach saying, "It sure is honey, be careful, I still have to search the upstairs bedrooms." Then he frowned with his left hand placed on Jaspers neck while his right hand was gripped on the butcher knife handle. He was thinking to himself, Jasper was getting stiff like a stuffed animal displayed in a museum when he snatched the butcher knife from his midsection. Once Jasper was dismantled from the wall, Maria said skeptically. "This should have been you, Bitch!" As Bobby immediately placed Jasper and the knife on the ground taking off slowly to Antonia's room with the gun extended out in front of him, Maria automatically knew with in her mind who was responsible for such an courageous cruel act. Bobby eased Antonia's door open with his hand while his right index finger was relaxed on the trigger cautiously working his way in. He slowly angled the weapon in every direction his eyes landed on, then kneeled down on his knees taking a quick peek under her bed and once it was clear he crept over to the closet. "Honey, you think I should call the authorities to set up an perimeter?" Maria asked, entering inside the room. Bobby didn't reply immediately from being in self thought snatching the closet door open, remembering her closet was chosen as a hiding spot the last time. "Babe, did you hear when I asked you if you wanted me to call the authorities?" She once again asked with a straight face. Bobby was more at ease once he seen the closet was clear as he finally answered. "No, Hon. We don't need the authorities to get involved, and have the media broadcast our home and situation over the news trust me the news will get involved, especially by me being a known attorney and you as my wife being the number one paranormal activity investigator." Maria gave it a quick thought nodding her head saying. "Yeah, you right babe. I'm going back outside to check on our princess, be careful." She suggested walking out of the room. Right before she was about to go down the flight of steps, she couldn't help but to stop and look a Jasper with an expected tear crawling down her right eye taking off down the steps. Bobby stopped at their bedroom door when he noticed more muddy footprints stopping at their door without going in. He knew he couldn't let that throw him off cause his heart wouldn't be at ease unless he did check the room. Maria pushed the disarm button on the car and immediately stopped in her tracks rooted to her spot, when she heard something within the darkness like a can had been kicked. Then she proceeded on realizing it could have been a stray animal in someone's trashcan. Maria quickly opened the back door, placed Antonia in her arms, armed the car and took off back inside the house. Bobby was on his way back down stairs to check the food pantry, plus get a green plastic trash bag to place Jasper inside while Maria slowed her pace coming through the door thinking he was still up stairs when she heard some noise coming from the kitchen area. "Babe, you frightened me a little. I you was still up stairs." She admitted breathlessly, once she saw him coming from the kitchen with a trash bag in his hand and the gun inside him back pocket. "Well, everything else seems to be pretty much alright, except for poor little Jasper that is. Honey I may have to sleep inside the study room tonight, and take off work tomorrow to fix the window." He assured her before taking off up stairs to Jasper. Maria turned around with Antonia's head relaxed on her shoulder to close and lock the door, then immediately laid her down on the sofa with her tiny arm over the tinker bell doll. Moments later Bobby came heading toward the kitchen patio sliding door with Jasper in the bag, and when he placed him inside the trash can on their porch right beside the patio door, he yelled back inside. "Honey, do you wanna do a ceremonial cleansing over Jasper for the family." Maria didn't have a problem at all, matter of fact she figured it wasn't even optional, being that Jasper was like a son they had. "Sure Babe. That'll be great!" She agreed without hesitation going over the patio. They both stood side by side in front of the trash can container underneath the glaring porch light, when Bobby calmly said. "Do you want me to say a short ceremonial, or do you Honey?" "I'll say it, you ready?" "Give it your best shot." He answered, as they both grabbed hands and bowed their heads. "Dear Father in Heaven of all things, we're coming to you with bowed heads on the behalf of our little cat Jasper, who was dearly like a son to us. We're hoping you look over him where animals go when they pass, so please send him to that favorite place with all the Gates love. Amen." Maria had to cut the ceremonial short from feeling that lump approaching inside her throat, from being very touched about God hearing their final words and farewell to Jasper. "You alright, Honey?" Bobby asked concerned putting his arm around her with his hand brushing up and down her arm soothing her to let her know everything is gonna be alright followed by a kiss on her forehead.

CHAPTER EIGHTEEN

THE VERY NEXT evening Britney and Tara was pulling out Britney's driveway as they both agreed last night to get a few items from the town grocery store. Britney needed to get anniversary flowers fro her foster parents burial site, like she normally had every year and for feeling bad about missing their last years anniversary. She sparked up a conversation with Tara when she powered her XM Radio off as they traveled up the road. "I can admit, this town be having some weird mysterious murders ever sense Mary got hung." "And you know what Britney? I honestly couldn't believe it when they told me Marilyn Woods, Terri Lovetts, Alicia Wagner, Melinda Simpson and Libby Copeland just stood there laughing and watched her strangle to death." Britney was quiet for a second with tense concentration feeling confused about if she should tell her best friend something she never knew. "Tara, I have something to tell you. Remember a few weeks before Mary was murdered, when me and her got into a fight in the gym?" Tara quickly nodded her head, yes, with her undivided attention. "Well, the day everyone was passing the note around about what they were going to do to her, I made sure I was the first person in the restroom to see if they were going to do what they said, and I'm not going to lie, I couldn't help but to laugh when I saw her legs stop kicking and hanging motionless. Once everyone saw her eyes become suffused with blood from her strangulation, we all vacated the restroom and that's why no one was caught. When I ran out the restroom I saw the janitor staring me dead in my eyes then he closed himself inside the janitor's closet." Britney yielded into the middle lane preparing to make her turn onto the grocery store parking lot. "Britney, I can't believe this. You stood there and watched her die too? How could you?" Tara fumed for explanation staring at her with a discourage look. "Why you looking like that? It wasn't like I'm the one who killed her!" Britney whined coming into a complete stop parking her vehicle. "Well you might as well had. You could have stopped it but you didn't, so you good as well as killed her." Tara barked getting out the car when they both exited the vehicle Britney put her hair in a ponytail with her pink bow and once they both was inside the store Tara grabbed a shopping cart saying. "Britney, while we're here getting some anniversary flowers your foster parents, I think you should buy some flowers for Mary also, just to let it be known her mistakable death is being mourned. You know?" Britney blandly nodded her head saying. "Yeah, that is good idea. You most definitely have a point." The moment they turned the corner on the last lane, they discovered some beautiful flowers real one and fake ones. "O-k, here we go right here. Go pick out some flowers while I grab a few tomatoes and onions." Tara insisted walking away from the cart, seconds later she accompanied Britney in choosing some flowers. "Britney, these look like some good flowers, at least they smell good." She said thoughtfully, while stealing another smell from the bouquet of flowers. "I think I'll get my foster parents these, and give Mary these ones." "Britney don't buy Mary no Carnations, get some of these." Britney placed the Carnations back inside the bundle of the assortment and grabbed the flowers Tara was handing her while saying. "Oh I like these, and they're nothing but six-ninety-nine plus taxes. I'll get Mary these, you ready?" "Yeah, cause my hubby chirped me on my Nextel saying he was only fifteen minutes away when we pulled off." "You didn't let him know we were going to the store?" Britney asked as they was approaching the cash register counter. "No, because we were only going to be gone a hot moment." After they purchased everything they needed, they was back inside of Britney's aqua color Legend pulling off the lot. "Do you think we should stop at the Cemetery first before it gets any later?" Britney asked pushing the fluid button to the clean her dry spotted windshield. "Yes. That'll be fine." By the time they traveled three lights from the grocery store a man in a Dodge Magnum accidentally ran the light coming from the opposite direction with his hand smashed down on the horn. He was two seconds away from colliding with them. "Britney! Did you see that man?" Tara shouted, grabbing the dash board all at the same time. "Did I? That stupid ass almost killed us, geez!" After the mere accident they both focused back to their conversation. "Tara other than what just happened, there have been a lot of times I wanted to take off and search for my real parents, and leave this Jinx town. What's here besides woods, oak trees, houses and murder victims that haven't been found, nor solved?" Britney asked surveying the scene to answer the question herself. Tara immediately shrugged her shoulders, "I'm sure anyone of us could up and move else where to start having just as many problems as we do here?" "No, refrain that. Other places will have other problems as well, but nothings near what we done had or yet to have. I shall add, besides it's some crazy willie stuff going on around here nowadays. Look what you told me last night about that news coverage on, what's that girls name?" "Darla Phelps." Tara reminded her. "Oh yeah. Look at her situation for example, you get what I'm saying?" Tara blankly nodded her head with approval turning her head to glance out the window.

* * *

Maria was just now checking her answering machine from yesterday evening of the two messages she forgot to check because of the terrible incident Jasper had gone through last night. "I wonder who these two messages is from?" She said beneath her breath pushing the playback button, while Bobby was in the study room fixing the window. The first caller was Richard saying in his raspy tone of voice. "Sorry, you missed my call Maria. This Richard calling at four-twenty-five pm and I was just calling to inform you that Mr. Zimmerman the Saginaw School District supervisor faxed me those materials we requested, so if you cold please give me a call as soon as you receive this message. Bye." After she heard the other message being a telemarketer from Verison, she immediately picked up the phone to dial his number. Once the phone rung three times, Maria heard a woman's voice pick up saying. "Hello." Maria was puzzled for a moment thinking she may had dialed the wrong number, then she finally said. "I'm sorry, I may have dialed an incorrect number. Is this Mr. Richard Owens residence?" "Yes you have the right number, may I ask who's calling?" Darlene asked while zipping up the back of her skirt with the phone rested on her left shoulder. "Sure. My name is Maria Gates, I'm one of his Colleagues." "Honey, come to the phone. You have a phone call from Mrs. Gates!" Darlene yelled to the back bedroom. A few seconds later, Maria heard him get on the phone line saying soberly. "Good afternoon, Maria. I was wondering when you was going to return my message." "Actually, I didn't get your message until now cause something terrible happened last night." She answered taking a seat at the kitchen table. "What happened last night?" He asked with sympathy in his voice. Maria took a quick breather before saying. "Last night Jasper got killed and I have a strong felling it was that damn messed over in the head Norman Gandy who done it." Then she added. "Excuse my French Richard but I'm still highly upset behind that." "It's ok, so you actually think Norman may be the one who done this to your cat?" He asked, while silently waving goodbye to Darlene after she blew a kiss to him heading out the door. "Yes, that's correct because where Jasper was stuck to our up stairs hallway wall with a butcher knife plunged completely through his midsection above his head with his own blood had a messaged written out saying. 'This should have been you Bitch!' And you know what Richard every since I moved back to this town taking the opportunity to work out the privacy of my own home for this special assignment, it seems like things been happening in a domino effect to cause me to go hack-a-berry crazy." She said with strong enthusiasm. "No Maria. Don't think that, cause believe me the same thing was making me think the exact same way. Before I retire on all those previous mysterious unsolved murder cases, ever since that young lady Mary Swartz got murdered. The town been getting swept clean, but then came those five kids in the woods waking the dead again. Which they never found out who was responsible for her hanging, but anyways. Not to be taking you on a roller coaster ride, I'm terribly sorry to hear about Jasper." "Thank you Richard, it'll be o-k. Oh yeah, I was doing some research about how long a ghost could exist. Well actually my facts came from the top existing records saying ghost are not immortal and according to the Gazeetteer of British Ghosts, seems to deteriorate after four hundred years. The most outstanding exceptions to this normal 'Half Life' are the ghost of Roman Soldiers three times reported still marching through the cellars of the Treasures house, Your Minister, England, after nearly nineteen centuries. The book's author, Peter Underwood, states that Britain has more reported ghosts per square mile than any other country with Borley Rectory near long Melford, Suffolk, the site of unrivaled activity between eighteen-sixty-three and its destruction by fire in nineteen-thirty-nine, so other than saying all that I hope generations to come we don't have to deal with Mary Swartz ghost for four hundred years. And I see somebody been getting a little sexual healing lately. No, I'm just teasing you." Maria said with humor cracking a smile. Richard laughed heartedly saying. "Oh, you mean. Darlene? "Yeah . . . !" "Yeah. She's an old friend of mines, oh. I have a few things solved right now as far as perfect matches of victims on this school list of ours. Maria can you hold on for a second while I get the list of names I yet written down?" "Sure." She countered quickly, then started tapping a classic rhythm on the kitchen table, as she heard him fumbling through some papers on the other end until got back on the phone. "Alright here we go, we have Shelly Ciera whom was murdered with her boyfriend. The young lady they found floating in the shallow lake, which doesn't have anything to do with what I'm about to say. Well we have Britney Levels, Melinda Simpson, Terri Lovetts, Marilyn Woods, Tara Peers, Alicia Wagner, Tracy Khan, Laura Baits and Las but not least Libby Copeland. That's really the only ones still living in town, besides guys that were also classmates of hers." He noted. "Richard. We most definitely have some big help here, great job. Would it be ok to swing by tomorrow afternoon to finish going over these notes with you?" "Sure that's fine, oh for the record those kids I just mentioned off my notes was the ones supposed to had participated in Mary Swartz hanging, but back when I was on the case. The school Janitor Mr. Banks let it be known to the principal. He saw every last one of these girls I named come storming out the girls restroom, except maybe one or two girls on the list that didn't participate with the bunch and that's Tara Peers, Tracy Khan and I shall add one more Laura Baits. Oops, I didn't see this name." "And who's that, Richard?" "Oh, it's another classmate by the name of Marissa Lopez." "Richard, so that means, if we don't capture Darla Phelps like we've mentioned once before in one of our meetings we'll have to say goodbye to these ladies also?" "Yes that's exactly what I'm getting at, but like I somewhat mentioned before she's on a far more mission than that. She wants this entire town to rest in peace, if you know what I mean. Well thanks for returning my call Maria. I'll see you when you swing by, bye." Once Maria placed the cordless phone back on the charger, she took off to the study room where Bobby was still fixing the window. "I just got through talking to Richard on the phone about some very important materials we requested from the school district." She said when she entered the study room. "I'm almost finished, but I hope I beat the darkness with this window." "Oh you will Babe. Mr. Handyman of mines." She added, then thought silently, 'Why did the conversation with Richard feel like De'Javu? Oh God, Maria, you're gonna need a physiological evaluation after everything's all said and done.'

* * *

Britney and Tara was just now parking along the curvy road on the Cemetery grounds from taking a detour drive to converse. Getting out of the car they both went looking for Britney's foster parents burial site. "If I'm not mistaken, I think their located over there by that tree." Britney said thoughtfully. "I never been inside this Cemetery before and we just live five blocks from here, it sort of reminds me of the Pet Cemetery. What's that building over there?" Tara pointed. "That building right there is where they hold the ceremonial service before someone gets buried, here we go. How could I ever forget they're located over here, amongst this tree? Maybe it's because we came through the other side." Britney took her foster parents flower's out of the bag then bent down to gather up the old stems to place inside the empty sack. She put the new flowers on both of the tombstones that are right beside one another. After that she stood there with a moment of silence saying to her parents. "I'm very sorry for not remembering to come and do what I promised to do every year, and may God forgive me for that." Britney opened her teary eyes from the sympathy of respect venturing through her body. Then Tara started rubbing her back with her right hand letting her know every things fine and it was ok to cry. Once she saw the first tear dancing from Britney's eye. "Thank you Tara, so are you ready to go place these flowers on Mary Swartz tombstone?" Britney asked, while wiping the running eye liner away from her bluish eyes. "Sure, why not?" When they found Mary Swartz burial site, they easily noticed she was only buried seven rows down from Britney's foster parents. Tara placed the flowers on the top of her tombstone, they both bowed their heads as they agreed for Britney to say a few words of prayer. "Dear Mary, you were a good friend to us all, and Mary, I also remembered when we both use to cheat with each other on our tab testing, until we finally got caught. Mary you use to tell me all your secrets about your boyfriend Michael. the things I always teased you about all the time. Mary me and Tara are here placing flowers on your tombstone today to let you know you are being mourned over and surely not forgotten. God please look over Mary as we are here hoping she didn't die in vain." Once Mary's name was mentioned for the fifth time a slight breeze blew the flowers off her tombstone, plus at the same time Darla's eyes popped open in the pure darkness of the mortuary storm basement. It was very abstruse to Britney and Tara on why wind was carrying on the way it was to cause the flowers to fall completely off the tombstone and onto the ground. "Tara, I think we better leave that didn't seem right." Britney said without malice in her voice. Darla quickly pushed open the storm basement doors and just stood there at the top of the steps to adapt her eyes to the daylight. Britney and Tara stopped in their tracks once they heard the echo sound from the wooden doors hitting the concrete ground. "What was that noise Britney?" Tara asked questioningly with their attention drawn toward the ceremonial building. Britney shrugged both her shoulders saying. "I don't know, but it sounds like a door slammed from that building." As soon as the chills raced up their spines they took off in a rush to the car. As Britney and Tara pulled off it was so quiet inside her car you could actually hear their heart beats pumping after each other making a five heart beat pattern. Darla came storming late around the building observing Britney's Acura Legend slowly pulling off around the curvy pavement. Darla stood at the front gate a half of a minute after they pulled off the Cemetery grounds watching them drive up the road, then she took off walking off side the road behind them. "I hate to say this Tara, but something's always was spookily about Mary Swartz. To tell you the honest truth, I think that's why Libby Copeland, Terry Lovetts and Alicia Wagner passed that note around to want to hang her." Britney said, while adjusting her rearview mirror thinking why her foster parents wanted to live up the street from the cemetery grounds. Tara just sat silently and speechless that rest of the way home, until she saw her husband Nelson's Nissan Quest SUV backed in backwards in their driveway. "Well I see my hubby back. Thanks for taking me to the grocery store with you Britney. I might come over to talk to you later, or it depends on what he had planned for us." Tara added, while grabbing the grocery bags from the passenger floor. Darla saw Britney's brake lights blare up a few blocks down, once Britney yield pulling into her driveway. The second Britney stepped through her front door Dorothy came skipping up saying. "Dang, Mom, why you take so long? Oh yeah, Mr. Nelson called looking for Tara, and I also cooked Anna some Fish Stick's and French Fries." "Thanks my big girl." Britney said with a smile advancing away to the kitchen.

* * *

Nelson was sitting in the living room stabilized watching the news lady broadcast. "Alfred Carbajal one of the Michigan State Prison escapees was apprehended earlier this morning inside the towns Greyhound Bus Station using the pay phone, after purchasing a bus ticket to Houston, Texas. This is Angie Lincoln signing off and have a great evening." Then he quickly muted the T.V. when he suddenly heard the door close. "I knew I heard the door, Precious." "I went to the grocery store and the cemetery with Britney to place some anniversary flowers on her foster parents burial site." She explained, then gave him a door and Dorothy told me already, oh. This morning they caught one of those prison guys that escaped at the town Greyhound Bus Station using the phone after he purchased a ticket." "Now why would he want to go to a Greyhound Station for, knowing he's been on Americas Most Wanted nearly every Saturday so far?" Boy these people now a days is getting bolder by the second, and I only could imagine if that new invisible experiment fall through and get into the wrong hands what this world would become." She scoffed, then walked off to the kitchen. Once she placed the tomatoes and onions inside their refrigerator vegetable pan she yelled out with enthusiasm. "Honey! What you wanna eat tonight?" Tara eyes got wide with girlish excitement.

"I though you was going to cook some Pepper Steaks, Rice and Onions when I got back. Why? What you have in mind?" "Oh nothing, I was just thinking girlishly that's all!" Nelson said after licking his lips. "That'll be good too. I'll hold that thought against you for after dinner dessert." He agreed ebulliently. While Tara was running fresh dish water drifting off to a blank stare from feeling confused about what her and Britney had witnessed inside the cemetery. The sound of the faucet water brought her back to the present. Darla was at least a block away from Britney and Tara's house walking and breathing strongly frowning deviously through the thick bangs of her hair that covered her entire facial area. People that was driving passed her kept staring thinking she looked familiar from the news, but unsure as they sped along up the road paying no further attention and getting to their destinations.

* * *

Maria was up stairs scrubbing the rest of Jasper's blood off the wall with sanitizer soap water while holding back tears. Antonia came scooting her Barbie sit down car up to her mom in the hallway saying questionly. "What's that Mommy?" "Its nothing honey, mommy wasted ketchup on the wall." Maria lied. "Ketchup?" Antonia asked curiously, making a cute frown scooting her Barbie car in reverse with her tiny feet. Then scooted forward into her room that was set up like a little house of its own with her toys in the form they were in. When Maria finally was finished scrubbing the blood off the wall she stepped up to Antonia's door with a bucket of soapy water saying. "Come on Princess Tonia, we're going back down stairs to Daddy. No, keep your car parked there in this little house of yours." Maria took her right rubber glove off to grab her hand and once they made it down stairs to the kitchen Antonia glanced on the chopping counter pleading for Jasper's cat treats saying while pointing. "Mommy, I wanna feed Jasper some cat treats. Please, Mommy, Please." Then she stormed into the living room to look behind the curtains where she always knew Jasper to be hiding at. A bit of nausea gripped at Maria's stomach when she heard her mention Jasper. "No, Honey, Jasper isn't behind the curtain." "Where is he Mommy, in there with Daddy?" Antonia asked, pointing at the far wall. "No, Jasper ran away. He might be back and he might not, but if he doesn't soon, Mommy will get you another Jasper, ok?" She lied again with saccharine sweetness this time. Antonia quickly nodded her head yes, then went looking out their living room window, saying in a concerned tone. "Come back Jasper, I need to feed you." Maria stood there silently staring at Antonia's body print behind the curtains, thinking to herself. 'She don't know how many lies she could keep telling her daughter about Jasper.

CHAPTER NINETEEN

DARLA STOPPED ACROSS the street in front of Britney's house in seeing Britney's Aqua color Legend parked in the driveway. Dorothy was sitting on the sofa next to the window looking at old re-runs of Lizzy McGuire, until she suddenly felt like she was being watched so she looked through the window by slowly opening the window blinds. She crotched onto her knees and spread the blinds with her index finger and saw Darla standing across the street in front of their neighbor Pauline's house. It was spooky the way she kept staring with her bangs hanging over her facial area. Quickly releasing the blinds with fright and said breathlessly. "Mom! Its a woman outside across the street staring at our house. She looks spooky to me Mom. Hurry up!" She added with hype excitement. Dorothy turned back toward the blinds as Britney came rushing over to the window. Dorothy said Amazingly. "Wait a minute! Where she disappear too?" "Dorothy your just trying to scare me." "Mom, I promise you on Grandma and Grandpa. I saw a strange lady staring at our house." Dorothy assured her. "You once said you saw shadow people with hats on in your room the other night, but were they there when I checked? No, so it may had been another figment of your imagination. A lot of that's been going on." "Mom, well just go out there and check for yourself. I know what I saw." Britney immediately got up from the sofa to step out on the porch pacing from one end to the other saying underneath her breath. "Now why would someone want to just stare at our house, amongst all the rest of the houses planted on both sides of the street." But I have no reason to doubt my daughter, she did feel quite a bit shaken, besides she never lied when it came to her Grandparents. Hum?" Dorothy let go of the blinds again asking throatily when Britney came inside locking the door behind her. "Did you see her, Mom?" "No, I didn't see anyone, but a stray dog sniffing along the curve." She answered her truthfully taking off calmly to the kitchen, when Britney's conscience made her take a peek out the kitchen curtain and got startled when Anna's soft voice caught her off guard when she asked. "Who out there, Mommy?" "No one hon. Go back in the living room to pick all your toys off the floor, Mommy will be in there." Britney said softly. Anna didn't hesitate in walking off to do what she was directed to do. After she watched Anna walk off, she once again went peeking out the window. Darla was kneeled down out of eye sight below the outside window ledge with her back pressed against the house, staring craftily up at the window. After finding nothing Britney got her self together and went walking back into the living room tossing the incident out of her mine and feeling more convinced that Dorothy was only trying to scare her with Halloween on its way.

* * *

When Maria glanced out their patio sliding door, she discovered the same dried up muddy footprints they didn't notice last night trailing up to the patio. Focusing her eyes far out where the footprints had came from and when she observed something lying on the ground by their big tree. Stepping out the patio door to see what it could be. Bobby was looking at her through the window as he drilled a screw into the window frame wondering what she was going to do by their tree and when she picked up the empty lunch meat package off the ground with two fingers and placed it in the trash can on their patio. Maria snapped the lid down tightly once she got a strong whiff of Jaspers decomposed body. "Babe, guess what I found out in our backyard." She said soberly coming through the study room door. "I saw you pick up something while I was here struggling with this window of ours what was it?" He asked concerned enough while she started clearing the document off the desk. "Can you believe it was empty lunch meat package?" She replied pausing what she was doing. "A lunch meat package?" he echoed with a pause then proceeded while listening. "Yes Babe, a lunch meat package. It might of been Normans." Bobby screed the last screw into the frame and when it snuged tight, he said. "There I beat the darkness by a long shot." Then he stood there opening and closing it testing the finish work. "Well its good as new." He added placing the drill inside the Black & Decker casing.

* * *

Norman was walking pass Mr. Dan's Food Dinner and discovered a old Nineteen eighty-four F One-fifty pick up truck with the windows rolled down parked on side the building on the blind side. He quickly circled around the block taking a short cut through the alley to see if he could hot wire it, and when he crept up to the truck from the backside of the diner he said underneath his breath. "It couldn't be anymore easier." Discovering the passenger and driver window rolled completely down with the dash wires in plain view. Looking around to confirm if anyone was coming or looking he then slipped on his dirty gloves, but as he put his hand on the passenger door handle he bent down beside the door when hearing a couple come from around the corner laughing and walking to their vehicle that was parked four cars away. Norman slightly braised his hand with the gloves on along his forehead and once the couple pulled off without noticing him he rush to open the door thinking to himself. "Ok no more wasting time hot wiring this here truck so I can get out of here." He slid into the driver seat to reach under the dashboard beneath the steering column to pull the wires out a little more. "Hum, lets see, red is hot, black is ground and this one is the ignition wire." He said thoughtfully. Taking his gloves off and placing them on the seat so he could strip the wires he chose. As soon as he was finished stripping the wires he twisted a couple together then started tapping the twisted wires against the hot wire. "Come on Damn it! Start for Daddy." He whispered when he heard the started turning as if it was trying to crank and when the engine fired up he was racked with relief like he cracked a multi-million dollar code. Then he snatched the steering column gear down in reverse to back out then took off hauling ass through the alley disappearing into the evening traffic.

* * *

Night time had finally settled in and Britney was sitting in the living room fighting her sleep from continuous times going to the kitchen window, thinking she was hearing scrapping sounds outside the house. Dorothy had dozed off to sleep on one end of the sofa while Anna was stretched out on the other end with her arm hanging motionless from it. Darla was in the backyard remembering through her conscience of Mary on what Britney participated in the hanging of her death, but now the vileness of Mary was contemplating vengeful acts with the Macabre leaves to destroy her. Britney became more tired by the moment from her eyes putting in over time fighting to stay open, but when they finally closed permanently, she immediately got bright eyes once she heard one of the up stairs bedroom doors slamming shut. "Oh my! What was that?" For a moment she miscalculated both of the girls weren't sleep on the sofa until she saw Anna's little arm hanging motionless from under the blanket as the rest of the blanket covered her entire body from head to toe, and that's when things became more vivid to her. "Now what could that had been? It sounded like one of the bedroom doors slamming." She figured thoughtfully, standing up on her feet aiming the remote control to the TV. to mute it so she could zero in while saying with a low voice. "Maybe it was Dorothy's door closing from the air through her open window." She concluded taking the mute button off when she saw the program C.S.I. Brazil coming on. Darla was in the backyard with her right arm stretched out in front of her, animating the oak leaves that was in a pile up to Dorothy's open window with a slight breeze. "Oh God!" Britney screeched with her hand placed on her breast in hearing the sound of glass bursting up in Dorothy's room above her that caused her nerves to also jerk with erratic violence.

* * *

After Nelson and Tara finished their Pepper Steak and Onions that still lingered in the air throughout the house, Nelson sits on the bed waiting for his lovely wife to come out the bathroom with the lingerie he surprised her with. With the anticipation on a little kid on Christmas morning. He started reminding himself on what he was thinking about on his way back home while he waited on what he was going to do to her in bed. It had been quite sometime now since they made love to each other under these circumstances. The kids nearly heard everything that went on that night, and when the next day arrived they were confronted by their daughter as they all were sitting at the breakfast table. When she said while making circles in her strawberry hot cereal. "You guys need to be a little more quiet and considerate on your love making." The second the bathroom door opened the thought disappeared instantly when he saw his beautiful petite wife in the short see through Teddy lingerie with one hand on the door seal while the other hand was relaxed on her hip looking like a million dollar pork chop to him with his mouth wide open. "So are you going to sit there and stare with your mouth open or are you going to tell me how I look?" Nelson was so amazed on how sexy and tasty she looked, he barely caught the last words that came out of her mouth. "Mommy, you look great! Now let Daddy get a closer examination on your luxurious goods." The he padded his right hand on the soft comforter that covered his legs.

* * *

Britney finally built herself up with courage, taking her first step up the stairs then she suddenly stopped in her tracks only to glance over to her daughters making sure they was still asleep. Then proceeded up to the top landing. Reaching the top she started to feel like it was more than her and her daughters in the house, and the night air breezing from beneath Dorothy's bedroom door from the window being open made the up stairs feel like a morgue. Britney slowly crept up the hallway, until she turned around with her heart steaming like a coffee pot making that whistle sound. Taking a deep swallow from feeling the knot in her throat when seeing the shadow of circles beneath Dorothy's closed door. "What in the world?" she said blandly with a touch of amazement in her voice, and a shudder racked her body. "Who's there?" As her bottom lip started to shiver from the combination of being cold and frightened on what she may encounter. Britney was so focused in on the shadows beneath the door, she didn't even recognize one of her square windows on her kitchen back door being busted. When Darla punched the door window out with her bare hand, Dorothy changed position without fully awaking to the noise she heard. Darla reached her right hand through the now open space and unlocked the knob she slowly opened the door like a thief in the night demanding to take a soul. Britney stood there paralyzed for a moment not knowing if this was a dream or reality, but either way. She was very desperate on finding out what was on the other side that had so many shadows and she was more afraid to go all the way back down stairs to the only phone her daughter Anna hadn't broken but if I did what would I tell the authorities? She thought silently Darla left the kitchen door wide open once she stepped inside making her way in the other part of the house and when she entered the living room she noticed Anna and Dorothy stretched out in a deep sleep on the sofa, then she stepped up to Dorothy with her right hand elevated in the air in a striking position, but right when she was about to strike she quickly drew her attention to the noise Britney had made up stairs from rambling through the hallway closet looking for a potential weapon that could be used to defend herself before opening Dorothy's door. Darla eased her hand down then slowly and desperately went walking toward the stairs with her bangs hanging over her face like a sheep dog. Dorothy softly started scratching her neck and sniffing in her sleep, when she began to smell a fetor stench smell from Darla's closeness. Then she relaxed back into her dream she was having of flying in the mid air with Harry Potter and a over sized Dragon. "I can't believe, I can't find anything harmful to use." Britney indicated grabbing the glass vase from the shelf stepping back over to Dorothy's door. Darla slowly crept up the stairs trying not to be heard as Britney finally reached out for the door knob with vase elevated in her hand, prepared to knock the sense out of whatever was behind the door. She slowly started turning the knob when she realized she was wasting far to much time then thinking to herself 'I wonder what ever was behind the door do it even know I'm on the other side about to open it?' But it was a little to late to answer her own question cause the door knob was turned as far as it could go. Britney took a deep breath exhaled then pushed the door wide open as if she was trying to catch whatever off guard. She stood there numb with her eyes and mouth wide open as the glass vase dropped completely from her hand. The sight she was seeing made her not even hear the vase shattering to the floor. Britney slowly stepped inside the room to get a closer look to see if her eyes was deceiving her from seeing the Macabre leaves circling six feet high in a bodily form Darla stepping inside. "Oh God! Who are you and what you doing in my house?" Darla didn't say a word, she just raised her right hand demanding the leaves to savagely attack. Britney screamed from the top of her lungs when she felt the first cut on her body from the Oak leaves point's as they completely shredded her clothes and sliced her body allover like razors whirling around her. Darla just stood there with a crucial smile on her face like she was enjoying the fainted cry agony cry Britney was letting out. When no sound was any longer coming from Britney she eased her hand down tilting her head to one side to another being fascinated on what terrible damage the leaves did to her body as she laid on the ground. It wasn't a single piece of clothing left on her skinless corpse all was left was a full corpse camouflaged inside a puddle of blood and a pile of leaves. The door opened on its own allowing Darla to vacate the room. Once Darla made it down stairs she passed Anna and Dorothy on the sofa without paying any further attention to them feeling very convinced about what Britney had brutally suffered and seconds later Darla disappeared into the outside darkness. As time elapsed by Dorothy realized in her dream it was starting to snow when her and Harry Potter was taking a nice walk to Mr. Wizard's castle. Then suddenly she broke her sleep when she heard Anna mention it was cold. Dorothy sat upright rubbing both arms with her hands and when she glanced through the hallway said in a worried tone. "Where's Mom?" Anna rubbed her eyes shrugging her shoulders she didn't know. Dorothy slid her feet into her house shoes anxiously wanting to close the door, but when she made it to the kitchen door she took a speculative glance out the door making sure her mom wasn't out in the backyard, then noticed the door the pieces of glass scattered on the floor she barked in disbelief. "Whoa, who did this?" Seeing her breath in the coldness of the kitchen front door being wide open reminded her how cold it was in her dream. When she closed and locked the door she thought to herself, 'what differenced did it make if the window was already busted to lock it?' The second she was about to yell out to her Mom she heard Anna scream like she never heard her before, it was the type of scream that made chills come upon her body instantly a second later she went rushing back into the living room only to find Anna was no longer sitting on the sofa and quickly strode up the steps nearly clearing three steps at a time to shorten her climb. Anna came storming out of Dorothy's room into the hallway shouting in tears when she heard Dorothy racing up the steps calling out her name. "Some things on the floor!" Anna yelled pointing then started shaking both her hands like her hands was on fire and she was trying to shake 'em out. Dorothy scooted Anna to the side fearfully rushing up to her door and screamed. "Mom!" At that point she panicked storming out the room nearly snatching Anna's arm out of socket by rushing her down stairs so they could get out the house. They made it to the front door. Dorothy unlocked the dead bolt snatched the door open then they ran out. When Tara heard some little kids call out her name repeatedly she jumped out of bed while Nelson was asleep with his head buried into the pillow from the good loven she had given him earlier. She rushed out of bed so quick she nearly forgot to grab her house coat to cover her nakedness going out the bedroom door. "Good gracious. Who could that be pounding on the door like that, especially this time of night?" Dorothy saw Tara's porch light click on, she impatiently yelled out. "Mrs. Peers, please hurry!" "Dorothy?" Tara said thoughtfully snatching the door open and when the girls raced up to her to hug her waist she said while feeling them shaking from being so frightened. "Calm down, girls. Now tell me what's going on?" "Mommy's in the house dead and we're scared!" Dorothy's voice was so loud and lament it awoke Nelson out of his sleep, when normally he could sleep through a tornado and a earthquake all at the same time. "What's all this hype ness about?" He asked when he stepped inside the living room. The second Tara recognized her husband standing there with his men's tight Speedos on she quickly pulled both the girls heads to her stomach to avoid them from seeing his bulge in his underwear. "Honey we need to call the authorities the kids said something happened to Britney, and put some clothes on for heaven's sake."

* * *

Once daytime arrived detectives was still doing their investigation inside Britney's home. When Maria pulled up and appeared the house she leaped over a wet spot on the porch ducking her head under the homicide tape entering the front door, and she immediately saw the camera flashes snap after snap glaring on the up stairs wall. The crime lab must of taken over two hundred snap shots of Britney's body while realizing they never experienced such brutal murder such as this caliber in their whole line of history. "Hello Mrs. Gates, good morning well at least for us, but before you go up stairs. I think you'll be needing one of these." Detective Fredrick said while pulling a mouth mask from the latex box. "Is it that bad?" She asked grabbing the mask from his grasp. "Oh yeah, the worse if you ask me. We already had two officers rush out the door vomiting." "Oh, so that's what that was on the porch. I had to leap over." Once Maria proceeded up the steps a young officer approximately in his early twenties came striding down the steps with a handkerchief held up against his nose and mouth area nodding his head to her as a indication of hello. Maria at least saw thirty more flashes being snapped from the glare of the wall, when she made it to the top landing hearing a officer saying to a Detective where the body is. "I've never seen nothing like this." Hearing that just made her want to take all day to approach where they was. Maria quickly stopped in her tracks when she observed the red skinless corpse lying on the middle of the floor helpless in a pile of leaves and partially dried blood, even part of Britney's scalp was ninety percent hairless. Officer Haynes slightly got shaken up once he realized Maria was standing in the door way behind them. "Hey, nice to see you Mrs. Gates. I didn't hear you approach." He said with a friendly smile. "Hello Everyone." If she didn't see the exposed breast on the victim, she would of thought it wasn't a human at all by the body of Britney being skinned so badly and curled up and the longer she stood standing there the more the smell of dry blood seeped through the edges of her latex mask. "So who else lives here with the victim?" She finally asked once they was through taking their photos. "I'll let Mr. Coleman here answer that for me." "I'll be delighted to show you Mrs. Gates, shall we?" He insisted angling his hand toward the bedroom door. "Sure." Maria was very happy to leave away from the scene, plus that's the only thing she hated about her job and that was seeing sights that's extremely un-natural photogenic.

Once Maria and Mr. Coleman made it to Tara's front door he knocked on it three times with his big solid gold college ring from Xavier. Mr. Coleman is a tall man at six-four, weighing about two hundred and thirty pounds, freckles, deep eye sockets and a reddish goatee mustache beard. When the door came open Maria instantly noticed two little girls sitting in the middle of the living room floor looking at cartoons. "Hello, Mrs. Peers. I'm sorry for interrupting you once again and I'm fully aware you had a rough night as well as a rough morning, but this is one of our Paranormal Investigating Officers Mrs. Gates and she was wanting to know if it was ok to come in and ask a few questions, if she may?" The whole time Tara was mind searching in her mind why Maria looked so familiar, the it struck her and saying soberly to Maria. "Oh, I remember you, I saw you on TV a long time ago about that crazy guy Norman Gandy. I'm sorry, where's my manners? Yes, please come in." "Great. I guess I'll leave you two alone so you both can talk. There's plenty of work to be done next door. Be easy on her Mrs. Gates." Mr. Coleman said with a smile then placed away. "You have such a nice home, Mrs. Peers. Maria said when she stepped inside. "Why Thank You, Mrs. Gates." "Is it ok to ask questions in front of the little girls?" "Oh certainly please have a seat at the table, matter of fact, there the victims daughters, and basically they're the ones who has the most part of the information what little there is to know. Excuse me, Dorothy can you come here for a moment please? Not you Anna, you can finish watching cartoons." When Dorothy came to sit at the table Maria noticed dry tears on her cheeks. "Hello Dorothy, my name is Mrs. Gates. I know this is a rough time for you and your sister right now and I can only imagine the grief your going through, but I must ask you these questions to help find your moms killer. Is that ok?" Dorothy quickly nodded her head yes. "Good. Do you know who or what could of did this to your mom?" Dorothy sat there with a blank stare mind searching cause the disturbing over lapping images of her mom kept on interfering with her thoughts, till suddenly Maria heard her innocent soft voice say. "I really don't know, cause last time I remembered my mom being alive was when we all were sitting in the living room looking at Malcolm in The Middle, until me and my little sister Anna fell asleep on the sofa. I must of gotten tired of my mom getting up saying she thought she heard some scrapping noise against the house." "Not to cut you off Dorothy, but did you ever see your mom go out the front or the back door?" Maria asked softly. Once again Dorothy had that same blank stare, that look like she was deeply concentrating on the question Maria asked. "No. I don't think my mom opened the door she didn't like opening the doors when it got dark. Wait. I did notice when I woke up from being cold that the kitchen backdoor was swinging wide open, and when I went to close it I found out the window had been broken out, but once I closed the door I heard my little sister scream out from the top of her lungs. That's when I ran up stairs where my sister was, and saw mom the way she was." Tears came running down her cheeks like rain drops on a windshield. "Its ok Dorothy. at least you and your little sister Anna wasn't harmed." Maria consoled her. Tara stepped to Dorothy's side to hand her a tissue. After she wiped her eyes and cheeks Maria suddenly saw her eyes get bright and wide as Dorothy said. "You know what Mrs. Gates earlier yesterday when my mom got back from the grocery store I called her to the living room window when I saw a strange looking lady standing across the street staring at our house." Maria flipped the page on her memo pamphlet then asked her if she could describe her. "Well. I really couldn't see her face clearly but I do remember seeing her long bangs hanging over her face though and when I turned back around to show mom the lady had vanished. Really that's about all I know." Maria reached inside her folder to hand her one of her business cards saying. "Dorothy, you're a very smart young lady and thank you for this very vital information you've given me. I wish you and your little sister the best and if there's anything I could do for you in the future, please see that you contact me and let me know. Mrs. Peers, thank you also ma'am." "Oh, it's all my pleasure Mrs. Gates. I'm a very big fan of yours." Tara countered quickly with a smile. From hearing that sweet comment Maria's dimples in her cheeks popped up instantly as she walked over to the door. "Bye, girls!" She shouted going out the door. "Bye, Mrs. Gate." They all choirly yelled back.

* * *

Three days later when Maria and Richard was having a conversation over the collective notes she had gotten from Dorothy, and once Maria got through explaining the facts, Richard scratched Britney's Levels name off their notes of the classmates. Maria placed her hot cup of French Vanilla coffee on the table to let Richard know what she suddenly realized. "You know what Richards?" "What's that Maria?" "It didn't dawn on me until now as I was going over our notes. I realized Tara Peers name, she's Britney's next door neighbor." She explained with a puzzled expression. Richard stood up from the table and started pacing back and forth saying. "If this is correct, what your telling me is you were in Tara Peers home and didn't even realize it until now?" "That's correct." She countered shortly. "Well, well, well. If that doesn't make things a little easier, I don't know what to tell you." He said lively while clicking his pen repeatedly with both hands behind his back, which Maria thought, was very annoying to her. Richard settled back down at the table saying. "I guess that leaves us five possible suspects left, and that's Marilyn Woods, Terri Lovetts, Alicia Wagner, Melinda Simpson and last but not least Libby Copeland." Maria's eye pupils dilated while saying. "I think we need to have a little chat with our friend Tara Peers to see what she at least knows about Mary Swartz and her possible murder suspects. That's still a crime that's unsolved you know." "It sure in the hell is Maria, it sure in the hell is." Richard agreed with a nod.

CHAPTER TWENTY

HOURS LATER MARIA and Richard pulled up in her SUV in front of Tara's house for questioning. They both exit the vehicle like the episode 'Cops' making a drug raid, but right when Maria was about to knock on the door Tara's daughter Rhonda opened it saying. "Yes, can I help you?" "Hello young lady. My name is Mrs. Gates and this is my partner Mr. Owens, we're here to speak with Mrs. Peers if it isn't inappropriate." When Tara daughter turned around to yell out. "Mom!" Maria and Richard glanced at each other feeling a instant relief to catch her at home. The second Tara approached the door Richard licked his dry lips to apply moisture to them from seeing how beautiful and lively she looked. "Oh, Hello Mrs. Gates. I didn't expect to see you, so soon." "I know Mrs. Peers and I didn't expect to come back on a short notice, but me and my partner here Mr. Owens was wanting to know if we could ask you a few questions concerning Mary Swartz?" "Mary Swartz?" Tara countered with a certain look on her face, as if she was shocked to hear Mary's name. "Is something wrong, Mrs. Peers?" Maria asked concerned enough after studying her face expression. "Oh no nothing's wrong. I was just amazed to hear her name, please once again come in." "Thank you." "You'll have to excuse the house this time, my son and daughter just got back from visiting their grandparents." She explained closing the door before guiding them to the dining room table. "Where's the other two little girls, Anna and Dorothy?" "Oh they were taken in by the Social Service. I feel so concerned for them." Tara replied with her hand upon her cleavage, where Richard's eyes were glued until she moved it. They all sat at the table Rhonda shouted out from the back room in anger saying. "You better stop hitting me!" "Excuse me, Mrs. Gates and Mr. Owens, both of you guys need to get somewhere and have a seat, I mean it!" "Shall we get down to business?" Maria asked opening her folder. "Sure, why not?" Richard couldn't stop staring at Tara, and he sure in hell was glad she wasn't paying any attention. "How did you guys know I knew Mary Swartz?" "Oh we checked into the old school records not long ago." Maria answered truthfully. "Oh, I see so what you need to know beside she been passed away quite sometime now? Matter of fact a few days ago me and Britney placed flowers on her burial site." "That was a very nice thing to do, but we was needing to know if you knew where anyone of these girls or ladies, I shall mention reside at? I can guarantee you whatever information you do decide to give up will remain confidential." Maria assured her. "I mean, I don't want to get into any trouble." Tara said rocking her legs underneath the table. "Oh no. You're not in trouble at all, and you wouldn't be if you do the right thing." Richard told her. Once Rhonda came walking into the dining room area Tara turned around immediately saying. "Hello, I still have company here!" Then a few seconds later they all heard Rhonda's bed room door slamming. "Kids, now you promised me no one would find out, whatever I tell you right now?" "That's one hundred percent correct." Maria assures her. Tara took a big sigh, then whispered. "I'm here to tell you guys I didn't actually see what happened to her with my very own eyes, but Britney told me Libby Copeland and another girl was going around the school with a note telling everyone what they were going to do to her. I guess everyone who received this note arrived in the girls restroom to see what was going to happen. Britney told me it all started out as a game to scare her until they started seeing her eyes being suffused with blood and her legs stop kicking. She said that's when everybody took off running out the restroom and basically that's all was told to me." "See that wasn't so hard. Now can you tell us where anyone of these girls live by the name of Marily Woods, Terri Lovetts, Alicia Wagner, Melinda Simpson and our one and only Libby Copeland?" "Let me see, well if you'll excuse me for a moment.

I could at least tell you where two of them live and their numbers. I have that info in my personal phone book." "Sure, that'll be great." Richard spoke up politely, while Maria managed a smile. A few moments later Tara came back at the dining room table with her pink phone book saying. "Ok, here's Alicia Wagner, her address is 71059 Mile Road and her number is five-five-five-one-one-seven-zero. Now here's Libby Copeland's, address is 1620 W. Dale Avenue, and her number is five-five-five-zero-zero-two-five. How could I ever forget hers?" Maria closed her folder on notes saying. "See that didn't take, no time. We sure appreciate your time and effort in this matter Mrs. Peers, I guess we should be leaving so you could pertain to your normal life." "You guys have a safe trip." Tara said very mannerly when Maria and Richard stepped over to the door to go out. Rhonda didn't waste no time coming in the living room after they left asking. "Who are they mom?" "No one, I'd ever want to see again." Tara responded gruffly lighting a Virginia Slim cigarette while peering out the corner of her dining room window watching them pull off.

* * *

Darla was walking on a deserted road when a Saginaw Police Officer was attempting to apprehend her. Officer Perry pulled over in front of her, exited his patrol car saying. "Excuse me young lady, you wouldn't happen so to be Darla would you?" He knew it was from the wanted photo drawing in his patrol vehicle. Darla stood there staring for a moment, then nodded her head no. "I'm sorry, but I think I'm a have to take you into custody." A lady citizen in a Nissan Altima was slowly driving pass looking being very observing like any ordinary citizen. Officer Perry tilted his uniform hat mannerly to her indicating that everything was under control and to keep going, but once he focused back to Darla reaching for his handcuffs. She raised her right hand toward the woods and trees animating the Macabre leaves to her command. Officer Perry couldn't believe what he was seeing to the point. He forgot to draw his weapon from his holster, instead he took off running to his patrol car. Once he slumped down into the driver seat fumbling with keys to make his escape. The animated leaves came blowing through the half raised passenger window cutting and slicing his body waist up as the leaves just kept whirling. Officer Perry gave out a loud scream, then instantly had a heart attack. Darla eased her hand down controlling the leaves to a halt as they laid scattered on the dash board, the floor and the half skinless bloody disemboweled body. Allowing her to escape with in the woods and the down trodden trees that was being blown by the wind.

* * *

Maria observed an unfamiliar primer down grey F one-fifty pick up truck pulling away from their house once she turned the corner on their street, and when she pulled into the driveway. She felt inexplicably uneasy when she thought about seeing the passenger front tire pop on the curve as it was pulling off. She exited her SUV going up to the front door; she noticed a note inside the screen door. "I wonder who that could of been?" She said beneath her breath. Grabbing the note from the screen door, she could admit that she felt a little queasy and nerves when she saw red spots on the note, until she realized it was nothing but ketchup. Opening the note the first words made the hair stick up like static on the back of her neck by saying. "I'm gonna kill you, sooner or later Bitch!" Maria crumbled the note looking toward the direction she seen the truck pulling off saying. "Yeah, Norman, if I don't get you first Asshole!." Then she unlocked the door and went into the house. Making it inside despite the house was feeling vacant it also seemed demand cozy from the clouds forthcoming outside from the rain and although she was brave. Still she didn't like being home by herself, especially sense psychopath Norman had escaped and out for revenge. Maria felt she needed not to think about it before the thought got her anxious and spooked out cause Norman was a great deal of a threat. He was someone who didn't have a heart at all, at least he made it seem so, she thought. Maria flinched to where she had to catch a shrill rush of air and swallow when the study room phone rung catching her off guard. The house felt so empty every time the phone rang it echoed throughout the entire house, coming to that conclusion as she easily approached the phone. "Hello, this is the Gates residence." At first she heard complete silence, then a loud breathing sound. "You damn pervert!" She fumed slamming the cordless phone down on the charger disconnecting the line, and right when she was about to walk away it rang again. She snapped rushing over to the phone saying. "Listen you Mother Fucker! You make one more call to my residence, I'll get in my car and find your ass! I sure will as mother nature be my witness!" "Babe, babe, its me. What's going on?" Bobby asked curiously. "Oh Bobby, I'm glad its you!" "Is everything ok at the house, Hon?" "Well now it is sense your on the phone. I just got a call from that perverted Norman. When you and Antonia coming home? I decided to come home early today." "Well that's why I called the house phone to let you know we was on our way. I tried your cell phone, but it went straight to the answering machine." Maria had to strain to hear Bobby after sound of the crackle of thunder and lightning that had begun. "I'll put dinner on Babe, and give our Princess a kiss for me, be careful." "I will, love you. Bye." When Maria hung the phone up she could of sworn she heard some constant tapping up stairs while she stood there for a moment in self doubt listening. Then she came to the conclusion to grab her nine millimeter handgun from the drawer just to be safe than sorry. When she made it to the up stairs top landing she firmly gripped around the rubber handle ready to fire at will at anything that has a life, though coming to find out it was just spattered raindrops tapping hard against Antonia's bedroom window sun guard. "Good, it was nothing but the rain drops on her outside window sun guard." She said with relief lowering her weapon looking out her window seeing the sky growing dark from the thick clouds and rain. Then reminding herself that she needed to go make a important phone call before putting dinner on. Libby Copeland rush fully wiped her hands on her cooking apron when she heard the phone ringing. "Don't everyone rush at once, I'll get it! Hello." "Hello. May I speak to Mrs. Copeland, please?" "Her speaking, can I ask who's calling?" "Sure. This Mrs. Gates, I'm an Investigator from the O.F.P.A. Office." Once Libby heard the word Investigator, irritation, fear and guilt of her past gripped her. "Hello, Mrs. Copeland, you still there?" "I'm sorry, yes I'm still here." "Did I catch you at a bad time, Mrs. Copeland?" "Oh no, it's ok. I'm just over whelmed on how hard it's raining outside, but anyways how can I help you Mrs. Gates?" "Well, I was wanting to know if me and my partner Mr. Owens could meet up with you for an interview?" "What is this meeting going to regard too?" "Actually its concerning to a young lady by the name of Mary Swartz, and your encounter with her." Maria heard Libby breathing get stronger on the other end. "And when would this interview be conducted?" She asked blandly. "Would tomorrow afternoon be fine?" "Sure, that's fine with me. I guess I'll see you then Mrs. Gates, bye." "Bye." Maria countered back, then took off to make a quick dinner.

* * *

Bobby turned his windshield wipers on higher to fight the heavy raindrops as Antonia was looking out the back window at the rain examining the under and lightning strikes, flinching and blinking her eyes wishing they make it home safe to mommy. Bobby turned his Bruce Springsteen Greatest Hits cd down glancing in the rearview mirror at her saying. "Antonia is Daddy's Princess still buckled down in her seat belt?" Antonia nodded her head yes, then turned her head back toward the window to further study the lightening. A few minutes later they was pulling up in the driveway. Antonia leaned up in the backseat in her seat belt saying happily. "Yah Daddy, there's mommy's car." Maria was sitting at the dining room table reading a Tech Now Magazine issue waiting for the Spinach to get done, but the horn from Bobby arming the car made her flinch breaking her chain of thought on the article about Honda Robot's. The second they stepped through the door, Antonia ran straight up to her breaking the good news. "Mommy look at the animal cage, Daddy brought us a new Jasper." She pointed backwards. Maria quickly scooted the chair back away from the table meeting Bobby in the middle of the living room floor to grab the small cage from his hand placing a soft peck on his lips. "Oh, he's so cute. He even has green eyes like Jasper had, different color fur than his though." "Mommy open the cage and let him out, please?" Antonia pleaded. "I sure will, little girl of mine." Maria bent down to the carpet to open the cage. "It sure smells delicious in here. What my gorgeous wife cook?" Bobby asked when he hung his coat up and loosen his tie. Maria stood up right walking over to the stove saying. "I cooked your favorite, Meatloaf, Macaroni and Cheese, Spinach and Jiffy Cornbread Muffins." As time ticked by and everyone had eaten their dinner preparing for bed time, Maria tucked Antonia inside her bed after she fell asleep on the living room sofa. Once Maria placed their new little kitten Jasper on Antonia's bed she calmly laid her tiny arm motionless over him then trained her soft hair behind her ear lobe landing a kiss on her cheek, before leaving out the room. Laying down in the bed Maria a smile of knowing spread across her face as her felt Bobby's erection pressing along her leg. Opening her legs to welcome her man to come closer to her. Putting himself between them. Placing his lips to her lips and gently opened them with his tongue as he slid it through to kiss her passionately and lovingly. Making her feel as she has always felt that his kisses are magical. Circling his tongue around hers in three full circles then reversing it sent her body into tingles of ecstasy drawing him closer to her. He trailed kisses from her chin down to her neck and over to the side nibbling on her earlobe, trailing his tongue down tasting her and smelling the sweet fragrance of Kimora Simmons perfume called "Goddess" on her neck coming to a stop on the lower part of her collar bone and planting two passion marks for remembrance of this night when she looks in the mirror. Feeling the hardness of her nipples against his chest brought his penis to pulsating making him more aroused. Wanting her completely naked he undressed her and then cupped her breast into his and gave her nipple a flick with his tongue, then placing his mouth to it while still tongue teasing her. Hearing her moans and feeling her body move as though it can't wait for him to enter her, he knew she was ready for him to fill her. Entering her always made him feel like he was at home and so right. Looking at her and seeing her and her body wanting him as much as he is wanting her brought him to another level of arousal and the tightness of her like that of O.J. Simpson trying to squeeze his hand inside the evidence glove took him to a further level of arousal. While thrusting inside her, her legs locked around his waist and her head leaned back into the pillow arching toward him with soft moans escaping from her inner throat. As their passion mingled and entwined with one another taking them to a world within each other he lifted to go deeper sliding up against her clit as they both joined one another in climax. He climaxed a second time as he stayed in her from the vibration of the pulsing of her secret garden. If felt as though they both was standing under a shallow aqua blue waterfall on Temptation Island and he was enjoying seeing her bottom lip shudder from coming down from the great explosion of essence. After that he slumped himself on his side of the bed as they both subsided limply beside each other naked under the satin sheets wrapped in each other's arms. Then he slid her long silky brown hair back, and kissed her forehead. Maria just closed her light brown eyes and snuggled underneath his chin with her right palm relaxed on his chest. No longer than a minute later she popped her eyes open when she heard the barrier sound of the lightening strike.

* * *

The very next morning a Saginaw Police Officer pulled up behind the parked stolen F one-fifty pick up truck Norman Gandy hotwired. The Officer approached the truck driver side door placing his weapon back into his holster when he saw the inside of the truck was clear, then he radioed in at the emergency switchboard as a code thirty clearance on the vehicle. Norman was coming around the corner of the White Castle Hamburger restaurant when he saw the police officer behind the truck. He immediately jumped back out of view placing his back up against the building saying underneath his breath. "Damn it! I just put a full tank of gas in that son of a gun, and not only that it leaves me back to square one, shit!" He whined zipping his pants closed then took off escaping from the backside of the building on foot.

* * *

Maria was washing the last few dishes they ate from a late breakfast before Bobby took off to work and Antonia took off to school. She stood there for a moment staring blankly with her hands dipped into the apple scented Joy dish water. Gazing at her three karat diamond engagement ring, and her one karat promise ring that was rainbow sparkling on the counter. She was reminiscing in deep thought thinking her and Bobby was made for one another, cause every time they made love it was getting better and better. Deciding she needed not to think about it cause the more she would had. The more she would want him to come home so they could rekindle things all over again blow for blow. She jerked with chills as if he had just blew the words I Love You inside her ear lobe from even thinking about it. After she got through rinsing off the last dish with the scorching hot water she realized she needed to get dressed and start her day off, and quit standing around like a lingerie model in her Victoria Secret G-String panties Bobby love seeing her in.

* * *

Once noon time sprung around she came pulling up in Richard's driveway to drink a cup of coffee before they had their meeting with Libby Copeland. When Richard opened the door from the alarming of his watch dogs, he said while she was approaching. "For some reason you look different Maria, is it because the sun is out today?" Maria smiled saying in her mind. "Only if you knew." then said shortly walking through the door. "Oh, nothing terribly significant." "But any how I brewed a fresh pot of coffee for us like you requested." He said while putting two cups and a box of sugar cubes on the table once she stepped inside. "Thank you. I sure could use a fresh cup right about now and this is what our agenda is for today. I already spoke with Libby Copeland last night to make the appointment to have an interview with her about her dealing with Mary Swartz." "Oh, you did?" she said surprised. "I sure did, so as I gulp down a few cups of French Vanilla coffee. I'll warn her with another phone call." She answered then took a sip of her scorching hot coffee blurting out. "Oh my, this is hot!" Right after she finished two cups of coffee, she picked up Richard's cordless phone, and quickly dialed Libbys number. When the other line picked up she heard a voice like it was being disguised saying. "Hello, who's calling?" "Good Morning this is Investigator Mrs. Gates. I was calling to speak with Ms. Copeland, is she available?" Maria heard Libby clearing her voice saying clearly. "I'm sorry, Mrs. Gates. This is she." "Was it a bad time to call you, Mrs. Copeland?" "Sort of Mrs. Gates, can I please, please meet you at a fast food restaurant for your guys interview?" Libby asked pleadingly. "Sure, would Arbys be fine in thirty minutes from now?" "That sounds perfect to me. Gotta go, bye." Libby agreed with a speedy whisper hanging up. "Well, what she say?" Richard asked when Maria powered the phone off. "She said the interview was more or less still good, but she'll rather for us to meet up with her at Arbys in thirty minutes. If you ask me she didn't sound to legit." Maria sat there for a moment entwining her brain, then stood up to pour another half cup of coffee before they took off.

* * *

Libby Copeland was sitting inside her Mountaineer SUV nervously tapping on her gear shift stick ball humming a old American Idol tune called, "A Moment Like This" by Kelly Clarkson, until she discovered Maria and Richard pulling up along her driver side. "Libby Copeland?" Maria said when she powered the window down. "Yes." "Shall we go in and have lunch? Its all my treat." Maria offered cutting the SUV off and stepping out to greet her with a friendly hand shake. Twenty minutes later as they all swept through their meals Libby sat there twirling a French Fri inside a pile of ketchup thinking about the question Maria just asked that reminded her suddenly and poignantly of Mary Swartz. "So you do realize its been some weird, mysterious activities definitely going around lately, right?" Maria added, studying her expression. Libby got a wave of goose flesh thinking back to the sighting of that day inside the girls restroom. When they all ran out the girls restroom after seeing without a doubt, she didn't mean the part she played in Mary Swartz hanging. "But for our last and final question. Are you the one who hung Mary Swartz or not? He asked with a spoon of impatient. She stuck the French Fri standing up in the pile of ketchup leaning agitatedly back in her seat while feeling inexplicably uneasy on what she was about to say. Then after a deep breath she said. "No. I'm not the one who hung her." Maria and Richard gave their famous glance at each other saying out of coincidence at the same time. "Your, not?" Libby nodded her head no. "Well, I guess your free to go. We do appreciate your meeting up with us for this meeting." Maria said calmly. "Wait Maria. Libby, can you tell us the person who did it?" Richard pressed a little further. "I'm sorry, but I don't remember a thing." She answered with a lie. Richard sighed then said. "Alright, Mrs. Copeland. Your free to go." Libby was glad their unpleasant questioning was precipitously over once she was finally allowed to walk away and when she pulled off the lot she mentioned to herself. "I don't never want to remember that nightmarish day every again."

* * *

It was a full month later sense the town had any mysterious activities until Gloria Madison woke up instinctively and immediately glanced over to her bedroom door mistaking she saw someone looming presence standing in the darkness staring at her holding an axe like the shadow people she once saw. Gloria relapse out of her nightmare in sweat, breathing hard feeling claustrophobic saying underneath her breath. "I would be having a nightmare on Halloween eve midnight." Then she reached over to her nightstand for her glass of water and took two big gulps but right when she heard someone wandering about down stairs beneath her she nearly drowned herself as she snatched the glass from her writhing lips choking. Gloria slammed the half glass of water on the night stand hoping it was her boyfriend James Faceson back from his computer consultant out of state meeting. Then she realized it couldn't of been him. He only been away for two days now and always was expected to be gone at least a week at a time. And that's when she started staring around the room in the darkness sitting upright feeling very defenseless. The house was so dark and quiet she could actually hear her heart beat and veins clutching from being in a frightening state of mind. Plus the more she sat there on the bed the more she started hallucinating thinking someone was crawling on all fours on the floor till suddenly she jumped grabbing both cheeks with her palms when she heard a loud thump sound down stairs beneath her. Thinking to herself. "I should of gotten the Brinks Alarm house system like James told her instead of being cheap about everything, and this is one time she wished she had listened." And the only phone in the house was in the downstairs computer room, she didn't like the phone to be upstairs in the room waking her up when she slept. Gloria slowly eased out of bed with her senses and attention feverishly heighten egger to get out the house or for the most part make it to the phone. When she opened her door she slowly eased her head out gazing straight down the spacious dark hallway, she flipped her bedroom light switch on so light could illuminate though out the hallway. Seeing that no one was standing in the hallway she felt a little more relieved controlling her strong breathing, whispering. "If someone was in the house wouldn't they have made it up stairs by now? Oh my, what was that?" She had a horrid suspicion someone really was in the house now, when she heard her silver wear clashing from the drawer being snatched open. Gloria slowly tiptoed back inside her room feeling very dehydrated. She snatched the glass off the table then guzzled the rest of the room temperature water down her throat. She suddenly came to a conclusion to go close the door and flip the light out to look out the window, and see if she could see someone either walking or riding down the street to holler out to for help. After she quietly closed the door and flipped the light out she whispered beneath her breath saying as she was going over to the window. "If I holler out the window for help and the intruder gets irritated and comes looking for m, what would I do then?" She took her hand from her breast feeling gracious she was indefinable in a great distance from whoever, or whatever that was now in her home unwanted and uninvited. She though insanely when she realized she said, "from whatever or whoever that was now in her home."

* * *

Libby Copeland was still up late sitting on the living room sofa with her blanket spread out over her long legs looking inside her old school year book, examining every old school classmate picture in Saginaw Township School. She suddenly thought her eyes were beginning to play tricks on her when she thought she saw Mary Swartz class picture in the year book five times. She flipped back to the page she first saw her picture on saying with thinly veiled hatred in her eyes flipping the pages. "This is Mary, here go Mary, another of Mary's pictures, again Mary." Libby took a quick sip of her cup of Jack Daniels slowly turning to the last page she saw her picture on saying after she scrutinized her picture. "Mary you just don't know how much I hate your guts!" The moment Mary heard the fifth calling of her name Darla's eyes extended wider. Libby started getting light headed from being over tipsy from her third glass of Jack Daniels and Seven-up soda. Anger take over her she flung the photo album year book to the far living room corner.

* * *

"I can't believe I didn't see anyone I could yell out too, of course not Gloria, look what time it is, stupid woman." She whispered to herself standing a few feet away from the window, but when she saw a glare appear on her wall from someone's car headlights she raced back to the window. "Son of a Bitch!" she cursed when she saw a mini van drive pass. The crumbling steps downstairs beneath her started sounding more vivid to her as she stood there frustrated thinking to herself. "I can't be feeling like a prisoner in my own home and to be trapped in my room like a fly in the web frightened waiting for a bid daddy long leg to discover me and take my life away for a meal." Then she questioned herself. "Or am I thinking this way to build my courage up to go down stairs?" She took a deep breath exhaled then paced over to her bedroom door. The quietness of the house made the door knob sound like a automatic hand gun being cocked back unlatching its release, and once the door was open she once again was happy her head didn't get cut off peeking her head out. "Now why couldn't this be Halloween day for my sister to be here?" She asked herself thoughtfully at the same time hating herself for ignoring her sister Angie's phone call before she dozed off to sleep. Gloria restored her senses then tiptoed over to their guestroom diagonally across the hallway remembering her boy friend James kept a stun gun inside the guestroom bottom dresser drawer. When she opened the drawer she immediately got relieved seeing the stun gun knowing she at least has something to work with and once it was in her had she coached herself real low. "He always told me to place it on the enemies nerve parts and let it rip." Then she crept her way out the room to the beginning of the stair casing. She slowly peeked her head around the corner into the dark stair casing, and seeing no one was coming up the steps she crept her way down trying to avoid from stepping on the squeaky step she remembered with her hand extended out in front of her with her right index finger slacked on the electricity button. The intruders hand was tightly gripped on the steak knife handle tucked away inside the down stairs darkness deliberately waiting to strike. Gloria suddenly stopped on the fifth step before the bottom landing focusing in to see if she could hear someone still wandering about but the more she struggled to see in the darkness chill bumps started to spread across her neck while thinking every image of a piece of furniture in her living room was someone staring at her lurking in the darkness while she stood there listening to the house settle. Part of her body wanted to take off running in the dark to make it to the phone and the other part made her legs feel like they had one hundred pounds of weight bags tied around her ankles afraid to move thinking to herself. "If all it takes for me to stand right here without anyone jumping out and morning arrives it'll be great. Then again I can't distinguish much standing here or maybe the intruder vanished presumably vacating the premises realizing someone was home. Oh Gloria, I don't understand the way you think sometimes." She silently added, taking the final steps down. The second she stepped her feet on the bottom floor she felt frightened when she thought she saw something move in the darkness to the left of her where their big sofa is located. Squinting her eyes siking herself out that it wasn't nothing. She slowly took off right of her a few steps only stopping once more to glance back for reassurance making sure she wasn't being followed and once she proceeded on the intruder rushed up behind her and grabbed her by the neck with the knife pressed against her throat. Gloria gave out a strong sigh dropping the stun gun from her hand. Norman quickly placed his free hand over her mouth area muffling her scream saying in her ear with the knife still pressed against her throat. "Shhhh . . . if you do what the hell I tell you may not die, got that?" "Yes, yes, please don't kill me." She thought in her mind. 'This man is very over baring in the way he is guiding me around." He reached over to the living room light switch and clicked it on. She instantly saw his black bag in the middle of her living room floor zipped wide open with a rope partially hanging out from it. Norman bent down to grab the rope with the knife against her throat making her bend down right along with him. Walking her over to a dining room chair and sat her down forcefully. Gloria once again thought to herself. "He is going to tie me down, torture me then kill me." Noticing the scratches and big birthmark on his cheek she got even more frightened recognizing he was once on America's Most Wanted for escaping. Norman tied her up double checked the knot making sure it was good and tight then assured her. "One scream and this goes over your mouth. Try to get away." Gloria took a dry swallow when she saw him sliding his right thumb across his own throat. "Got that?" He asked mean fully and she quickly nodded her head with approval as a tear rolled unexpectedly down to her lip. "Good!" He added taking off to the hallway where he remembered something dropped from here hand. "Hum, what do we have here. Ah, hah. This bitch was going to taze me." He said thoughtfully standing upright with the tazer gun in his hand pacing back over to her. He straddled himself over her legs guiding her head back with the shiny pointed tip of the steak knife underneath her chin. Then started slithering his tongue out at her fast like a human reptile. Gloria started panting strongly while slightly turning her head away from his long tongue and the hissing sound he was making right along with it. When he kept slithering his tongue toward her closed mouth the phone started ringing. He hurried un-straddling himself taking off to the computer room where the phone was crazily ringing. She took a deep breath saying "Thank God." Looking around to see if she could locate something that could get her out from being restrained, but it was to late Norman was coming. when he came back walking up from looking at the call I.D. on her phone, he didn't hesitate not one minute on asking who was Angie Madison? She stifled a gasp saying. "That's my older sister everyone is being expected over my house first thing in the morning to celebrate Halloween." Norman exploded. "What! They're going to be here first thing in the morning?" He then stepped behind her leaning menacingly over her right shoulder calmly saying in her ear. "Now what you going to do is tell me where your car keys are and the pocket changed of the house." "I can tell you where the car keys are but its only one problem." "What's that?" He asked raising up stepping around to the front of her so he could study her beautiful face and delicate olive tan complexion. "There's not much house change." She said with a grave expression when he stood in front of her. "There's not!" He snapped. Gloria flinched back saying quickly. "It's only sixty dollars total." "Aye, ye, ye." He grumbled surprisingly and to Gloria. The house had began to feel like a huge sound proof interrogation room the way he kept gagging her with questions. Norman arrogantly felt there wasn't no need to keep screwing around with precautions and get straight down t business about things.

CHAPTER TWENTY-ONE

DARLA WAS ABOUT three minutes away from Libby Copeland's house walking along anxiously to act out her next retaliation kill from the vengeance she held within her. Libby fell into a deep sleep as the glass of Jack Daniel's fell from her hand onto the carpet and her arm remained motionless from the sofa. She was so tired and intoxicated she started having rapid eye movement. Libby drank half of the fifth of Jack Daniel's celebrating Halloween eve sense it seems to had been forever since she had the entire house to herself, being that her three kids were away for the holiday. Dreaming that she had a beauty salon that was so crowded people was little kids crying and some little kids fighting each other, but they all was faithfully waiting as if they was waiting to purchase a daily lotto ticket worth ninety-nine million dollars. Darla kept observing scary Halloween decorations lit up in peoples yards and windows as she walked dangerously like she was out sporting her scary costume early in the darkness fog of the streets alone on a prowl.

* * *

Norman grabbed Gloria's car keys from his tan baggy corduroy pants pocket to open her two thousand and ten Grand Prix driver door helping himself inside. In the driver seat he tossed the tazer gun into the glove department and powered the window down when he started the engine up taking a quick glance at her and James photo on her key chain then ripping it off and tossing it out the window onto the driveway, then sped off into the midnight of the fog.

* * *

While Libby was still deep off into REM (Rapid Eye Movement) sleep tossing and turning. She persistently raised up out of her sleep soberly with her eyes wide when hearing her SUV alarm sound off. Quickly getting up staggering off to her bedroom to get her keys and walking shoes saying. "I already told them I was coming with the car note next week, geez." She raced her feet into her shoes snatching the keys from the ironing board. When she opened the front door she said thoughtfully trailing off the porch without looking right of her. "I'm glad I don't see a tow truck man or a repo man well let me make sure it hadn't been broken into." Darla stood there within the darkness of Libby's porch staring at her going around her vehicle then she quietly stepped into her house. Once Libby did a full inspection around her vehicle. Resetting the alarm when her teeth started to chatter indicating she needed to go back where its warm. Stepping inside she closed and locked the door behind her then swiftly rubbed both hands on her arms for instant warmth, an when she came around the couch she cried out. "Oh no! My carpet is all stained now." She couldn't believe the big brown spot the Jack Daniels made from her dropping her glass. Getting through scrubbing the stain from the carpet, she put everything away, clicked the light out in her bedroom and living room. She opened her living room blinds so she could keep an eye out on her SUV stretching herself out on the couch by the window. The house was so dark. The only light was glaring was the flame of the fire at the bottom of her wall heater. Libby laid there in the dark gazing at the ceiling, until her eye lids got heavy from opening and closing. Then she was back off into her sleep. It was twenty minutes later when Darla crawled out of Libby's closet on her knees and hands standing upright when she observed the iron on the ironing board. Libby opened her eyes in the darkness when she heard the heater reset itself she slowly closed them back again once she realized what the clicking noise had been. Darla absolutely wasn't in any mood for waiting around this time. Especially being the villainous person she became wickedly creeping camouflaged inside the darkness of the hallway with the iron handle tightly gripped in her grasp as the cord hung freely. She stopped a feet away from where Libby was lying asleep. The plug on the bottom of the iron cord hit the empty glass on the floor beside the couch sounding off a crystal clear ting sound. Libby opened her eyes instantly bulging wide in fright staring directly at Darla's a looming presence, unable to say a word. Then came the bright light from the powerful impact to the face with the iron repeatedly. When Darla bashed her face in with the iron the third time, blood squirted across the blinds and Darla's face while leaning over her then she released the iron from her hand to wipe off the blood from her face before vanishing out the house leaving the front door ajar.

* * *

When Halloween morning finally arrived, Angie Madison, her two daughters and a friend Carol Came pulling up in Gloria's driveway on the cell phone constantly ringing her phone. Angie said to the girls cutting her car off. "She had to be here, and where is her car? Oh maybe, it's in the garage, you girls sit here until I see if she's here." The second she exited the vehicle she went walking to the back of the car to see what it was in the driveway that she avoid from rolling over. "This my sister photo keychain of her and James, what's this doing lying in the driveway? It looks like it's been ripped from the key ring, at that." She pondered thoughtfully taking off to Gloria's door. Angie placed the photo keychain in her pocket saying while knocking on the door with four continuous knocks. "If she can't hear this then she done went plain deaf." But as she stood there for a moment realizing no one was coming to answering the door. She glanced at the girls in the car having a girly conversation focusing her attention back to the door with hesitation tired knob, while the girls waited patiently talking about Kenneth Ingram their school most handsome guy. Angie thought curiously to herself when the door knob kept turning. "Why is her door unlocked?" And once the door was opened she discovered her sister tied up to one of the dining room table chairs faced away with her hair scattered shaggy. Angie took a breath of relief saying calmly approaching her. "Gloria, it's to early to try to scare me and the girls." But once Gloria didn't respond Angie continued saying approaching the front of her. "Hello, Gloria. Did you . . ." Her words being cut off by a scream of the highest note like the Blue Alien in the classic movie the 5th Element from seeing her sisters throat slashed wide open, and her entire front of her a night gown soaked with her own blood. "Wasn't that you guys mom? Screaming like that?" Carol asked meekly. Janice responded happily. "That means our Aunt is here after all, she must of scared mom. She always scares us on Halloween." But Angie came storming out the door with real horrified terror in her eyes.

* * *

After the authorities arrived the 10th Precinct Homicide Detective Mr. Dean was sitting on Gloria's living room sofa with Angie going over her statement with her. "Alright. I'm about to repeat everything I've written down of what you told me to make sure its correct. Ok. You said you been calling your sister on her house phone since eight thirty last night. You and the girls arrived at nine this morning to begin your yearly Halloween get together, and you knocked on . . ." "Excuse me Detective Dear sir, I didn't mean to interrupt your report session, but the intruder seems to have entered through the basement window, we discovered." Officer Phil explained. "Great job, I'll be right with you." Detective Dean said genuinely. "No problem, sir." Detective Dean focused his attention back to Angie saying humanly. "I'm sorry for the interruption, shall we proceed? Great. Alright, you knocked on the door four times and no answer. You then reached out for the door knob out of curiosity and just like you tuition told you the door was unlocked. You then opened the door and discovered your sister tied up in the chair faced away. You thought she was playing one of her practical scares until you realized she had been brutally murdered. Is that correct 'ma'am?" Angie stopped biting her nails to give him a blandly nod of approval while saying. "Yes. That's correct sir." "Thank you ma'am for your information and cooperation in this matter. We're terribly sorry of what happened to your sister as well, and you and the kids are free to go if you like." Angie gave him a lopsided short smile wiping her tears then stood up and walked out the front door with a crushed heart. Detective Dean stood there twirling his pen watching her walk out the door, until Officer Phil approached him saying. "Mr. Dean, do you think we need to contact the O.F.P.A. unit?" Detective Dean instantly stopped twirling his pen saying. "Non, I don't think this is one of those cases. I think this is a common murder, and not a paranormal killing." "What makes you say that, sir?" Detective Dean turned glancing over at the covered body, then professionally explained. "Because if you notice on the left side of her neck she had shock veins visual as day with two stun gun post marks in that same location, and usually that's a sign of a stun gun in my career, beside the knife slash across her throat." Officer Phil nodded his head blankly at the covered body saying. "Yeah. I did notice those marks now that you mentioned it."

* * *

Mr. Wallace stepped inside of Twenty-nine Palms City Hall to have a quick meeting with Captain Aversa about his progress on the missing victim Bryan Smith mysterious abduction. "Good evening, Mr. Wallace and Happy Halloween." The Captain clerk said respectfully. "Oh, hello Mrs. Datson. Happy Halloween to you too, Sweetie. Is the Captain still in?" "He sure is." Mrs. Datson pushed the button saying. "Sorry to bother you Captain, but you have a visitor here to speak with you. It's Mr. Wallace." "Of course, send him in." He insisted. "Go right in, sir." "Thank you, Mrs. Datson." Captain Aversa swiveled around in his chair from staring out the window at the large crowd saying. "Hey, big money, you're not taking a break for the holiday?" "Oh no. I'm not to fond of celebrating Lucifer's birthday, besides I can't afford too." "All that's non-sense, so what you got for me big shot?" Mr. Wallace slid a confidential informant statement across the Captains desk saying. "It's not one hundred percent, but its a start." Captain Aversa scanned over the contents of the CI letter saying Bluntly. "This isn't enough Mr. Wallace. I'm here to tell you sometimes police work involves democracy more than anything else, well I'm going to give you an example. You see all those people on the outside of this building daily holding a rally over that kids long disappearance? Besides you once told me the first lead you got from this Derrick Akins character who sent you on a coyote trail of poop balls now you saying you have suspicion on where he could be by this letter. Well Lt. Wallace, I'll give you seventy-two hours to come up wit some hardcore evidence. Is that understood, my friend?" "That's very understood sir, and I promise I won't let the town of Twenty-nine Palms down." He said very sharply. "Well I hope not Lt. or it'll be some fired asses around here. Including mines." Captain Aversa countered with a straight face looking sincere then swiveled his chair back around toward the window indicating the short meeting was adjourn. Mr. Wallace walked out the door with no further words, but though silent to himself. "He was the one who offered his help, and now his job is on the line for a missing kid he had no clue where he could be.

*   *   *

As the Saginaw sun set the Trick or Treater started their Halloween night and Libby Copeland's body was still lying on her living room couch unfound like Darla left her. Kids was going door to door dressed in their most scariest costumes laughing hollering talking and exchanging candy, enjoying the holiday, except for those who had their bags snatched by some bully teenagers. Two parents and six kids in their costumes came walking up on Libby's porch while one little girl dressed up as Chucky's Bride started pounding on the jarred open door. "Don't knock so hard, Linda." Claudia told her, when she saw the door opened a couple of feet wide from the hard knock. Linda stood there gazing straight seeing if someone was going to approach the door, then shouted as the kids sound off behind her voice. "Trick or Treat!" Then Linda added turning around smiling to her mom. "This is a spooky house mom." "Hello, is anyone home?" Claudia yelled from behind her. "Hum, this is strange Sharron." Linda curiously took a peek inside the door glancing at the couch to the right of the inside door, then dropped her trick or treat basket screaming out fearfully. "Mommy some ones on the couch!" Claudia hurried up to the door cuffing both hands over her mouth area when she saw flies flying around the thick blood of Libbys face, sofa and blinds. One of the little boys amongst the crowd of trick or treaters took off running yelling out. "A dead lady, a dead lady. I saw her through the window!" Another little boy vomited on the porch when he cuffed his hand on her living room window and saw her himself.

* * *

Maria, Antonia and Bobby was over one of their neighbors house attending a neighborhood Halloween party that was fit for the children and grownups with the intention to forget about everything that had been going around lately in Saginaw, Michigan. Maria was sitting on the sofa having a nice chat with Jesse's wife Sandra until her ring tone on her cell phone started sounding off. "Oh, my God! You like that song too? I love that song "U Take My Breath Away." Sandra blurted out excitedly. "Will you excuse me for a minute Mrs. Houston? This is a business call." "Hello Mrs. Gates speaking. How can I help you?" She answered stepping out the sliding door patio where little kids was taking turns dunking their heads into the shallow swimming pool trying to bit apples with their teeth. "Hello Maria." "Oh, hello Richard. Happy Holidays." She said tucking her hair behind her right ear lobe." Like wise, Maria. Oh yeah, the reason why I'm calling is to let you know no more than two hours ago a breaking news coverage broadcasted that two murders was committed today and one of those victims was our little friend Libby Copeland." "What!" "She was found murdered by some Trick or Treaters around seven this evening, ain't that something?" "Its sure is." Maria answered sounding amazed. "Oh, and our other victim that was found by the name of Gloria Madison was found nine in the morning with her throat slashed." "Mother of God! This really done gone to far now! So I'm confused a little. Did they say these murders were done by the same suspects?" She said covering her right ear to eliminate some of the yelling of the party. "No, they didn't really say. If it was left up to me I'll say it wasn't." "Alright." She said convincingly enough. "Well, I'm not going to hold you up Maria. I'll be speaking with you after Halloween, have fun!" "Thanks Richard for your consistency of awareness once again. Bye." Maria flipped her cell phone closed cracking a smile. When she saw fun and joy in Antonia's eyes, as she ran around the backyard shouting with all the other kids. Maria could see herself in her when she was little all over again. "Is everything ok, Babe?" Bobby asked softly when he crept up placing his arms around her from behind. She broke her chain of thought leaning her head back realizing it on his broad chest saying. "Of course every things ok. I have you and Antonia in my life." then he kissed her hair with a smile saying. "Um . . . your hair smells good to me, Mommacita." Rubbing both her arms with his hands un-tensing her. "And that new Kenneth Cole smells good on you Babe." "Thanks to you, Mi Amour." He replied. "All babe, Te Amo." She assured him that she loved him. Seconds later Antonia came happily running with a big bag of candy in one hand and a prize that she won in another saying. "Look Mommy and Daddy, look what I won. I'm going to give this to little Jasper when we get home." Then she stumbled taking back off. "Honey be careful!" Maria yelled shortly when she saw her catching her fall.

* * *

A few days after Halloween Mr. Wallace was making his last few rounds on the seventy-two hours Captain Aversa had given him to come up with some hardcore evidence. Far a minute he thought to himself he never should of taken this over pay opportunity to come all the way to Twentynine Palms, California to search for a kid that may of been abducted by an alien race or dead already by some punk hands. He thought it would be quick, fast and a hurry in finding him within such a small pioneer town. Pulling up to the stop light on Adobe Road and the Sixty-two Highway facing Southbound he lit the tip of his fresh Marlboro cigarette, then strolled onto Dennys lot when the light turned green. As he pulled up he noticed two Marine women and a guy walking out heading to their vehicles. "Excuse me, may I have a minute of your guys time?" He yelled putting his cigarette out four respect. One of the Marine women approached his driver side door saying with a friendly leer in her voice. "Sure. How can I help you, sir?" "First of all allow me to introduce myself. My name is Lt. Mr. Kirk W. Wallace. I'm from the O.F.P.A. office out in Los Angeles County, and I'm here doing an Investigation in Twentynine Palms on the missing kid Bryan Smith." The young lady hung her purse on her shoulder saying. "I'm pretty much familiar with that issue." "You are?" He said excitedly until she said. "On television from the news, sorry." "Don't worry thank you for your generosity ma'am, your free to go." "Good luck." She said. Mr. Wallace nodded his head with a smile then pulled off the lot. He ended up driving through El Paseo Apartments which was a common area. When he parked his truck in front of the rental office he saw a quite a few people of mixed races walking all about enjoying the refreshing mild day after Halloween. He hit his alarm button when he exited the vehicle and stopped a young couple walking toward him on the side walk holding hands. "Hello young lady and young man." The young teenage girl off the bat knew exactly who he was when she took a glance at the mirror on his vehicle door. "I know who you are. Your that one guy that be getting advertised over the news, looking for, what's that guys name? Oh yeah, Bryan Smith." "your one hundred percent correct young lady." "For a minute, I thought you was one of those narcotic jump out guys." Brandon said thoughtfully. "But what I was meaning to ask is have you been hearing any rumors on where this missing kid maybe, or being held captive? I can fully guarantee you your name and information would be kept secret and pretty much confidential." Brandon took a quick glance at Mr. Wallace's gun holster for the third time then blurted out. "Man, I ain't no snitch. Even though it don't have anything to do with us, but people get killed or come up missing behind that type of stuff. You feel me? Come on Boo, we outta here." Mr. Wallace nodded his head watching them trail off behind the rental office and through the small park. A group of white guys was smoking on some chronic inside a cigar when one said. "Man, put that down he look like police." Mr. Wallace came walking up saying "Hey fellas. I don't mean to invade on your guys session here, but I was wanting to know if any of you have heard anything about the missing kid Bryan Smith?" Everyone shook their heads no, nearly at once, while one of the guys still had the blunt lit in his hand cuffed. "So no one knows huh? Now if I bust you guys for smoking Marijuana I bet you would pop an undisclosed answer then." He said as his smile deepened. "Listen man, fuck you!" One of the guys cursed him before they all took off running in separate ways. "Hell, let me get out of here before things jump into another situation." He said underneath his breath striding off to his vehicle. No later when he pulled off from the rental office he heard a bottle bursting behind him. "I'll handle you guys later, little buggers!" He yelled punching over the speed bumps screeching his tires leaving out the apartments. Later that evening his cell phone was receiving a phone call from the confidential informant he received the letter from. "Hello Mr. Wallace speaking at his best and may I ask who's calling?" He answered while walking back to his Motel room from getting a bowl of ice and a few pastries. "Hello Mr. Wallace this Andy remember me? The guy who gave you that letter and the one you paid a hundred dollars too. Well, I climbed over the fence yesterday morning and peeked through the warehouse windows." "Wait a minute. I thought you said he was in a house that you know of?" Mr. Wallace challenged him. "I know, I know. You don't have to get all excited about it." Andy said on the other end nervously twirling his hair. "Get all excited! Listen son of a Bitch, you made me walk in the Captains office with some evidence that wasn't even accurate and you telling me don't get excited?" Mr. Wallace muted the TV once he heard a muffle sound on the other end of the line. "Andy what was that noise I just heard?" "What noise? But anyways Mr. Wallace that's not your worst worry. Your worst worry is before I tell you where his location is it'll cost you one hundred thousand dollars." "One hundred thousand dollars! Listen dude, just tell me or show me the location and where do you think I can come up with that type of money anyways? Why don't you give me the location like a good citizen would and except a good citizen platform for telling me where this damn kid is. We're running out of time." "And you right about that Mr. Wallace your running out of time." Andy snapped slamming the phone down disconnecting the line. "Wait! Wait! Damn!" Mr. Wallace said hitting his fist on the round Motel table. Moments later he heard somebody pounding on the wall saying with a deep voice. "Hit the pussy a little softer and take your time. Asshole!" "Ah, shut the hell up!" Mr. Wallace shot back heatedly, rediaing the number that appeared on his phone of Andy's phone call, but only to find out he called a payphone. "Shit. I'm getting a funny suspicion about this Andy character." He said thoughtfully taking the mute button off the Sci-Fi Channel.

* * *

After Mr. Wallace sat up all night doing his homework the very next day he went to Captain Aversa's home to talk to him about his hardcore evidence he finally stumbled across. Mrs. Aversa opened the door with a smile saying in a benign tone of voice. "Hello, Lieutenant." Mr. Wallace grabbed his hat from his head out of generosity saying. "Hello Mrs. Aversa, It's nice to see you again. You looking younger every time I see you, is the Captain home?" "Sure, please come in. Your always welcome." When she went to go get her husband from his study room or his quiet chamber as he likes to call it. Mr. Wallace started smelling a sweet Cubin cigar burning freshly to his nostrils then he stood up from the sofa when the Captain came walking up. "Hello Captain." "Hello lieutenant. You look like you have some good news on your mind, so tell me about it." The Captain insisted while pouring them both a glass of Bacardi on ice. "Captain, for what it's worth I wanna video that C.I. letter I presented to you a few days ago, due to it was false information." "You better have a good excuse behind this one, Mr. Wallace. Mr. I can find him less than two days, explain yourself, sir." His tone full of sarcasm. "Well first of all, Captain. I never said I'll be able to find a lost chewed up sucker that's been thrown in the middle of the street in two days. I told you when I first came out to be assigned to this case, being its such a small town, that its likely for him to be found in two days from my expertise, and accountability of work." Mr. Wallace corrected sharply. Mrs. Aversa was inside their master bedroom listening to their whole conversation thinking to herself. "My husband is going to explode." Knowing he didn't like anyone being sarcastic especially having a conversation with him never the less in police work. The Captain sat his glass of Bacardi on the private bar, then said with an attitude. "First of all Lieutenant you need to watch your tone of voice in my home, second of all you have many admirable qualities Lieutenant, and that's why I called you personally as a friend to come and dress this sandwich of a case up for being sort of a little payback when I helped the O.F.P.A. Officer Mr. Owens to try to crack a few cases. Which to your knowledge you knowing how it went. So I don't have to go into further detail on that subject." The his expression turned even harder when he continued. "I'm sure your aware on how much its costing this little town daily to find this kid, right?" Mr. Wallace placed his partially filled glass of Bacardi on the coffee table answering shortly. "Yes Sir." While using formality to distance himself from a potential argument. "So what did you necessarily come to tell me, Lieutenant?" The Captain's voice turned soft. "Well with no further arguments I came to tell you my hardcore evidence ends up coming up hardcore easy at the last minute. I got a phone call yesterday evening from that confidential informant Andy and I stood up all night coming up with the conclusion that he's our possible suspect if you ask me." He said holding back his second real thought. Captain Aversa attempts his glass up to his lips, then quickly placed it on the bar as his expression brightened saying. "I didn't hear what I thought I heard, did I? "If you heard me say Andy could be our possible suspect, you did." He assured the Captain. "So how you come up with this art piece of conclusion?" "Let's just say the only person that'll be asking for one hundred thousand dollars to give up more information, or even this kids where abouts could only be the one who's holding this kid ransom or hostage himself either on. To be honest I don't think these guys so bright." Mr. Wallace pointed out clearly. "Oh so you're telling me this Andy guy tried to give you a confidential letter to cover up his trail then had the nerves to phone you asking for one hundred thousand dollars for further info. Oh I see. Well Lieutenant, I must admit that's some hardcore evidence you came up with. What do you say the old buzzard still has it in him after all." Captain stated proudly. "It isn't what's in the old buzzard its how long the old buzzard could keeping going." Mr. Wallace corrected rising to his feet taking a glance down at his Ostrich boots then glance back over to the Captain saying. "So Captain all it gonna takes is the next phone call and I should have this son of a gun, dag nabbed."

* * *

Andy slammed the building door closed with the back heel of his foot sense his hands was occupied carrying a heavy box of dry foods and two gallons of Arrowhead water. Setting the box on the table he went to place the jugs of water inside the mini refrigerator then he took a glance at the eyes that are scrutinizing him sharply. Andy is a Caucasian guy in his early thirties, six feet tall, two hundred pounds, brown hair and eyes a bad case of acne and a thick brown handle bar mustache to go with it. His G.P.A. grade level was that of a six grader. When the sharp scrutiny of the eyes that are following his moves say Andy staring they quickly glanced away trying to avoid direct eye contact. Then the puppy soft eyes glanced back at Andy only to have cigarette as water flung in his face.

CHAPTER TWENTY-TWO

AS SOON AS Mr. Wallace made it back to his Motel room, he called the main operator switchboard to confirm where the pay phone was located that Andy used yesterday evening. "Hello, this the Main Operator Assistant Mrs. Cook speaking, how can I assist you today?" "Hi, this is Investigator Mt. Kirk W. Wallace. I was doing some major follow ups here in Twenty-nine Palms California and I was desperately needing to know where this particular pay phone is located? If I may be assisted with that." "Sure. What's the area code and number, sir?" "Thank you, its area code seven-six-zero-five-five-five-one-one-one-one." Mr. Wallace started hearing repeated taps on the computer keyboard on the other end then a final tap. "Sir?" "Yes, Ma'am." "This particular pay phone is located outside Twenty-nine Palms Desert Ranch Market off of Sixty-two Highway and Yucca Avenue. Is there anything else I could assist you with, Mr. Wallace?" "No Ma'am, that was perfect. Thank you once again, and have a blessed day." "Thank you for choosing the main operator information line, have a nice day." Operator Mrs. Cook said with dignity before disconnecting the line. Mr. Wallace closed his cell phone realizing the info she just gave him wasn't enough evidence for him and he'll just have to sit and wait for the big fish to bit again by ringing his phone for the one hundred thousand dollar fish steak.

* * *

Maria was sitting in their study room scanning over the top news paper articles on the two murders that were pronounced on the news Halloween day. She read out loud in a low voice. "Halloween morning a woman by the name of Gloria Madison was found dead with a deep laceration to the throat and visual shock veins from a tazer gun. This case is under investigation." Then directed her eyes down to the obituary section stopping on Libby Copeland's name as she continued to read in a low voice. "Halloween evening a lady by the name ob Libby Mariah Copeland was found dead and the cause of death was continuous beating to the face with an iron. This case is under investigation." Maria closed the news paper then placed it on the des leaning back with her legs and arms crossed contemplating on what she just read about. Hearing Antonia's little feet trucking up the hallway changed her train of thought. Coming through the study room door yelling. "Mommy, look what little Jasper did to Tinker Bell!" "Oh Jasper." Maria said incredulously getting up to go take a closer look of her old doll which she's had since she was a little girl herself and ended up handing it down to Antonia when she was born. "That's it young lady. I'm putting him back into the cage for the rest of the evening." "No mommy, he didn't mean it!" Antonia pleaded. "I guess he didn't mean to tear my flowers either." Maria added. When Maria made it inside the living room and observed the curtains moving she thought it was cute the way little Jasper was hiding behind the curtains the way big Jasper use to do. "Come on, little Jasper. Back in the cage little man." But as she was placing him inside the case she happened to peer over at the patio sliding door, viewing the outside darkness thinking she saw someone gazing straight at her. Bobby was up stairs sleeping so Maria said to her daughter. "Antonia go up stairs and climb in the bed with Daddy and Mommy will be up there to tuck you into your own bed. Ok?" "Ok but can Jasper please sleep in my bed with me Mommy?" She asked in her irresistible voice. "Ok although I said he was going to be in the case for the rest of the evening, but if you run along now I'll bring him up with me." "Thank you Mommy." She said running off doing what she was told too. Once Maria heard Bobby tell Antonia to climb in the bed she swiftly marched her way into the study room pulling the nine millimeter hand gun from the drawer to take a look out the patio door to ease her conscience. She came walking in the kitchen cocking the gun slowly so Bobby and Antonia couldn't hear it, but right when she was about to reach out to grab the patio door handle she turned around drawing her full attention to their living room window when she heard a car pull off screeching its tires. Bobby quickly rushed out of the bed racing over to the window that looks out over their front yard when he heard the sound. "Who's out there Daddy?" Antonia asked curiously enough sitting upright. "It's no one Honey lay back down, every things ok." He assured her calmly remembering not to get her rounded up but when she saw him pacing over to the door heading out the room she climbed out of bed storming off behind him. "Who was that honey and why you have that out?" He asked when he got down stairs and saw the hand gun in her hand. Maria immediately placed both hands behind her back seeing Antonia come trailing up behind him. "It was someone here at our house Babe. I saw them through our patio door and the only person I could think of is that damn Norman Gandy." "Ooh Mommy said a bad word." Antonia echoed absently. "I'm sorry Honey, Mommy just a little upset." Bobby reached out to grab the gun from her and put it back in the study room so Antonia wouldn't see it. Once her returned he could see in her eyes that she was tired of Norman Gandy's frequent visits to their home and in their life. "I know, I know." He said thoughtfully to her as if he was reading her mind through her eyes then he thought to himself. "If Norman ever came again he'll get in his Charger and stop at nothing to kill him at all means necessary."

* * *

Darla came walking pass Jerry's Bar when a drunk man staggered out the door onto the sidewalk with a Bud Ice in his hand saying when she passed him. "What you looking at, you ugly Bitch?" Darla stopped in her tracks when she passed him from hearing his rude statement. Continuing to stand there faced away from him as her tense breathing breezed through her bangs. "Ah what the hell." He said waving his free hand at her then went walking along side of Jerry's building to take a leak. The second he zipped his fly down with his free hand Darla crept up behind him unnoticed and grabbed him by his penis ripped it off then snapped his neck like it was a chicken neck with no hesitation, with her speed and accuracy he had no time to utter a sound. The beer fell from his hand and burst on the ground. Everyone in Jerry's Bar was laughing, dancing and drinking their lives away until the man's body came crashing through the front window. The customer by the window quickly jumped up snatching his pitcher of beer out of reflex as the man's body came flying through the window and crashing down on his table. "What the!" The man from the table said extending the pitcher of beer out in front of him when some of it splashed out. The music had stopped, people started to crazily run out of the bar when they realized it was Fred a regular but by that time Darla had vanished.

* * *

Once the authorities arrived and started questioning Jerry he didn't know where to begin then he went to say after tossing a couple of cashew peanuts in his mouth. "Well, all I know he was having a few harsh words with his girlfriend Rebecca when he saw her dancing with John Earl, while Kate was singing Karaoke from one of Paris Hilton's songs I believe it was a song called 'Stars' anyways, I was about to sock him good for spitting a noggy on my floor with the slugger bat of mines but he stepped out moments after that his body came flying through my window like a dickless test crash dummy." Jerry said ten tossed a few more cashews in his mouth. "Did you see any one leave out the door behind him?" "No, not at all. The only thing left out this door with him was a ice cold Bud Ice in his hand." He answered with a monotone voice. "Corporal, I have a young lady witness right here claiming she saw exactly what happened from the time our victim stepped out the bar door." Officer Dan stated. "Ma'am, would you?" Corporal Mitchell stood up angling his hand to his chair, then told Jerry thank you for his cooperation. "No problem sir." "Hello Ma'am. I'm Corporal Mitchell from the fifth precinct do you mind stating your name or we could keep your name confidential if you like." "Yes, that'll be great. I rather not state my name." She said meekly. "Alright then shall we get down to the questions?" "Sure." "So please tell me what all you saw from top to bottom." "Ok. I came out of Momma Joes Bar and Grill next door to sit in the truck to get some fresh air and I must of dozed off to sleep for at least five minutes but I instantly woke up when I heard the music from Jerry's Bar get loud when that man came staggering out the door. Suddenly I saw a lady or girl, I couldn't quite make out much of her cause her whole face was covered with her hair. I didn't hear exactly what was being said between the both of them, but I did se that man wave his hand at her as if something didn't make sense. Then he took off walking on the side of Jerry's building. It looked like he was about to take a leak, to be truthful. Well at that point I slumped down in the passenger seat of the truck when that lady or girl came behind him ripped his man hood off and snapped his neck and boy was she strong. She picked him up like a rag doll and there he went flying through that window over there." She said with no exaggeration in her voice. "So did you see where she took off too?" Corporal asked with a calm tone. "Sure right through this alley that separates Jerry's Bar and Momma Joe's." Corporal Mitchell reached his hand out to give her a friendly hand shake. "I'm sorry sir, but I don't shake hands." She said with a smile. "Well thank you ma'am for this interview. I guess that'll wrap things up from here." "Isn't it quite strange for all these murders to be popping up on a full scale out of no where? You watch and see the murder rate is gonna out do New Orleans in a minute." She said with a worried look on her face. "No Ma'am. I don't think it'll ever get that worse, at least I hope not."

* * *

The very next day Corporal Mitchell decided to update Maria on the latest incident that took place last night at Jerry's Bar. "Now who could that be?" She said unloading the groceries then took off to the study room phone. "Hello, Mrs. Gates speaking." "Hello Mrs. Gates, this is Corporal Mitchell." "Oh hello, Corporal." "Hi. I called to the O.F.P.A. Office after I couldn't get through on your cell phone and they told me your handling matters from the privacy of your own home. So they gave me your resident number." "That's right Corporal. I fully earned the special assignment investigation part of the Union, basically I just picked up where Mr. Owens left off." "That's nice to hear Mrs. Gates, but if you don't mind me bugging you with our latest and if you like I'll get right with it." He said while flipping through his report book. "Sure, be my guess, sir, that's what I'm here for." She answered with charm in her voice. "Here we go. Last night approximately twenty one-fifteen hours we had an emergency one-eighty-seven call stating someone had been murdered. Then thrown through Jerry's Bar window, and could you imagine who we're thinking is responsible for it?" "Sense you said it like that don't tell me Darla Phelps." "Bing! You hit it on the parrots head." He pointed out then added. "Oh yeah. I went over the Captain's head and walked the chain of command to the Chief of Michigan. I asked him if she should be shot on sight or be brought into justice, and I couldn't believe he said brought in to justice so medical could examine her. Due to she's not the average deranged person. Boy I tell you Mrs. Gates sometimes this job makes me wanna go join those G.I.S. workers Mrs. Barbra McBeta and go around taping ghost voices on tape recorders." "Well I know one thing that son of a bitch Norman Gandy needs to be shot on sight and have you ever seen the movie Exorcist?" Corporal Mitchell nodded his head saying. "I sure have, Mrs. Gates." "Well. That's great cause it happens and its happening now. If we kill the body the body dies and only the devil knows what Mary's soul would do. The possession of Mary within Darla most definitely given her razor intelligence to find any victim or non-victim she needs and I'll advise you not to say the name Mary to many times. Even you could become a victim of her circumstances." Then Maria laughed when she heard him clearing his throat. "I'm here to tell you Mrs. Gates we need to come up with something real quick before this town be renamed after the "Ghost Trail and be called the "Ghost Town." He said thickly. "Yeah I know what you mean and its sort of strange. I once thought about the same thing before I shall add." "Alright, Mrs. Gate's. I think I held you up long enough. I'll be letting you go now and its always a pleasure to be talking to you as well. Bye." "Bye Corporal." When Maria hung the phone up she leaned back in her chair putting her hair into a pony tail thinking to herself. "Will the nightmare ever stop or are we in hell now? If so, Heaven has to be a better place." Once she broke her chain of though she picked up the phone to dial Richards number. "Hello, Richard Owens speaking." "Hello Richard. I was just calling to let you know heads up cause I was on my way." "Ok that's fine with me boss lady." She blushed with a smile saying. "See you shortly, bye."

* * *

Mr. Wallace pulled on K.B. Liquor parking lot when he saw an Asian man standing outside the store smoking a cigarette. Mr. Leeman flipped his lit cigarette into the parking lot preparing to assist his customer. "Hello sir. I don't mean to bother you but do you mind me asking a question or two?" Mr. Wallace said with a friendly leer getting out of his Excursion truck. "Not at all what can I help you with, sir?" Mr. Leeman said with his strong Asian accent walking in the store making his way behind the counter. "Well first of all let me purchase a pack of Marlboro's to give you a little business." Mr. Wallace pulled out a twenty dollar bill sliding it over the counter. "It'll be four dollars and twenty-five cents, I'm sorry you wouldn't happen to have a smaller bill than that would you? No change, we haven't had to many customers today." Mr. Wallace calmly reached out and grabbed the twenty dollar bill form his hand then handed him a ten. Once Mr. Leeman handed him his change Mr. Wallace came out and said. "I was told by a certain person a gentleman by the name of Andy works here as your cooler stocker, is that correct, sir?" Mr. Leeman's eyebrows arched in surprise. Then he answered with his accent. "That's very true, but what's the reasoning asking that? If you don't mind me saying." "Well let's just say it was told me through the grapevine and I was desperately needing to get a hold on him." Mr. Wallace demurred. "Wait a minute his Parole Officer isn't looking for him again is he?" he asked sounding very concerned. "No, no, that I know of at least. Not yet I might add." "Well then, his days off are Wednesday and Sundays and I'm sorry today is Wednesday." "Is there anyway we can keep this a secret between us? We don't want him to get all over excited if you know what I mean." Mr. Wallace noted. "Sure, why not." He agreed easily.

* * *

Richard was in the blue room posting up the new pictures he received from the crime lab of Libby Copeland and Gloria Madison. He stood there shaking his head from seeing the bloody condition they was in until he heard a horn blowing outside the house. Richard quickly clicked the bright light off closing the door behind him then opened the front door as Maria approached. Foxy and the other watch dogs must have gotten use to seeing her cause they usually bark their lungs out when someone pulled into the driveway. Though now she just sat there wagging her cut off tail like a dog on strike. "Sorry it took so long. I had to turn back around to close all the windows. I can't be expecting any unwanted visitors anymore before they come out to install the alarm on the house. If you know what I'm trying to hit at." She said with a little humor in her voice as she walked through the door. The aroma of potatoes, Roast Beef and onions assaulted her noise as she walked inside. "Um. It sure smells good in here." She admitted sliding her purse off her arm placing it on his coffee table. "Would you mind having a plate? Lets just call it a business meal." He yelled from the kitchen taking the roast out to place it on top of the stove. "I would love that, do you need a hand?" She asked walking into the kitchen and over to the sink to wash her hands. While Richard was slicing his way through the tender roast Maria placed two plates on the counter thinking to herself. "He was looking like Chef Boy-o r d without the hat. then she cracked a smile for thinking about it.

* * *

As time went by they both got through with their meal when done Maria wiped her mouth with her napkin getting up to go get her folder next to her purse. When she returned to the table she immediately pulled out her report she jotted down from Corporal Mitchell. "Richard. I got a call from Corporal Mitchell earlier letting me know Darla struck again." "You don't say." he said shortly. "The location was in the fifth District at Jerry's Dance Bar. She broke the victim's neck and through his body through Mr. Jerry's window, and that's not the least of it. He also told me he had a talk with Michigan Chief and the Chief let it be known he wanted Darla captured alive to medically exam her being she's not our averaged deranged person." Richard's eyes got bright with surprise. he was stunned to hear the Chief would rather for Darla to be captured alive only to examine her. Coming back to his senses he said. "Well, our friend Ethan D. Witchata said if we need his hand again just give him another magical ring." "That'll be great, cause I think we'll be needing him again." She agreed ebulliently picking the dirty dishes off of the table and taking them to the sink.

* * *

Thursday morning when Mr. Leeman opened the liquor store he called Andy to warn him to not come to work cause Mr. Wallace was parked across the street on Kentucky Fried chicken lot looking at the liquor store through a pair of binoculars. Andy raced over to the phone. "Who the hell is it?" "Andy. You don't come to work that man I told you about yesterday is across the street on Kentucky Fried Chicken lot to surveillance the store, I guess expecting you to arrive. Where's that damn kid at?" "I took him to another location last night after you called me." "Another location?" Mr. Leeman snapped. "Wait, wait, wait calm down big boy. This here was your whole damn idea anyway from starts and if I don't get my couple pounds of crystal meth soon from our agreement on kidnapping this kid to hold hostage, so you can get ransom money to save your store. He's not the only one that's going to mysteriously disappear." Andy yelled furiously disconnecting the line. Mr. Leeman's frown vanished while slowly putting the cordless phone on the counter when he heard his Asian automatic greeting voice bell sounding off at the door from Mr. Wallace stepping through it. "Was we telling someone about our little secret, Mr. Leeman?" He said casually enough approaching the counter. "Oh no, that was my sister-n-law." He ejaculated with a lie. Mr. Wallace leaned over the counter playing if off as if he was interested in purchasing a half pint of Paul Mason Brandy and at the same time jotting the number down in his membrane from the back of the phone that was last dialed. Mr. Leeman turned toward the wall shelf waiting on his last request. "And let me have a small bottle of that After Shock, I guess I'll have some heated Cognia tonight with a special friend of mines." The second Mr. Wallace got back into his Excursion he tossed the brown paper sack on his backseat to scribble down the number then he fired the engine, reversed out and accelerated off the lot heading back to the Motel.

* * *

When Maria made it home, Antonia climbed out the dining room table chair and ran straight up to her when she saw her coming through the door. "Mommy, mommy, look what I did." She anxiously shouted holding the art paper out in front of her. Maria received the picture front her tiny little hands to scan over the drawing of a tree and falling apples. "Mommy, you can have it. I'll make another one for Daddy." "Oh. Thank you princess, where's Daddy at anyways?" "Uh. he's in the backyard cleaning the bar-b-que grill." "He is?" Maria said with sugar can sweetness glancing over to the half open patio door, then went advancing over to it. "Hello Babe." "mmmm, hello Momma. I knew I heard Antonia talking how your morning go Mi Amour (my love)?" He said with concern after receiving a kiss. "Oh, this morning was fine we covered a lot of plans. We also figured it was time to bring out the infrared video camera, the electromagnetic field detector and the thermal imaging camera." "You guys about to get down to business." He pointed out. "We sure are Babe." She answered then added. "Although, I've eaten a little over Richard's house, what you was about to cook, Babe?" "You did? Well I was about to cook some El Aros Con Pollo (rice and chicken) and a few other dishes." He answered in Spanish. "Um. Mi Gusta El Aros Con Pollo (I like rice with chicken)." Maria replied back in Spanish rubbing her stomach. "So finish doing what you doing and call me if you need a lady's assistance." She said giving hi another peck on his lips before walking off to the study room. Maria unlocked their safe that contained her high tech camera and detector thinking to herself. She never thought she'd ever have to use the gadgets at all. Holding the camera she peeped through the lens placed it on the table and did the other one the same. She lowered the thermal imaging camera from her eye, when Antonia came through the door in fright talking in Spanish. "Mommy. Hay una aranya en la pared (there's a spider on the wall)." "It's not gonna get you honey. Tell Daddy to kill it for us, ok?" "Si" She replied yes storming back out the door to tell Daddy to kill the spider on the wall. Maria couldn't shake Norman off her mind and it wasn't a day that went pass she wished if he was still in Saginaw, Michigan that she saw him get shot down or captured on the news.

* * *

A week later Mr. Wallace was having a meeting with Captain Aversa and a few Officer's from the Twentynine Palms Police Department inside the City Hall on what their plan and operation was gonna be to capture Andy and rescue Bryan Smith alive. "Alright, with a little help from my operator friend Mrs. Hinkie. I finally located the empty building where the call had been made too from Mr. Leeman's liqour store to our suspect Andy." "Ah so we're ready to bust this guy." Captain Aversa blurted out feeling relieved that they finally are down to the bottom of things. The president could find someone being held captive in the Middle East, but it was unbelievable they couldn't find one guy inside a small town. Mr. Wallace started flipping through his note pad where he pretty much had everything mapped out. Their room was covered with complete silence from knowing what this meant for the Captain and that was a big raise and a lovely retirement plan for finding Bryan Smith alive. "Alright, it's right here. The building is located off the South end of Adobe Road, inside an old building that use to be a Auto body shop of his fathers, whom lost the battle with Prostate Cancer." "Hold on Mr. Wallace. Is this the building that sits along side Adobe Road, by Bar Lumber?" Officer Dixon asked disbelievingly. "It sure in the hell is." Captain Aversa answered quickly before Mr. Wallace could fix the words to answer. "Thanks, Captain." He said politely but sarcastically enough. "Well, as I was saying, when we approach this here building in a moment we need to be very cautious and wait for the cue from Captain Aversa or myself to make the move, and remember we need to get this kid out safe as possible and alive. Do anyone have any questions? Great, lets go make things happen fella." After Mr. Wallace was finished giving his directions, everyone stood on their feet double checking their weapons.

CHAPTER TWENTY-THREE

MR. LEEMAN CLOSED his liquor store earlier than usual to prepare himself to make the transaction for the kidnapping in order to save his liquor store with the ransom money. "Hum, it'll be good to make a call first. I can't afford to make another dry run with this meth in the car." He said beneath his breath with the phone on his shoulder as he listened to the constant rings. Andy unstraddled himself from the chair he was sitting on staring into Bryan's eyes. "Shit, who could this be again?" He disguised his voice pretty much sounding like his old man. "Hello." "Andy?" "Oh, it's you. Good." Andy sounded relieved to hear it was Mr. Leeman. "Andy. I was making sure you were there this time. I'm getting everything ready right now." "Wait a minute! I thought you already had everything allswuared away." Andy fumed. "I thought I did." "Listen you piece of shit! If you're not here within the next half an hour, I'm blasting this little turd and I'm coming looking for you for messing with my intellitense." He meant to say intelligence. "But!" Mr. Leeman couldn't get his next words out from Andy madly slamming the phone down again disconnecting the line. "Now I'm really pissed!" Andy said loudly advancing back over to his chair that's sitting right in front of Bryan where he's tied up and duck tapped at the mouth. When Andy restraddled his chair. He leaned over to the milk crate to grab his German Lugar 9

Millimeter. Bryan's eyes got wider when he saw Andy cocking the gun then blew the tip.

* * *

All the patrol vehicles that convoyed behind Mr. Wallace's Excursion truck yielded along side the road twenty yards away from the auto body shop where Andy held Bryan captive. The moment everyone exited their vehicle they all huddled into a circle to hear Mr. Wallace's final plan of operation in approaching the building. "Alright gentlemen. This is our final location and I also wanna mention our suspect maybe armed I do believe, so we need to be safe as possible. Is that clear to everyone?" Then he continued when he saw everyone's heads nodding with approval to his question. "good. May the action begin with everyone mounting themselves to their position, but remember no one makes a move without my cue, lets go." Mr. Wallace was just excited as Captain Aversa was to finally come down to the last moment of the search that seemed like a lifetime in progress.

* * *

Mr. Leeman was at least three blocks away from the auto body shop stuck at the light. He was impatiently tapping on his steering wheel for the light to change, and when it did he screech both of his back tires punching off knowing Andy meant business about his thirty minute time limit.

* * *

While everyone was tucked away and rooted in their positions as planned, two officers crouched down on both sides of the front entrance door, three officers was tucked off behind a old classic Vega Station Wagon and Mr. Wallace was next to Captain Aversa behind a van on the lot with their guns drawn like everyone else. Andy hopped up quick with the German Lugar nine millimeter when he heard some noise on the outside of the building. He made it to the front window, using his right palm to clear some of the buildup dirt on the window to take a glance out the circle. For a minute he thought it was Mr. Leeman approaching but then again he couldn't quite fathom what it may had been from the lot looking calm and peaceful as usual sense everyone was camouflaged behind the abandon vehicles and up against the building. "What I'm tweaking for? Maybe it was someone walking pass on the street. Boy I sure wish dad had put a fence around this lot before he passed away for times like this." he said thoughtfully beneath his breath advancing away from the window. As moments passed, Mr. Leeman was about to pull up on the lot until he saw the building was covered by cops in their positions. Then with a quick decision he sped off screeching his tires. Upon hearing the screech of the tires Mr. Wallace yelled to Captain Aversa. "Damn it. That was Mr. Lee!" Then quickly took off running to his Excursion truck leaving everybody still rooted to their spots. Mr. Wallace hopped into the driver's seat rushing the key into the ignition with no hesitation, as if it was part of a marathon of some sort for timing. Firing up the engine he snatched it into drive peeling off. Mr. Leeman was speeding recklessly up Hatch Road yielding in and out of the opposite lane passing up vehicles that was cautiously driving on the road. "Ah, got to hell!" He yelled out with an attitude when hearing a car smash on its horn. Mr. Wallace pressed down on his gas pedal nearly making it touch all the way to the floor causing all the barrows on his engine to open up with him. People was yielding to the side of the road when seeing the emergency code three lights flashing as Mr. Wallace came up behind them.

* * *

Andy quickly paced over to the door when he realized moments ago he heard tires screeching outside the building and didn't hesitate one minute in unlocking and opening the door. He frightenly tried to slam the door closed when he saw the two Officers posted on both sides of the door, but Officer Dixon forced it back open with his foot and stepped back to his position. Andy immediately raced over to Bryan and with no remorse "Pow!" he shot him in the center of his chest. "Drop the freaking weapon!" Officer Dixon yelled. Everything happened so quick to where Bryan didn't have a chance to make a sound. His chair flipped backwards from the powerful impact of the close range blast. Both Officers immediately opened fire when seeing Bryan get shot and Andy angling the gun at them in the doorway. "K-pow, K-pow, K-pow, K-pow, K-pow, K-pow, K-pow, K-pow, K-pow!" Between both Officer's they unloaded nine bullets inside his body knocking him off his feet and onto a homemade weak table. This table collapsed in two when his body came crashing down on it as the handgun went air born. And was dead. Captain Aversa grabbed his radio from his shirt strap to call the emergency dispatch. "Thirty-three-twenty-five to the emergency unit." "Go head, Thirty-three-twenty-five." The emergency dispatch replied instantly. "yes. We need a couple of ambulances in route to the location of seventeen-sixty Adobe Road at the AutoBody Shop right across from Bar Lumber." "That's affirmative sir, paramedics is on its way." "Than you, over and out." Officer Dixon read over to Bryan where he laid and saw his eyes half open with one single tear rolling down to his ear. "He's still alive!" Officer Dixon yelled with relief, when he pulled the duck tape from his lips. He cried out concisely for an answer. "I'm gonna die aren't I, aren't I?" "No you're not gonna die, just hold tight help is on its way." He assured him propping his head on his knee.

* * *

"Lt. Wallace, to the back up unit." "Back up unit, go ahead Lt. Wallace." Officer Green responded right away. "I have a known suspect fleeing recklessly heading west bound toward the Sixty-two Highway on Hatch Road, set a perimeter road block in route." "That a copy sir Over and out." Mr. Wallace slid the receiver back on the metal clip on his dash panel then snatched his hat from his head tossing it in his backseat. "I knew it, I knew it, I knew it. We screwed up now!" Mr. leeman yelled out regretfully still doing seventy mile per hour in a thirty-five miles per hour zone.

* * *

Shortly after the paramedics was called they pulled up with their siren blaring. "Here's the paramedics now, hold on little fella. We gonna get you to the hospital, right now." Officer Dixon said tossing up an assuring smile at him then stood up on his feet to step to the side so they could place him on the gurney bed. "Those marks on his wrist came from the rope I cut off him myself." "Alright, that's fine." paramedic Ms. Stevens noted.

* * *

Mr. Leeman slammed down on his air brakes trying to avoid from crashing into a station wagon that was slowly crossing from a side street in an opposite direction of Hatch Road, but it was to late. His Camry went sliding with smoke burning from his tires into the station wagon, barely missing the middle section of the car. When his car impact with the vehicle back passenger quarter panel he caused the station wagon to jack knife to a complete halt. Mr. Leeman's Camry went tumbling off the side of the road three times, until it landed on its driver side in a thick cloud of dust. The back passenger wheel was still freely spinning while he was barely knocked in to subconscious with the air bag inflated from the steering wheel. When Mr. Wallace witnessed the accident occur he snatched the radio receiver from the dash panel to call for the medial emergency units while pulling over a few feet from the station wagon. "Lt. Wallace to the medical emergency unit." "This is the medical emergency unit, go head Lt." "I need a fire truck and a couple of ambulances routed to east bound on Hatch Road in Twenty-nine Palms, over." "That's affirmative sir, they're on the way." Mr. Wallace slid the receiver back onto the clip and exited the vehicle to make sure the woman inside the struck vehicle wasn't severely hurt. "Are you alright man?" "Yes. I think so, but its blood coming from my head. Oh God!" Ms Casey cried in pain. "Don't move ma'am. The ambulance is on its way. You gonna be perfectly fine, just hold tight." He consoled her then took off on the other side of the road where Mr. Leeman was trapped inside his Camry, and as he was crossing the road he heard the emergency response team sounding off in the back ground coming to the rescue.

* * *

Bryan was breathing hard like a fish out of water, until he started shaking going into shock iwth a thick dark blood sobs spitting up from his mouth. "Darrel, we're losing him." Ms. Stevens hollered to the front. "Oh no, his heart stopped. We lost him." Adrenaline rushed through her veins when she saw his eyes freeze once his heart stopped. The she extended her hand out to close his eyes and although she didn't know

Bryan it still didn't stop tears from falling knowing he was someone's son. "Damn! We only had a little more ways to go." Darrel said beneath his voice reaching for the rear spot light switch shutting the light off, which let Officer Dixon know they lost their patient.

* * *

Mr. Leeman was just now coming around when he heard and felt glass shattering down on him. Mr. Wallace climbed up onto the car knocking the rest of the glass out the passenger door window. "Why in the hell you tried to escape from me, Mr. Leeman?" He asked curiously reaching inside to release his seat belt so he could be pulled out. "Good their just in time." Mr. Wallace added soberly, once he saw the Fire Department and Ambulances pulling up to the scene.

* * *

The crime lab zipped up the black bag Andy's body was placed in then rolled him away on the coroner gurney so the detectives could start their investigation. "I still can't believe as many times as I've driven pass this building on duty or off duty this is where Bryan was being held captive all this time." Detective Nunley said to Captain Aversa in total disbelief. "I know exactly what you mean, but like they always said. 'Do things under the cops nose and they'll never find out.' Which is half and half true, I shall admit." The Captain said with an affable voice, reaching for his radio. "Excuse me Detective Nunley, go ahead twenty-six-nineteen." "Sir, I hate to say it, but Bryan didn't make it." "He what!" The Captain fumed. "Sorry, sir." Officer Dixon apologized. "No need to apologize it's not your fault. Thank you for the news Officer Dixon, over and out." "You bet sir, over and out." "Well we lost the kid." "Yeah, I heard." Detective Nunley said congenially.

* * *

Once Mr. Leeman was pulled out of his vehicle and transported off with Ms. Casey to get emergency medical treatment, the Fire Department worker Mr. Hamilton yelled out to Mr. Wallace, while he was standing by Ms. Casey's station wagon having a conversation with Officer Green. "Excuse me Officer Green, I guess you can help the two truck company while I see to things over here." "Sure." As soon as Mr. Wallace made it to Mr. Leeman's vehicle where Mr. Hamilton was holding a large zip lock bag he said. "Don't tell me that's what I think it is." "I'm not. Only if you're thinking its meth or a whole lot of paraphernalia." He replied with forced enthusiasm. "Oh, now it's making perfect sense on Mr. Leeman's arrival at the shop, and his reckless evading." Officer Green tuned his ears to where he heard a radio sounding off then yelled. "Lt., your radio's going off the hay wire!" "Oh shit! I the kid." He said with concern taking off to his Excursion saying to Mr. Hamilton. "Make sure that makes it to the evidence room!" "You got it boss!" Mr. Wallace couldn't remember when the last time he had so much excitement happening all at once. Everything was barrowed down to it was going to be ugly and not easy. He snatched the driver's door open and slid the receiver off the metal clip. "Lt. Wallace, go ahead." "Lt. everything's went wrong. The kid is dead." Captain Aversa said quickly. "The kid is dead?" "I'm afraid so, plus our suspect wasn't too lucky either. Once the door was open and he saw my men he fired a single shot into the kid's chest and that's when my Officers returned fire and killed him on the spot." "Well so much for our happy ending. I'll meet up with you Captain to tapper down our reports and to let you know what else I just discovered on our second suspect Mr. Leeman for conviction." Mr. Wallace inquired. "Sounds like a plan, see you in a bit. Over and out." "Over and out."

* * *

Two days later the investigators at the forensic office decided to release the D.N.A. report to Maria, letting her know who was responsible for Gloria Madison's murder. "I'll get it Babe!" She shouted out placing her champagne glass of Sherry on the coffee table when she reached over to grab the phone. "Hello, the Gates residence. How can I help you?" "Hello, Mrs. Gates, this is Homicide Investigator Mr. Dean and I'm hoping I caught you at a good time." "Oh sure. I wasn't doing anything particular, so what you got?" She said with alacrity from the nice buzz that was settling in from the Sherry. "I promise I won't hold you up, but the results are in on the Madison case." "Oh they are? Well this gonna be good." "We all here at the forensic office just discovered the D.N.A. we found in her vagina was semen from Norman Gandy." "Norman Gandy?" "Yes, ma'am. Norman Gandy, so basically not only did he murder her he brutally raped her savagely as well." "Poor lady didn't have a chance with such an animal, so do you all have any leads on him as we speak?" She asked curiously. "Actually its funny that you asked, we also found out by the victim's boyfriend James A. Faceson her car was stolen prior to this crime so we came up with the conclusion he may be mobile in her twenty-ten Grandprix." "You know what Mr. Dean?" "What's that Mrs. Gates?" "A few nights ago, someone screeched their tires away from our house. Now that I look back it just may had been him for sure." "Yeah, we gonna do everything we can to get this guy." "Creep." She corrected shortly. "Your right and finally end his days once and for all. Well it was a pleasure providing you with this up date and I wish you and your family a good evening Mrs. Gates." "Likewise. Thank you Mr. Dean, Bye." When she hung up the phone she appeared honestly startled from the news she just heard about Norman. Bobby came walking into the living room with his Champagne glass of Sherry in his hand and when he saw the uncharacteristic expression on her face he said. "What's wrong Honey?" "Oh nothing." "Are you sure?" "I'm positive." She quickly countered airily. "Alrighty." He said lifting his glass up to his lips looking unconvinced. Maria picked up her champagne glass from the coffee table and guzzled the whole glass of Sherry down trying to avoid eye contact with his trancing gaze.

*   *   *

The second Mrs. Tucker closed the door behind her taking off to the grocery store and pay a few bills, Juan raced over to the dish rack to grab a butter knife so he could pick her bedroom door open to find some loose change for gas money. He couldn't stand a chance in asking her for any when he gave her his promise he'll stick around, until she made it back. He reached out for the knob only to find out it was locked and without wasting anymore time he slid the butter knife between the seal and the latch between the wood. "Yes, works every time." He said convincingly racing over to her dresser. He opened and closed each one of the drawers until he located a brown wooden box. "Hum. What could this be?" He said out of curiosity opening the box. He got suddenly amazed when he saw his deceased father's handgun. "Just what I need in order to get more money, momma. I think I'll borrow this for a second." He said beneath his breath placing the box back in the drawer where it belongs then stood upright to make sure it had bullets inside the three-eighty clip. Releasing the clip from the handle he immediately saw the bullets lined up through the slit side of the clip weighing down on the spring. "Yeap seven bullets mean a full clip." He said readily placing the small three-eighty inside his waistline below his stomach, and then locked the door back before he left out so his mother wouldn't know off hand what he did.

CHAPTER TWENTY-FOUR

ALICIA WAGNER CREPT quietly up to the gaped open bedroom door to eavesdrop on Michael while he was sitting on the bed faced away with the one photo he could never get off and that was Mary Swartz's after she died. "Boy do I miss you Mary and whom ever did that to you really needs to pay for it." He whispered underneath his breath glancing at the photo with a blank stare. "What the fuck!" she snapped with an instinctive grab in her voice at the same time barging through the door. Michael jumped and stood indecisively while tucking the photo inside his back pocket. "How long you been standing behind the door, eavesdropping? See now you see why we have our trust issues?" Michael elucidated. "But anyways i been standing there ever since you decided to walk away from our argument that you thought was so childish, and enough time to hear your fucking ass say you missed Mary." "So we're eavesdropping on folks now?" "What was that you nearly killed yourself trying to put in your back pocket? The truth this time." She asked heatedly. Michael calmly reached in his back pocket instead o f replying in words and handed her Mary Swartz picture. "What the!" "Look Alicia, you gotta believe me." "I don't have to believe anything!" She corrected. "You srue know what Buttons to keep pushing." He considered grimly. "You can try to change the subject or say whatever you want, but it still doesn't explain what the hell your doing with this dead bitches picture especially after all these years." Michael just shrugged his shoulders morosely not knowing the exact words he could say without putting more gasoline on the fire. "Alicia." He murmured sulkily. "Yes. I'm waiting for a good explanation, Michael Arron Stearns." She responded automatically with both arms crossed in front of her with the picture clinched between her left index finger and thumb. A glimmer of comprehension light her eyes when she saw his face expression turn amazingly bland and showed the sign he was about to explain himself. "Well first of all just like when we were in the living room you made it seem as if I'm using you." "Of course you're using me and now I see why!" She replied tranquilly then threw the picture at him storming off angrily out the room. Michael stood there momentarily with his mouth pride wide open when the picture bounced off his forehead. He then took off behind her.

* * *

Mrs. Tucker made it back home from doing her errands. Contemplating putting all the dry groceries in the cabinet or should she call the authorities when Juan was gone to let them know his whereabouts. Cause she figured if he'd turn himself in he may end up getting a lighter sentence. "Yeah, that's what I'll do cause the dear creator knows I wanna see my son free the correct way someday." She whispered low, convincing herself then advancing away to her bedroom phone. She sat on the edge of her bed with her hand relaxed on the phone, exhaling visually she picked up the phone and dialed 911. She was about to change her mind until she heard the operator lady say. "Thank you for calling Atlanta Emergency 911, my name is Ms. Cooley, please state your emergency." "Good evening, ma'am. My name is Juanita R. Tucker and I just want to say first my life is in no danger at all and it's more or less me calling on my son's behalf." "We'll be glad to assist you Mrs. Tucker. What can we help you with?" "Alright. I believe my son is being wanted by Michigan City Prison for escaping." Oh your son escaped?" Ms. Cooley answered sounding honestly confused. "Ok. I'm gonna ask you a few questions in order for us to help your son." "That's fine." "Good. First off, we need to know if your sons there at the house now?" Mrs. Tucker took a quick glance at her bedroom door as if expecting to see her son standing there. The she said over a rippling sigh. "No he's not, ma'am." "Ok, I have another question. Is your armed with any weapons?" "No Ma'am!" She responded soberly. "That's fine, that's fine. That's a good thing. Alright we need to know is your son driving, if so, what's the make and year of the vehicle? And after that I'm going to need you to verify your address." Mrs. Tucker retraced her mind saying. "If I'm not mistaken it's a green Monte Carlo and I'm not too sure on the year but I'll take a guess at it. Let's see it may be a two thousand and five or six, ma'am." "Great, so just to verify your address on our computer. It's five-five-five-eight-zero Luca Court in Castle Brooke Apartments." "That's correct." Mrs. Tucker declared truthfully. "Thank you for your emergency and your patience, Mrs. Tucker. We're going to get everything on the ball about getting you and your son some help. Have a great evening." "You too, bye." When she hung up the phone her pulse was rapidly pumping then she experienced a sharp stab of guilt at what she just did. Feeling like she just betrayed her son.

* * *

Alicia out of reflex broke away from Michael when he tried to put his arms around her to comfort her then he said when he saw her eyes shoot angry sparks at him. "Babe. Please let me explain, will you?" "I even resent you asking that question cause its over Michael!" She said with a touch of hauter. "It's over?" "Yes, over. O-V-E-R-, over! All I know you could of been pleasuring yourself off the dead bitches picture." She attacked accusingly. "How could you say that to me?" Michael cocked his hand backwards out of hurt then backed handed her in the cheek. "Oh God Alicia, I'm sorry!" He stated regretfully reaching out to sooth her from his mistake. "Get your fucking hands off of me, damn it!" She yelled furiously taking off upstairs with her left hand on her cheek.

* * *

Once night descended upon Atlanta City, the U.S. Marshall was twelve deep in under cover vehicles driving in castle brooke apartments with their lights out trying not to cause to much attention to themselves to capture Juan. He was still driving around Atlanta City down town seeing if he could catch somebody slipping or vulnerable enough to rob with his handgun. "It sure is a lot of people walking around at this time of the night, but it'll be might hard to rob somebody without anyone seeing especially amongst this crowd." He whispered thoughtfully to himself accelerating from the green light.

* * *

Sergeant Marshall Mr. Steel huddled with everyone once they all was parked and out of their vehicles. "Alright, I need everyone to huddle for a second." He said with the sting of authority rippling through his voice. He was a tall Caucasian middle age man with broad shoulders deep eye sockets with a clean cut facial area that made him look three or four years younger than what he is. He also used to be a professional NFL Football player for the Atlanta Falcons, before he got injured in his right knee. Once everyone surrounded his undercover Cavalier, he said with his raspy deep voice. "Alright, ladies and gent's. As we all do know we're dealing with an escaped convict so we need to treat it at that same measurement like all the rest of the cases. Marshall Kendell, you don't mind if I borrow your cell phone for a hot second do you? I need to make sure our suspect hasn't slip into his mom's house from the last time I've spoken with her." "No, not at all. Be my guest." Mr. Kendell reached for his cell phone on his waist handing it over. "Thank you." Mr. Steel said calmly stepping a few steps backwards to reach and grab Mrs. Tucker's number from the sun visor. "Here we go." Mrs. Tucker quickly twisted the top back on her two liter Pepsi bottle then stormed off to her room to catch the call. "Is that you Juan?" "No ma'am. This is Marshall Steel, well I see that answered my question. I was just calling to make sure your son hasn't arrived already." "No sir, he hasn't. You guys gonna help my son right?" She asked concerned. "Sure ma'am. That's our job to do so." He replied truthfully. "Good, I sure appreciate it." "Ma'am, don't worry. Everything's gonna turn out perfectly fine, and just to remind you Mrs. Tucker you made the right decision, well until further notice. Have a good night." "Thanks you too." When she hung up the phone she had another funny feeling inside her stomach, she did the wrong thing by getting the authorities involved. "Alright everyone, I just confirmed the kid hasn't arrived yet so I need everyone to pursue their positions. We can't afford to blow this one." He concluded.

* * *

Alicia and Michael's telephone was ringing off the hook as they both sat in different parts of the house ignoring it, until the answering machine intercepted the call. "Sorry we missed your call, but you did reach Alicia and Michael's number, so please leave your name and number. Bye, Beep." After the beep Maria said. "Hello Ms. Wagner, my name is Mrs. Gates. I'm an investigator from the O.F.P.A. Office. Sorry I didn't get a hold of you, but it'll be highly appreciated if you reach me at your earliest convenience at five-five-five-one-zero-zero-one, thanks." When Maria disconnected the line she immediately grabbed for her temples from feeling a headache coming on. She also was happy she didn't directly get in contact with Alicia from how she's starting to feel as the entire room started to spin in circles.

* * *

Juan quickly reached for the cell phone that was sounding off on his front pants pocket saying. "Hello." "I hope you know I told the police what state you was heading to, all I was trying to do is be nice and you wanted to jack me for my car. I'm gonna make sure you get the biggest sentence you can't handle!" Carmen cried in tears. "Listen lady! I asked you to do me a favor from the jump, you know what? I don't even know why I'm even explaining myself to you." Juan said thoughtfully while driving on the highway heading back to Castle Brooke Apartments. "And I hope you had a good time with my phone also cause it's lined up to be turned off in the . . ." He closed the cell phone cutting her off, then tossed it on the passenger seat to blast the factory radio to drain out the ringing it was doing from Carmen's calling.

* * *

Darla had been hiding inside the Davisons farm barn house for two days now, busting open chicken eggs with her mouth draining them dry from the shells. The Davisons was still traveling on the road on their way home from Cleveland Ohio after spending a whole weekend there for their twelve year old daughter Pam's horse pageant competition. Mr. Davison adjusted his driver door mirror making sure their horse trailer wasn't swinging on the back of the truck. Then he powered his window up. Mrs. Davison was out cold asleep in the passenger seat exhausted from nearly driving the entire way to Michigan City. She had her head buried into the pillow that was prompt up against the corner of her seat and the window snoring to the Angels. Their two daughters Pam and Elain were in the backseat looking at a DVD movie called "Head of State." staring Chris Rock on their five inch screen hanging from the ceiling. Elain is ten years old and was very jealous of her older sister Pam, cause she's been winning competitions with her horse Starburst ever since she was known to enter one and it seemed like it was taking forever for her to turn twelve so she could compete. "Once we make it home, I guess you girls can relax for the rest of the evening. I'll just leave Starburst and Fastcloud inside the trailer overnight. Hell, they have enough hay back there to nearly last them a week. But make sure you both take all your bags in with you and straight up to your room." He instructed through the rearview mirror as he accelerated on the gas pedal. Then he stole another glance at his door mirror monitoring the trailer.

* * *

Juan punched in the apartment gate code that his mother gave him to come and go into the apartment complex. He didn't notice anything out of place making it around to his mother's court, but then again he thought to himself. It is sort of strange the way people just lodging in their vehicles spread out, especially for nine at night. He further thought out of paranoia preparing himself to park where he was before he left. "Alright. Don't nobody move from their positions, until I pull up and trap his vehicle into the parking slot. Ok, here we go." Mr. Steel said in his radio snatching the gear into drive and cutting his emergency code three lights on. "Oh shit! I knew it." Juan echoed hoping himself back in the driver seat locking himself inside when he saw the code three lights. Sergeant Mr. Steel slammed on his brakes barricading him in, jumped out taking cover behind his vehicle with his weapon drawn. Mrs. Tucker ran over to her living room window when hearing Mr. Steel's tires screeching out front. "Oh Lord! What have I done?" She yelled taking off out the door to make sure everything goes right with justice, instead of injustice. The rest of the Marshall's response team had the whole parking court surrounded taking precaution. Juan grabbed the three-eighty gun from under the driver's seat firmly gripping it in his hand. "I repeat, Mr. Tucker, please put both hands up with the keys out the driver window, and your hands where I can see them!" "I'm not gonna do it!" Juan objected truthfully. Mrs. Tucker ran out to the curve in front of the car where Juan locked himself inside screaming. "J.T.! Give yourself up!" "Ma'am! Step away." Marshall Kendell yelled, running out of nowhere rushing her to the side away from the vehicle with his right arm around her. "Momma!" "Mr. Tucker we're not here to harm you, all we want to do is help!" Mr. Steel yelled from behind his car. "Juan listed to them!" Mrs. Tucker cried.

* * *

When the Davisons finally made it home Mr. Davison backed his suburban in on the side of their ranch home positioning the horse trailer where he normally kept it, so he'll always have quick access to hinge it to the back of the truck. The barn sits forty yards away from the back of their house and parking it right there buys him some time on various occasions. Once everyone exited the truck and made it in the house Pam and Elain went racing up to their room to the only computer they had access to. Darla sat down in the barn house corner behind a large stack of hay after devouring through at least twenty raw chicken eggs. "That's not fair Pam. Before we left off to the horse competition you were the last one on the computer!" Elain accused heatedly. "But you're the one who said whoever makes it here first and now you wanna complain." Pam pointed out looking her dead in the eyes then focused her attention back to the lite computer screen to tap in her password. Elain angrily strode off to her bed on the other side of the room and slumped herself down with her arms crossed deviously frowning. Pam could admit she sort of felt uneasy seeing her little sister through the computer screen reflection just staring at her with an evil expression.

* * *

Sergeant Steel came up with the conclusion to use Mrs. Tucker as their negotiator to get her son to surrender. Juan cocked the active bullet in the chamber with the nose pointed toward the floor between his legs. The first thought ran through his mind was to jump out and shoot one of the Marshall's, if not one Marshall per bullet if he only was straight enough. He thought insanely. Sergeant Steel reached for his radio saying. "Sergeant Steel to Marshall Kendell." "Go head, sir." "Can you carefully escort Mrs. Tucker to my vehicle, please?" "That's an affirmative, sir." Marshall Kendell acknowledged latching his radio back to his waistline saying to Mrs. Tucker. "Excuse me ma'am. You don't mind if I escort you over to the Sergeant's vehicle do you? I think he has a backup plan to help your son." "Of course! Anything to help my son." She said precisely taking her hands from her waist. "Sure. Anything to help my son." She added with a sweet whisper taking off behind him. "What's Momma doing?" Juan said underneath his breath watching her being escorted to Mr. Steel behind the car that has Juan barricaded. "Alright Mrs. Tucker. I have a plan of action." "I know, that's what Mr. Kendell said." She announced stiffly. "Thank you Kendell, you may resume you post. Well Mrs. Tucker my plan is to use you as our negotiator, are you up for it?" "Why wouldn't I be? This gonna help him right?" She asked questioningly. "Sure, I hope so, anyways." He responded with a smile. Mrs. Tucker took a deep breath then said after she exhaled. "Ok, I'm ready." And at the same time hoping Juan do exactly what she says. "Go whenever you like Mrs. Tucker." "I'll do it now." She said shortly walking around his vehicle heading over to the driver's side of Juan's car. "Yeah, like this is gonna work to use my mom against me." He said underneath his breath watching her approach through the rearview mirror and when she stepped unto the driver side door she immediately said. "J.T., we can't go any further with this so please surrender son, you have too!" he yelled back from the other side of the window. "Momma, I told you I can't go back to that place, and I'll do anything to prove it!" He explained while holding his hand with the three-eighty palm on it under his right leg. "I know son. But maybe we can get your prison term switched out hurr to Marrietta Cobb County, Georgia." "That's still a slight possibility Momma! What part of that you don't understand?" "Don't raise your voice up at me, boy. I understand every part of it!" She snapped then added. "Juan, open the door right now. You're making this worse on yourself and if you truthfully wanna know how they knew you were here." "I already how they knew. It was that woman who this caar belongs to." "No. I'm the one who called and told them." "You what!? That's it!" He fumed. "He's got a gun!" Mr. Steel yelled out to everyone. Juan squeezed his closed then pulled the trigger. "Pow!" He blew part of his brains out the back of his cranium. "No! No! No!" She cried furiously while pounding on the window with her bare hands trying to get to him. Blood was splashed on the back seat and dripping constantly from the wound of his mouth area as his body laid slumped over the passenger seat. Sergeant Steel raced to her side guiding her away from the vehicle while Marshall Lohan paced up to the passenger door window and shattered the glass with the handle of his weapon.

* * *

Maria was on the phone having a conversation with Richard about the conversation she had with Alicia Wagner, when she finally returned her call. "Richard, she also was telling me, Melinda Simpson had gotten married and still living here in Saginaw, but for some reason she wouldn't answer my million dollar question." "Why what's you ask her?" He asked curiously enough. "I asked her did she see who hung Mary or was she possibly the killer?" "And what she say?" "She said she didn't wanna talk about it." "She said she didn't wanna talk about it." Richard blurted out in disbelief "Yeap. She didn't wanna talk about it, at least at that moment." "I hope she's fully aware she still could be accountable for conspiracy of murder. If not murder." He concluded. "Yes she very much could be." Maria agreed shortly. "So where you think we should go with this, Maria?" "Well actually the only thing we can do is wait to see what happens unless someone finally comes clean." "I sure hate that's our only option." "At least for this conversation Richard." Richard exhaled then said. "Yeah." "But I also have been thinking Richard. It's not going to make a difference if

Darla or shall I say if Mary tracks down her killer underneath our nose, would it be the end or will she keep on killing? Because when a derange persons figment of the imagination subdued, it's pretty much no point of return for that one's imagination cause we have to look at it like this. This is the real world and not a fairy tale and believe me the imagination can go out of this universe, galaxy this way of life as we know etc. etc." "So when you're saying the for to us track down Mary Swartz's killer before she do things would be okay and in all you was totally wrong." "Totally, because if you do the math, Britney participated in her hanging and she ends up getting murdered, but still yet the murders still continue. Then we have Libby Copeland whom also participated, and she was murdered and yet the murders continued. So you see Richard with that I came up with the final conclusion we're gonna have to destroy Darla and hence Mary Swartz from her." "Well, what about the Chief's decision about bringing her into custody to medically examine her?" "Lets just say we never got that news." "You bet, cause there wasn't anyway we were going to bring her in, especially without a fight." He conspired. "Oh yeah. I also came up with the theory on how the leaves are being animated by Darla's command." "Oh yeah. Well that's what I been wanting to know." "I found out its through Mary's spirit so once the leaves are animated that's when her spirit exits the body and in order to keep her expelled from her. We must fate Darla." "You know what. That's why I always leave things up to you, cause that makes perfectly good damn sense and not only that we have no other choice." "You damn right, we don't!" She countered quickly.

CHAPTER TWENTY-FIVE

ONCE DINNER TIME was over at the Davison's residence and everyone was sitting around the table preparing themselves to enjoy some German Chocolate cake and Ice Cream, Elain sat at the table staring blankly at her dirty plate with her right fist cuffed into her left palm contemplating on what she thought she saw before it got fully dark. "Can I be excused from the table, Ma?" "Sure, but aren't you going to eat some dessert?" "No, I'll have some later." "Alright, you're excused. Leave your dirty plate there I'll get it." "Thanks Ma, thanks Pa." She said sliding her chair away from the table heading off to her room. "What's gotten into her? She never turned down her favorite dessert." Mr. Davision asked looking over at Pam. "I don't know." She responded shrugging her shoulders holding back her real thoughts. She may still be mad at me from earlier. Although Elain couldn't see anything in the outside darkness it still didn't keep her from pacing straight over to her window that face out to their barn house to see if she could see someone sticking their head out the barn doors again. "I can't see a thing besides maybe it wasn't anyone from the get go. The barn house does sit a little ways from the house. I could have mistaken. So there's no need in telling anyone to get them startled for nothing. Alright no I'm ready for dessert." She whispered beneath her breath then took off heading back to the dining room.

* * *

"Hold on Richard my line is clicking someone's on the other end." "Sure." Maria clicked over and said. "Hello. This is the Gates residence how may I help you?" "Mrs. Gates. I'm ready to talk." "Oh hello Alicia." Maria said with a friendly leer. "Is this a good time?" "Sure. Give me one minute while I clear my other end." "Hello, Richard." "Yes I'm still here." He responded easily. "I need to phone you back that's Alicia Wagner. She's ready to talk." "What? Well why you still on the line with me? Phone me back when you get through, bye." "Bye." She said before clicking back over. "Ms. Wagner." "Yes, Mrs. Gates?" "I'm back, and I'm all ears. So what we need to talk about?" Alicia exhaled after a deep breath then continued saying. "Well I understand I wasted your time earlier by saying I didn't want to talk about Mary Swartz but it's something that's been haunting me for years and I thought about coming clean and doing the right thing by telling you." "By telling me what Ms. Wagner?" "What I know of Mary's hanging that took place in the girls restroom." "So what your saying is you want to tell me you had something to do with her hanging, is that correct Ms. Wagner?" "In a way, but not quite. You see me and mary were best of friends at one point. Let me just tell the story like this Mrs. Gates. Mary had a boyfriend named Michael Stearns whom I madly fell in love with and pretty much still in love with. We'll when she found out me and Michael started hitting things off she started acting really weird in many ways especially toward our friendship." "Ms. Wagner can you be a little more specific on how strange she was behaving?" "Ok. She was making crazy looking voodoo dolls of people she didn't no longer like or wanted to be friends with." "Can you tell me the people's names she made olls off? But if you can't remember don't worry." Maria asked gently. "Let me see. I'll try to remember but first Mrs. Gates, I want to let you know why I'm coming clean with you." "Why are you now deciding to come clean, Ms. Wagner?" "Well. Not long after I had that short conversation with you earlier I end up having the most weirdest dream ever. I dreamt Mary was in our home hiding wih the plan to kill me for what happened to her, and I never once thought about her in any way since she died until I spoke with you." "But either way Ms. Wagner your doing the correct thing right now." "I hope so Mrs. Gates. Well, the voo-doo dolls she made was me, Libby Copeland, Britney Levels, Terri Lovetts, Marilyn Woods and its only one more I can remember, and that's Melinda Simpson. Mrs. Gates just to remind you. Melinda is no longer Melinda Simpson, she's a Davison now." "Oh, so that's her new last name." Maria acknowledged simply enough. "Yes ma'am." "Ms. Wagner you wouldn't happen to have her address or number would you by any chance?" "I'm sorry but I don't Mrs. Gates." "That's fine, I have my ways of getting it. Finish telling me the story." "Alright, just to shorten the story I'm gonna come out straight forward like this. I'm the one who passed the note around about scaring her Mrs. Gates." "I mean why would you want to scare her in the first place?" "Because I was living to hater her back, besides I'm not the one who hung her." "Excuse me? If you're not the one who hung her then who did?" Alicia took in a breath then exhaled to say. "It was Melinda." "So Melinda was the cold blooded killer?" "I suppose so, I watched her do it." Alicia responded convincingly, then added. "Thank you Mrs. Gates for allowing me to get this off my conscience." "No problem, Ms. Wagner. I'm just as thankful as you are, so is there anything else you need to add before we hang up? "No not at all." "Alright, once again thank you and goodbye." "Bye." Disconnecting the line Maria tossed up a convinced smile with relief, speed dialing Richard's number. "Hello Richard Owens speaking." "Richard. I got it, I got it, I got it." "Got what Maria?" "I finally got the name to Mary Swartz killer." "You did? I can't believe it!" "I sure did." "So crack the egg to me who did it?" "Just take a wild guess, Richard." She said with an continuous smile. "Why was it Ms. Wagner?" "Close but not even. It was Melinda Simpson whom is now married and to be called Melinda Davision for now on." "I still can't believe it." "You minus well and once I'm finished talking to you I'm gonna call information and get her address and phone number under her." "Well need not to waste any more time jaw japping to me." "You right. I need to get on that right now, so I'll talk to you later." "Alright, bye." "Bye Richard." Maria hung up whispering underneath her breath while dialing four-one-one. "I sure hope information can provide this information to me." "Hello. Thank you for calling four-one-one my name is Eric Drake, please state the name city and state please." "Hi. I need the address and phone number to a Melinda Davison in Saginaw Michigan." "Is that Melinda with an 'M-E'?" "yes sir. M-E-L-I-N-D-A." "Thank you. the number is five-five-five-nine-one-one-one and the address is eighty five-sixty five Des Monte Road." "Thank you very much, sir." "No problem, ma'am. Thank you for choosing four-one-one at your convenience have a great evening."

* * *

"Honey, the dessert was delicious and I think it's time for me to lay it on down. You girls don't be up late on that computer." Mr. Davison said rising to his feet than headed off to their bedroom. "Is something wrong Elain?" Melinda asked curiously enough when she noticed her uncharacteristic expression. "No ma'am, there's nothing wrong at all." Elain replied looking into her mom's eyes with a weak smile. "Mom. I think I'll call it a night also." Pam said while grabbing her napkin from her lap placing it on the table. "Me too, Ma." Elain insisted as well. "Alright. You girls have a good night sleep." Both girls came around the table and planted a soft kiss on her cheek, then headed off to bed. Melinda gathered all the dishes from the table and soaked them in the premade dish water she prepared before they ate dessert. Hearing a noise echoing from the back of the house she noticed as she stood there silently staring out the kitchen window trying to detect the sound. "Hum, that sounded like barn doors." She said thoughtfully underneath her breath. Melinda placed the dishtowel on the sink counter, and rushed open the end miscellaneous sink drawer to grab the flashlight. "Oh yeah, the batteries, good I see." She said when she clicked it on and saw the light brightly glaring to the floor. Melinda slowly unlocked their kitchen back door with her senses feverishly heightened. "I wonder why I'm just now noticing this noise?" She whispered opening the door to head out to the barn and as she moved along she glared the light all around her. The closer she was making her way to the barn the more she realized the noise was the doors swinging freely hitting up against the barn house. When Darla saw the distant light glaring from the flash light she quickly stood on her feet making her way over to the wall and grabbed a pair of large scissors from it to use as a weapon. "I should of gotten Greg to come and close the barn doors. How did they get open anyways?" She thought dryly out loud as she continued approaching with the flashlight glaring at the barn's opening. Darla hid herself back behind the haystack in the pitch darkness with the large sixe shears spread wide. While both hands was firmly gripped on the wooden handles pointing the weapon out in front of her but when she opened the shears wider to its full extent Melinda stopped in her tracks inside the doorway the noise heightening her senses. "Did I just hear something make a echo sound? Of course you did its animals inside, duh. But that didn't sound like noise from an animal. That was a material sound. She whispered insanely then said out loud while she slowly extended inside. "Is anyone in here? If so, I advise you to show yourself at once. Wait a minute, I think I see something." Elain came walking out the private bathroom in her sleeping pajamas and her days cloths neatly folded in her arms. Easily noticing a bright light glaring in the barn house when she took a quick glimpse at her reflection through the window as she was making her way over to the closet. "Now I really know I'm not seeing things." She said peering out the window. "What the hell happened here?" Melinda incredulously asked herself raising the light from the cracked egg shells and over to the far left corner when she heard something brush up against the haystack. She automatically knew something was wrong when she saw the cracked egg shells in the middle of the walkway near the chicken coop, but she just couldn't expand her mind to think what may had been the cause. "This is your last chance to show yourself, or I'll be forced to notify the police." She yelled while slowly approaching the haystack with the flashlight aimed at it. Darla tossed up a devilish look the closer Melinda's footsteps got. Melinda stopped rooted to her spot on the side before turning where Darla was deviously standing with the large shears gaped wide open. Melinda had a strange feeling it was something on the backside of the haystack that wasn't right, but then again she had numerous feelings about a lot of things ever since Mary Swartz died and this was the one that felt like De Ja Vu to her. She thought crazily, though only if she knew it wasn't so crazy. She glared the light directly in Darla's face then dropped it glued to her spot unable to move as Darla came charging toward her shearing off her head from her shoulders before Melinda could scream. Her head hit the ground and rolled as her body fell to the ground. Darla straddled over her body with the closed shears elevated in the air, and without any remorse jabbed it through her abdomen. Every animal in the barn started fussing in their own language as Darla repeatedly jabbed the shears in and out of Melinda.

Elain rushed over to the window when she heard their animals going wild and discovered someone coming out the barn and vanishing into the darkness of the moon light. "Who was that coming out of the barn house?" Pam opened the bathroom door after taking a shower saying. "Who was who?" "Pam, i just saw someone coming out of the barn and I see a bright light inside it too. We need to tell Ma and Pa." "It's a light?" Pam countered soberly taking off behind her. The moment they made it down stairs Elain couldn't help but notice the kitchen door being opened as a shiver from the cold air hit her. "Ma." She said concernly enough entering into the kitchen and when she took a peek out the door and didn't see no sign of her, they both took off to their parents room. Mr. Davison got bright eyed when he heard Pam rushing through the door saying. "Pa! Where Ma? Elain said she saw someone coming out of the barn!" "She what?" He barked tossing the covers off him to go grab his house coat and shoes. Making it to the kitchen he automatically figured it was Melinda out in the barn house, when he saw the kitchen door open and the flashlight missing. "You girls stay right here while I check things out, I think its your Ma out there in the barn." "But why would she be?" Elain said cutting her question off when their Pa went storming out the door but in his mind he was asking the same exact question and that's "Why would she be out here in the barn at this time of night?" AS he strode along he clearly could see the glare in the barn from the flashlight. He began to pace quicker under the full moom that nearly illuminated the entire ranch. "Melinda Honey! You in there?" He yelled when he finally made it to the barn doorway. Mr. Davison glared his flashlight directly where he saw the other flashlight glaring from the ground, then angled it to the dark shadow oa few feet away. "Honey! Is that you?" He asked while slowly walking up to her body but once he saw her head in the glare of his light before he reached her body he screamed out. "Oh God. No!" Elain dropped her glass of juice from her hand, frightened by her Pa's scream that echoed with agony throughout the entire ranch.

* * *

Two days later Maria decided to give Melinda an unexpected phone call to let her know she wanted to meet up with her to ask a few questions.

Finally after the phone rang five times she heard a deep grave voice say. "Hello." "Hello. Is this the Davison residence?" "Yes, it is, how can I help you?" "Great. My name is Mrs. Gates." "Excuse me for cutting you off but this isn't another one of those new reporters is it?" "No sir. I'm an Investigator from the O.F.P.A. Office and I was just wanting to know if I could have a word or two with Mrs. Davison?" "I'm afraid that's not possible." "It's not?" She responded noncommittally. "No its not. My wife was murdered two days ago." "I'm sorry to hear that Mr. Davison. You don't mind me asking you what happened do you?" Maria asked smoothly to see if she could get him to talk. "I'm sorry Mrs. Gates but I'd rather not, goodbye." "But . . ." She couldn't speak out quick enough from not believing what she just heard with her own ears. Maria laid the cordless phone back on the charger saying. "Oh, my, God. Now it's really too late. I need to phone Richard."

* * *

Lisa was in her bedroom sitting with a couple of her friends having a conversation about going back to the house in the ghost trail woods although she told herself it would be a cold day in hell she'd ever step another foot back in those woods again. Katie's expression turned bland from having second thoughts about going with Ronnie and Lisa to set the house on fire, till Ronnie talked her into it by saying. "Katie everything's gonna be just fine. We get there set the house on fire and we're out of there. No one would ever know we did it." "Katie, we really need to do this for Kent, Ricky and April to prevent anyone else from falling victim of that house as well. Katie you think I'm anxious to go back to those woods? I even coached myself once upon a time by saying. It would be a cold day in hell if I stepped another foot back in those woods again period. But something always told me the only correct thing to do. Lisa said convincingly. "Yeah, that's true. After all Ricky is my Cousin." Kattie agreed with no further restrictions. "So well all game for it or what?" Lisa asked determinably then witnessed them both nod their heads with approval.

* * *

Maria pulled up at Richard's house after telling him on the phone she needed to talk to him in person about the message she received from Mr. Davison. "I'm coming!" He yelled out from his bedroom when he heard her pounding on the door. The moment the door was open she rushed right in hanging her own coat on the coat rack and headed straight over to their meeting quarters. Which was his dining room table without saying a word. "Something's really got to be going on Maria. You never hang your own coat up." He said pulling his chair out form the table accompanying her. She took a quick deep breath leaned back in her seat putting her hair in a ponytail, then said finally with a straight face. "Richard something terrible has happened that tell we don't have no more time to waste. If we haven't ran out of time already." "Maria. What in the world is going on?" "I was just told by Melinda's husband Mr. Davison. Melinda was murdered two days ago." "She was murdered two days ago?" He proclaimed standing up to his feet. Maria danced her brown eyes up to his eyes saying calmly. "Now, what shall we do?" Richard silently eased himself back down to his seat slowly nodding his head in disbelief, then said. "We need to contact Ethan to find this girl and put her out of her misery once and for all." A month ago, Maria couldn't see herself harming the innocent Darla she once interviewed at Patton State Hospital, but things most definitely took a curve ball on that thought cause she was all for what Richard said and that's to put her out of her misery once and for all. "Richard I think that's a good ideal get Ethan back on the spot to find this girl." "You mean woman." He corrected her. "You right agian." "Oh Maria you never explained to me how Melinda gotten murdered." "Richard, your guess is as good as mine. Mr. Davison didn't want to give up that information. You believe me right?" "Of course I believe you, why wouldn't I?" "I'm sorry it's the way you said it, that's all."

* * *

"Alright. The gas can in the trunk just held ten dollars worth of gas, and I think that'll be more than enough to make that house a burnt wood skeleton." Ronnie said sliding the gear shift down to drive pulling off the Chevron lot. "I hope so." Lisa whispered underneath her breath glancing out the window. "I heard that. It will, trust me." Ronnie countered quickly stealing a glance at Lisa. Katie drew her attention to the rearview mirror from the back passenger seat, staring directly at Ronnie's reflection and said. "Ronnie how long you think this is going to take?" "I can't say but I can say the quicker we make it to the house and set it to blaze the quicker we'll be out of there." He answered. "Let me add to that you guys. As long as we stay on the ghost trail to the split we shouldn't have any delays and for the most part we won't get lost if you know what I mean." Lisa said thoughtfully. Ronnie's eyebrow lifted from the thought of being lost knowing if they didn't take the trail to and from. They will end up lost and may end up like Ricky, April and Kent, and that's dead. He exhaled the thought right out of his mind accelerating on the gas.

* * *

Mr. Adams entered Mr. Baily's bedroom suite where he was in his chair with his eyes closed momentarily resting after reading the entire news paper. "Excuse me sir. May I please have a moment with you?" Mr. Bailey folded the newspaper when his concentration was broken. "sure, most certainly. What did we need to discuss?" "May I?" Mr. Adams said pointing to the chair that was once Mrs. Baileys. "Why not?" "Thank you. Mr. Bailey sir, I was wondering if you heard some strange noises last night around two in the morning?" "Sense you've mentioned i, indeed I did, but I thought it was you or Mrs. Adams perhaps." "Oh no sir. These were noises and even whispers from your son Jason coming from the guest room he was brutalized in. And this wasn't the first time either one evening I vacuumed the guestroom and left the door wide open to answer the door bell when I soon returned the door was closed and there wasn't a single draft to cause it to do that sir." "So you telling me the mansion may be haunted by my son, or my wife perhaps?" "I honestly believe so Mr. Bailey or it could be something else." "Something else like what?" "I don't know sir. It seems as if it's something very dark even now when I travel through that wing of the house. The hair on the back of my neck stands up and for the most part, I feel the tension throughout the entire mansion sir." "Well that's not hard to believe, after all several people was murdered by a house intruder. That's what gave us the fine deal on the mansion." "Sir, so you knew this house was haunted the entire time?" "Why certainly

John." "Sir, you should of informed me and my wife about this before we was hired, my wife and I are terrified by ghost. I guess that's explains how I was locked in the basement by some nullify ghost. I'm sorry sir, but my wife and I quit. We'll be gone before sun down." "No John. You can't quit!" Mr. Bailey said rising to his feet, "I most certainly can sir. Good day." Mr. Adams walked away with his chin high out the room without looking back.

* * *

"Alright Ronnie make a right off the road where that sign is up ahead." Time relapsed with a flash when Lisa read the sign as Ronni yield onto the ghost trail road. "So this is the ghost trail road everyone always talked about?" Ronnie said as if he was a little kid for the first time stepping on the Disneyland Amusement Park grounds. "Boy isn't it." Lisa responded blandly and thoughtfully dancing her eyes up to the sky to see how bright it was although she knew it was still early in the day. It was the thought of being lost in the darkness that was bothering her. But after being lost for that life or death moment is what will take her to and from the house but I have to guide us by the ghost trail." She added thoughtfully. "So where do I need to park?" "Ok it should be a pathway into the woods right about here." Lisa pointed. "And right here it shall be." Ronnie killed the engine to his Jetta studying Lisa frustrated expression then whispered. "Lisa is everything alright? We don't have to do this you know." "No we have to!" She blurted out abruptly. "Katie make sure you have the lighter we can't afford any dry rund to that house." Lisa added. "I have it right here, so are we ready?" "We sure is." Ronnie assured her stepping out the car to grab the gas can from the trunk and they was off following behind Lisa up the trail like she was a human navigation system.

* * *

"Well we back on. Ethan said he'll be over first thing in the morning." Richard said placing the phone on the table reclaiming his seat. "Good. I'm glad we always have his support to rely on Richard, how could we ever repay him?" "Believe this or not Maria he actually gets a kick off this case." "I see why. This case load is very very intricate or to be straight blunt its puzzling." "Yeah you can say that again. I'm going to be very honest Maria. At first I wasn't a strong believer in the paranormal or in ghosts. But when this case load came along years ago as you know when you was just born I been a number one firm believer ever since. Everyone has to realize this is the real world like you said once before. Anything can happen especially like what we're facing today." Maria tossed up a closed mouth smile from seeing the belief of what he said appearing in his bluish green eyes. "I guess I'll cut this meeting short Richard to go grab a few things from the grocery store, besides I can't wait to meet up with Ethan here in the morning." She said rising to her feet to adjust her skirt. "I sure can say one thing Maria. You sure be having some good valuable information I know that's for sure." He said walking her over to the coat rack. "Thank you Richard, but you also have to give yourself half the credit here, cause you been phenomenal." "Have a safe trip Maria and I'll see you first thing in the morning." He said while handing her jacket over to her. "Thanks bye."

* * *

Everyone stopped on the split of the Ghost Trail looking all around them to make sure they remember every little detail they saw. "Alright. We need to be heading in this direction." Lisa said pointing to the right of her taking off as Ronnie and Katie followed lead. Lisa was doing a great job by not letting them see in her actions that everything was gradually replaying in her mind on what happened the day Kent, April and Ricky was murdered. She didn't want them to renege on their mission, and leave the house to stand prey to victimize another victim.

* * *

"Honey pack your things together." "Why?" Mrs. Adams said wiping her hands on her apron studying his facial expression for a good explanation. "Because not long ago. I told Mr. Bailey we quit." "You what? We can't just quit on him, we're all he has left. We've become a family to him. Do you understand? A family and we promise him that after Mrs. Bailey died."

She sympathized. "I know honey, but look. The house is haunted." He agreed brusquely. "How do you know this John?" "Because he told me with his own mouth." He replied without hesitation. "He did?" "Yes. So we need to quit and get out of here, before we're the next ones to die. Look, I have some extra money hid in a savings account from all the tips Mr. Bailey gave me throughout the years. We can take that money get us a place buy whatever you need, hell even take a small vacation to your mom and dad's in Utah. Whatever, but we need to do what we have to do and that's get the hell out of here." Cindy was seeing a side in her husband that she experienced and that's what made things more real on what he was saying. "Alright John. but do we have to leave today?" "Honey put it like this the sooner the better." He told her then added with a kiss on her forehead. "Alright, hun?" "Alright John." "Trust me everything is gonna turn out fine." He consoled her with a hug.

CHAPTER TWENTY-SIX

LISA BENT DOWN to pick up an old smashed plastic Mountain Dew liter bottle and a nice size stick that fits the pore neck of it to use as a marker, just to be safe than sorry again. She thought sticking the stick in the ground placing the two liter bottle on top. "What's that for Lisa?" Katie asked curiously enough. "It's just to secure our direction back out of here that's all." Lisa explained. "I see the house over there you guys!" Ronnie yelled back to the girls' forty feet ahead while they was planting a marker. "Come on Katie. I knew it wasn't too much farther from here, we have work to do." Once Lisa and Katie skipped up to Ronnie, he said with in a whisper. "That is the house right?" "It sure in the hell is. That's the house that took April and Ricky's lives." Katie glanced straight through the scattered leafless trees at the house when she heard Lisa say her cousin Ricky's name. "So what's the plan?" She finally asked. "I don't know, ask Lisa." "Lisa so what's the plan?" "I heard you the first time. We're about to set this mother on fire only if we don't waste no time right here any longer." "Andy we off." "Hold up Ronnie, me you and Katie need to walk closely together." The closer they got to the house Lisa could clearly see that the front door had been closed. She then thought that maybe the rescue team who found Ricky and April's bodies were the ones who closed it when they were there. "Wow! Why would someone want to build a house smack in the middle of the woods?" Ronnie asked placing the gas can on the ground as they all now was standing ten feet from the front porch. "Katie hand Ronnie the lighter so we can get the job done and get the hell out of here." "Here Ronnie." "Thanks. Alright girls go stand over there by that tree, while I pour the gasoline around the entire house. I don't want anyone to get caught by the flames." "Fine but be careful Ronnie do not go in the house through the back and promise me you won't." Lisa said concerned with a serious expression. "Ok, ok. I promise now get away." "Come on Katie lets stand over by the tree like he asked." Ronnie slowly crept his way around the house pouring the gasoline as he moved alone making his way to the back of the house. He was trying his best not to spill gas on his clothes or shoes so he wouldn't end up going in flames with the house. The gas was so strong even the girls could smell the strong fumes of unleaded as the slight breeze carried it bringing water to their eyes. "Boy, this house does look spooky. It looks like a house that belongs on a Texas Chain Saw Massacre movie." He thought out loud coming to the last spot on the right corner of the porch. "Well, here goes the fun part." Ronnie dropped the burning paper from his hand and once the flame touched the gasoline it immediately ignited a large trail of flame racing around the house. Ronnie tossed the gas can on the porch, before he took off running toward the girls. "Come on guys we got to get out of here!" Lisa yelled leading the way back up the trail and once she saw the marker she stuck in the ground. It made her even more relieved knowing her dream finally came true about setting the house on fire and knowing they're going to make it out the Ghost Trail Woods safe.

* * *

Night arrived and everyone in the Baileys residence was sleeping. Cindy finally broke her sleep when she heard someone's voice for the second time outside their open bedroom door in the hallway darkness. It appeared to be a lady's voice calling out a name she couldn't make out, but it sure was a lady's voice she heard not only once, but twice. "Oh my! Who was that." She said flinching to her husband laying beside her. "Who was that sugar?" "John. I swear I just saw someone's presence zoom pass our door in the hallway." "Honey are you serious?" "John, you said this house was haunted earlier right?" "Now why would you doubt that?" "It seems like ever since you brought that to my attention I been noticing things or even expecting things. I think you at least should check things out in the hallway." "Alright and then can I get some sleep?" He said sounding exhausted. John sat upright sliding his house shoes on and went to turn their bedroom light on to illuminate the hallway a little. "No way!" He said sticking his head back in the room looking straight over to the chair where the clothing they once wore earlier was laid upon before they went to bed, but he realized the clothes that was once on their bedroom chair is those that was now scattered outside their door in the hallway. "What's wrong John, what you see? How our clothes we took off before we went to sleep get all scattered in the hallway?" He asked incredulously. Cindy quickly focused her attention over to the chair tossing her right palm up to her mouth area and when she herself saw that their clothes was no longer there she said. "John where you going?" "I'm just going to pick them up, you don't want your panties to be part of the hallway, do you?" He said with a little enthusiasm heading out the door. He bent down to pick up his shirt then stood upright focusing his attention down to the far end of the spacious hallway when he felt he was being watched. But when he didn't hear anything or see anyone in plain sight he proceeded along picking up their wardrobe. Cindy snatched her right index finger out of her mouth from biting on her polish nail, when John came walking through the door with their clothes tightly gripped in his arms. "Now do you believe me?" He said placing them back on the chair. "How can I not? Seeing that happen." She answered in a deceptively calm tone of voice with a taste of worry in her eyes about what she saw zoom pass the door herself. Then she thought for a moment or was it the clothes in mid air going out the door in the darkness and the last part of them going into the hallway had appeared to me being someone? But wait. What about the voices I been hearing? "Honey are you alright?" He asked when he saw her expression amazingly bland from deeply contemplating the matter. "Yes I'm fine, come and get your rest honey." "Well I'm a see if I can get back to sleep." He said clicking the light switch off.

* * *

When morning arrived Bobby was awaked by the phone endless ringing. "Hello, this is the Gates residence." "Hello sir, my name is Mr. Avery. I'm a homicide detective and I was desperately needing to speak with Mrs. Gates if she's available." "Sure. Hold on sir, she'll be right with you. Honey, honey, wake up. It's Detective Avery on the phone, he needs to speak with you." Bobby whispered to her tapping her on the shoulder. "What you say Babe?" "I was saying Detective Avery is on the phone. Here." "Oh!" Maria sat upright grabbing the phone from his hand and once her back was relaxed up against the base board she said with a clear voice. "Good morning Detective Avery." "I'm terribly sorry for waking you out of your best sleep Mrs. Gates and I would of gotten this message to you yesterday evening but things were a little bit excited and complicated and I'm here to tell you half our battle is over with." "What makes you be so sure Mr. Avery?" "You see yesterday evening the house in the Ghost Trial woods was wet to blaze and not only did we discover that but I think we may stumble over a mystery as well." "Mr. Avery. This is surreal for me to hear you say that house was set to blazed, and I can't wait to see or hear what you guys came up with." "Well the Fire Department found three bodies inside the house after they put the blaze out. It was three remains in the kitchen floor basement, a basement that was made to be secretly hidden underneath the floor tiling. "Did you say bodies were found?" "Yes ma'am three bodies and by the bodies being so badly burned we can't make an immediate I.D. so I'll try to get you that information soon as possible." "That'll be highly appreciated Mr. Avery and believe me I'll be impatiently waiting on those results." "No problem Mrs. Gates, until then I'll talk to you later. Bue." "Remember. I'll be waiting." She said with a smile reaching over Bobby to place the phone on the hook. "You'll be waiting on what Honey?" "Some good news, hopefully." She answered happily then added. "Oh God, I forgot. I have to meet up with Richard and Ethan this morning. Honey can you." "Yes I'll drop Princess off at school on my way to work. You just hurry up and get dressed so you won't keep them waiting any longer." She leaned over gave him a kiss and said. "Thank you Babe. I always can count on your support forever." "You sure can. Well you better get ready."

* * *

"So I wonder what's the hold up on Maria? She's never late for a meeting, I guess she's not a robot after all." Ethan said after blowing the steam from his hot cup of coffee. "Trust me, she'll be here shortly. Do you want another jelly, bacon and egg sandwich while we wait?" "I don't mind if I do." Ethan responded easily. "One more jelly, bacon and egg sandwich coming up." "So Richard! Wait you think the plan is gonna be today?" "I don't know but I'm sure going to have something for us!"

* * *

Heading to Richard's house Maria couldn't get the thought out of her mind about the Ghost Trail house being burned down and not only that three anonymous bodies were found also. She couldn't stretch her mind to think who those bodies belong too, but that didn't really matter cause they still was bodies of someone and she was very anxious to find out. Also thinking to herself while turning the corner on Richard's road, whenever they have a right on the case, here comes two wrongs. "Well here comes the boss lady pulling up!" Ethan yelled to the kitchen, while glancing over at the three tv camera monitors. "You don't mind showing her in do you? My hands are full." "You got it." Ethan placed his half cup of coffee on the taste to answer the door. "Hey boss lady, we thought we was going to have to have the meeting without you." "Good thing you're not cause I'm here now. It sure smells baconlicious in here." She said hanging her coat on the rack behind the door. Ethan closed the door saying. "Care to join us on breakfast? Richard make some terrific jell, bacon and egg sandwiches." "Why not? As long as the egg is sunny side up." "What! You're joining us for breakfast Maria?" Richard yelled from the kitchen stove. "Why you sounding like that's hard to fathom? I always joined you for meals from time to time!" "So what do we have planned for today? Tell me something good." Maria sat at the table with her legs crossed saying. "Well Ethan. Things sort of been placed on a stand still since early this morning." "They did?" Richard asked skeptically wiping his hands entering into the dining room area. "Yes it did. I got a very important breaking news from Detective Avery. He called and told me this morning that the house in the middle of the Ghost Trial Woods was burned down yesterday afternoon and that's not all. After the fire was put out by the Fire Department they discovered three burnt bodies inside as well." "You got to be kidding me." Richard echoed absently slowly taking a seat at the table wearing a blank expression. "Like they always say. I wish I was, but this not my real feeling of words. I'm glad it is." "I mean yeah. So am I. I'm just puzzled about the three bodies that were found." "I think you better go check the sizzling bacon on your stove before your house be the next one on fire." She said with a smile. "You ain't lying I nearly forgot the quick. Hold your thought Maria."

* * *

Seven in the evening that evening Ronnie phoned Lisa to let her know what he heard on the news last night. "Hello." "Lisa this Ronnie, I need to speak with you really bad." "Hold on Ronnie let me close my door. Alright I'm back so what you need to speak with me about?" "Listen last night me an my dad were watching the news inside the garage having a few brew together." "You drink with your dad?" She interrupted him. "Look, just listen." "Ok go ahead." "well you know what went down in the woods that we took care of right?" "Of course." "alright I'm just gonna be blunt with it. They found three bodies burnt in the house." "Are you serious?" She blurted out shockingly. "More serious than I ever been." "Listen to me Ronnie. We can not let anyone know we're actually the ones behind the scene of that. I need to call Katie and let her know." "Been there done that." I already informed her on what's going on not even ten minutes ago from speaking with you." "Ronnie. If someone finds out we done." "Hold on Lisa. I'm on the phone hang it up." He yelled when someone pickedup another phone in his house, dialing a number unaware that he was using it. "I'm back, look. I already know what your going to say. and without saying it. I think we should talk about this some other time." "I know what you mean, bye." "Bye." He countered before they both disconnected the line.

* * *

A week later Maria was called down to the Forensic Department to finally hear the news she had been impatiently waiting on. "Hello Mrs.

Robinson. Remember me? I'm Investigator Mrs. Gates." Maria introduced herself to the clerk again. "Why certainly Mrs. Gates. Mr. Grant told me to buzz him once you arrived, can you excuse me for a second please?" "Sure." "Thank you, Mr. Grant your visitor Mrs. Gates is here. Mr. Grant your visitor Mrs. Gates is here." She repeated over the intercom. Then smiled at Maria saying. "Mrs. Gates. He'll be right with you." "Thank you, Mrs. Robinson." "No problem, make yourself welcome." The second Maria was about to grab up another coffee cake like the last time she visited, Mr. Grant came walking through the corridors. "It's nice to see you again Mrs. Gates, do you care to follow me back to my office?" "Sure, I don't mind." When they both entered his nine by twelve office he angled his hand down to the visitor chair making his way around to his own. "Mrs. Gates, Detective Avery told me to notify you first on the I.D.'s of those three bodies we ran test on. He said you'll be very, very relieved find out and here we go." He explained opening up the clear yellow folder on his desk. Her eyes grew bright and sober as it seems as if it was taking him forever to slide the results out from the folder. "Alright Mrs. Gates. One of the bodies was Chris Cunningham, another one was Mikey Furgerson. Let's see and the other body they found in the basement with these other two was Carlos Bledsoe." Maria's heart started beating fast and nearly stopped when she thought he was going to say Norman Gandy. "Why don't you have this copy right here for yourself." he said pulling an extra copy out of the folder handing it over to her. "Thank you, thank you, thank you Mr. Grant. This is the best news ever! I'm sorry Mr. Grant, but I have plenty of work to do."

CHAPTER TWENTY-SEVEN

"JOHN, HONEY, I really feel awful about leaving the mansion and leaving Mr. Bailey by himself." "Cindy, you're telling me you regret leaving the mansion?" "It's not only that. John, I have something to tell you." "You been holding something from me?" Cindy wiped the fallen tears from her cheeks sobbing finally saying. "Yes I have." "And what possible could that be?" He pressed. "I've been having an affair with Mr. Bailey." "You what?" He snapped smacking her across her cheek. "How long this been going on, and when?" Cindy cried out. "Since Mrs. Bailey been deceased and it happened at certain times, when he set you off on certain errands." "I can't believe you. You disgust me!" He yelled snatching his coat off the couch of their new home and slammed the front door behind him. "John I didn't mean to hurt you!" She yelled out to late.

* * *

Maria decreased her speed down to forty-five miles per hour to dial Richard's number a few rings later she heard him say. "Look Rent-A-Center. I told you I'll get that computer payment to you tomorrow sometime!" "Hi Richard this is Maria." "I'm terribly sorry Maria. I thought you was Rent-A-Center calling me for the third time today, so what you got going on?" "What I have, once again you wouldn't believe. Look. I'm less than six minutes to your house and how about me explaining it all to you once I get there?" "Fine. I'll be waiting." "Bye." She said with a friendly leer closing her cell phone increasing her speed. Her hormone that stimulates her involuntary nerve actions couldn't stop rushing through her body knowing a piece of their missing person puzzle had been solved. "Boy do I hope this get better." She whispered looking at the names highlighted on the printout she received from Mr. Grant. Minutes later she was pulling up Richard's driveway and she wasted no time approaching his door. "I'm coming Maria!" He shouted out when he heard her knocking on the door. "We are really down to the wire and it's a case solved in it for you too." She said hanging her coat while Richard closed the door. "It is?" "It sure is, here I'll show you." Richard anxiously followed her over to the dining room table and once they both took their seats she said. "Richard, do you remember those three guys that came up missing in the Saginaw Woods the three guys that were on your case load years ago before you retired by the name of Chris Cunningham, Mikey Furgerson and Carlos Bledsoe?" "Yes I do. Those were the guys who came up missing when Amy Bailey was murdered." "Exactly. Those were the three bodies that were found in the kitchen basement hidden and I thought they searched that place inside out." "So that's why I couldn't never find their remains in the woods at that period of time. Norman must of had lured them in the house and murdered them when they approached him for help after running from whatever they saw that Amy and Daria seen." "You know what Richard, your exactly right. I can't see them getting locked in that kitchen floor basement in any other way. Except by that creep Norman himself and he had to kill them first cause there wouldn't of been no way. He could of put all three of them in there alone if they were still alive." "And that's exactly how I see it Maria." "So that only leaves us and this town with only one problem." "I know and that's Darla Phelps."

* * *

Meanwhile Mr. Adams came pulling up at the Baileys mansion to have a few words with him, but he just couldn't find the correct words. Something told him to check the door handle to see if its locked or not before he ringing the doorbell and true enough it was unlocked. The moment he stepped inside he called out his name. "Mr. Bailey. It's John! I'm here to speak with you and grab a few things." "I'm in the family room John, come and join me!" John was growing even angrier from the inside by hearing the calm tone in Mr. Baileys voice like nothing out of the norm wasn't going on. "Hey John entered the room. "Nice to see you again too sir." He countered back with a false smile thinking while giving him a handshake. I should ram your head into the plasma tv that's on that wall and watch you bleed like a turkey after his head been cut off. "So. What brings you back so soon?" I can't believe this. I don't even have the guts to say it. "Oh. You said what brings me back so soon?" John quickly searched his mind again but only to find a lie. "Cindy and I left a few things and I came back to retrieve them for us." "That's fine help yourself. You know Cindy will always have a place here, of course you too, so you take your time in doing whatever." "Yeah I bet my wife is always welcome old man." John said to himself silently walking out the family room heading to the kitchen.

* * *

"Alright this is the plan Richard. Whoever gets a lead on Darla, meaning whoever hears about her location must immediately contact Ethan for our tracker and the police for backup. We cannot let her get away this time." "You know what Maria? I'm very proud to have you back." "What do you mean by that?" "Well what I meant to say was this and you may admit it. Ever since Norman's been lost and on the prowl a big part of you was lost from knowing he was free. "Alright Richard, I will admit I was lost as long as he was walking the streets. So without saying all of that. Thanks for having me." She ended it with a happy smile. "That's the Maria, I know."

* * *

"Excuse me, John! Are you in the kitchen?" "Yes sir I am, do you need anything?" "Why certainly! Can you please bring me a bowl of that beef stew and a nice piece of cornbread?" "No problem its coming right up!" John yelled back to the family room. John grabbed the pot holder mitten so his finger prints wouldn't appear on the rat poison box. When he grabbed the box from the bottom shelf in the big long length cabinet. He knew off the top he had to immediately erase his previous hand prints from it of the various times he did use it for good causes. "Good. A single fingerprint shouldn't be on this box." He said placing the dry towel back on the refrigerator door handle proceeding along with his mission. Mr. Bailey didn't think not one minute to be suspicious on how long it was taking Mr. Adams to bring his bowl of beef stew while he sat there patiently sipping on a half a glass of French Brandy on ice. "Here you go sir, a big bowl of stew like you asked. Is there anything else you need me to get for you before I leave?" "No thank you John, don't keep that beautiful young lady waiting on you any longer." John immediately thought in his mind if only he would of been any smarter a long time ago to read between the lines the way Mr. Bailey directed his words when it came to his wife Cindy. "Your right sir. I think I need to be going enjoy your meal." "John." Mr. Bailey called out stopping him in his tracks. "Sir." "Thank you." "No problem sir." John replied dropping his eyes to the carpet walking away when he saw Mr. Bailey take a large bit of his bowl of stew.

* * *

"I guess that sums our meeting up, oh by the way when we do get another break to get on her trail don't forget to make sure our radios have a fresh battery connected." "How about you taking your radio battery with you ahead of time that way we'll be a step ahead." Richard went walking over to the radio battery charger, double checked the cells and handed it over to her. "I guess you can keep it off for not, it does spare the batter a little." He said succinctly, when she grabbed it from his hand. "And that I will do." "Well I guess this meeting adjourned." "It was nice talking to you Richard, bye."

* * *

Mr. Bailey's head was leaned back on his chair with a thick foam of saliva driveling down to his shirt with his eyes rolled back in his head and mouth wide open with the half eaten bowl of stew spilled in his lap. Mr. Bailey was D.O.A. dead on arrival.

* * *

Cindy flopped down on her bed to write in her diary. "I never thought I'd fall in love with another man in my life, other than John. But I was wrong. I guess I was tired of being accused and abused. I often wish myself to death at times. It seems as if no one would ever care what I think, what I feel or know or even what I would ever want. But Mr. Bailey always made me feel important no matter what." Cindy slammed her diary closed just like the front door she heard when John came in with the same attitude he left with. "Cindy are you back there?" For a minute he thought she packed a few things and left with how quiet the house was. She raced off the bed rushing her diary in between their mattress when she heard his foot steps approaching on the oak wood waxed hallway floor. "I'm back here in the room!" "Oh here you are." "Where did you take off to? Can we please talk about this without violence?" "I just want to know how could you do me like this? Is this your little way of getting back at me when I and your sister slept together when you and I first started dating?"

* * *

Bobby dropped his suitcase bag the second he stepped through the door, as Maria glanced over at him from the sofa wondering fleetingly what could be wrong, when seeing his uncharacteristic expression. "What's wrong babe?" "I lost the client murder trial, alright!" He barked passing her without giving her a kiss like he normally would have. Maria appeared unperturbed by his icy tone as she said underneath her breath. "Well excuse me, for asking." Then she thought to herself is this the right time to tell him we no longer have to worry about the three missing guys that were found? "Yeah I think I will." She said with a low tone placing the coffee mug on the end table heading off to the study room. Bobby's expression softened when she entered the room. "Honey, before you say anything. I apologize for my mysterious demeanor a moment ago, and I mean this from the bottom of my." "Shhhh." She said cutting his words off with a soft passionate kiss. "Well that just made me feel full of life again." He mimicked cheerily. "I figured it would . . . Oh Babe, I have the most exciting news ever and this should put the icing on the day." "Why, what you hear?" "They found the three missing guys burnt to death in Norman's old house in the middle of the Ghost Trial woods." "Are you serious?" He said very excitedly standing on his feet lifting her off the ground with a strong hug. When he eased her down back to the floor a tear of happiness nearly rolled from his left eye, knowing how much this meant to her, as if what happened in his client trial seemed to even out after all on his conscience. "Babe, this causes for a celebration. What you think?" "You're the boss around here, Daddy." "Well celebration it shall be." Bobby stormed out the room to grab a fresh bottle of Sherry from the food pantry. Maria suddenly got another feeling Alicia lied to her about Melinda being the actual person who hung Mary and as their conversation replayed in her head. The more she realized her story didn't sound right or even add up. Melinda didn't necessarily have a personal problem with her, she did. She was the one who stole her boyfriend from her so that's motive right there. "Hum." She breezed thoughtfully. "Honey, a nice champagne glass of Sherry in here waiting on you!" "I'm coming!" She responded quickly taking off to accompany him at the dining room table.

CHAPTER TWENTY-EIGHT

WHILE CINDY WAS still home alone sitting on the edge of the bed staring at the cell phone contemplating if she should call the police and let them be aware that Mr. Baily may need some emergency attention at his residence. She grabbed the cell phone from the pillow breaking her concentration and once she powered it on she pressed star sixty-seven to block her number so she'll be an anonymous caller. Dialing nine-one-one the emergency operator instantly picked up the line saying with a professional tone. "Thank you for calling emergency nine-one-one my name is Gale Scott and how can I assist you with your emergency?" "Hello. I'm calling to let you know someone maybe badly hurt at a mansion on one-zero-seven-one-two Edgewater road." "Excuse me ma'am, but your number appeared on our line blocked is there anyway you could state your name?" "Sorry, ma'am, but I can't, bye." Cindy quickly powered the phone off and tossed it on the bed before they traced her number by another source.

* * *

Once morning time arrived and Maria took a hot Skin So Soft bubble bath after her and Bobby made love, before Antonia and he took off on their daily schedule. When she fully got dressed, she made up her mind to give Alicia another phone call to get to the final truth of this matter. "Let's see, her number is right here, five-five-five . . ." She whispered dialing the last four numbers to her extension silently. "Hello, may I ask whose calling?" "Hi, my name is Mrs. Gates. I wanted to know if I could speak with Ms. Wagner?" "Sure." Michael covered the receiver whispering over to the living room sofa. "Alicia, it's that lady again." "What lady?" "Mrs. Gates." "Ooh, tell her I'm not here." "I can't I already told her you was her." "You did not, you said sure." "Same thing when she asked to speak with you." Michael lifted the phone back to his ear saying. "Hello. I'm sorry here she goes." "Give me this dummy! Hello. Hi Mrs. Gates, what's going on?" "Well we seem to have a problem here Ms. Wagner, and just so you'd know Mrs. Davison was murdered not too long ago." "Oh my. She was murdered?" "That's correct. Ms. Wagner before I ask you this I honestly want you to know murder do carry a lifetime sentence in the State of Michigan, but if you wanna come clean right now today, I'll give you a proposition that you can't refuse." "And what would that be?" "I'll keep it between me and my partner Mr. Owens and don't let other authorities know, and you'll have to do us a favor in capturing a young lady by the name of Darla." "And after that you promise to never bring this up to anyone." "I promise and believe me, I'm a woman of my word." "You got yourself a deal Mrs. Gates, but can you please hold so I can go into another room with a little more privacy?" "Sure, be my guess." After a few seconds Maria heard a door close in the back ground and Alicia saying. "You there Mrs. Gates?" "I'm here." "Man, I never thought I would ever tell anyone this. But you have to believe me it wasn't done intentionally at all." "I believe you, you know what Ms. Wagner? You did a good thing now in making a lifetime wise decision so tomorrow afternoon me and my two partners will pick you up to chop up our plan to you. Alright?" "A deal is a deal Mrs. Gates, and I'm a woman of my word too bye." "Bye. Yes!" Maria said happily pressing stop on their recorder phone.

* * *

Maria got the cameras out and ready, plus loaded an extra clip to take with her on her mission tomorrow afternoon. Phoning Richard when she came up with their final ultimate plan to get Darla to come to them, now that they have bait to work with other than themselves. "Hello, Richard Owens, speaking." "Richard I don't think we have to wait until Darla strikes after all." "What makes you be so sure Maria?" "Well. A little while ago, I somewhat coerced our friend Alicia Wagner into coming clean and telling the final truth, by cutting her a deal she couldn't refuse." "How you coerced her to do that?" He asked questioningly managing a smile. "First of all I kept getting this gut feeling that she wasn't being one hundred percent honest with me, and that lead me to do the math. So I called her up letting her know in the law of Michigan City, you can get life for the crime of murder, and if she wanted to come clean, I'll cut her a deal by not taking her guilty pleas to the higher authorities and she would have to cooperate with us on catching Darla." "And what part will she play in that?" "Answer this Richard. What's your main ingredient in catching a big fish?" "Bait." "Correct, and that's exactly what she's gonna be tomorrow evening." "That's a genius idea cause she will show up to meet her killer eye to eye. Well, Mary will show up to meet her killer." He corrected. "Exactly and once dissociate Mary Swartz soul from her." "And I can't wait." Richard stated calmly. "So I told her me, you and Ethan will be over to pick her up tomorrow afternoon to get this rolling." "That sounds great but I only have one more question." "Shot it." "What if she decides to go bowlegged on us?" "Then we have a murder suspect, cause I tapped her confession of the crime while we were having our conversation and was smart enough to conspire with her not to repeat her confession. "That was good thinking." "Now. That was just common sense." She said unselfishly, then added. "Well Richard, you still have her address still noted that Tara Peers gave us right?" "And that will be a yes." "Great, cause I want you and Ethan to meet me in front of her residence at eleven forty-five tomorrow morning on the dot." "And that's a copy. I'll call Ethan as soon as we get off the line and have him all ready to go, plus fill him in on the plan of operation." "And that's exactly what I need you to do. I guess I'll let you go so you can get right on it, bye." "Bye Maria, see you tomorrow." After they both disconnected their lines, Maria said to herself real low. "I can hear and feel peace around here already." Maria paced over to the desk where she kept her gun to place it inside it, when she heard Antonia calling out to her coming through the front door with Bobby. "Mommy where are you?" "I'm back here in the study room honey!" "Ah here you are. Mommy I'm hungry, Daddy told me to wait until we got home. He wouldn't buy me no Jack in the Box." "Honey you just had Jack in the Box yesterday. How about mommy fry you up some shrimp and French fries?" "Can you mommy please?" "Hey Honey did our little princess just come in here and tell on me?" Bobby said landing a kiss on her lips. "She sure did, but she know you truly knows what's best for her, don't you princess." "Yeah." She answered with an innocent tone.

* * *

The very next morning couldn't come quicker for Maria, as she tossed and turned throughout the entire night thinking about their plan. She quickly dialed Richards number but reached his answering machine. She knew without a doubt he was waiting on her with Ethan at their meeting point. After she got dressed, she didn't waste not it me going down stairs to the study room to place the cameras inside her black traveling bag and mount her gun in her holster. Looking at her wrist watch she read eleven ten a.m. She was out the door. "Let me radio check Richard." She whispered reaching in the bag for her radio pulling away from the house. "Maria to Richard, over." Richard reached in Ethan's middle console cup holder where his radio was sitting and responded. "This is Richard, go ahead Maria." "Are you guys at the meeting point?" "That's an affirmative, and our friend Ms. Wagner even came out to offer us a cup of coffee." "Good. So that means she's all set to go too." "Just as ready as we are, if you ask me." "Well I'll be right there in a little bit, over." "That's a copy, over and out." Richard placed the radio back inside the cup holder taking a glance at Michael peeking out the living room window. Maria pulled up in her SUV, Richard and Ethan exited the vehicle they were in to approach her. "Good morning Maria." "Good morning guys. So where our friend at? Speaking of the devil, here she comes right now." Maria answered her own question. Maria exited her vehicle to introduce herself in person for the very first time. "Hello Ms. Wagner, it's a mighty pleasure to meet you in person." "Like wise Mrs. Gates." She countered quickly with a warm handshake. "Alright, before we take off, it's only right to tell you what you'll be used for." "What will I be used for?" She asked curiously enough taking a glance at them all standing in front of her. "Let's say you'll be something like bait for us." "It's gonna be perfectly safe isn't it?" "Of course it is. All we need for you to do is when we get everyone in their positions to say. Mary wake up five times continuously, and once she arrives we'll put you in total safety and we'll just handle the rest, is that alright with you?" "Yes I guess, what other choice do I have? A deal is a deal." "Alright then, come and ride with me and you two follow us." "You got it." Ethan said heading back to his vehicle as Richard followed lead. As they all was driving up the road. Maria Grabbed her radio to say. "Come in Richard." "Go ahead Maria, over." "I think we should find a location by the woods being that's the path she likes traveling to and from. I'll call in for back up to standby with us, before Alicia do the calling." "Just keep leading the way, over." "Over and out." "Mrs. Gates will this person actually show up if I say what you told me five times?" "That's what we're about to find out so only time will tell." "Hypothetically speaking Mrs. Gates. What will happen to our deal we made if this such person do not show up?" Maria adjusted her rearview mirror saying. "You'll be scot free, cause technically you would have done your part." Alicia didn't ask another question for rest of the duration to their destination. Ethan pulled right behind Maria where she yield to the side of the road parking. Woods and Oak trees was planted out all around them, Maria easily noticed. She chose that location being it had tremendous blind spots they could camouflage themselves into. "Ms. Wagner can you please hand me that cell phone in my glove department please? I need to call for our backup unit to this location." "Sure." "Thank you." Maria said grabbing the phone. "Saginaw Michigan Police Department my name is Mr. Ross, how can I help you?" "Hello Mr. Ross. My name is Mrs. Gates. I'm an Investigator from the O.F.P.A. Office. I was wanting to know could I be transferred to detective Mr. Avery?" "You sure can. Please hold while I transfer your call." After she heard the line beep twice Mr. Avery, this is Mrs. Gates." "Oh hello Mrs. Gates, it's nice to hear from you." "Thanks. I was contacting you to request a ten man back up unit." "No problem, and where will is the back up united requested too?" "It would be westbound on Hunts, the woody area center of this town. By the way. This is the operation for Darla Renee Phelps." "Need to say no more, help is on its way Mrs. Gates." "Thank you Mr. Avery." "No Mrs. Gates, thank you. bye." "Bye." She closed her cell phone, grabbed the radio and said convincingly enough. "Back up is on its way boys, we're that close to the party." "And that's just marvelous, over and out." After thirty minutes shot by they all saw five patrol vehicles with two officers inside each car pulling up and parking behind one another on the opposite side of the road exiting their vehicles. "Come on Ms. Wagner so we can get you all set." Maria grabbed the radio as they both exited the SUV once everyone was out their vehicles standing in a circle Maria started explaining to them all. "Alright guys. Today is a very dangerous task we're dealing with here. This is the task to finally end the mysterious murders that's been going on in this very town, underneath our noses. This is also the opportunity to promise our children of young youth to have a future instead of being scared to play in parks, walk to school or even go to school period. So me and my partners right here came up with a great plan to stop this insane madness that one can do. We decided to use our special friend right here to help us get Darla to this location, by calling out a special call. Once the call is made while everyone is camouflaged in their positions. The only thing we could do after that is wait for her arrival, and if this plan works, to get her here. Please don't shoot until I express that through the radio receiver. Mr. Avery what channel is your radios on?" "That'll be channel twenty-five." "Thanks." Maria and Richard switched their radios to channel twenty-five to be in line with everyone else's. "Mrs. Gates. It didn't dawn on me until now. Didn't the chief of police say, he wanted Darla to be captured to medically evaluate her?" "I'm afraid he did. But he also didn't understand how big of a threat she is either so it's all left up to us to end this once and for all. This town has suffered enough." "Yeah, that's a damn good answer to my question." Mr. Avery said sounding convinced. "So. Shall we all enter the woods to set our positions and get this started?" "You bet." "Lead the way." "Let's do it." They all answered. "Ethan, you can tag along with me. I'm going to be needing some extra firing power while I aim the thermal imaging camera and the radio to let everyone know when to fate her. This camera will show me Mary's soul leaving Darla's body, once she animates the leaves. Trust me, she gonna use the leaves to her advantage." Maria said then walked off to her vehicle to get her camera while everyone talked amongst themselves waiting on her return. "Alright guys, let's hope this works." As they all moved along deeper in the pool of woods and trees each Officer branched himself off into a spot in a angle where no one is in firing range. Maria, Ethan and Alicia stopped by a three feet wide tree to get Alicia set up and explained to her once more what to do. "Well Ms. Wagner, this is where the Polar Express Train stops. Are you nervous?" "I can't lie. I'm very nervous." She answered truthfully. "You shouldn't have anything to worry about cause the second she do show up and animate the leaves everything will be over for her and ours deal of our will be personally sealed. Alright?" "Let's do it." "Ok the minute we leave off to our positions and I'll holler out to you, start, I want you to stand comfortably right here alongside this tree, and begin the calling five times in a row." "Ok." "Well Ethan, let's take our positions." Maria couldn't see not one officer the way they was tucked into the woods, she notices as her and Ethan crouched in their positions. "Alright Ms. Wagner, you can start!" She yelled. "Well. Here I go." Alicia whispered. to herself thoughtfully, then said. "Mary wake up." five times like she was instructed to do. Darla stopped in her tracks looking back over her right shoulder instantly, once Mary heard the calling of her name and without a doubt she redirected herself to the calling. Alicia flinched turning her head to the direction she was hearing broken twigs being crunched from the hidden officers feet until she realized it was them who was causing the broken twig sounds. "Oh that's nothing but the Officers." She eased herself. Maria glanced at her wrist watch saying low to herself. "It's one zero five p.m." With that Maria periodically glanced at her watch. Everyone heard the same distant noise as the wind started gradually picking up. "What was that?" Alicia said out of curiosity from hearing the distant crunching sound of twigs near her, as if someone was making their way through them. "Oh, my, mother fucking stars." Officer Payton said being the first through one to see Darla pass his position without discovering him. "Ethan look. There she goes, it worked!" Maria whispered amply, turning the thermal imaging camera on and grabbed her radio from her coat pocket to give everyone the cue when its time. Alicia's nerves jerked taking cover behind the tree on the opposite side, once she heard someone fire off a single round. Maria flinched herself from being caught off guard from the shot someone took at Darla. "Damn it. I told them to wait!" She fumed. Darla was still unaware of all the officers who were still planted in their positions. "So much for this camera, look she's animating the oak leaves. Everyone release fire, I repeat, release fire!" She shouted through the radio. "Ahhh!" One of the guys yelled out in agony while the leaves swarmed around him skinning him alive. When done he was elevated five feet in the air and flung into the tree. Bullets just kept flying hitting Darla nearly in each part of her body, as she was being brought down to her knees. Alicia was sitting on the ground behind the tree with both hands on her ears to muffle the multi-gun shots. "Stop firing! Stop firing!" Maria yelled out when she saw Darla lying face down on the ground and once the life leaked out of Darla so did Mary's soul from the leaves. Everyone came out of their hiding positions one by one once they saw Ethan and Maria cautiously walking up to Darla's body. "Be careful Ethan, she may still be alive." The second they was standing over her body. Ethan bent down while Maria still had her weapon pointed and ready. "Yeap. She's dead." He said while searching for a pulse. When Ethan stood upright Maria couldn't help but give him a hug from being so relieved since she's been on the case. "Thanks Ethan." She said releasing her arms from him. "No problem boss lady." "She's dead everyone!." She yelled. Officer Payton extended his hand to Alicia where she was glued to her spot with her hands on her eyes. "Oh, I'm sorry." She said opening her eyes reaching for his hand. Once everybody was standing around only a few feet from Darla's body. Maria searched amongst the officer and said. "Where's Richard?" "Oh no! That may have been him screaming out." Ethan concluded taking off to the spot where he remembered Richard hiding himself off in. Two Officers was instructed by Detective Mr. Avery to stand posted by Darla's body, while they all took off behind Ethan and Maria. "I remember very clearly, this was the exact same spot he hid himself off in." "I found him! Oh god!." Offer Wade yelled from twenty feet away. Maria was the first one who rushed over to the Officer and Richard's body laid. "Richard!" She yelled nearly fainting from seeing her best friend brutally skinned on the ground with leaves partially covering his naked corpse. Maria dropped down on both knees in tears saying. "Richard. I never got the chance to tell you, you are my best friend. God why Richard, why?" She cried out in tears on her knees.

THE END.

BY: ANTHONY WAYNE FACESON   DISCOVERY DATE: 6/25/2004

RONALD GOENS, PEN NAME.

PROLOGUE

TWO WEEKS LATER after Richard's funeral and Darla's body was reportedly buried inside the Sunnyside Mortuary after Mary Swartz's soul was henced from Darla's body and everything appeared to be back to normal. Multi-millionaire Mr. Fester Tiggs was over infatuated on what the town of Saginaw had gone through and experienced. He also was thrilled on how the Saginaw Michigan Governor kept everything so secret from the nationwide media until other reporters got a hold of the coverage story. Mr. Tiggs is a specialist in Artifact's, Relica's and other devilish scared materials with priceless values. But the far most priceless devilish scared material to him is to receiver Darla's skull. On this very day Mr. Tiggs was inside his office of his huge estate home in Grand Rapid, Michigan holding a dangerous heist conference with the two qualified people he personally picked to steal expensive relics from Kenya Africa in the past that was worth millions of dollars and their names are Beverly Coontz, whom is a very virile woman and Max Winthrop, whom is a money hungry man that will pursue any job, hard, medium or soft for a solid buck. "Like I've mentioned once before. I hired four good men that are digging up the burial site preparing it for you guys arrival, but they made it very clear they didn't want anyone to know their names and identities other than myself or even have anything to do with what you guys are being hired to do." Mr. Tiggs explained conversationally, then he clipped the tip of his cigar and instantly fired it up. Beverly quickly swatted the thick smoke rings from her nostrils, then asked once the smoke cleared. "So this isn't a catch 22, is it?" Max asked "Of course not." Mr. Tiggs replied truthfully. Then Max continued. "Basically your telling us once we arrive at the Sunnyside Cemetery, Darla's burial site is gonna be good and dug out?" "Basically." Mr. Tiggs answered shortly raising his cigar back up to his lips and once he did, he twirled it in his mouth for a sweet taste. "Well, when the sun goes down tomorrow, the butchering begins." Max said easily sliding his right thumb across his own throat. "I guess we'll go and prepare ourselves." Beverly suggested. Max stood from the table and they both headed toward the door. "Hold on guys for a minute." Mr. Tiggs said, then added. "Please be careful and this time make sure no tools aren't left behind on this one like the last time in Kenya. Which could end our careers." Mr. Tiggs smothered his cigar inside his twenty-four karat ashtray looking directly at Max indicating he was personally speaking to him. "It won't happen again sir, I promise." Max spoke up before they both left out the door to prepare for their lifetime opportunity to butcher Darla's head.

CHAPTER ONE

THE VERY NEXT day when the sun went down, Beverly and Max was pulling through the Sunnyside Cemetery gate not a minute to late on their schedule to butcher Darla's head. "It's going to be mighty hard in finding her burial site with all this fog." Max said. "Max, we have flashlights you know. Besides, I was told her burial site would be somewhere along the right side of the curve up ahead." "Maybe it'll be a good idea if I turn my brights on. I can't see a damn thing in front of us." "The curve should be coming up." Beverly said thoughtfully. "Oh shit! I almost ran off the pavement." "At least we know it's right here, quick. Pull over and park right here." She said impatiently. Beverly immediately grabbed the razor sharp meat cleaver from the middle consul of the van, before they both exited with their flashlights glaring in front of them. The air brought instant chills to their flesh as they continued swimming through the thick fog heading directly toward Darla's burial site. Max swiftly spun around with this flashlight penetrating the fog, once he heard a rodent of some sort moving around within the thickness of the fog. Beverly also stopped rooted to her spot when she heard him gasp for air. "What's going on, Max?" "I thought I heard something that's all. Beverly let's just find the burial site, do what we came to do and get the hell out of here." He said passing her and leading the rest of the way. When they finally found Darla's burial site,

Beverly stood there with the flashlight glaring directly on Darla's casket then said. "Boy are you lucky, the dirt had dug out already or we would of had a hell of a job on our hands." "I know, tell me about it." Max agreed blandly glaring his flashlight at the pile of dirt next to them. "So what are we waiting for? We have work to do." Beverly said placing her flashlight on the ground preparing herself to climb inside the burial to open the casket. "Wouldn't it had been wise to have brought the plastic bag with us?" "You didn't grab the hefty bag?" She blurted out staring directly into his big green eyes. "Wait a minute, I'll go get it. Just put your flashlight on the ground here and point it this way so I can find my way back straight through this fog." Beverly picked the flashlight up from the ground saying. "Here, you put it where you need it." Max grabbed the flash light without hesitation, placed it on the ground and took off to the van. As time crept by Beverly didn't no longer want to wait for his arrival, so she placed the flashlight on the ground and the meat cleaver on her back side at her waistline then jumped six feet down onto the casket sounding off a thud sound that echoed when she landed. Beverly reached her right hand along side the one foot space trying to fill out the casket latches to open it. "Here's on latch, here's the second one and the other one should be right about here." She whispered to herself unlocking the last latch, then she said as an afterthought. "Here goes nothing." Beverly opened the casket and once she cracked it open she planted her feet along the seal of it to open the top completely. "Damn that was awkward, ooh she smell." She said with a frown once the casket was wide open. The wind started blowing hard causing her flashlight to fall into the casket. "Damn, that scared me." She grabbed the flashlight quickly once the light glared on three dead German Shepherd dogs in the casket. "What the?" Darla wasn't dead after all and her family had been lied to by being lead to believe her body was too much to bear to be seen that a closed casket funeral was mandatory before placing the casket into the ground. The day of Richard's death while the coroner was escorting Darla's body, she murdered both Coroner Transportations and escaped. Mary's soul lives on and so does Darla Phelps . . .

RONALD GOENS, PEN NAME